Meet Me
in Mumbai

Meet Me in Mumbai

A Memoir

Lovelace Cook

First Edition December 2023

Cover design by Radu Muresan
Interior design by Tabitha Lahr

Manufactured in the United States of America
Library of Congress Control Number: 2023901989

Paperback ISBN: 979-8-9877038-0-9
eBook ISBN: 979-8-9877038-1-6

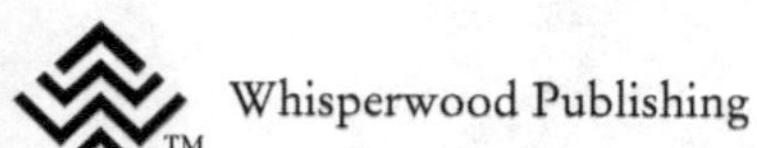
Whisperwood Publishing

In memory of Lisa Bard Carpenter,
whose love affirmed me,
and who said, "Yes! Go to India."

Anthologies

Work in Progress
Iron Fist in a Velvet Glove

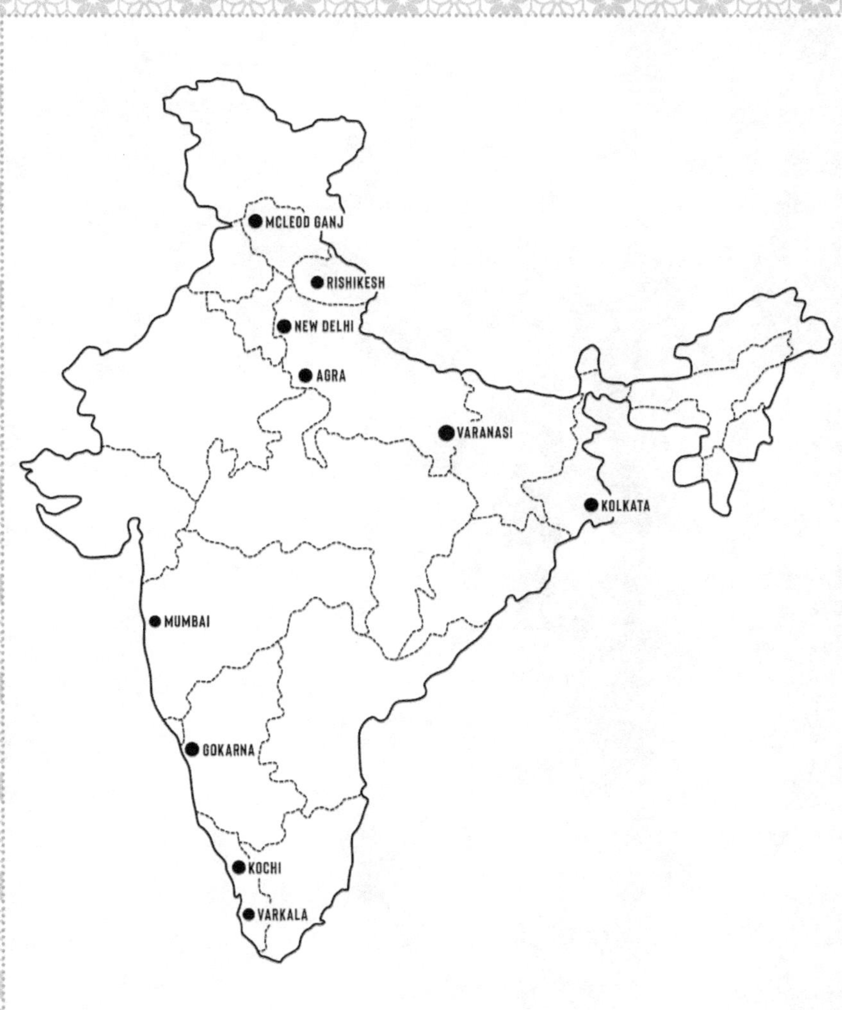

MCLEOD GANJ
RISHIKESH
NEW DELHI
AGRA
VARANASI
KOLKATA
MUMBAI
GOKARNA
KOCHI
VARKALA

"I seek the truth . . . it is only persistence in self-delusion and ignorance that does harm."
—MARCUS AURELIUS

Ram Dass was right. Be here now. You have to be in the moment in India. Otherwise, a tuk-tuk will run into you. A motorcycle will knock you off your feet. A taxi will flatten you. A car driven by a madman will mow you down. The cycle rickshaw will graze you. A pickpocket will rob you. An eager shopkeeper will assault you. Pedestrians will push you out of the way. And beggars will tear at your clothes as well as your heart. If you're on a train or a bus, then anything goes. Just get out of the way. Shove or be shoved. Your survival depends upon being in the moment. And that goes for just about any place or any time in one's life. Be here now.

Preface

*M*eet *Me in Mumbai* is a personal account of my travel experiences, with my point of view, beliefs, and recollections. It is important to note that the experiences depicted in this story are solely my own and may not align with the views or beliefs of anyone mentioned.

Through the narrative, I recount interactions and observations involving individuals from diverse cultural backgrounds, religious beliefs, and affiliations. My intention in sharing this story is not to defame, offend, or disrespect anyone. Instead, my goal is to present my unique journey with transparency and honesty.

The characters in this story are not real people. They are fictional characters who represent the individuals who were a part of my transformative journey. My hope is to foster empathy and understanding among readers, encouraging them to embark on their own explorations and seek a deeper appreciation of our global community. Let us celebrate our shared humanity, and may my narrative serve as a catalyst for unity, respect, and harmony.

If any unintentional errors, misrepresentations, or unintended offense arise within the pages of this nonfiction narrative, I sincerely apologize. I extend an invitation to readers to reach out to me with any concerns, corrections, or clarifications they may have.

Thank you for understanding the spirit in which I wrote *Meet Me in Mumbai*—one that embraces and honors the diversity of faiths, cultures, and spiritual beliefs.

Namaste,
Lovelace Cook

<h1 style="text-align:center">Prologue</h1>

Ten years of MRIs after the neurologist discovered my brain tumor, I celebrated the doctor's news. No more MRIs. The tumor hadn't grown, and, as far as I was concerned, it was merely a shadow about which I rarely thought. My life changed in that decade. I lost the musician lover, had a handful of forgettable dates, spent hours staring at the computer and writing the same old same old for clients, adopted three mischievous cats and two quirky dogs—one of which was part wolf—and experienced a horrifying epiphany: my life was boring.

This unpleasant awareness rocked my world on my birthday. At sixty-two, I was eligible for Medicare. I was old. No, wait. I didn't feel old. I had to shake off the shadow, the malaise I had allowed to color my life gray for ten years. Where had I gone? That woman was not who I was, and I was the only person who could change her. Instead of a birthday wish, I implored the gods to help me find the gypsy-heart I had lost somewhere along the way. I was ready to receive the gifts of the universe. William Blake wrote, "Arise and drink your bliss . . ." And so I did.

On reflection, maybe I should have been more specific. I learned it's never too late for love or a rite of passage.

I thought I'd picked him up at the smoothie bar. He stood at the counter beside me and sorted the dimes, nickels, quarters, and pennies for his peanuts. He wore a small orange backpack and had strange brown suede shoes with pointy toes.

"You're not from around here." I smiled and helped him sort the change.

"Cheers," he said in an unmistakable British accent. His white hair was in a peak like Tin Tin and his shoes were odd, but he wore an easy smile that emphasized his laugh lines, and his eyes crinkled when he asked, "Care to join me for a coffee?"

He was easy on the eyes, though he seemed a bit old for a backpack. "Sure."

He pointed to his shoes after he noticed me staring at his feet and explained, "Winklepickers . . . from the Irregular Shoe Company . . . in London."

"What's a winklepicker?" I couldn't help laughing.

It was an unlikely meeting, and although he spoke English, it could have been a foreign language. A winkle was a sea snail and mods wore winklepickers, the longer the toe, the better.

"Mods?"

"Rock-and-rollers," he answered.

The orange backpack was a rucksack—an Osprey Daypack, I learned. Standard gear for an outdoor-loving Brit. An Englishman with a rucksack and winklepickers in Fairhope, Alabama, I marveled. "How is it you're in this little town?"

"Visiting a family I met whilst fishing in Barbados."

Later, he admitted he had followed me up the street from Fairhope Auto/Marine. He liked my red hair. I liked his smile. He had fumbled with his change to get my attention, but he was glad I'd already paid for my smoothie. He lived in Cornwall, England, and was visiting. He was charming, funny, and intriguing. He came into the winter of my life. He showed me photos of his travels in India. I introduced him to Capote and Steinbeck. He showed me how he had learned to cook from Thai women on a barge trip in Thailand. I seduced him with a snack-sized cup of Ben & Jerry's Chocolate Fudge Brownie ice cream.

Nine ecstatic and bumpy months later—after his two trips and six months with me in the United States—he dared me to meet him in Mumbai.

Georgia O'Keefe said, "I've been absolutely terrified every moment of my life and I've never let it keep me from doing a single thing that I wanted to do."

It was time for me to get out of my comfort zone.

Contents

PART III — INDIA 2014

PART I
India 2013

CHAPTER 1: *Mumbai*

India. I should have known to expect the unexpected.

I pulled out my passport as the line of foreigners snaked its way through Immigration, and I felt something sharp stab me in the back. Startled, I dropped the passport, bent down to pick it up, and rammed my head into the generous buttocks of the turbaned Sikh standing in front of me. He glared.

I mumbled an apology. "Didn't mean to get familiar."

What had stabbed me? I turned and saw a little girl with beautiful brown eyes. She giggled and held up her doll for me to admire. An Indian Barbie's stilettos. Was this my welcome to India?

The airport was a colorful madhouse, the noise deafening, and the chaos exotic. Swarms of people surged past Immigration. I was delirious with excitement and fueled by adrenaline. I rushed with the crowd to the baggage claim, where Indian families piled mountains of suitcases on large luggage carts. I grabbed my suitcase, passed through Customs, and headed to the main terminal. Where was Trevor?

When I stepped outside, heat and humidity enveloped me. The night reeked of stale urine. Families shouted, waved, and jostled one another for the best positions behind control barriers. It was thrilling and terrifying. I saw Trevor wedged in the crush between saris and turbans, and I breathed a sigh of relief.

"You don't look like you've been traveling thirty-seven hours, Jesse." Trevor kissed me.

"I had a layover in Paris."

He lifted my small backpack off my shoulder. "Crikey, babe, you got rocks in here?"

We walked to the row of parked taxis and waited for one to be assigned to us. I said a silent prayer for a new taxi. No such luck. Ours was ancient, a beat-up black-and-yellow cab, its trunk filled with plastic containers of gasoline and tied down with a rope.

The young driver took my bags from Trevor. "Uncle, let me."

He put my suitcase in the passenger seat. We climbed into the back. Nasty ragged towels punctuated by faded red flowers covered the seat.

"Happy birthday, babe." Trevor nuzzled my neck. "You smell great."

"Duty-free Chanel." I thought about Rodin's sensuous sculpture *The Kiss* in the exhibit at the Charles de Gaulle airport in Paris. I kissed him.

The driver turned to us. "I'll take you on the scenic route."

Backseat odors assaulted me. The air conditioner didn't work. I rolled my window down. Streetlights cast a strange yellow glow like the sky before a storm, and hundreds of people slept on the sidewalks. Dogs lay beside people who were covered head-to-toe with saris, scarves, and blankets, or not at all. I was mystified. What was scenic about bodies lined up on sidewalks, block after block for miles? It was an apocalyptic landscape.

Our driver couldn't find the hotel, and Trevor didn't remember the address. We were lost. A barricade blocked the road ahead.

"Slight detour, madam," the driver said.

The cab turned into a shadowy alley. A group of men huddled under a light outside a brick building and exchanged money.

I panicked. "Drug dealers!"

"No, Auntie," our driver said. "They're playing the stock market."

The taxi turned down another dark alley. A few meters ahead, I saw a blue building surrounded by sandbags and uniformed guards with machine guns. Trevor, the driver, and I spoke simultaneously.

"I know where we are," Trevor said.

"Oh my god!" I freaked out.

"Our hotel is around the corner."

"Machine guns!" My muscles tensed.

"Security is tight after a bombing at the synagogue." Trevor patted my hand where it gripped his arm.

"It's a Mumbai landmark," the driver announced.

"Here it is, Jesse. The Hotel Lawrence."

The taxi stopped but I didn't see a sign for a hotel. The headlights shone on wooden steps leading to an open, dark hallway off the alley.

"The lift isn't working," Trevor said.

The lights weren't working either. I didn't know whether to laugh or cry.

"Bloody hell. My torch isn't working." He shook the small flashlight.

I heard the batteries rattle around, and a faint beam of light shone on the steps. A large roach scuttled out of the way.

"At least the cockroaches here aren't as big as the ones on the Gulf Coast," I said.

Trevor cut me a glare. His lips pursed in disapproval. I hadn't meant to be sarcastic.

The driver took my suitcase and backpack from Trevor. "Uncle, I'll carry the bags."

The building smelled musty, like the inside of an old wooden warehouse. Trevor led the way, his flashlight useless in the dark. We walked up three flights of steps worn down by the years. We stepped over people who slept on each of the landings. I was horrified. I thought our hotel, if it could be called that, must be a flophouse. I heard a loud crunch. Trevor had smashed someone's glasses.

When we reached the third floor, he said, "This is it, Jesse."

I didn't see a reception desk but at least the overhead fluorescent light worked. Two battered wooden chairs with faded cushions sat next to a crude bookcase filled with dog-eared paperbacks. A sleepy Indian man opened the door opposite and peered out of an office. His mat lay on the floor beside a desk. He mumbled something and shut the door.

"He's the night guard," Trevor said.

We walked down a long corridor with a cracked linoleum floor and grimy walls. Only a handful of the overhead fluorescent bulbs weren't burnt out. Trevor unlocked the door to our room.

I looked around and saw a small rotary fan mounted on the wall over the bed. The screened windows were open. The furnishings included an old wardrobe, a wooden table, two white plastic chairs, and a wooden bed. At least the sheets looked clean. Trevor's orange backpack leaned against the wall, his gray sleeping bag lay open on the bed, and a copy of Lonely Planet's *India* was beside it. A harsh strip light threw the room into stark relief. It was awful.

"I can't wait for a shower." I waited for Trevor to tell me what I already knew. The sad little hotel room had only one door.

"The bathrooms are at the far end of the hall." He paused. "We won't have hot water until morning."

I wandered back down the hall to brush my teeth, carrying the bottle of water Trevor had given me after warning me not to drink the water from the tap. Three communal wet rooms, each with different doors, served the no-star hotel. The showers rained down on moldy tile floors and splashed appalling toilets and sinks. Water drained out through a hole in the floor. I hoped nothing stopped the drain. The open windows didn't have screens, and bugs circled a naked light-bulb suspended from the high ceiling. Where was the toilet paper? The Hotel Lawrence might be every backpacker's dream, but I hadn't traveled on five dollars a day since the 1970s.

Back in the room, Trevor lay on the bed wearing nothing but his wicked grin. God, I'd missed him.

"I brought you a surprise." I pulled Mark Twain's *The Innocents Abroad* from my backpack.

"Brilliant." After he stopped laughing, he said, "I haven't bought your birthday present."

I saw the hint of a shadow cross his face, but I forgot it as soon as he wrapped his arms around me. Chanel's Allure Sensuelle perfume delivered on the promise of its name. We reveled in holding each other and fell asleep to the sounds of crows, cats in the alley, and dogs barking.

I awoke before dawn and saw a full moon over Mumbai. It was quiet and cool. Trevor slept soundly. I traced the line of his cheek with my fingertips and wondered how much it would cost to take a return flight home the next day.

CHAPER 2: *Gateway of India. Celebrating Freedom*

We left the hotel the next morning to explore Mumbai's historic Fort Area. The night's fears over sleeping bodies on the staircase landings gave way to wonder. Naked toddlers shouted and danced around a young woman who wore a faded red sari and bathed a squalling infant in a yellow plastic bucket of water. Another woman cooked on a small coal-fired brazier. The sidewalk was home, downwind of foul-smelling public urinals. I breathed through my mouth.

We walked along a tree-lined street with a brilliant green feathery canopy, past an art school surrounded by a wrought-iron fence—an outdoor gallery for students' paintings—and stopped at the Gothic Prince of Wales Museum inside the Victoria Garden.

I lingered. Trevor stirred from one foot to the other. "Another time, babe."

We walked out of the shade. The blistering sun stunned me. Heat rose from the sidewalk and the asphalt. The cacophony of city traffic washed over, around, and through me.

The newness thrilled me. "It's exotic." I mopped my face with a bandana.

"You're like a little kid." Trevor grinned and took my hand to cross the street.

We dodged motorcycles and taxis, horns blaring. He pointed to the Gateway of India, where people lined up to enter—women in one queue, men in another, small children clasping their mothers' hands. Barricades surrounded the enormous landmark overlooking the Arabian Sea. A band played under its arch. Armed guards watched us pass.

"Trevor, there are so many people."

We faced the harbor where Indian families waited for sightseeing boats to Elephant Island. A breeze off the water stirred a rainbow of saris, and women in the queue stepped onto boats in a colorful parade. The past and future didn't exist. I felt an intoxicating freedom.

We walked past the magnificent Taj Hotel next to the Gateway. A horse-drawn white carriage draped in flowers stood next to the hotel; a new Mercedes wrapped in satin ribbons stood behind it. "Look, a wedding." I was enthralled.

The streets were noisy and jam-packed with tourists and Hindus in festive clothing to celebrate India's Republic Day. We walked down sidewalks, squeezing past tourists and vendors' stalls. Swept along in the sea of people, it was impossible to stop.

"The Colaba's a scene," Trevor said.

I saw a copy of Harper Lee's *To Kill a Mockingbird* for sale in a vendor's stall. "Trevor, I can't believe it."

"Watch your bag, babe." Trevor grabbed my hand and led me out of the Colaba onto a side street. We stepped around gaping holes on a hazardous sidewalk and stopped at the New Apollo Restaurant in Akbar House.

"They serve great grub," he said.

It took a moment for my eyes to adjust once we entered the Muslim restaurant. The men stared at me. I didn't see other Westerners or women.

"Is it okay for me to be here?"

"Don't worry, babe." Trevor reassured me.

The restaurant was simple, clean, and a welcome respite with its ceiling fans. The waiter brought us glasses of ice-cold soda with lime.

"What is this?" I asked.

"Veg curry with rice, *dal* fry, and tandoori *naan*."

The food was delicious.

Mumbai's traffic was astonishing—a kaleidoscope of colors. Black taxis with yellow roofs, bicycles, cars, and buses—an orange, yellow, and green sherbet blur—raced like greyhounds from traffic lights. No lines marked the lanes. Horns honked nonstop.

"It's mad."

Trevor laughed.

We walked to Victoria Station, an extraordinary dark-red brick Italian Gothic structure. "It's a monument to the British Raj," Trevor said.

We stood under a massive clock inside the station, a kinetic melting pot of Hindus, everything in colorful motion. Beautiful, brown-skinned women with long, shiny dark hair and dark brown eyes wore vibrant saris and tunics—purples, reds, oranges, and yellows. Loudspeakers blared announcements in English and Hindi about trains and tracks. People shouted at one another. Families slept on the concrete floor beside enormous parcels wrapped in white plastic. The parcels doubled as tables half-naked toddlers used to steady themselves.

"Why are there armed guards?" I shouted. The machine guns made me nervous.

"Terrorist activity."

"Oh." I hadn't considered danger.

We walked for hours. Little altars to Hindu gods, draped with golden-orange marigolds, were everywhere—even in the folds of trees. The newness of it all whetted my appetite for more. Vendors cooked on the street, colorful umbrellas shading them from the sun, food set on red plastic oilcloth covering portable tables. A man stripped the leaves from sugar cane with his knife and put it in a press to squeeze out the sweet juice. He powered the wheels for the press with an old treadle sewing machine.

"How ingenious." I wiped my face with my wet bandana, astonished that the heat and humidity didn't affect Trevor. Crumbling colonial mansions intrigued me. "Just imagine what life was like."

"Look at 'em now," Trevor said.

Derelict buildings housed multiple families. Laundry hung from balconies, and gardens with hints of former splendor suffered from neglect. Massive trees grew around wrought-iron fences. Their roots buckled sidewalks and pushed walls from their foundations.

"Let's go to Marine Drive, Trevor." I read aloud from the Lonely Planet guide about the Art Deco buildings.

Trevor put his arm around me. "Fancy a break for tea and cakes first?"

We stopped at the small bakery next to Gaylord Restaurant, where I eyed sugary confections.

"Pick out what you want," Trevor said. "A waiter will bring the food to our table."

The waiters wore black slacks and white shirts with black bowties. A doorman wearing a red jacket and a small black cap with a red brim held the doors for us to enter the restaurant. Instead, we had tea outside on a covered porch where latticework and tall potted palms screened the dining area.

My first bite of the little Indian iced cake was a surprise. It was spongy, and the icing that looked so tantalizing wasn't sugary.

"Welcome to India." Trevor laughed and poured a cup of tea from a little pot. He paused a beat. "Milk?"

We walked back toward the India Gate on Marine Drive, where Art Deco buildings overlooked the Arabian Sea. "The architecture is fantastic," I said. "I could live at St. James Court."

I fell in love with Mumbai's vibrancy but found it impossible to ignore the poverty. A legless beggar on a board with roller-skate wheels pushed the ground with gloved-hands and propelled himself along the busy thoroughfare. Women put naked and crying babies on dirty cardboard on the hot sidewalk and gestured with their hands for us to feed them. A bloodied bandage draped over one baby's forehead.

My heart ached. "Trevor, I have to give them money."

"Don't fall for it, Jesse. It's a scam."

It was devastating to turn away from their toddlers who grabbed at me. How could I possibly help them all?

The Hotel Lawrence felt like a womb to which we retreated at day's end.

CHAPTER 3: *Last Day in Mumbai*

The next morning, we decided to visit Crawford Market before our train to Gokarna. While we waited in the queue at a city bus stop, a large, sweaty Indian man pushed me aside and stepped between Trevor and me.

"Babe." My voice shook.

Trevor turned, a look of anger crossing his face when he saw me behind the man. "How dare you push my wife!"

The man gave Trevor a sullen look, then moved behind me, jostling me with his shoulder.

The bus was crowded, hot, and dilapidated. Wedged between other passengers who were standing, I clung to a strap hanging from the ceiling and stood with my feet apart for balance.

"Why did you say I'm your wife?"

Trevor didn't reply. The bus stopped abruptly. I bumped into the woman in front of me and apologized.

"Let's get off, Jesse. We're near the market."

We crossed an alley where stray cats and kittens dodged under a fence. An emaciated dog slept curled on the springs of an old car seat.

"I want a haircut, babe."

We stopped at the barbershop—an open-air affair without a door—a tiny space with a mirror and a barber chair protected by a rusting tin roof. The barber had a moustache and wore a diamond earring; he talked on his mobile phone and cut Trevor's hair at the same time.

Crawford Market was a three-ring circus. Women and children crowded around stalls where vendors arranged fruits and vegetables and sold spices piled high in artistic mounds—red, yellow, brown, and white. We squeezed through narrow aisles in the hectic market, its shops crammed full of saris and exotic materials.

My dull T-shirt, baggy gray cargo pants, and trainers were the wrong wardrobe choice against the backdrop. "Trevor, I don't feel smart in my clothes."

He nodded and stopped to buy a sculpture of fresh-cut melon, pineapple, and papaya from a vendor's rainbow display. The vendor pulled several plates out of an old paint bucket filled with dirty water that sat next to the table.

Trevor handed me a plate. "The fruit is delicious."

"Is it safe?" I asked.

He gave me a cheeky grin and popped pieces of fruit into his mouth.

"In for a penny." I stuck the plastic fork into a melon slice, held it near my mouth, and took a small bite.

"Let's get our bags at the hotel and head to the train station," Trevor said. He flagged down a taxi. "We'll call in to Fabindia, Jesse." He smiled and his eyes twinkled.

The store was cool and spacious, filled with beautiful, handcrafted clothing. I felt out of place next to a group of young women dressed in designer casual yoga-to-let's-do-lunch clothes, their New York City sophistication unmistakable.

I found a beautiful tunic and put it back quickly when I saw the price tag, but Trevor noticed.

"Try it on, sweetheart," he said.

I waited for a dressing room and asked the young woman ahead of me. "Where do you live in the city?" She lived in Brooklyn, worked in the city, and was in India for a yoga retreat with her friends. They were going to a flower festival in Mumbai.

"Do you live in New York?" she asked.

I shook my head. "Once upon a time, when I worked in the city. I live on the Gulf Coast now."

Trevor bought me the silk tunic, a scarf, and Punjabi pants. "For your birthday, Jesse."

CHAPTER 4: *Leaving Mumbai.*
A Sacred Cow Stampede

We got out of the taxi at Lokmanya Tilak Station—a far cry from majestic Victoria Station. The parking lot was red clay, pockmarked with deep ruts. Tuk-tuks, taxis, rickshaws, bicycles, carts, people, dogs, cats, and cows blocked the way to the tracks. Trevor parted the crowd, his massive orange rucksack swaying with his sleeping bag on top, higher than his head. I hauled my little olive-green suitcase on wheels behind him, and we edged our way toward the trains.

"Let's hope nobody bumps into you, babe," I said. "You'll topple over with all that stuff on top of your skinny legs."

"Swan Vesta." He shouted.

"What?"

"Matchsticks, Jesse. They're matchsticks."

I heard him laughing. Heat waves rose from the concrete ramps and platforms. I didn't see any signs for the trains or tracks. All at once everyone in the crowd behind us shouted an alarm. A dogfight had startled the cows, and without warning the cows were rushing up the ramp toward which we walked. Trevor's backpack wobbled, and we dashed out of the way within a hair's breadth of disaster.

"Fuck me," Trevor said. "A sacred cow stampede."

My heart was racing but I had to laugh. "Where's the train?"

Trevor pointed and led the way. "Here. Our names and ages are posted outside the carriage."

"You're kidding!" I was hot, thirsty, and sweaty, and I wanted something cold to drink. "Watch my bag." I dashed off to the station, an unattractive gray concrete building opposite the platforms and tracks. A crippled beggar writhed across the platform and tried to grab my legs. I rushed back to Trevor.

Panic clouded his face. "Our train's about to leave, Jesse."

I spent my third night in India on the train to Gokarna—an overnight express and my worst nightmare. It was a third-class sleeper car without air conditioning, and the late-afternoon heat was oppressive. We were on the cheapest possible train journey, our tickets discounted because we were older travelers and foreigners. The third-class sleeper was the poor relation of a six-berth couchette in France. Designed for eight people to occupy each of the open compartments, two three-tier berths faced one another and were across the aisle from two-tier berths along the length of the carriage.

I sat next to the window on the hard bench seat and smiled at the Indian women who sat across from me, and they smiled back. Hot air blew through the windows—only metal bars in the openings. Leaving Mumbai, we passed through slums—unbelievably dirty shantytowns with a film of dust coating all. Tent cities mushroomed side-by-side with tenements. Tarps, sticks, bamboo, and every conceivable material pieced together grim dwellings where millions lived. Enterprising families planted vegetable gardens on the no-man's land around the train tracks littered with trash, utterly filthy.

Outside Mumbai the air was cleaner. The leaves on the trees suggested they had once been green rather than gray, but the landscape looked burnt. A haze softened the edges of the barren land. I watched a family walk toward a shelter with tarps draped over bamboo supports, the crude dwelling next to a small garden.

I turned to Trevor. "My life is so soft."

Trevor patted me on the knee.

Our railway car was an adventure in determination. People boarded without tickets, crashed onto benches, and claimed seats. It was a game of who was most stubborn. Six people sat on a bench meant for three. No other Westerners were on the train, and the Indian men stared at me. I tried to ignore the stares. I thought it was my clothing. Then it hit me. It was me and my red hair. I was so white.

I gazed out the window, lost in a reverie, and the landscape blurred. I had started to nod off to sleep from the rhythmic clickety-clack of the wheels on the track when I felt something brush across the top of my thigh. It wasn't Trevor's hand.

"Mouse!" I screamed. Everyone jumped from their seats to search.

When it was dark, I had to move because the Indian women had the bottom two berths. We helped them raise the middle berth and attach it to the fixed top berth. They lay down on the hard benches and covered themselves, head to toe, with scarves and saris. Trevor and I had the top berths, rock-hard platforms on either side of the open compartment.

He pulled out a length of chain, wound it through our luggage underneath the bottom platform, and put a padlock on it.

"We don't want anything stolen while we're sleeping, sweetheart."

" . . . didn't see that coming," I said, and paused a beat. "Babe, I need the loo."

"Jesse, the train has Western and Indian toilets. There's no toilet paper, you need hand sanitizer, and take bottled water to brush your teeth."

The signs for the doors were missing. I opened the door to the Indian toilet—my first encounter with a squat toilet. "Oh my god." The Western toilet wasn't in any better condition. Both were disgusting and smelled dreadful. I let the door slam shut and went back to the Indian toilet. I knew there must be an art to using a squat toilet since it was tricky to hold on with one hand and prevent my clothing from touching anything. The waste just dropped onto the train tracks. "Heaven help me." I exited the stinky compartment.

Using metal rungs at the end of the bench seat, I climbed to the top berth and sat on the hard platform, my head close to the ceiling.

Trevor said, "You're quite spry."

I dangled my legs over the side to untie my shoelaces and tried not to kick the Indian woman who climbed into the middle berth beside her two small children.

"Put your trainers in a plastic bag, Jesse."

"Why?"

"So no one can steal them when you're asleep."

"Jeez Louise," I muttered and put my small backpack with my laptop, phone, and camera under my head. I tried to get comfortable, but it was a lumpy pillow. On the top berth, the air was stifling. Two small electric fans were fixed to the ceiling. One worked, although it only blew the hot air around. I baked at 350° on the top berth of the open compartment in the third-class sleeper car.

CHAPTER 5: *Shock and Awe in Gokarna*

We reached Gokarna Station in the wee hours and endured a bumpy thirty-minute ride in a tuk-tuk. The auto-rickshaw, like a three-wheeled golf cart with a noisy lawnmower engine, drove to a small group of huts in a jungle where faint moonlight shone through tree branches. Trevor, the tuk-tuk driver who carried my suitcase, and I walked past the huts to a field of sweet-smelling plants. My shoes sank in the sand path, and we reached a group of palm trees.

"This is Ananda House," Trevor said.

"Where?"

Trevor's torch shone a faint light on small masonry buildings and palm huts with thatched roofs. We were in a camp on the beach.

We walked through deeper sand to the treehouse where Trevor had stayed since early January. He hadn't offered details during our Skype calls, and I hadn't thought to ask. I climbed a makeshift bamboo ladder and pulled myself up through a hole onto a piece of plywood—the treehouse floor. The tuk-tuk driver pushed my suitcase up through the hole, and Trevor passed his orange backpack to me the same way. It was another challenge after the train journey, the tuk-tuk ride, the hike through the jungle and the sand, and, lest I forget, the sacred cow stampede in Mumbai.

A single lightbulb dangled from a bamboo rafter in the middle of a small room with a thatched roof. The wiring looked dangerous. Trevor had decorated the spartan dwelling with a colorful Tree of Life spread on the bed, a mattress on a plywood platform surrounded by mosquito netting. The crude bamboo-and-palm structure had no running water. Trevor had camped all his life. I had been a miserable Girl Scout.

I heard waves breaking on the beach. The Arabian Sea was just a few meters away. Trevor stood behind me and put his arms around me. Moonlight sparkled on the water, and the cool breeze was refreshing.

I stirred from a brief but dreamless sleep I'd enjoyed for a few hours when a rooster crowed nearby. It was cool in the wee hours before dawn, and I snuggled next to Trevor under his down sleeping bag.

Nature called. I climbed down the bamboo ladder and made my way through the dark with the aid of a flashlight to the toilet, a crude tin outhouse with a porcelain squat toilet set in a block of cement. I shone the light into every corner of the outhouse, terrified of large spiders or other creatures. It was the jungle after all.

Later I awoke coughing. Trevor stood next to the bed. "Morning, sweetheart."

"What is that noxious smell?"

"The villagers burn rubbish every morning. Here, babe." Trevor kissed me and handed me a cup of ginger, lemon, and honey tea.

The sun was up, and I had my first look around the treehouse. I walked out onto the plywood porch with my cup of tea, stood under the palm frond roof, and looked out at the beach, the water sparkling in the morning sun. A tiny kitten stood on the peak of the thatched roof of a building nearby, hissing at squawking crows that tried to land.

Trevor laughed. "She's guarding the restaurant."

It looked like a picnic shelter.

"I'm going to shower, Jesse. I'll show you around."

A sign leaned against the trunk of a large coconut palm tree and was wedged between large sandstone rocks. *Ananda on the Beach. Rooms Available. Gokarna Beach.* We stood in front of the lime-green outhouse surrounded by lush tropical plants with dark green and variegated leaves growing in the sandy soil. In the light of day, I surveyed its construction. The back and sides were built with rust-colored sandstones collected from fields, and its funky wooden door, wrapped in tin on which the word "Toilet" was painted in crude white letters, was at a slight angle, and the letters were at an opposing angle to the door.

When Trevor opened the door, I examined it in its glory from a safe distance. Slightly elevated on a concrete pad sat a once-white ceramic squat toilet with convenient places to put your feet on either side of a hole. Wooden boards separated by large gaps made up the questionable roof with a view of the trees and sky, and a dodgy-looking lightbulb hung from two electrical wires affixed to a glass condenser where the two wires joined on the front of the building.

"It's disgusting."

"Some wanker didn't clean it, Jesse."

"Hope I won't be fried in an outhouse in India."

"Right." Trevor laughed and filled a small pail of water from the nearby tap around which grew even more plants. He handed it to me. "Splash the water on the concrete and the toilet."

A five-gallon bucket of water sat next to the toilet. "What's that?" I pointed to a large plastic measuring cup hanging by its handle over the lip of the bucket.

"To wash yourself after . . . "

"Oh, a gravity bidet."

Trevor laughed. "Use the small pail to fill the bucket and rinse the toilet for the next person."

"Squat toilet etiquette." Mastery of the technique seemed doubtful. Thank heaven I had bought Coleman biodegradable bamboo wipes. "Who knew."

The outdoor shower was a concrete slab surrounded by woven palm screens, a tattered floral shower curtain for a door.

"Hmm, not much privacy."

"I'll stand guard." Trevor winked at me, a big grin on his face.

It was only 9 a.m. and the day was hot. Cold water flowed from a shower head and felt good. How glorious to be clean!

The open-air restaurant looked like a picnic pavilion with a concrete floor and thatched roof. Concrete benches with colorful pillows and cushions lined two sides of the structure; the front side was open to the sea. The kitchen was no larger than a broom closet, with a single propane burner and a small refrigerator.

"That's it?" I asked.

One of the boys, dressed in jeans and a T-shirt, took our order, and promptly sat down with two other boys at the table with their iPhones. Two young girls in saris cooked behind the small counter.

"It'll be a while till we get our omelets," Trevor said. "Want to go for a swim?"

I shook my head and lay in a hammock strung between wooden posts at the front of the restaurant. I stared at the waves and must have fallen asleep until Trevor surprised me with a kiss.

"Breakfast, sweetheart."

The food at Ananda House's small restaurant was a wonderful surprise. Sugary chai jolted me awake, the omelets were delicious, and the bowls of fresh fruit were beautiful.

Later, we crossed the field through which we'd trudged in the dark. It was a gorgeous vegetable garden. We passed through a stone stile into the jungle village and sidestepped chickens until we reached the road. We walked on hard-packed red sand while bicycles and an occasional tuk-tuk beeped at us. Old women, rail thin, carried bundles of twigs on top of their heads.

My heart broke when I saw two dead kittens in a pile of refuse on the dirt road, and I wanted to weep. Stray dogs, puppies, cats, and kittens were everywhere, hungry, skinny, and scavenging through the trash side-by-side with bony sacred cows. I pressed my bandana over my nose to stop the overpowering stench from garbage and dead animals that clogged the drainage ditches.

"There's no spay or neuter program in India?"

"Different culture, Jesse."

Sweat rolled down my forehead. It had to be over 100 degrees outside. I watched a little girl swing a kitten by its leg in the air, as if it were a teddy bear.

"Stop that!" I said.

The child ignored me. It was Mardi Gras back home, and I would miss the Mystic Mutts of Revelry parade, the fundraiser for our no-kill animal shelter.

We came to a fork in the road. To the right was the beach, and on our left was a small bridge over a canal filled with refuse. I couldn't see the water. Rubbish littered the streets. One of the Hindu pilgrims threw an empty plastic bottle on the road.

"Babe, why are the Hindus who came for a religious pilgrimage throwing trash and bottles wherever they walk?"

"Ain't got a clue, Jesse."

The disregard for the beach town was appalling. I struggled to understand.

We walked through a narrow cobblestone lane, on either side of which were open-air storefronts—your basic concrete boxes with clothes in vibrant colors hanging from the bottoms of roll-up metal doors. At the end of the short lane stood a whitewashed temple where pilgrims removed their shoes and sandals before entering.

"We're here," Trevor said.

I wasn't sure where "here" was when a beautiful young woman ran out of a shop set back from the lane under a canvas awning.

"Major Tom." Her long honey-blonde hair swung when she hugged Trevor.

"Anna, we made it," Trevor said. "This is Jesse."

"Major Tom?" I asked.

"We called him Major Tom when our group hiked in Dharamsala," Anna said.

"When I was in India two years ago," Trevor explained.

"Want an espresso?" Anna grinned at him.

"Anna manages the Internet Café for the Indian owner and sells espresso to earn a bit of extra dosh."

We sat outside, our backs against a gray masonry wall. It was cooler in the shade under the canvas awning. So this was the Internet Café where Trevor had called me on Skype in the weeks before I joined him. It appeared to be a hotspot of sorts, judging by the backpackers crowded there for the Wi-Fi. I thought calling it a coffee shop was a stretch. It was a hole in the wall in the marketplace.

Anna handed Trevor a small cup of dark coffee. "Did Trevor tell you about his harem?"

I nodded and realized Anna was one of the young women backpackers who hung out with Trevor, although he was old enough to be their grandfather. His humor and charm cemented friendships—with the young women and men backpackers. Was I self-conscious (threatened) when I met the gorgeous, svelte, estrogen-producing young woman? Well, hell yes, but I'd be damned if I'd let Trevor know.

I wasn't paying close attention when Trevor warned me, "Watch out, babe."

A sacred cow had wandered into the café from the travel store next door, a stream of warm piss splashing dangerously close to my new trainers. It wasn't quite a baptism by fire, but it was close.

"Ram Naam Satya Hai. Ram Naam Satya Hai."

Two weeks earlier, faint chanting had interrupted our Skype call. It was after midnight. I lay in bed, wrapped in a flannel nightgown, socks on my feet, under a down comforter pitched like a tent, blue light reflected on my face from the computer. It was bitterly cold that January night, two weeks before my sixty-third birthday.

"What's that?" I had asked.

Trevor turned his iPad toward a crowded lane in the marketplace. A massive white Brahman cow with a large camel-like hump walked past the spot where he sat. Trevor called it a coffee shop. He perched on a ledge, his backdrop a dull gray concrete wall.

The chanting grew louder. Six men, dressed in white tunics and trousers, carried a bamboo stretcher bearing the body of a very old man, also dressed in white, with long white hair and a long white beard. Golden-orange marigolds blanketed his body. He looked so peaceful. Sunlight reflected from the white clothing, the man's soft, white beard and hair, and the glowing marigolds draped over his body. An ethereal light bathed the entire procession, and the beautiful simplicity resonated deep in a primal part of my soul.

"Where are they going?"

"To the beach . . . to burn his body."

"That's a funeral in India?" It was stunning. "I want to be dressed in white, draped in marigolds, and carried out on a bamboo stretcher."

"I miss you, sweetheart," Trevor said. "Are you coming or not?"

I hesitated a moment and caved. "Okay, I'll meet you in Mumbai." No sooner had I agreed to join him than a wave of terror washed over me. "Carpe diem."

Now I sat on the same ledge, my back against the gray concrete wall, and watched the parade of people on the narrow lane. Hindu Pilgrims, Russians, and French backpackers filled Gokarna. I saw disheveled and dirty older white men who looked like wandering hippies not aging well and stoned out of their minds, a throwback to the 1960s. A disheveled woman wearing jeans and a tunic walked past us with a puppy in her arms. She mumbled to herself, but the puppy wasn't moving.

A young French couple stopped at the café to post photos of clothes they sold on Facebook. Their online business supported their travels. A woman from Philadelphia who seemed part Indian, spoke fluent Hindi, and had lived five years in India studying to become a monk, bought an espresso and talked with us.

"India is hard living," she said. She was leaving after five years. "I'm a mass of contradictions, afraid to leave India and apprehensive about going home."

So many people on different quests. I just wanted to see what I was made of.

We walked past the temple where pilgrims' shoes and sandals were piled higgledy-piggledy and to a wide main street packed with hardened red dirt, shops on either side.

"What's that?" I pointed to a large, two-story wooden structure on wheels in the middle of the street.

"An Indian temple chariot, Jesse. It's at least 350 years old."

Gokarna, I learned, was a sacred temple town whose name meant "cow's ear."

We stopped for lunch at a small restaurant where we were the only foreigners. People stared at us. It was a relief to get out of the hot sun, but it wasn't cool, even with ceiling fans. Trevor pointed to a communal sink with a grubby-looking bar of soap. The sink was next to the open kitchen. "Wash your hands here, babe."

The waiter handed me a dog-eared laminated menu. Why had I bothered to wash my hands? The menu had photographs of food, the names in English.

"The pictures don't help."

"I'll order, Jesse."

"Nothing too spicy."

When lunch arrived, it looked like it was in a pancake wrap.

"This is *Masala Dosa*? A wrap?" I asked.

"It's not a wrap. It's a dosa." Trevor laughed. "That's Sweet *Lassi*."

The wrap held a tasty potato concoction, and I enjoyed the refreshing yogurt drink.

As we walked back out of the town, sweat poured down my forehead. I wiped my face with my "peace and love" bandana—pink hearts and peace symbols against a white background.

"How's it possible to be so hot in January?" I asked.

"It can go up to 100 degrees Fahrenheit in March."

At night, I huddled under the orange sleeping bag with Trevor. Early mornings were cold, but the heat was sweltering at midday, like Alabama Gulf Coast August heat. The days and nights melted into a blur.

One evening we ate dinner at Prema Café, a crowded vegetarian restaurant near Gokarna's marketplace. A handsome young Russian and his girlfriend shared our table, and he told us he taught yoga at Om Beach.

His girlfriend asked, "Where are you staying?"

"Ananda House," Trevor replied.

The young man said, "We call it the Russian ghetto."

"No kidding," Trevor answered.

After leaving the restaurant, Trevor and I walked down the beach holding hands. It was cool in the evening and peaceful listening to the waves breaking on shore. We stopped, and he put his arms around me. "You're a trooper, babe."

I welcomed the evening's romantic moment since the day's heat hadn't encouraged much closeness. Unfortunately, the peace didn't last. Before we reached Ananda House, we heard ear-splitting Russian pop music. A disco ball, strung up outside a palm hut, sent a rainbow dancing across the sand. Its flashing lights guided us back as surely as the North Star.

As we walked toward our treehouse, I saw a young girl who wore a thong, and nothing more, bare her ass to three men who sat outside the hut. The disco-ball Russians were a rough-looking lot.

"That's obscene," I said.

"For fuck's sake!" Trevor said. "They're wankers."

The music kept me awake until the wee hours, but Trevor slept through it all. I got annoyed while I lay there, thoughts churning. During the night, I heard a scratching sound, the palm fronds in the roof rustled, and an animal squeaked. I turned on my flashlight—two large rats crawled in the rafters. *Oh, God, what's next?* I wondered. I didn't want to wake him, so I curled my body around him. He didn't stir, and I lay awake in tears until almost dawn, when I finally fell asleep.

I awoke coughing; the noxious smoke from burning trash irritated my scratchy throat, and I felt achy. The sun was up, and I was alone in bed. Tears rolled down my cheeks.

"Babe, what's wrong?" Trevor handed me a cup of the ginger, lemon, and honey tea he made for me every morning.

I waited twenty minutes for the communal outdoor shower while one of the Russian men stood under the shower and sang along with the godawful pop music on his iPad. Two young Russian women stopped me on my way back to the treehouse.

The young women spoke to me in broken English. "We're not all so rude."

"No apology necessary." I smiled.

Trevor joined us and we chatted for a few minutes until one of the Russian men, with a bandage on his leg, stormed out of his hut and launched into a vitriolic attack.

"Fucking Brit and American," he said. "You woke me."

The guy got up in Trevor's face. The young women and I stood frozen. Trevor said nothing but he put his arm around me and, wearing a stoic expression, led me away. It was over the top, but then everything was extreme in Gokarna.

"Let's get a cup of chai," Trevor said.

I needed down time. Alone. I shook my head. "I'm going for a walk." I took a shortcut through the restaurant and out to the beach in near meltdown. I felt like Al Pacino in *Dog Day Afternoon*. It was all too much. I needed a break from Trevor. I was exhausted from the heat and tired of mosquitoes biting me under the net. I'd had enough of peeing in a jar at night because I didn't want to fall down the bamboo ladder. The rats and the hungover Russian's over-the-top tirade were the last straws. I was amazed I'd lasted eight days in a treehouse.

I hadn't walked far on the beach in the opposite direction of town when I saw a sign, *Chez Christophe.* It was a laid-back French restaurant open to the sea. The restaurant had low tables and soft bench seats. Inviting cushions covered platform swings hanging from the rafters. A lovely ocean breeze blew through the restaurant, and a young man with dreadlocks played an acoustic guitar and sang softly. The French restaurant was heaven. What a surprising find.

A handsome young Frenchman said, "*Bon jour, madame.* Can I get you something to drink?"

"Yes, thanks. Do you have a cold lime soda?"

He nodded and asked if I'd like the Wi-Fi password. After getting a signal, I sent a WhatsApp message to Maggie to ask if she had time for a Skype call. The twelve-hour time difference meant it was 10:30 p.m. back home. Thank heaven she was awake and had time to talk. The moment I saw her face I started crying.

"Jesse, what on earth is the matter?" Maggie asked.

"Where do I begin?" I sobbed and recounted how unprepared I'd been for the challenges of India with Trevor.

"You can always come home."

I nodded and blew my nose into the bandana. Still sniffling, I said, "I know, but . . . "

"You wanted a challenge, right?"

"Yeah, out of my comfort zone and into fucking hell." I struggled to stop the tears rolling down my cheeks. "I need to see what I'm made of."

"In a treehouse?"

"I can't quit." I paused a moment to catch my breath in between a fresh round of sobs. "I love Trevor, and I don't want to give up."

"Good Lord, Jesse. Roughing it on the beach is great if you're twenty and love to camp. Have you told Trevor you're miserable?"

"No." I sighed. "I didn't want to complain."

"Oh, for heaven's sake, Jesse. Say something."

The waiter set the lime soda on the table and walked back to the bar.

"Who is that gorgeous man? And where are you?" Maggie looked astonished.

I took a sip of the ice-cold drink and turned the phone around to show her Chez Christophe.

"It's beautiful," she said.

" . . . brings back memories of a romantic getaway to St. Barth's . . . many years ago," I said.

"Graham and I took the ferry over from St. Maarten for a day trip, and we loved the island."

"That was four-star then, and this is no-star now." I sighed.

Maggie laughed. "Hang in there, Jesse."

"I'll talk with Trevor after lunch."

The waiter brought me a veg tali—a huge plate with delicious curry, a chickpea concoction, cottage cheese-onion-peppers, soup, and *chapatis*. It was too much food, and I swiped a tear away.

"*Quel est le problème?*" the waiter asked.

" . . . next door . . . the treehouse."

"*Je comprends.*"

I sniffled and wiped my nose with my bandana.

After my experiences in Gokarna, the restaurant felt chic, and I felt like a slob, eaten up with insecurity. I was dismayed. When I went back to Ananda House, I heard Tchaikovsky's *Swan Lake* coming from the Russian women's hut. Classical music playing in a jungle hut on a beach in India made sense.

I told Trevor, "Eight days in the tree house is enough."

He put his arms around me. "Okay, babe."

We walked into town and on the way discovered Naga Palace. It wasn't a palace, but we looked at a room with an en suite bath. It was cool, there was no mosquito net, and it had electricity, an air conditioner, a fan, and Wi-Fi. Although it was not clean by Western standards, it was the Ritz by an Indian yardstick. We had room to move without bumping into each other, and we had a covered balcony with chairs.

"Trevor, let's stay here tonight."

He nodded in agreement. "We can move our things from Ananda House tomorrow."

The treehouse cost only $2.50 USD a night for the two of us. Thank goodness we were on the same page.

It was heaven. I finally had a good night's sleep after a clean, cool shower. The bath and shower were private, and the electricity stayed on most of the night, though the AC didn't work. Trevor and I enjoyed a lovely morning cuddle at Naga Palace.

We returned to Ananda House and ate breakfast at the restaurant before we moved our belongings. I fed the scrawny resident kitten my scrambled eggs and bits of Trevor's hard-boiled egg. While we weren't paying attention, the kitten snatched up a pat of butter and gobbled it. Trevor went for a swim. I lay in the hammock, watched waves break on the beach, and listened to the lovely accents of the Frenchmen who sat at a nearby table. The kitten slept next to me. The cheeky little scrapper would probably make it.

CHAPTER 6: *Carrying on Tradition Older Than Time*

Women were beasts of burden. No matter what age. An old woman walked through communal gardens near Ananda House every day to weed and water the vegetables. She filled a clay pot with water at a spigot. Indian women worked diligently in the fields. Women carried loads of firewood balanced on their heads. One day we watched a construction site where a woman walked with a heavy sack of concrete that required two men to lift it to her head. Hindu men and boys slept in hammocks.

Trevor said, "They watch telly on smartphones."

Men walked into me if I didn't move out of the way. I walked behind Trevor in the crowd—sometimes in front, as brazen men took pleasure in touching my derrière. It happened more than once and disgusted me. I was the only redhead I'd seen in Gokarna. Women and men stared. It was a different world. I felt overwhelming gratitude for having a cozy home with central air and heat as well as two bathrooms and water I drank from the tap. My electricity worked all the time. We enjoyed clean streets and flowers all year round. My hometown didn't have dusty roads littered with plastic bags, bottles, and trash. The dogs and cats back home were well-fed, even the feral cats in the woods at Magnolia Beach.

We were walking into Gokarna, heading to the post office, when a young woman walked toward us and shouted with excitement.

"Major Tom!" She spoke with a thick German accent. She had shoulder-length dark brown hair and eyes to match. She was pretty and in her twenties, I guessed.

"Blimey, Elsa, it's great to see you." Trevor gave her a hug. "Have you seen Anna?" She nodded and he introduced us. She was one of four young women in the harem of girls Trevor had charmed two years earlier. We made plans to have dinner since we were traveling to Kochi the next day.

That evening Elsa directed us to a dreadful place, a dark restaurant somewhere out of the way, not in the familiar part of Gokarna. I felt like we were in a cave, and we were the only diners. Not a good sign.

"Where's the menu?" I asked.

"The restaurant doesn't have one," Elsa said. I noticed she spoke in a loud voice.

When the server came to our table, I asked, "What vegetarian dishes do you serve?"

He shook his head.

Elsa said, "You have a choice, fried chicken or fried fish."

Why was she so loud? I wondered.

I thought what I ate was chicken, I hoped what I ate was chicken. The bones looked weird. I ate all the rice after a few bites of the maybe-it-was chicken. The fried fish were so small they looked like bait dragged in the cast nets off the Fairhope Pier. Trevor picked through the bones on those little puppies with remarkable skill. How he managed to find enough to eat defied understanding, but he did eat another full plate of rice. We walked back to town for chai and Badam milk. I learned that Elsa was deaf, or hearing impaired, and a loud, nonstop talker. By the end of the evening, I was exhausted.

I had an upset tummy the next day, although I wasn't sick. The antidote I found was a cheese naan. That, and what looked like Indian grits—tasty semolina with green and red peppers and a side of hot sauce like wasabi that I set aside.

I sent an email to Maggie:

We are traveling by train to Kochi tomorrow—overnight, of course. It saves the cost of another night at Naga Palace. I passed the acid test. I survived eight days in the treehouse on the beach. Trevor and I are still together.

CHAPTER 7: *On the Express Train to Kochi*

We boarded the express train to Kochi at Karawar. It was almost seven hours late. We had tickets for a third-class sleeper car, and I was in an upper berth again. I got the giggles when I couldn't climb the ladder to the top berth on the first or second attempts. I was tired and, yes, I was truly out of my comfort zone. I might have slept two hours before the vendors started chanting through the train cars. "Chai, chai. Chai, chai." After a night of very little sleep, I concluded that everyone in India had smartphones. The ringtones that chimed through the night played an annoying range of songs. Even more annoying were the loud conversations, hopelessly animated, and, since families tended to be very large and extended in India, I was certain the passengers in our car spoke with every living relative throughout the night. Trevor slept through it all.

I sipped chai and thought about the night before. We had waited seven hours at the station from dusk till the wee hours. An Indian gentleman gob-spat every few minutes to rid his cheeks of the *paan* he chewed. It was disgusting and I felt nauseous. A large sign posted in the station house read *Please Do Not Spit*. If I'd wanted to avoid it, I could have joined the Indian women in the Ladies' Retiring Room, but the facilities were so unsanitary I felt safer next to Trevor, who guarded our luggage. Three puppies on the train platform sucked at their mother's teats. It was nearly time to wean them. They looked fat and healthy, unlike their poor emaciated mother, whose rib cage showed.

When I went into the Ladies' Retiring Room to use the toilet, an Indian woman in a sari pointed at me and said in a stern voice, "Ladies. Ladies."

My travel costume consisted of long olive-green pants, a shirt over a racer-back tee, sports bra, and trainers. Did she think I was a man with my very short hair and travel outfit? I pointed to myself and declared, "Lady. Lady." Embarrassed, I thought it was past time for me to look for more feminine travel attire. The squat toilet in the ladies' room was foul. I photographed it for posterity, but Trevor's photo of the Western toilet in the gents' proved beyond a doubt that the men's toilet was far worse.

I doubted I would ever see the world again as I had once seen it. Beggars fine-tuned performances. When they spied us, they rushed forward with hands outstretched. Terribly crippled beggars crawled and scooted through the train cars using their hands to drag useless knees and legs along. I saw a child whose arm appeared to extend backwards out of his shoulder, the rotator cuff protruding. Spina bifida? Women pinched children to make them cry and carried them naked through the streets, or they draped bloody bandages over the children's heads.

Beggars rarely approached other Hindus, I noticed, but they watched us wherever we went. If we wanted to buy a bar of soap and pulled out our money, they appeared, one after another. It was heartbreaking. The beggars had their turf staked out. At one stop on the journey, a fragile old woman stood before me with palm outstretched. I shook my head. I'd given money to the crippled beggars on the train. I was annoyed and wondered at my ability to detach. I questioned my annoyance. Did I feel guilty because I had so much and they had so little? I could not help them all.

Our "express" train stopped at every station. The train car was filthy, and the squat toilet, my only option, was beyond disgusting. I thought about my mission to get out of my comfort zone. I had succeeded in my first two weeks in India. Was it only two weeks? It felt like a lifetime. I didn't know if I could make it three months.

It was impossibly hot. The cool mountains and tea plantations we planned to visit could not come soon enough for me. Trevor didn't suffer from the heat as I did. In fact, I seemed to be the only person who had perspiration dripping down her forehead every day, almost all day long. It was early February, but it felt like a hot summer day. Where Trevor guided us, we rarely found air conditioning. I thought about yoga trips to the Motherland and the arranged tours of India where people like me, my age, traveled by air-conditioned car or coach and slept in resorts with hot and cold running water, clean sheets, maid service, and AC. Did they pay to tour the Mumbai slums made famous in *Slum Dog Millionaire?* Facebook friends said the photos I posted were like *The Best Exotic Marigold Hotel.* No way! The Marigold Hotel was a four-star resort in comparison.

Trevor and I stayed in a tiny two-room hotel in the historic Fort Kochi area. Bell House called itself a boutique hotel. I'd booked our stay online before we left Gokarna. Although our room was the size of a postage stamp, it was immaculate, with lovely clean linens. The en suite bathroom was brand new and beautifully tiled.

"Hallelujah. Hot and cold running water, and a real toilet." I was over the moon. Unfortunately, the weather was so hot that I didn't want hot water showers. "It's awfully hot, Trevor. Let's turn on the air conditioner."

Trevor frowned. "Air conditioning costs four hundred rupees extra."

We had a beautiful 800-rupee room with all mod cons, but Trevor didn't want to pay more for AC because the cost of our $12 room would increase to $17. Travel with Trevor was proving to be a steep learning curve. Bell House may have been pristine, but it was hot and humid.

"Let's leave the fan on high, babe." Trevor wasn't bothered much by the heat, but I roasted slowly under the ceiling fan that blew hot air on high speed.

"Jesse, I'm cold when it's on high speed."

"How is it possible?" I'd never met a man whose body temperature was so different from mine. I couldn't wait until we headed into the mountains, to Munnar, where we planned to stay and visit the tea plantations. It was said to be blessedly cool.

The next morning, we explored and walked to a park on the water where we saw the Chinese cantilevered fishing nets. Four- and five-man teams of Indians pulled ropes weighted with large rocks to lower and lift the nets. One of the men with the team that pulled the Chinese fishing nets wore a garment that looked like a cross between baggy shorts and a diaper. He walked barefoot out on one of the poles to weigh the net down into the water.

"What is that man wearing?" I asked.

"It's a *mundu*, Jesse. A long skirt the men wrap around their waists and tie up to work in the fields or on the Chinese nets. It's traditional dress for Southern India."

Women in colorful saris sold trinkets in the park. Dirty children played near their mothers. One crippled toddler held onto her brother's finger to walk. It was a hardscrabble existence for so many Indians. Traditional dress seemed to change in the cities. Older Indian women wore saris, younger women wore tunics over leggings or jeans, and teenagers dressed in Western attire. Most men wore Western clothing—jeans and a T-shirt. American television and movies likely influenced each generation's cultural changes.

"Amazing." I pointed to a sign for *Kerala's Clean Street Campaign, Keep Kerala Green*. "There's official action here." I was excited to see Kerala promoted environmental awareness. "What a difference from Gokarna."

"Jesse, I don't want to burst your bubble." Trevor rolled his eyes. "Their campaign probably has more to do with tourism. The fort area is a popular tourist attraction."

I studied our Lonely Planet *India* and researched online to learn that Kochi, in the Indian state of Kerala, had become a port after a huge flood in 1341, and then was an important city on the spice trade route. The Portuguese had settled in the city and left a Catholic heritage.

CHAPTER 8: *On the Bus to Munnar*

The bus station was a red-clay parking lot with vendors' sheds on either side. I wasn't sure what I had been expecting, but it wasn't the wasteland that lay before me. Our bus to Munnar was ancient. It was hot as hell and smelled like pee. My initiation to a bus trip in India didn't look promising. I sat on a hard bench seat toward the back of the bus on the right side. Trevor dropped his daypack on the seat beside me and raced off.

"I'll be back in a few minutes, Jesse."

The bus wasn't air-conditioned, a single metal bar the only barrier across open windows. More people of all ages crowded onto the bus than I'd imagined possible. The driver climbed aboard and started the engine. Indian music blared from speakers, and I panicked.

"Wait!" I shouted. Heads turned. I peered out the window into the parking lot and watched Trevor make a mad dash to the door. The driver opened the doors to let Trevor and an older Hindu woman board the bus. Trevor made his way down the aisle carrying a small paper sack and a large bottle of water.

"Where the hell have you been?" I asked.

"Buying *samosas*, babe."

Passengers filled every seat on the bus except ours, and the sari-clad Indian woman who had boarded the bus after Trevor sat beside him. The three of us squeezed together on the seat built for two. Unfortunately, the woman was well-fed and had a remarkably broad derrière. Trevor was sandwiched between the two of us.

"Bloody hell, she's got a big arse," he said.

I elbowed him and leaned my head out the window. I was mortified. Didn't he consider she understood English? She got off the bus a few hours into the trip.

The bus ascended to Munnar through a forest primeval. The driver seemed to be on a suicide mission as the bus raced around perilous curves, overtaking cars and horse carts around blind spots.

"This is either terrifying or thrilling," I said. "Thank God we have travel insurance."

"If we die, it won't matter, Jesse."

"Pretend it's a carnival ride, Trevor."

"Right. And a dodgy driver is torturing us with Indian music blasting through shite speakers."

Trevor handed me a samosa. It was petrified, a rock-hard missile. I threw it out the open window and down into a ravine that was too close for comfort. The bus climbed into the hill country where I reveled in the cool mountain air and marveled at Munnar's tea plantations. We survived the memorable six-hour trip.

I hadn't booked a room online in Munnar, but after a brief recon we chose a hotel that looked decent on the outside. It was dreadful. It didn't have hot water, then no water full stop. The electricity shut off throughout the night, and, every time we lost electricity, a loud generator cranked up outside our room. The generator sat below a large ventilation opening near the ceiling and we couldn't block the opening in the wall. A single lightbulb on the ceiling illuminated the room.

"We survived the bus trip, babe," I said.

"Right. Now carbon monoxide in this shite hotel will kill us."

"There's only one thing to do. Make it a Kodak memory." I turned the camera at an angle because the room was just plain cockeyed.

"Jesse, I'd cry if I were here alone."

We survived the night, but when Trevor came out of the bathroom the next morning, he said, "I can pee faster than the water in the shower."

He wasn't exaggerating. My shower experience was no better. A little hot water dribbled out pitifully, the cold water didn't work, and the faucet handle fell off.

"Don't you think the mold on the walls gives the bathroom character?" I laughed.

Other hotel guests turned out to be a group of loud men next door. One man cleared his throat. The sound punctuated the morning along with bird calls.

"He's gob spitting," Trevor said

"Disgusting."

"Get used to it, Jesse."

After a soothing and delicious breakfast at Rap, a town restaurant with a good mix of Western and Indian foods, we moved out of the one-night-stand hotel. I tried to retrieve copies of our passport and visa information, but the dodgy desk clerk wouldn't return them. The night before, we had filled out lengthy paperwork with our life history and signed in blood before we had the privilege of paying for the shite room. We learned an important travel tip: always check to see if the shower really works and the handles don't fall off.

We wanted to visit Top Station, the highest point in Munnar, but we missed the bus in town. A tourist at the bus stop suggested we pay a jeep driver to take us. Trevor negotiated with the driver, and we waited while the owner of the jeep recruited other passengers. We didn't consider how many other passengers might join us. That was mistake number one. Trevor and I watched nine Hindu men launch themselves into the front and back seats of the jeep, a couple of skinny guys sat on the other men's laps.

"Fuck me," Trevor said. "I didn't pay for a clown car."

"Where do we sit?"

We climbed through the back window of the jeep into the cargo area, the only more-or-less free space remaining, and squeezed our bodies into unnatural shapes to fit on top of and between large sacks of rice. Remarkably enough, it was a wildly fun ride. We were a merry crew in the jeep hurtling around hairpin curves, through the tea plantations, with ear-shattering Indian tunes blasting from the speaker that was quite literally under me for thirty-five kilometers to Top Station, a mountain 7,400 feet above sea level. Trevor's hat blew off somewhere along the route because the jeep didn't have a back window, but we enjoyed a gorgeous sunny day. The landscape was beautiful, with terraced tea plantations on incredibly steep slopes on either side of the road. We didn't have a plan to get back to Munnar, but that was part of our adventure. We had a ball, laughing all the way and waving to the cars that passed us.

It was cool, blissfully cool, in the mountains. We joined tufted birds in the clouds. I smelled woodsmoke from the fire where a man shucked cobs of corn and threw them into a cast-iron pot of hot water along with the husks. We sat on a log at Top Station drinking chai and eating roasted corn on the cob.

"The people in India are so enterprising, Trevor."

"Look at all the Indian tourists here, babe."

I nodded. The corn salesman did brisk business on the mountain.

On the way back down the mountain, we shared a tuk-tuk with a young French couple from Lille in Northern France. We stopped several times along the way, first to see wild elephants grazing in a meadow and then to watch Indian women who picked tea leaves by hand and carried bags of tea leaves on their backs. The hard work was a way for a woman to earn a living. The lady tea pickers were enterprising, as well, and asked us to pay a gratuity for the photographs we took. The driver stopped for us to see a fantastic tree with hanging beehives. He said he had a shrine under the tree. I left fruit as an offering, but Trevor and the young couple didn't notice.

We ate dinner at Saravana Restaurant, across a steep alley from the hotel of the same name where we stayed the second night. The French couple joined us for our meal. An attractive young Indian couple came into the restaurant. The man wore a UCLA T-shirt, and we struck up a great conversation after he learned I'd lived in Los Angeles and attended classes at UCLA, where he had earned his MBA. They lived in Singapore because it allowed him to travel easily from India to Asia and to New York for the businesses he owned.

Our new hotel room was heaven. The bathroom had a marvelous hot shower. The bed had two starched white sheets, a blanket, and a thick mattress.

"Thank God," I said. "A real bed."

At last we were in a hotel room conducive to a romantic interlude, and it was cool enough to snuggle. *How easy it was to take things for granted in a comfortable life in America*, I thought. Trevor and I enjoyed our romantic adventures and each other's company. It was wonderful to share intimacy in such relative luxury, but we splurged at the hotel and upgraded to a room that cost less than $15 USD per night. Trevor complained it was too much money.

We planned to take an early morning bus down to the coast and then travel by boat through the backwaters of Kerala to Varkala. Trevor said the beaches were beautiful. We were closer than ever. It brought back fond memories of the early days we shared. I was having the time of my life.

CHAPTER 9: *On the Bus to Alleppey*

We were up and ready to leave the hotel at 4:30 A.M. Since there was no lift, we carried our bags down several flights to the lobby and discovered four Indian men sleeping on the marble floor.

"Blimey," Trevor said.

"Quiet, babe." We tiptoed to the doors, pushed them, and discovered they were locked.

"Christ," Trevor said. "We have to wake somebody."

The manager, who was one of the sleepers, awoke and opened the door to free us. I realized that the workers at the hotel had no accommodation other than the lobby floor. It was pitch-black dark when we walked down the steep narrow path and steps to the town center. Buses were rolling in and unloading passengers in two different locations in the market square.

"Where's our bus, Trevor?"

"Ain't got a clue, Jesse."

We didn't know where we needed to board our bus to Allepey. We stood next to Gandhi's statue and looked lost. As luck would have it, tuk-tuk drivers thought we had just arrived in Munnar and flocked around us vying to take us to a hotel.

"Go away," Trevor snarled.

We lugged our bags up and down the street, wandered up and down it in increasing frustration, and desperately tried to find someone, anyone, who could direct us to our bus. One man sent us on a wild goose chase in the wrong direction.

"Well, fuck me," Trevor cursed.

Finally, someone took pity on us and told us which bus we needed. The early-morning drive down curving roads was akin to rides at the fair in which you were convinced you'd meet certain death. You screamed and prayed your seatmate didn't vomit on you because they looked a bit green, but an amusement park ride would come to an end. Our ride seemed wildly out of control. The bus hurtled down hairpin curves at breakneck speed, heading directly toward oncoming buses, cars, tuk-tuks, motorcycles, cows, carts, and people. I looked out my window and saw the edge of a cliff only inches away. It was a sheer drop-off.

"Oh, jeez Louise," I said. We had so many near misses in overtaking slower traffic that we couldn't watch the road ahead. It was too frightening.

"Blow me," Trevor said. "He's a maniac."

"Just look out the window and watch the scenery, babe."

It was the less frightening choice. The upside of our bus having no glass in the window openings meant we had a spectacular view. On the downside, the bus didn't have a bathroom. We stopped twice at big stations and used grim public pay toilets, a necessary bargain at five rupees. We met three precious boys from Brazil, college students who had come to India for a couple of months of volunteer work and had a few free weeks to explore the country before heading home. Trevor gave them the scoop about the places we had stayed and entertained them with funny stories about our travels.

CHAPTER 10: *Alleppey*

Travel in India was confusing because the same place might have two, or even three, names. Alappuzha and Alleppey were the same place. Go figure. We were exhausted after the six-hour bus ride and our descent from cool mountain tea plantations to heat, humidity, and Alleppey's canals. We didn't have a hotel reservation. We found a restaurant in the Hotel Yuvaraj near the bus station. Our plan was to eat and then go on the recon mission to find lodging. The place was jam-packed with Indians but no other foreigners. Our waiter was terribly rude. He dropped menus on the table without a smile and served diners at the tables surrounding us. We waited. And waited some more.

I was hot, irritable, and hungry. I stood up and stopped the surly waiter. "Why are you ignoring us?"

The waiter curled his lip under a droopy moustache, and maybe I imagined it, but I could have sworn he snarled at me. Trevor's eyes widened and he pressed his lips together in a tight line. Uh-oh. Not a good sign.

"Jesse, you're not in New York anymore."

I thought it best not to tempt fate, and I said nothing more. However, the waiter served us a short time after I'd spoken to him. I admit I wasn't at my best. In fact, I'd been downright bitchy. Trevor remained silent through lunch.

✺

Trevor walked ahead of me as we crossed a metal bridge over one of the canals. In an awkward attempt to wrangle my bags and haul the suitcase down a set of stairs, the clasp on my watch opened. I watched it disappear into the backwaters. It was the watch he had bought for me at a boot sale.

"Damnation."

"What now, Jesse?" Trevor said in an unmistakably angry tone.

After I told him, we walked in silence. I didn't want a disagreement. Just ahead, we saw a sign advertising "Palmy Residency, Rooms Available." An arrow pointed us down an alley.

"Let's take a look, Trevor."

It was a lovely old villa with spacious rooms, high ceilings, ceiling fans, a mosquito net if needed, Wi-Fi, covered porches, and a shady courtyard where kittens dashed into hiding. Perfect. Well, nothing was perfect. There was no air-conditioning, which wouldn't have been a problem, but smokers sat in the courtyard outside our room. It was unpleasant. I detested cigarettes and smoke. My throat was scratchy, and I felt more irritable than usual. I caught a bad cold and coughed all night the first night.

The next morning, after a great breakfast on a covered porch, Trevor shuffled bits in his daypack and said, "Want to explore?"

I shook my head. "Babe, I need to sleep."

After my nap, I felt better and caught up on emails. I learned that my sweet friend back home had lost her sister to cancer. Later, Trevor and I walked around the neighborhood and stopped at Thaff Restaurant. The owner and staff welcomed us with smiles. We enjoyed a delicious dinner at the small restaurant, a recipient of the 2012 Trip Advisor Certificate of Excellence framed and hanging on the wall.

One amazing thing I discovered in India was the coexistence of churches, mosques, and temples, all within spitting distance of one another. The Palmy was near a Hindu temple, a Muslim mosque, a Jacobite Syrian Church, and a Catholic Church. I heard the temple bells, the Muslim call to prayer, and the church bells from our porch, and I marveled at all the faiths existing in harmony near one another. I had noticed the influence of Catholicism when we visited Kochi and Munnar, Kerala. I saw Hindu altars everywhere, and, so far, I had witnessed nothing but acceptance of all faiths. One restaurant we visited had a painting of Jesus, a shrine to Ganesh—the elephant-headed god—and the moon and star of Islam. I posted a Facebook photo of a billboard with pictures of Abraham Lincoln, Gandhi, and Nelson Mandela.

"Trevor, I really like the Palmy," I said. "Let's stay awhile."

It was the perfect place for me to stay for a month and write. At 600 rupees (about $11 USD) a night, it was a bargain. Our breakfast, included in the daily rate, featured an omelet, toast with butter and jam, and a pot of chai a waiter served us on the veranda. Bicycles were available, the sheets were clean, and we had a real Western-style toilet in our en suite bathroom.

"It's an oasis," I said.

"Babe, I'm ready to go to Varkala."

I was enjoying the peace, but he was itching to travel. Despite Trevor's restlessness, we had loads of fun. We researched the ferry and the houseboats for the six-to-eight–hour journey through Kerala's backwaters south to Varkala and its beaches.

"Varkala has good restaurants and great small cafés on cliffs overlooking the beach, Jesse."

It sounded like a good place to relax. Since we'd been on the go for five days nonstop, I was glad to hear we planned to stay somewhere for a while.

CHAPTER 11: *On the Canals of Kerala*

Kerala had canals like Venice. Well, maybe not just like Venice, but we traveled by water through the state. We left Alleppey on a ferry at 10:30 a.m. to travel on Kerala's backwaters to Varkala, sitting with other tourists on the covered upper deck. It seemed a pleasant way to travel. We introduced ourselves to Christian from London, Nello from Tuscany, and Mary Jane from Amsterdam. I chatted with Christian for an hour until I saw Trevor's face. *What was the deal with his annoyed expression?* I wondered. I didn't understand why he could be irritated with me. After all, Christian was a delightful gay man. We passed villages along the canals with little mud huts and old ladies doing their wash in the water. I photographed the scenery and fishermen in the water with Chinese fishing nets. I was startled to see a high-rise building in the middle of the jungle.

"What's that?" I asked.

"Amma's Ashram," Trevor said and laughed. "We spent two days there and escaped."

"Why escape, Trevor? People love Amma."

Trevor didn't answer.

I hadn't realized we'd pass her ashram on the way to Kollam, and I certainly hadn't imagined modern construction. The eight-hour trip with stops for lunch and later for tea was about five hours too much of a good thing for me. It was remarkably boring after a while. Nothing like the *African Queen* experience I had envisioned. We reached Kollam at 6:30 p.m. and needed transportation to Varkala.

Trevor said, "We can take the bus to Varkala from Kollam."

"The bus ride takes two hours, babe." I wasn't looking forward to a hot, crowded bus ride.

Thank heaven, a couple we met on the ferry suggested we share a taxi. Trevor agreed because we could split the cost. I wasn't convinced it was the best decision because it turned into a harrowing one-hour drive for the thirty-five-kilometer trip to Varkala. The driver was a maniac with a lead foot on the accelerator and an equally heavy foot on the brakes. The taxi dropped us off on the tarmac at the helipad on Varkala's North Cliff. No sooner had we gotten out of the car than the electricity went out along the entire cliff. We were in the dark without a hotel reservation, and it was after 8 p.m.

CHAPTER 12: *Varkala*

Fortunately, the couple had reservations at Tina's guesthouse. We followed them with flashlights down a narrow sand path away from the cliff, and we asked the owner if we could get a room. We were in luck, kind of. Trevor was fit to be tied when he found out it cost 1,000 rupees, almost $15 USD.

"Twelve quid for this place," he complained in front of the owner, "and it ain't great."

Our room was spacious, with tall ceilings, and we had a large en suite bathroom. Even though the flashlight provided the only illumination, I could see torn mosquito netting around the bed and water stains at corners of the ceiling. A wooden wardrobe missing one of its doors stood against one of the walls. On the plus side, the bathroom had the first roll of toilet paper I'd seen in a hotel. Spying the toilet paper was so exciting, I promptly dropped it into the toilet while juggling the flashlight and the roll.

"Damn!" I fished the soggy mess out of the water and dropped it into the waste basket.

"What now, Jesse?" Trevor called from the other room.

Thank heaven for small mercies. He hadn't seen my klutzy, one-shot dunk with the TP in the toilet. I was torn between despair and humiliation. I went downstairs to request another roll from the German woman who owned the guesthouse, only to find I had to buy it. I trudged back up the worn wooden staircase to our room. Sometime during the night I awoke to the crash of thunder. Heavy rain beat down on the roof, and flashes of lightning lit the room while Trevor, as usual, slept through it all. It stormed all night, and I slept very little. By morning, I couldn't breathe. My nose was stopped up. *How could I have caught another cold?* I wondered.

We ate breakfast at a small, crowded café on the clifftop, the music too loud for early morning. After a brief stroll on the cliff walk—a trendy location with overpriced shops—I couldn't stop myself. "I hate this place." It was the first crass commercial tourist magnet I'd seen in India. I was unhappy. Judging by the pinched expression on Trevor's face, I knew he was unhappy with me.

"I'm ready to go back to Alleppey."

"Jesse, sit tight." He sounded fed up. "I'll see if there's a room at a small hotel on the beach road where I stayed before."

Thirty minutes later he returned wearing a big smile. "Babe, I got us a room."

"Great!"

"I ran into friends staying where I stayed two years ago," he said.

We hauled our gear back to the helipad, where we found a tuk-tuk to take us to Om Beach Resort. I had high hopes with a name that included "resort" at the end. We turned onto the beach road and drove past a huge temple and water tank. Om was on the beach road that leads from the 2,000-year-old temple to sacred Papanasam Beach.

No sooner had we arrived at Om than Trevor introduced me to his friends—Israeli sisters Esther and Emma.

Esther nodded at me and laughed, saying to Trevor, "Remember . . . "

"Let's not go there," he said.

I wondered if, on his earlier travels, he'd only hung out with women travelers. It was beginning to feel that way. I let it go. That was then.

Om was by no means a resort, but it was clean, and the manager, Sanjay, was kind. We got the last room available—small, with twin beds. The sheets were clean, and we had an en suite bathroom, a wet room like all the bathrooms I'd seen since Mumbai's Hotel Lawrence and Gokarna's Naga Palace.

It was a short walk to sacred Papanasam Beach, where Hindu pilgrims came to pray and toss the ashes of a loved one on a banana leaf to drift into the sea. We passed an invisible dividing line that separated the Western-style beach at the foot of the cliffs from the Indian beach at the end of the beach road. We could swim at the Western beach if we dared face strong waves and undertow.

One day, when we walked down the beach, we came upon Esther.

"Oh my god," I said.

She was sunbathing topless, and it was a dreadful sight. Rail thin, with weathered, wrinkled skin, Esther had dried-up little mounds where her breasts should have been. Nonetheless, the teenage Hindu boys who ventured down the beach in the hope of spying young foreign women in bikinis bumped into one another, pointing and laughing. It was appalling.

"Crikey, she should know better," Trevor said.

Indian women who went into the sea wore saris or tunics and jeans. They didn't wear bathing costumes, as Trevor called swimsuits. They showed a sense of decorum, of modesty. In fact, I didn't see young men and women holding hands or displaying any form of affection in public. What did surprise me, however, was seeing young men holding hands.

"What's that about?" I was curious.

"Indian men and women can't hold hands in public unless they're married," Trevor said.

"Why do the men hold hands?"

He shrugged his shoulders and said, "Practicing, I guess."

I took off my tunic and slacks, determined to go in the water, but I was unprepared for the force of the waves. My folly! I should have known after seeing surfers that the water was rough. I felt my feet give way and tumbled head over heels into the sea. As I struggled to my feet, I realized I had a wardrobe malfunction! Yikes, the strap on my swimsuit top had unattached itself and, in the process, one of my breasts slipped out of its modest cover. I was mortified. I pulled up my swimsuit and got out of the water with as much dignity as I could muster under the circumstances.

Trevor couldn't stop laughing. "Babe, you gave 'em quite a show."

"Shut up." I scowled and yanked the tunic over my head.

Despite my embarrassing moment, I was glad we had moved to the beach road. My impression of Varkala changed. It was beautiful and dramatic with its high cliffs overlooking the Arabian Sea. Since it's far south down India's coast, it was hot and humid. It's the jungle.

Trevor loved it—the heat, the beach, and Sanjay. People spend four to five weeks at the hospital for Ayurevedic treatment, and Om had an Ayurevedic healer on site whom Trevor had seen during his first visit.

When we walked up to the North Cliff, I watched brahminy kites soar and crows protest by dive-bombing the graceful raptors that captured the wind currents off the cliffs overlooking the beach. It was quiet on the clifftop, but motorcycles and tuk-tuks whizzed by on the beach road next to the hotel. That proved to be a problem. It was noisy. Surely there was a quieter place in Varkala that wasn't on the beach road or on the commercial North Cliff. Crows cawed. Horns beeped constantly. Monkeys hooted and howled.

One day, the noise and the heat were godawful. I wiped my face with the bandana, my clothes sticking to my skin.

"It's time for lunch," Trevor said.

"I'm too hot to eat."

"Get over it." He was annoyed with me for complaining.

I ate just to keep the peace. The grizzled old hotel manager crept around behind me, spying on us. I tried to avoid him.

After a few days of the heat and humidity in the jungle, I was ready to move on. I told Trevor I wanted to go to Calcutta when we left Varkala.

"I want to visit Mother Teresa's tomb," I said, "and I'm fascinated with the poet Rabindranath Tagore."

"We ain't flying," Trevor said, but he was game. "You need to come up with the plan."

Of course, he didn't want to spend the money to fly, and I began to understand how much he struggled with technology and depended on me to help navigate. It finally occurred to me that Trevor's prior travel in India had always taken place in the company of another. Anna had helped him get to Gokarna in January. He had traveled with a young Frenchman to Varkala from Gokarna. I had made the travel plans to Munnar. It was up to me to be our guide. Talk about the blind leading the blind.

It was difficult to make travel arrangements by bus and train in India. Following India's independence from the British, they had changed the names of towns. I found it especially confusing with small towns because people used all the names interchangeably. A travel agent helped us in Gokarna when we wanted a train to Kochi—also Cochin, but the destination was Ernakulum. One did not ask why because the logic defied understanding.

One evening, a big festival was scheduled at the 2,000-year-old temple in Varkala. Trevor and I planned to walk up the beach road to the temple to watch the festivities. Earlier in the day, we had taken the local bus into town so we could make our train reservations for Calcutta, or Kolkata. Trevor wanted to avoid travel agent fees. We were hungry, and someone we met recommended a restaurant called Ganga. We hopped off the bus and went into the small restaurant, just a short walk from the train station.

I didn't see a menu—not in Hindi or English. Trevor chatted with the waiter and ordered, nodding his head at everything the waiter said.

"What did you order for us, Trevor?"

"Ain't got a clue," he said.

Uh-oh, I thought. It was not the first time I had experienced a mystery meal on my travel with dear Trevor. The waiter set a beautiful tomato curry on the table before us with accompanying *parotta*—a kind of layered pancake-y bread—and sticky noodles. It looked wonderful. We didn't have knives, forks, spoons, or napkins. I broke off a piece of the parotta and mopped up a big bite of the tomato curry. My first bite was delicious. Then, oh my god, moments later my mouth was on fire. No kidding!

"My lips are burning!" I said. "My tongue is singed. The roof of my mouth stings and my throat feels like it has a bad sunburn." It was an unnamed Indian dish I would forever call Dante's Inferno. Aargh.

Trevor laughed and polished off his plate as well as mine while I nibbled on the parotta and asked for another 7UP.

"Your mouth must be made of Teflon, Trevor."

The same thing happened at dinner one evening at another local eatery with no menu in English. Trevor ordered Chicken Curry and Chicken Fried. At least, that's what the waiter called it. I know the Chicken Curry was chicken, and not another animal, because I recognized a drumstick in the sauce. It was unbearably hot.

"Trevor, I'm sticking with the Chicken Fried." I was skeptical because it didn't look like any fried chicken I've ever seen. Whatever seasoning was used to coat the chicken was fiery, too. I concluded that the locals should not try to fry chicken.

Overall, we had a pleasant stay in Varkala, but it was hotter than blazes the whole time.

CHAPTER 13: *Fifty-four Hours on the Train to Kolkata*

After I booked our train tickets to Kolkata, I was in heaven. After a bit of discussion—albeit somewhat tense because it cost more—we finally agreed on paying for an air-conditioned carriage. It was a two-day trip from Ernaculum, aka Kochi aka Cochin, the terminus where we had transferred after the four-hour non-AC trip from Varkala. I refused to endure fifty-four hours in a third-class sleeper car. Naively, I hadn't envisioned the reality of two days and two nights on a train crossing India. I didn't have a clue how vast the continent was.

Shortly after we boarded the train, an incident took place. A large, overweight Indian man lost his temper. Excitement, a big commotion, and a screaming match followed. The fat man didn't want a younger Indian man, who had an upper berth, to store his luggage under the fat man's lower berth, although there was plenty of room for both men's luggage. The argument lasted for over an hour and freaked me out because I hadn't seen anyone in India explode in off-the-charts anger. A few days earlier, on February 22, terrorist bombs in Hyderabad had killed 16 and wounded 119 others. We had to travel through Coimbatore—one of four cities on high alert for terrorist attacks.

"Trevor, you think the commotion might be a ruse?"

"I don't know, babe. It's weird."

Fortunately, no bombs exploded, and the argument didn't escalate to a fistfight. The men had gone into testosterone overdrive in the AC train carriage. Military officials with machine guns boarded the train somewhere along the way, and although I felt some alarm seeing their weapons, I was relieved at the same time.

We were thrilled to have air conditioning and our own little private compartment, such as it was. A tatty curtain fastened together with Velcro and safety pins separated us from the rest of the folks in our train car. We were fortunate there were only two bunks behind our curtain because the rest of the two-tier compartments had four beds, two on either side. I slept on the bottom bunk of our little two-bed compartment. We even had a sheet and a blanket supplied when it got dark.

I awoke in the middle of the night when I heard the fat man scream again. I said in a very loud voice, "Good God! We're trying to sleep!" Trevor didn't stir.

When I awoke during the night again, I was startled to find a couple of bloody morons sitting on the end of my bed with their bags in our little compartment.

Maybe I shouted, "What the hell!" I scared the bejesus out of them and miraculously woke Trevor.

"Don't yell, Jesse. Have you taken your tablets?"

"That's insulting. I was terrified."

"When I'm sitting in my caravan in Cornwall in April, I'll be thinking about how absurd this was," Trevor said.

The only problem—which did not seem to be an issue at the time but turned out to be a big problem for me—was that my clean sheets and wool blanket must have hidden bed bugs or some manner of small, blood-sucking creature that chose me as a succulent menu item. By the time our fifty-four-hour journey ended, bug bites covered my legs, back, and stomach. I itched like crazy. Trevor didn't have one bite. I told Trevor I needed a chemist's shop. I bought tubes of cortisone cream and the closest thing to Benadryl tabs I could find our first afternoon in Calcutta.

The irony of the bug bite debacle was that we had paid four times as much for our train tickets to get AC and the two-tier sleeping arrangement. I was covered in bites. We'd traveled on third-class sleeper cars with at least six people, no linens, no curtains, just six berths and no AC, unless you counted fresh air since there was no glass in the windows. It was hot during the day, cooler at night, but we had no privacy. We slept in our clothes, but I didn't get bug bites. We were the only non-Indian travelers I saw on the entire train trip. It felt so odd to be a fair-skinned redhead in India because people stared all the time. When the train stopped at small stations, I got off a couple of times to buy snacks from vendors and was the only person on the platform who had white skin. I experienced a disquieting realization: I felt what it was like to be a minority for the first time in my life. I finally covered my head with a scarf so no one could see my red hair. Camouflage helped.

I awoke to hear men clearing their throats—gob spitting—in the early morning. We ate *poori* for breakfast and met Linu from Miami. He told us about Tirumala and Tirupati—a sacred temple that receives 100,000 visitors daily. The pilgrims—women and children as well as men—shaved their heads in personal sacrifice. Colorful altars and temples punctuated the landscape everywhere I looked.

I watched old women carry heavy loads on their heads. Then, in contrast, I saw men driving new Range Rovers, and advertisements for jewelry shops with ornate gold jewelry worn by beautiful models. The adverts were in stark contrast to the poverty we witnessed on our train journey across India. The cows were bony; the goats were fat. The rice paddies were the greenest of greens. India didn't appear to be all muddy dirt roads and beggars, but we saw countless beggars.

People swept up bits of coal and coal dust with brooms or their bare hands and filled bags with the black leavings near the power station at a railroad crossing.

Trevor said, "The old blokes, women, and kids scrape up the coal to use or to sell."

Meager leavings were whatever fell off the trucks and train cars as they were loaded. Several dirty, barefoot little boys, maybe five years old, jumped on the train to sweep for rupees. The gang of little beggars eluded the conductors, who slept while on duty as the train rocked along down the tracks. It was a game to the children. I didn't think I'd ever forget the sounds of the men gob spitting.

CHAPTER 14: *Kolkata aka Calcutta*

When we reached Calcutta, we got off the train at a track in a remote location. We didn't know where to find an exit or even the station itself. I followed Trevor through a parking lot filled with taxis. The taxi drivers clamored for our attention and irritated Trevor. He told them, "Go away." He stepped through a hole where several boards were missing from a fence, and I walked through the opening after him into an alley.

"We're lost," I said.

We stopped at a small vendor's shack to ask for directions, but the owner didn't speak English. I spied a small refrigerator in the corner. We bought a cold fruity drink at the tiny shop constructed of mismatched old boards. The school day must have ended because children in neat uniforms paraded past the bench where we sat outside the shop.

"Hello," one little girl said and launched a chorus of hellos from almost every child who walked past us heading home from school. We were an oddity, as no other Westerners were anywhere in the alley. The children who spoke English wanted to chat. We were entertainment for the curious youngsters until we saw mothers poke their heads out of doors of the houses that fronted the alley and call the children, who waved goodbye and ran home.

"Let's go," Trevor said.

We walked back through the hole in the fence into the parking lot, where at least twenty taxis were parked. The drivers surrounded us, each shouting louder than the other, to take us to our hotel. We chose one man who turned out to be the taxi driver from Hades because Trevor tried, unsuccessfully, to negotiate a price before we got into his taxi.

"Right!" Trevor said. He was furious. "That's it." He stormed off through the hole in the fence back into the alley.

I followed him. "What now?"

We spied a cycle rickshaw in the alley and asked the driver to take us to a hotel we had read about in our Lonely Planet guide. The rickshaw driver cycled back through the alley where we had had the cold drink. Indian women and children peered at us from rundown houses lining the less-than-scenic route.

"Oh, for Heaven's sake!" I said. "This is going to take forever."

Trevor glared. "Have you ever taken a cycle rickshaw?"

I looked at the thin driver who was struggling to pedal with our combined weight and the weight of our bags and said, "Poor man."

"Not after we pay him," Trevor said.

Sometimes Lonely Planet proved to be a good guide. Unfortunately, the Sunflower Guest House, at $24, was a major disappointment. The guesthouse was on the fifth floor of what looked like a boarding house or decrepit apartment building. Ancient wooden steps offered the walk-up to the hotel. The alternative was an elevator, or lift, out of the *Casablanca* era. An old, skinny Indian operated the lift. We paid more for a room with AC and an en suite bathroom. We were past due for showers. The bed had one sheet—on the bottom. The room was old, rundown, and none too clean. We decided one night was one too many and told the manager we would check out earlier than planned—the next day.

We roamed the alleys and warrens of Calcutta as the city awoke. We ate breakfast and lunch with Ume of Japan, a Buddhist artist who was studying intricate mandala painting. We met Maya from San Francisco, who told us about the Modern Guest Lodge. At 500 rupees, $7.35, it was basic but friendly. Later, we drank cups of chai at Mughal Darbar on Free School Street at 42A Mizra Ghalib. I learned that Mughal Darbar was the son of the last Mughal Emperor of India. Everything was new and bustling in Calcutta. I couldn't take it all in.

We went to a barbecue restaurant for a Chinese and Tandoori dinner. Trevor had met the waiter, Bryan, earlier in the day, and he had encouraged Trevor to come to his restaurant for dinner. First, Bryan seated us at a nice table with a good view of an upstairs room. Moments after we sat down, the manager asked us to move to a table in a dark corner. Two wealthy Indian businessmen took our table in the more desirable location.

"This is unpleasant," I said. "Let's leave." I wasn't used to being treated as a second-class citizen in a restaurant.

Trevor said, "We're here."

And that was that.

We paid extra for an en suite room at the Modern Guest Lodge that was anything but modern. San Francisco Maya must have been a rough and ready traveler to stay in her downstairs room off the courtyard. Downstairs guests shared a single outdoor communal sink. Maya's room didn't have water. Our room looked out over the courtyard. I considered it acceptable until 10 p.m., when we were jarred awake by the loud noise of something sawing metal.

"What is that?" I asked.

Trevor peered out the back window, conveniently covered so we hadn't looked out when we agreed to stay in the room.

"We're next to a sheet metal shop," Trevor said.

We both started laughing.

"This place is a dump," I said and grabbed my earplugs.

The sheet metal shop began work every night at 10 p.m. After our experience in the cock-eyed room in Munnar, we always checked a room to make sure the shower worked, but we never thought to check the toilet to see if it flushed. This one didn't. We had to fill a water bucket and pour it in the commode to flush. The pull handle was broken. There was no sink per se in the quasi-bathroom—just a faucet. It was a dreadful place, albeit cheap.

We awoke early the next morning, 5 a.m. to be precise, to a huge argument in the room below us. Heaven knows what was taking place. The angry voices woke other guests and a couple of the backpackers, including Maya, who left their rooms and ventured into the courtyard out of curiosity. We went for breakfast to a hole-in-the-wall restaurant called Taj Continental on Sudder Street off Stuart Lane. Two young boys bussed tables in the cheap neighborhood eatery. We had omelets for 13 rupees each, about 35 cents. I asked why the young boys weren't in school. They were bright and chatty. The manager didn't answer.

We were planning to go to The Mother House of the Missionaries of Charity to see Mother Teresa's tomb. We also wanted to visit the Victoria Memorial—a beautiful marble building. According to the Lonely Planet guide, Calcutta was a city that celebrated the arts—music, dance, writers, and visual arts. I thought Calcutta was a friendly city filled with rickshaws, tuk-tuks, old Ambassador cabs, bicycles, motorcycles, cars, trucks, and people. It was bustling and noisy. The crumbling colonial architecture was lovely and intriguing. The city exuded an air of renewal—building renovation was the watchword.

Everything was going splendidly one afternoon. We stood on a corner under the balcony of a building, and I felt something drop on my head. I put my hand up and wiped away pigeon droppings.

"Oh no!"

Trevor laughed and pointed up to the balcony where pigeons nested. "It's good luck."

We walked to the South Park Street Cemetery, founded in the late 1700s by the British East India Company, where we saw graves and mausoleums for the British. Each of the graves told a story—the lives cut short; the hardship people faced. There were extraordinary tombs and mausoleums, some of which told heartbreaking stories of infants who didn't survive, young women who came from England and married only to lose a beloved husband within a few years, young officers lost in a battle in the Bay of Bengal. Although restoration was taking place in the cemetery, parts of it looked like a jungle.

On the way to the Mother House, Trevor and I got lost. We wandered into a Muslim bazaar where there were no other Western people. We found a shopkeeper who spoke English well enough to recommend a place near the market where we might buy a cup of chai. We thanked him and bought his multicolored scarves for friends back home. It was a brilliant shopping adventure—ten beautiful scarves.

We found Kallu Tea Stall and met Mr. Kallu, chai maker extraordinaire. We asked him for cups of tea. Mr. Kallu was a showman. Nothing would do but that he showed his artistic abilities in tea making. He was a master practicing his magic. He was proud of his tea and his skills, and he allowed me to video him making the chai. By the time we had drunk three cups of chai each—Mr. Kulla insisted—a crowd of fourteen or fifteen men had gathered to watch us. I thought it curious there were no women around.

During the show at the tea stall, a Muslim with a henna-orange beard drove up on his motorcycle. He was Mr. Halim—clearly an important person in the community because all the bystanders and Mr. Kallu deferred to him. Mr. Halim pointed to my red hair and his red beard. He wanted his photo taken with me. He called me his sister and I called him my brother. Trevor and I took photos of Mr. Kallu and Mr. Halim and drank several more cups of delicious, sugary chai. Mr. Kallu added a sprinkle of Nescafé on top of the chai as the final ingredient. We drank from little clay cups—there were no paper cups. After we finished each cup, Mr. Kallu threw it in a pile where it shattered, along with other broken cups next to the tea stand. Trevor and I hoped we could sleep after all the caffeine and excitement. What an amazing experience when we wandered off the beaten path!

We were hungry after our adventure in the Muslim Bazaar, so we stopped at a small neighborhood restaurant. There were no other Westerners. The other diners stared, and I thought I would never feel comfortable with the stares, but the fish curry was delicious.

We finally found what we were looking for—the Mother House and Mother Teresa's tomb. We rang a bell at a closed gate and a young Filipina nurse greeted us in fluent English. She was a nun at the Mother House, the name of the convent according to the locals we had asked for directions earlier. At first, she said the site was closed for workmen to make repairs. I pleaded with her, told her about the two-day train trip to Calcutta, and said I didn't know if I would have a chance to visit the city again. The pretty young nurse relented and allowed us to enter; we had the remarkable convent to ourselves. First, we saw the courtyard and the grotto where the nuns prayed. The courtyard where the grotto sat was below the balcony where Mother (that's what the sisters called her) used to stand when she became too ill to come down to the courtyard for prayers in the evening. The nun said the balcony was where Mother Teresa delivered homilies to the residents.

I entered the room where Mother Teresa's white marble tomb was to be found. It was so very quiet and peaceful and cool in the room—in stark contrast to the noise, dirt, and chaos in the streets. There were no workmen, although I saw their tools and wooden sawhorses. I knelt at the foot of her tomb and prayed. A profound sense of peace filled me—something extraordinary I had not expected. I was grateful for the experience and knew there was, without a doubt, a powerful presence in the room. After our long day, we took a cycle rickshaw through narrow alleys back to our hotel on Stuart Lane. Calcutta is the City of Your Imagination, I decided. Whatever you wanted it to be, it could be yours.

There was poverty all over India, and I wrestled with my own moral dilemma to ignore beggars. On the streets just outside Stuart Lane, a woman with a sleeping baby approached us and pleaded for rupees so she could buy milk to fill the bottle.

She said, "No money. No money. Come with me." She gestured toward a small shop. "You buy food for my baby—no money, just food." She showed us the empty milk bottle—the baby was listless in her arms.

It was a hideous scam on the streets of Calcutta. Shortly after an unknowing tourist paid for powdered milk for the starving baby, the woman returned to the small shop to sell the milk back to the shop-keeper—less a large discount for the shopkeeper, of course. We saw the same woman another day with a different sleeping baby. The babies were drugged, and the women lived in a camp where they worked for men. They were slaves. It was survival on the mean streets and a bleak existence. We gave to lepers, to the men without legs who pulled themselves down the aisles of the trains, and to the very old.

I got poisoned in Calcutta. We ate at a small restaurant that had no kitchen, although it wasn't obvious. Someone prepared the food at another location and waiters brought our meals to the tables after runners delivered trays with our dishes. The long wait for our food ought to have been a yellow caution light. I was sick as a dog during the night. The first day, I just wanted to be back home in my own bed. I slept all day despite the constant sawing at the sheet metal shop that was outside and just below the window of our room. Thank heaven for Trevor. He was a wonderful nurse who brought me 7UP and crackers.

Trevor went on an adventure with Levy, who had lived for thirty years in New York City. They went to a market, returned, and then went out to dinner. Trevor ate mutton, and I think that was probably a mistake because he got sick, too. I slept and dozed the second day. I thought, after two days, I might be able to return to the land of the living. I had another problem—the bug bites from the train journey itched like crazy. I used a full tube of cortisone and found a little relief. It was a hell of a rough time between the food poisoning, the bug bites, and the slum with a toilet that didn't flush. I had said I wanted to get out of my comfort zone, and I had gotten my wish—replete with the good, the bad, and the ugly.

We drove across the Howrah Bridge at night to the Howrah Railroad Station in Calcutta. The traffic was bumper to bumper—horns honking, people shouting. I watched a sea of flowing humanity sweep alongside the cab in which we rode. Where were all those people going? Where did they come from? We were taking the train to Varanasi.

CHAPTER 15: *On the Train to Varanasi*

While I waited on the platform—exhausted, itching, and propped up against all our bags—I met Ting Ling from China and an Indian couple who had studied at Tuskegee Institute outside Montgomery, Alabama. How amazing! I still couldn't keep food down, but I took anti-diarrheal pills that worked. There was still so much to see in Calcutta, and although we had missed a lot, I was glad to leave. It was hot in Calcutta, but not as humid as the south.

We boarded the 12333 train to Varanasi and were on a two-tier AC sleeper. Trevor spied a wee mouse before we went to sleep. A loud and rude family in the adjacent compartment woke me and talked nonstop between midnight and 1 a.m. Did I say they were loud? I had discovered that Indian travelers showed very little concern for others in overcrowded situations. When I awoke the next morning, I was covered with more bites, and I hadn't used the blanket provided. I itched like crazy. There were monkeys on the platforms at the stations we passed, and I saw entire families living by the railroad tracks. Naked, dirty children raced around blue plastic tarps that served as mean dwellings. Later that morning, the Loud Family surprised us with their generosity. They shared *bira*—the number-one sweet in India, they said. The children offered us a guava with salt. How could such loud, rude folk by night transform themselves into such warm and kind people by day? It was India—full of contradictions and surprises.

Varanasi is the holiest pilgrimage site and perhaps one of the oldest cities in India, known for its cremation of the dead. We checked into India Guest House with its rooftop restaurant overlooking the Ganges. Boys flew colorful kites over the temple spires. Boats ferried pilgrims across the river. Ghats, or steps, led down to the river. Our hotel was next to Manikarnika Ghat, the burning ghat, the sacred place where untouchables burn bodies on funeral pyres. There were temples, large and small, in every nook and cranny, wherever we looked. We got lost in a warren of alleys just wide enough for a cow and, unfortunately, motorcycles. We watched men carry bodies draped in flowers on bamboo stretchers. First, the men submerged the body in its shroud in the Ganges, and the untouchables built a funeral pyre with logs family members bought. What a powerful experience it was to watch!

Trevor said, "The explosions midst the flames are brains exploding in the skulls."

"No way." Who knew if it was true? It was sensational and unforgettable.

We walked for hours in the hot sun by the ghats and saw monkeys—lots of monkeys. Later, we explored the market and looked for a pharmacy where I could buy antihistamine or cortisone cream. My bug bites itched like crazy. My legs were covered in angry red blotches. I had an allergic reaction to the bites, so my legs looked like boiling lesions had scarred them.

We got lost and wandered with thousands and thousands of people crowding the streets. It was utter madness—the remnants of 100 million Indians who had come for Maha Kumbh Mela—the Super Kumbh Mela that takes place once every 144 years when the stars align just so. They were all in Varanasi. Hundreds of people stood in line behind a barrier of rope to go to the Vishnu Temple.

We watched the sunset on the Ganges from the rooftop restaurant. Four green parrots perched on the tops of pennants on the temples. They were tame. Swallows flew against the backdrop of a rose-gold sky. Did pollution create such a beautiful sunset? Perhaps it was smoke from the burning ghat and the funeral pyres.

During the night I couldn't stop itching from the bites. Bed bugs had to have been in the sheets on the train. I thought I would die. I got up and took the first of four cold showers to relieve the itching while Trevor slept. I squeezed the last bit out of the tube of cortisone cream, but it offered no relief. Finally, Trevor awoke.

"I need to go to the hospital and see a doctor," I said.

"What?" He looked startled.

"This morning, Trevor." I showed him the red-and-purple lesions.

"Oh my god, Jesse."

We walked past the ghats along the Ganges, and although it was quite early, it was brutally hot. We made our way through the marketplace and reached the spot where the tuk-tuks waited. No one seemed to know where the hospital was. In our experience, we had found that that meant any driver who told us he knew inevitably didn't have a clue. He just wanted the fare.

"Why don't we walk, babe?"

I gave him a look he couldn't mistake. We found a driver.

It turned out to be a long ride. We reached the hospital at 9:30 a.m. The hospital was efficient. A doctor saw me almost as soon as I walked through the front doors, while I noticed that Indian patients waited. I thought he was going to treat me, but I was mistaken.

"You'll have to wait until the lady dermatologist arrives at noon," he said.

We ate breakfast at a small canteen outside and waited for several hours in the heat, albeit under a canvas awning, where we watched countless monkeys. They crowded onto the limbs of the banyan trees and scrambled up the balconies of apartment buildings. They swung from the rooftops of sheds across from the hospital and raced along walls and ledges. At least one hundred poor people crowded in the shade of the banyan tree, waiting on the street, I supposed, while relatives and friends received treatment in the hospital.

At last, the doctors admitted us into a large waiting room filled with families sitting in rows, facing a wall with a large television screen. The examination rooms were small private offices and rooms off the main room, the doors around the walls facing the rows of seats.

The television in the waiting room featured Indian music videos with scantily clad young women, and the dances were sexy. The contrast with modesty and decorum surprised me. I couldn't reconcile it with the older Indian women who wore saris going into the sea at Papanasam Beach in Varkala or Trevor's admonition not to kiss in public, that it was verboten in India. Plus, the Indian videos I saw that morning were awful takes on American music videos. I hoped I wasn't disenchanted about Bollywood, but it was probably my anguish with the bug bites. When my name was called, a blockhead Indian on our row would not get up or move his fat legs to let us pass. I wanted to shoot myself to be put out of my misery.

I paid a receptionist for my ER visit, $10 USD, and we went into one of the examination rooms where a young woman sat behind a desk. A young boy sat cross-legged atop the gurney and played video games on an iPad. The dermatologist, who spoke fluent English with only a slight accent, explained that she had had to bring her son when the hospital phoned her because his school was on holiday. She looked at my insect bites, confirmed they were bed bug bites, and prescribed antihistamines as well as a cortisone cream and antibacterial cream. All the medication, including two-weeks-worth of antihistamines, cost another $10 USD. I was stunned.

"Trevor, my co-pay just to walk into the emergency room back home would be $150." The medications were all from US pharmaceutical companies.

By the time the visit was over, it was time for lunch. We climbed in a tuk-tuk and asked the driver to take us to Kerala Restaurant— recommended by the Lonely Planet guide. We hopped out across the street from the restaurant and discovered it was nearly impossible to cross the street. Young children darted between cars, tuk-tuks, motorcycles, and cycle rickshaws. I closed my eyes at one point, certain the vehicles would smash into the little ones. A collision between a cycle rickshaw and a tuk-tuk in the insane intersection stopped traffic. We dashed across the street during the brief lull.

The Indian diners didn't have menus. I noticed the waiters gave menus to foreigners. Lesson learned: tourists paid a great deal more than Indians who dined in the same restaurant. I ate Tomato *Uthappam*, and Trevor had curry. The food was delicious. Trevor griped about the cost. Some things just don't change. I felt miserable in the heat when we walked back to the hotel along the ghats, where we ran into Ting Ling, the young Chinese girl we had met at Howrah Station in Calcutta. She told us she had been robbed in the general sitting section of the train. A young woman had bought her a cup of tea, and Ting Ling had fallen asleep. We were sure there were drugs in the tea—a dangerous scam—and we tried to give her money so she wouldn't be without any cash, but she refused our help.

Two naked ash-covered men in a tent—holy men—laughed at us and asked for money. I showed them my legs with the allergic reaction and all the bites and told them I needed money. They laughed and asked us to come talk with them. We didn't take them up on their offer to share the hashish they smoked. I decided one of the long-haired, stoned, and naked Nagas was a bloke from Brooklyn rather than a holy man. It seemed there was to be a convention of sorts on March 10 with Sadhus and Nagas, naked men covered in ash. Varanasi would be swarming with holy men and women garbed in saffron or naught at all.

One afternoon, we spied a tuk-tuk with a bamboo stretcher and body tied on top. I found dark humor in such a lowly conveyance serving as a death chariot. The tuk-tuk drove past us and stopped at a point close to the burning ghat. Paid bearers, we learned, came to take the stretcher and the body while the family of the deceased followed behind the procession. The men chanted *Ram Naam Satya Hai* repeatedly. I heard the translation was, *"You were born with nothing. You die with nothing."* We live our lives suffering under illusion—*maya* in Sanskrit—and the allure of material possessions.

J.P., an older Indian gentleman who hung around the hotel, gave tours of Varanasi to guests for 500–1000 rupees. It wasn't much money for the hour-long tour ahead of us. However, a cheap tour in India always meant we would visit a shopkeeper, or several shopkeepers, where we would politely refuse the sales pitch for whatever goods the shopkeeper displayed. First, J.P. took us to a home where we saw a temple with an altar two stories below ground. Then, he guided us to a former palace on the Ganges, a spectacular building that had once belonged to a Maharaja. Arched windows overlooked the Ganges, and a marvelous temple to Saraswati, the Hindu goddess of wisdom, the arts, and music, took center stage in the courtyard. The palace, with unparalleled views and grandeur gone to ruin, was a slum dwelling for impoverished Indians. A baby slept in a little swinging hammock. Motorcycles and bicycles were parked on the marble floors. It felt like a tragedy, but I suppose it was a blessing for the inhabitants. J.P. guided us to a Muslim mosque built on the site of a Hindu temple, and then to a small Hindu temple where Indian men chanted. It was lovely but I didn't have the courage to enter the temple and join them, although J.P. assured us it would be okay. We walked past another tiny little temple where young women went to pray for husbands. The last stop was a fabric shop where we declined the offers of the specials the shopkeepers offered.

One morning's stroll along the ghats turned into Dante's Inferno. India was unbelievably hot. We ate brunch at the Kerala Café, where I washed my hands with Dr. No Wishy-Washy Soap. The walk back to the hotel was hell as we squeezed through crowds of pilgrims in the heat. We sat down in a stable in the marketplace to have a cup of tea. Horses lived in one part of the derelict building. We perched on wooden planks, waiting for a cup of chai—hot chai. The stable offered shade.

One experience from the day haunted me. Something extraordinary happened. In our wanderings, we passed a building where I saw several older men who wore turbans and sat cross-legged under an awning that shaded them from the brutal midday sun. One of the men looked directly at me, and although it may sound unbelievable, I knew him—not in the sense of an acquaintance—but a knowing in which we communicated our familiarity without words. It was a brief encounter that transcended earthly bounds. An echo of a vision I had experienced in my twenties in Virginia's Blue Ridge Mountains. It was a special moment I would never share with Trevor.

The Maha Kumbh Mela hangers-on meant utter chaos in Varanasi. The translation was *the festival of the pot holding the nectar of humanity.* I'd never seen so much humanity. Little had we known when we planned our visit to the sacred city on the Ganges that we would encounter remnants of the 2013 celebration, the largest gathering of human beings on earth—100 million in Varanasi. Sadhus arrived in droves in saffron robes, and more naked men covered in ash set up makeshift tents on the ghats. The Nagas had arrived. Later in the evening we stopped by Kashari Restaurant and dined on Vegetable Manchurian. Once again, I noticed the waiter gave us the menu with foreigners' prices.

I gave my silent thanks to all the Hindu gods and goddesses. After two days the itching was almost gone, although my legs looked as if I'd been scalded by boiling water. I hoped I wouldn't be scarred for life. The huge gathering was a celebration for Shiva. The Sadhus in saffron outfits and the naked men covered in ash painted a colorful backdrop. One day we came upon a crush of Hindus waiting to get into the Golden Temple for another celebration. Varanasi was insane with people and cow shit. According to J.P., cow shit is good luck. We must have been thrice blessed. Cow shit was everywhere, as were flies, bicycles, Indians who pushed us out of the way, motorcycles, and tuk-tuks that nearly ran over us. And it all happened at once and at the highest possible volume.

We got lost in the warrens of Varanasi. Motorcycles flew down the narrow streets built a thousand years ago. The streets, such as they were, were barely wide enough for two people to pass one another—streets a basketball player could lie across and would have to double up to fit. They wound around and made no sense whatsoever. Varanasi was a maze of ancient buildings, dotted with temples and altars, and doors leading into dwellings that belonged to the mean streets of poverty. We rounded one corner, trying to find our way out of the labyrinth, and came upon a snake charmer. It was too great a temptation not to put money in the basket and watch him play his instrument to call the cobra. He lifted the top off a woven basket, smiling in a way that alarmed me. I found myself enthralled by his terrifying sky-blue eyes. Afterwards, I didn't remember the cobra—only the snake charmer's electric eyes.

Kumbh Mela pilgrims hung around. Thousands lined up each day to visit the Golden Temple. The city was swimming with people like tadpoles in the shallows. It was unbearably hot, and I was irritable. We were tired of the crowds and decided to visit Sarnath—Buddha's Deer Park where Gautama Buddha first taught the Dharma. Then we planned to escape Varanasi and head to Dharamsala and the Himalayas on the train. We hired a tuk-tuk for the drive and, after fighting insane traffic and dusty roads, finally reached our destination, despite deafening chaos. Pigs wallowed in the mud by the road, finding relief from the heat, while barbers gave shaves to men who sat beside the mud holes. We reached what I could only describe as an Indian truck stop, although it was on a small, dirty, makeshift scale. We ate momos for a snack before we walked across a street to visit the beautiful Buddhist temple where Gautama Buddha first taught the Four Noble Truths after he received enlightenment at Bodh Gaya. It was peaceful, clean, and cool. Green grass and flowers, clean sidewalks, and order delivered peace in a world turned upside-down. A few other tourists toured the temple. It wasn't crowded.

"Blimey, babe," Trevor said. "This ain't the mob in Varanasi."

"Hmmm." I thought about Buddhist mindfulness.

When we returned to Varanasi, it was dark, and we stopped at one of the ghats where a massive *puja* ceremony was taking place. At night, the place came alive with dancers waving feathers, burning incense, and music to entertain huge crowds. The Ganges flowed dark against the night sky, punctuated only by the light of burning candles floating down the powerful river. Ripples in the fast-flowing river reflected light from the funeral pyres near the shore. Sparks flew from funeral pyres into the air.

We went to the railroad station to get tickets for our escape. It was a no-go. The station was a beehive, with no tickets available. The agents told us we couldn't leave for several more days. I met the Indian version of *Seinfeld's* Soup Nazi. He stood behind the counter at a restaurant in the Varanasi railroad station. He gave a hard time to everyone who came through the line to order.

"You must be the Indian Tali Nazi," I said when I stepped up to the counter to place our order. He grinned devilishly. "I don't suppose you've ever watched *Seinfeld?*" I was glad Trevor wasn't witness to the scene.

When we left the train station, we had an unwelcome and unexpected adventure on the way to IP Mall. We wanted to find a Vodaphone shop to add minutes to our cell phone. *How difficult could that possibly be?* I wondered. After all, it had been a simple errand in the other cities we visited, but this was Varanasi. The auto-rickshaw driver, who had a statue of Jesus on display, said he would charge 70 rupees to take us to the mall, but when we reached the destination, he demanded double the price—140 rupees.

Trevor went ballistic and refused to pay extortion money, handing the driver only the amount he quoted. "Bloody thief!"

Holy? What was holy about Jesus on the dashboard of a tuk-tuk? Everyone had "a hand out for gimme." I was tired of getting ripped off. Later, we ate dinner on a bench in the marketplace and bought material for a tailor to make a sleeping bag for me. I wanted a barrier between me and the linens on the train.

We asked the front desk manager, who doubled as a dodgy travel agent, to help us get train tickets. The thief at the India Guest House successfully booked our train reservation, since we'd had no luck on our own. They took 1,250 rupees from Trevor to handle the transaction for 400-rupee tickets. Trevor stormed up the steps to our room on the third floor, too disgusted to say anything. I stood at the front desk and demanded the manager return 850 rupees. He refused. The hotel manager said he had to bribe the railroad ticket agent for our seats on the train on Sunday. Who knew what was true?

We were biding our time until we could get out of Varanasi. On Saturday afternoon, Trevor got sick and had a high fever. Despite the heat, he zipped himself into his down sleeping bag and downed Gatorade to replenish his electrolytes. We had train tickets to Delhi the next morning. I was terrified, knowing full well how difficult it would be to get him to the hospital. It was impossible to think about home while I was in India. I was in a time machine—two hundred years in the past in Varanasi.

Meanwhile, a massive Vishnu celebration started Saturday evening and was supposed to last through the entire next day. The crowds made it difficult when I wandered out solo to Chowk Road to fetch cheese and tomato sandwiches and egg noodle soup from the hotel restaurant where lazy Indian boys watched Indian television. It was unimaginable to me. How could more pilgrims fit into Varanasi? It was more crowded than I would have believed humanly possible.

Thank heaven I felt good, and I prayed it would last until we got up north to the Tibetan quiet, peace, and cleanliness I hoped to find in Dharamsala. It was hot, hot, hot, but a drier heat in Calcutta and Varanasi—not as humid as the south. Climate change all over the world made it hotter in India, too. I looked forward to our time in Northern India. The weather would be much easier on me. Fortunately, I had walked enough over the past six weeks that I imagined the steep walks Trevor described in McLeod Ganj wouldn't be too bad.

Sunday marked Varanasi's largest festival celebrating Vishnu. Maybe we missed out on Varanasi's most important festival, but our only thoughts were to escape the madness. The guesthouse manager made a habit of price gouging. India was all about bait and switch. Our agreement was for 700 rupees per night but when we checked out, he raised the price to 800 rupees per night. It was a lie, all about greed, and we were beyond angry when we left the hotel.

"They fuck you coming and going, and don't think a thing about it, Jesse."

I took Trevor's arm. "Let's go, babe."

All the roads around the center of town were blocked off. It was impossible to find transportation to get into or out of the part of the city where we stayed, unless it was on foot. No tuk-tuks were available because the police had shut down all the streets. We learned we couldn't get a tuk-tuk nearby, nor could we find a porter willing to help us with the luggage. The streets were absolutely jam-packed. It was almost impossible to walk, much less get our bags out to the main road. All my proper home training flew out the window. I morphed into the ugly American I abhorred and felt ashamed of my behavior afterwards. I barged through the masses like Joe Namath, taking down Indians right and left. I had to get out no matter whom I plowed into or whose toes my rolling suitcase squashed. Trevor trailed behind me.

I turned to check on Trevor. "How ya doin', sweetheart?" I asked.

He shook his head and gestured for me to keep moving. He must have felt lousy. Hundreds of police filled the streets and monitored parades of people waving red flags. We navigated our way out with the help of one policeman in charge. At last we got a tuk-tuk to the railroad station after we had hauled all our bags solo from the cow-shit-covered warrens through the streets where thousands gathered.

I never did figure out why he took on the responsibility of helping us out of the melee, but we were thankful.

On reflection, seeing the greed was mind-blowing and life-altering. I knew the pilgrims who came to bathe in the Ganges had pure intentions, but it seemed as if the rest of India was on the take when it came to naïve, older tourists. At times, I felt disheartened by the Indians who were selling something, and it seemed like everyone had something to sell. Vendors were in-your-face-won't-leave-you-alone selling it, whatever it was. From the different menus and prices for foreign tourists to the price gouging at hotels, ticket counters, and tuk-tuks, I wondered, *Where are the holy, enlightened, spiritual persons in India?* Was I naïve or just misinformed? Maybe truth, beauty, and lessons were learned at the feet of gurus and holy men in the 1960s, but now it felt as if it were one voracious commercial enterprise with charlatans and tricksters.

CHAPTER 16: *A Day in New Delhi*

For all the greed and thievery of Varanasi's merchants, the simple, older Indians in the third-class sleeper car in which we traveled had generous spirits, were kind-hearted, and restored my faith in India. It still broke my heart to see the squalor and poverty in the dwellings by the train tracks. When we arrived in New Delhi after the long overnight journey, I was beyond exhausted after not sleeping well, given the dreadful experience.

In the wee hours, I'd stumbled down the aisle to the Indian loo with its squat toilet. I rocked and rolled to the rhythm of the *Delhi Express.* The metal soap dispenser was empty, and the washbasin was dry. Not a good sign. The rubbish bin on the wall overflowed with Styrofoam containers, plastic bags, and liter bottles. As the train carriage swayed unpredictably—its metal wheels thumping, grinding, and clickety-clacking on the rails—an empty Coca-Cola bottle rolled back and forth across the floor. I turned the tap. No water. What had I expected? I had entered the Indian-style squat toilet by mistake—an error in judgment, the result of sleep deprivation after a man wearing a turban woke me shouting into his mobile phone. It was still dark outside. Trevor slept like the dead through it all. He was clever like that. I'd pulled my shoes out of the plastic bag, climbed down the ladder at the end of the bench, and gone to the loo.

I shook the door handle. "Oh, hellfire and damnation!"

I managed, without grace, to use the squat toilet—feet firmly planted on either side of the hole, hanging onto the metal bar on the wall for dear life while the train pummeled and pounded along. Of course, there was no toilet paper, but I came prepared—biodegradable wipes from the camping store where I had puzzled over survival gear before travel to India. I pulled the chain after, and water splashed onto the floor instead of flowing into the metal pan that emptied onto the tracks. The loo stank. God only knew what else was on the floor. I tried the door handle again. Nothing. I was trapped in a squat toilet, less than five square meters. The plastic bottle stopped rolling when it hit my foot. I threw it down the hole. Bob Dylan's song ran through my head, " . . . can this really be the end, to be stuck inside of Mobile with the Memphis blues again?"

I pounded my fist against the door. "Help!"

Outside the loo, someone shouted—a one-way conversation in Hindi. Maybe it was the guy on his mobile phone who had awakened me while I roasted slowly in the heat on the top berth. I shouted and beat on the door with both fists. His voice faded. No! He walked away. He probably couldn't hear me over the noise of the train.

"Bloody hell!" I yelled and kicked the door, twice for good measure. It was hotter than Hades inside the metal cube. The electric fan was broken, and the window was stuck. What would Elizabeth Gilbert have done if she had been stuck in the loo on a train in India? Meditation. That was it. I chanted my Deepak Chopra mantra and sucked in shallow breaths, my mouth open. My mind wandered. Train journeys were watershed events in my life.

The train slowed. Were we approaching a station? I opened my eyes and saw faint daylight through the opaque window. Trevor stood outside the loo, along with the conductor, who had a key, and a gaggle of Indians, paparazzi with iPhones snapping photos. My face turned bright red.

"You don't do anything by half, do you?" Trevor asked.

"Next time we fly!"

"I hear that lonesome whistle blow . . . " Trevor laughed so hard he choked on Hank Williams' lyrics.

"It's not funny!" I snapped, but I couldn't stop laughing either.

I was a proper mess when we got off the train. I had to clean myself up before we faced the day. I went into the women's toilet. It was a tad short of a nasty outhouse. I locked myself in the last stall because it had a spigot with running water and a squat toilet. The only thing missing was a bucket. I stripped in the disgustingly dirty stall, leaving my socks on my feet as a barrier to the floor, while splashing water from the spigot all over myself. After my semi-splash bath, I decided the best course of action was to leave my socks and my underwear in the toilet stall. I wasn't presentable but some of the road dust was off, and I was in a fresh change of clothes when I appeared.

I sat next to Trevor on a bench in the station and thought of the impish young beggar we had met in the New Delhi station. He wouldn't go away. First, he leaned into the train window, eyes sparkling. I couldn't help but think, *With an education, he could rule a small country or run a major corporation.* He was remarkably resourceful, and he'd learned his lessons well in the school of life's hard knocks. I slipped him a dollar bill while Trevor wasn't watching.

Three beautiful young Muslim women with perfect manicures and pedicures, gold jewelry, and gorgeous silk saris sat next to me. I was mortified. They were dressed to perfection. I spoke to the young woman closest to me and told her how embarrassed I was by my appearance. There was nothing to be done, however. I felt overwhelming humili-ation. Not because the young woman said anything unkind. On the contrary, she and I had a delightful conversation. She thought what I told her about our travels was very funny. She was articulate and spoke English beautifully. Thanks to Trevor's reluctance to part with rupees, we were traveling as cheaply as possible through India. I no longer had a New York City expense account. Still, I wished I were invisible.

New Delhi's Bazaar—the Pahar Ganj—looked good to me. It was crowded but not at all like Varanasi. Hotel prices were low. We were burned out from Varanasi and the crowds, and I was thrilled to find a guesthouse in the district near the train station.

"Jesse, I don't want to stay overnight."

"I'm exhausted, Trevor."

"I want to go to Dharamsala. Tonight." He gave me a dark look.

"I want a shower and I need a good night's sleep."

I was firm, but he wouldn't budge. Tears filled my eyes. There's no other word for it—I sulked. Trevor ignored me. I followed him to a travel agent shop. He insisted we take an overnight deluxe bus—whatever deluxe meant—from New Delhi to McLeod Ganj near the Himalayas. I agreed we needed R&R from the crowds, filth, and chaos of Varanasi's many celebrations and pilgrims, not to mention the extra stay for five days too many since we couldn't get out; but I wanted one night in New Delhi before we traveled to McLeod Ganj. Trevor booked seats on the deluxe AC bus scheduled to leave New Delhi sometime around 5:30 p.m. from a location somewhere just outside Pahar Ganj—nothing was entirely clear to us. *That was never a good sign*, I thought.

CHAPTER 17: McLeod Ganj, Dharamsala

Before we left New Delhi on the deluxe bus, the conductor warned us not to put any of our luggage in the aisles. We thought it must be for safety reasons. No.

We reached a dark bus station at 4:30 a.m. Our scheduled arrival time was supposed to be 7:30 a.m. We decided the driver and conductor had made good time; although while we were sleeping, they had made several stops to pick up rolls of carpet that completely blocked the aisle of the bus. The deluxe bus didn't have a toilet. We had stopped once or twice at perfectly dreadful places for which we had the pleasure of paying a few rupees to pee in a squat toilet so dirty it would have made an abandoned outhouse look like the Taj Mahal.

"Blimey, babe," Trevor said as he struggled with his bags over the rolls of carpet.

"Now I see why we couldn't put anything in the aisles."

The driver and his mate picked up extra cash transporting goods up the mountains into McLeod Ganj. Indian opportunists had been at the helm of the deluxe overnight bus. Why was I surprised?

One of the vendors turned on the light in his shop—an open stall on the concrete platform at the back of the open-air station. I drank three cups of the hot, sugary chai and felt slightly warmed in the cold mountain air.

"It's freezing," I said. What little sleep I had had on the overnight trip had been interrupted by my coughing. I had a fever and felt sick as a dog.

Trevor nodded in agreement, but he was on a mission. "We need to get a taxi to Dharamkot."

"We're not staying in McLeod Ganj?" I asked. I desperately wanted to be in bed. We shared a taxi with a young Indian musician from Ireland and New Delhi, and drove on a curvy road up the mountain to the little village—Dharamkot.

"Is this where we're staying, Trevor?"

He shook his head. "We have to walk from here." He pointed to a rough sidewalk leading past storefronts and a restaurant. Nothing was open. It was too early.

Trevor said, "Let's go."

"How far is it?"

He didn't answer. Every muscle in my body ached. I couldn't stop coughing, and I felt worse by the minute. We hauled our luggage up and down over the uneven path. It seemed never-ending. We wound around and walked up the path on what proved to be a difficult, steep climb and descent. And then I saw a concrete staircase leading to another quasi-sidewalk. I was out of breath. I'd had enough. Trevor stood on the sidewalk at the top of the staircase. He turned and eyed me, a scowl on his face. I sat down on the steps and sobbed. I had a complete meltdown, and I couldn't move another inch.

"Just leave your bags, Jesse." Trevor spit out the words between his gritted teeth. "I'll carry them to the sidewalk."

After composing myself, I wiped away my tears and, with a final sob, made my way to the top of the steps. Fortunately, it was downhill and mostly flat from there. We hauled all our bags to a place where Trevor had stayed two years earlier—a guesthouse in the middle of nowhere. I saw a goat on the roof of a little stone house.

"We're staying there." Trevor pointed up another hill.

Tasha, the Tibetan woman who owned the guesthouse, rushed outside.

"Trevor!" She was delighted to see him.

Had I been Heidi, or in the cast of *The Sound of Music*, I'd have burst out with an enthusiastic *Yodelayheehoo*. I was numb and didn't have the energy. Thank heaven, Tasha hauled my bags through a gap in a stone wall and up a muddy path to her guesthouse—as isolated a place in the back of beyond as I could imagine.

When she left, I turned to Trevor and said, "How in the name of all that is holy did you find this place?"

Trevor was furious.

We were in Dharamkot, home to the Dalai Lama in exile. If I hadn't been sick, I could have breathed the crystal clean air in the remote, albeit beautiful, mountainous setting. I was astounded when we got an Internet signal outside on the porch of our guesthouse. And then the rain came. We made up after the sidewalk disagreement and tried to cheer one another, despite the rainy and windy start to our first day. Since dust didn't cover everything in the mountains, I hoped I'd be right as rain soon. The guesthouse had no heat. We were in the foothills of the Himalayas. We had hot water on demand, merciful Jesus, and an en suite bathroom. The room was $4.45 USD per night. What could I say? It was no small wonder Trevor wanted to stay in Tasha's guesthouse. I went to bed as soon as we got settled and slept for the entire next day and then most of following day. I coughed until I thought my ribs would break. I hadn't been so sick for years. I read *Papillon*, *In Cold Blood*, and *Cannery Row*, and I started *Other Rooms, Other Voices*—two Capote stories. I slept, coughed, and blew my nose. I stayed in bed. I wanted to get well. I wanted to leave the guesthouse. I was unhappy.

"I have the rainy-day blues," I said.

Trevor grimaced. "I'm more depressed than you."

"At least you sleep a solid eight at night," I said.

I felt as if I had to do penance every night because rock-hard beds made sleep nigh impossible. Each night I made a vain attempt to get comfortable and sleep on the ironing board *cum* lumpy mattress on a plank. We begged for a single towel and our bed had only a bottom sheet that was none too clean. I was anxious to leave Tasha's guesthouse.

The next day, I felt better, and we walked from our guesthouse in Dharamkot to the top of the hill where the Tushita Meditation Center was. Later, we walked down the paved, winding road to McLeod Ganj where the Dalai Lama had his residence. I lost my peace-love handkerchief on the way. I felt sure a little white monkey I saw that afternoon must have spied it and decided to wear it around her neck as a scarf.

She must have been a female because a big male monkey mated with her—and, to my disgust, it was astonishingly quick. No dilly-dallying. During the day, McLeod Ganj was a fascinating madhouse filled with monks, foreign tourists, and Tibetans, young and old. The town felt overbuilt, with too much motor vehicle traffic.

The following morning began sunny and cool—great walking weather. We walked from Dharamkot down a very steep, rocky hill with no defined path to Bhagsu. The downhill slope to the little town was better suited for mountain goats. I longed for my Patagonia hiking boots back home. Bhagsu was Israeli-to-the-max. Posted signs had information in English, Hindi, and Hebrew. Afterwards, we walked to McLeod Ganj by way of a small, busy road and found ourselves with an international crowd in the bustling town. We ate lunch at Nick's Italian Restaurant, a Tibetan restaurant and bakery, with a beautiful terrace overlooking the valley below. Snowcapped foothills of the Himalayas painted the backdrop. Eagles soared on wind currents on the blue-sky day. I marveled at the stunning beauty, and the Tibetan food was delicious. We enjoyed the sunshine as a welcome companion on the chilly day. *What a striking contrast to the unrelenting heat in Southern India,* I thought. When we left McLeod Ganj, we walked up the mountain by way of a former forest road, only partially paved, back to Dharamkot. We took it slowly, as we were both just getting over colds.

We enjoyed perfect weather in the daytime. Since the guesthouse didn't have heat and only a screen covered the bathroom window, it was freezing cold at night. That posed a challenge. It was warm under the covers but OMG cold when I had to get up during the night. We had a sunny start the next morning, but I zipped myself into my down puffer jacket, as it was windy and cool. Trevor and I ate an omelet and luscious Tibetan brown bread at a little restaurant just beyond Tasha's home in Dharamkot. One of her goats stood on the roof of the hut where her ancient father stacked twigs for firewood. The whole family lived together in the stone house. Somehow. We sat in the sunshine for a while and decided to walk to Bhagsu. It began to rain, and Trevor mocked me when I started to walk down one of the goat paths.

"It's okay for the goats, Jesse, but it's slippery after the rain."

After cautiously picking our way down the steep, muddy, and rocky slope, we reached Bhagsu and walked to the swimming pool next to a temple. A stream descending from the famed waterfall filled the tank with icy water. Without warning, an unexpected downpour soaked us, the temperature dropped dramatically, the wind blew, and it was freezing. We caught a tuk-tuk to McLeod Ganj and Nick's Restaurant, my favorite place, and ate steamed Tibetan momos—dumplings filled with crispy vegetables. Later, we stopped by a secondhand bookshop where I picked up George Orwell's *Down and Out in Paris and London* and a copy of Paulo Coelho's *The Alchemist*. We walked back to Dharamkot.

Trevor phoned his older daughter, who planned to arrive in India a few days before we were scheduled to leave. Trevor's Polish friend Anna would arrive in Bhagsu or Dharamkot on Monday with her Indian boyfriend Rishi. It was much colder that night, so we tucked in and snuggled under lots of covers.

The next day, we walked to McLeod Ganj, where we had lunch on the terrace at Nick's. After lunch, we walked through town to the Dalai Lama's residence. Although he was not at his home, there was a great gathering of folks for a special puja. I found it fascinating. Massive brass prayer wheels sang when I turned them. What an extraordinary place!

We walked back to the guesthouse by way of Bhagsu. The only way to reach the guesthouse from Bhagsu was by foot or, preferably, mule. The last thirty yards or so we squeezed through a stone wall—to keep cows out—climbed down a few rocks, walked on a dirt path, clambered over a few more rocks, and walked through terraced areas planted with wheat and oats for the goats, cows, and water buffalo; and the pièce de résistance was that I hauled my derriere up a slight incline with—you guessed it—a few more rocks. Finally, we reached our no-name guesthouse where Trevor had stayed two years earlier.

That night, after our beautiful day, Trevor and I had a major communication breakdown.

"I hate this guesthouse," I said.

Trevor turned away from me but not before I saw disgust written on his face.

"Tasha's spying on us," I said.

The woman crept past our waist-high windows along the stone terrace, stopped, and peered into our room daily. God only knew what the woman did when we were away for the day.

"She's making sure there ain't a portable heater in the room," Trevor said.

"Whatever. Sure puts a damper on a romantic mood."

"Leave it." He snarled at me.

He didn't speak to me the rest of the night and turned away from me when we got in bed. I felt confused and hollow. Not every day was a diamond, but that evening felt weird. I couldn't wait to get home to my own bed and see good friends and familiar things. Trevor and I were both tired.

"I'll never come back to India, Jesse."

Memory had a way of softening the edges of bad as well as good experiences, I thought. I hadn't fallen in love with gap year travel through India, and I was eager to enjoy modern conveniences. I wanted to visit McLeod Ganj again—the mountains, the Himalayas' snowcapped peaks, the fresh air, and the Tibetans: monks, old and young, the villagers who were exiles from Tibet with their extraordinary art and textiles. It was a special place, but I could see it fast becoming overbuilt with no planning or forethought. That was India.

The next morning . . .

"Look, Trevor," I stood stiff, feet apart and threw my book on the bed, "I want a place with heat and privacy."

"We're not moving." He went into the bathroom and slammed the door.

When he came out after his shower, I confronted him. "What is the problem?"

"I ain't moving." His lips pressed tight together.

"I'll pay for a place away from Miss Nosey."

"We're leaving next week." He raised his voice—unlike him.

"I'm not comfortable here."

He said, at one point after our heated discussion, "Do you know how close we've come to breaking up?"

Well, I didn't know. I was stunned at how angry he was because I wanted to move to a different hotel. I didn't understand.

"You never had disagreements with your wives?" I asked.

He glared. "No!"

I thought it strange he had never exchanged harsh words or had conflicts throughout his failed marriages. I kept my thoughts to myself.

Trevor and I went on a three-hour hike to the small village of Nadu. After our difficult morning, we hiked up a steep, rocky incline and had tea on top of the mountain behind our guesthouse in Dharamkot. The views were beautiful once I huffed and puffed my way to the top. We followed a mountainous trail past Tibetan prayer flags waving in a gentle breeze. Bird songs were the only sounds. It was beautiful and the long walk was well worth it.

The village had spectacular views, with a panorama of snow-capped mountains in the foothills of the Himalayas. We enjoyed a wonderful lunch at a little restaurant on the mountain—vegetable momos and dal curry. By the time we returned to the guesthouse, it was warm enough for me to take a hot shower and wash my hair. Trevor and I enjoyed cuddles at last. It was not an easy day with him, but the strenuous hike dispelled the tension.

Anna and Rishi arrived later in the evening.

Trevor and I tried to figure the next move. Would he come to Fairhope? Should I go to England? We both needed to go home to our respective countries and tend to business. It was impossible to figure it out from India.

We walked down to McLeod Ganj on the mostly unpaved mountain road on what started as a lovely, bright, cool afternoon. The weather changed unexpectedly, and we got caught in heavy rain, thunder, lightning, and hail as we descended the steep forest road from Dharamkot. We ducked into a small temple with a low roof, where I banged my head and avoided several aggressive monkeys that wanted to get out of the rain as well. They took shelter under the eaves of buildings close to McLeod Ganj. The monkeys were a bit too close for comfort.

After the storm, the streets in McLeod Ganj were a muddy mess—crowded with motorcycles, pedestrians, and tuk-tuks. Later that evening, Anna, Trevor's Polish friend, prepared a delicious borscht for us. She told us Rishi spent 10,000 rupees (about $135.00 USD) on hashish instead of supplies for the little coffee shop they planned to run near the Israeli hotel where a lot of young people stayed and were celebrating Passover. The coffee shop was a roofless cinderblock shell of an abandoned one-room building with only three walls. *Oh, Anna,* I thought, *run, don't walk, darling.*

Later that night, the metal roof crashed against the doorframe to the rooftop and startled us. During the night, we had heavy rains, thunder that shook the building, lightning, and hail. The roof thundered, too. It sounded like the end of the world up on the mountain in Dharamkot. We lost electricity and pulled out our flashlights to find out what was banging on the floor above us. I slept in three layers of clothes, my cashmere cap, and gloves to stay warm. I shivered with cold throughout the night without heat.

Trevor and I sipped hot ginger, lemon, and honey tea and read aloud from Mark Twain's *The Innocents Abroad* outside our guesthouse. It was a sunny, crisp morning after the storm. It was also our last morning since we had to pack and return to New Delhi, the plains, and the heat on another overnight bus. I'd seen crystals for sale, and I wanted a reminder of the Tibetans and the Dalai Lama in McLeod Ganj. I felt a peace in the beautiful mountainous setting—something that had eluded me. The cool air energized me. The invigorating and difficult hikes in the mountains had built my confidence as well as my stamina. In my heart, I knew I wanted to return and study at the Buddhist Meditation Center near Dharamkot. The Tibetans in McLeod Ganj had gentle spirits reminiscent of Quakers I knew.

We walked to Bhagsu in search of crystals and then to McLeod Ganj. I found a small amethyst crystal a Tibetan woman displayed in the market near the Dalai Lama's restaurant. I believed it was imbued with the magic I felt there. We ate dinner at Nick's in McLeod Ganj, where we watched a beautiful sunset and the eagles soaring over the valley below. It was our last supper in the foothills of the Himalayas. We shared momos and I ate a fabulous Tibetan *thukpa*—a noodle soup rich with vegetables. Trevor ate a special vegetable curry. We had a 7:45 p.m. overnight bus to New Delhi, where we planned to spend a couple of nights to avoid travel during the celebration of Holi, an all-India fest, we heard, but didn't really understand. After Holi, we planned to travel to Mumbai at 5 a.m. by train for 24 hours. My flight home was on April 3. Trevor would head back to England and snow. I hoped he would come back to Fairhope soon to enjoy fishing.

CHAPTER 18: *Surviving the Bus Ride from Hell*

The bus was dilapidated, an antique. Trevor and I boarded it with three other passengers. Since it was already dark, it was difficult to see the exterior, but the interior was a relic that reminded me of a 1950s school bus. It was dirty and had hard bench seats with metal grab bars instead of headrests.

"This doesn't look promising," I said.

"It's shite," Trevor said.

"I wonder why there aren't more folks on the bus?" I asked.

I knew Trevor would veto my request to wait a day and find less dodgy transportation. I didn't bother to ask. The other passengers sat near the back of the bus, but we chose a seat close to the front. Honestly, I wanted to keep an eye on the driver. We careened around hairpin curves and had little, if any, sleep. Thank heaven it was night because we only saw the near misses with the headlights of oncoming vehicles. The trip would have been more terrifying if we'd been able to see the steep drop-offs. The mad bus driver screamed over the engine noise at the ticket taker all night long. India's roads were an unending pothole. We stopped a few times at places with disgusting squat toilets and paid for the privilege to pee in the filth. I would have preferred to stand behind a bush.

Throughout the night I prayed that, if we had a deadly collision during the hellish bus ride, both Trevor and I would be killed. In the light of day, when we reached New Delhi, we saw the exterior of the bus. It looked like it should have been retired sometime after Rosa Parks disembarked with Montgomery's police in 1957.

"We survived," Trevor said.

"The bus ride from hell," I said, and paused a beat, " . . . I didn't want to have to ship your body back to England."

Trevor laughed. "I thought the same thing!"

We booked into the Arjun Hotel in the Pahar Ganj of New Delhi and lucked out with a lovely room with a real bed, clean sheets, an en suite bathroom, and hot water. The room featured a large window overlooking the street. The next morning we watched rainbow mayhem on the street of the Main Bazaar below. People threw powdered dyes of different colors on one another, and others squirted large water guns to drench their victims and ensure the dye stayed in place. People shouted, "Happy Holi!" Trevor and I were safe three floors up.

"I'm hungry," Trevor said.

"I don't want to be trapped in the room all day," I agreed.

The colors, used to dye fabrics, stayed on the skin several days. It was a conundrum! I wanted to find a large garbage bag to hang over me like a poncho, but they seemed to be in short supply in India, as the streets were full of litter.

We walked through the colorful streets of the Main Bazaar. Paint and dye were everywhere—on dogs, cows, kids, grownups, and especially tourists. Young travelers with multi-colored dreadlocks and faces blurred with the mix of paints looked like zombies.

"How do you think the zombies will get the dye out of their dreadlocks?" I asked.

It was nuts in the street. Absolute crackerjacks. Rainbow people zigging and zagging, dashing about, shouting, laughing, screaming.

"Blimey, babe." Trevor ducked when several young guys threw dye at him.

"Please don't throw the dye on me," I begged the young men, to no avail. One of the boys threw yellow dye on my back after my plea not to include me in the rainbow mayhem and revelry. I turned around, scolded the young guy, and tried to whack him on the shoulder with my purple brolly. The young men laughed.

"What are you doing, Jesse?" Trevor grabbed my hand, pulling me down the street.

What was I doing? *Holi* was an ancient Hindu religious festival. It welcomed spring and celebrated new beginnings. Wasn't that what I'd hoped for before meeting Trevor a year earlier? What had happened to me to make me even consider retaliating with my umbrella? All the people, young and old, were enjoying a splendid time. India had tried and tested me, and at times brought out the worst in me. I'd lost my temper more in three months than I had in decades. What was wrong with me? On reflection, I was embarrassed by my behavior. I didn't understand Holi and its significance to Hindu religion. I had behaved like the Ugly American Tourist—not as a traveler. Lesson learned: I needed to understand and accept cultural differences even if I hadn't embraced what I had perceived as madness. Holi was a celebration of life.

CHAPTER 19: *Mumbai. Back Where It All Began*

We boarded the Punjabi Mail Train #12138 at 5:15 a.m. to Mumbai for a 26-hour trip in SL (sleeper class), and I had an upset tummy. That was all that I needed. We arrived at Mumbai CST at 7:35 a.m. and planned to stay for a few days in the tired but familiar Hotel Lawrence.

"Don't ask me if I want curry ever again, Trevor." I didn't like my attitude. What was I to do about it? We took the metro train from Church Gate to Grant Road to visit the Gandhi Museum. There were such striking parallels between Gandhi's life in India and Martin Luther King's in America. Seeing the dioramas was a profound experience, although chilling at the same time.

Trevor and I both lost our tempers more as we approached the last days in Mumbai. I felt ashamed when I lost my cool and my serenity. Unfortunately, we met Indians with no sense of boundaries. Two plump sari-clad Indian women boarded the train in Bhopal on our trip from New Delhi. They took my seat and insisted we move our luggage. One of the women didn't have a ticket and pretended they didn't understand English. It was a nightmare. Later, they asked Trevor, in perfect English, what country he was from. Go figure.

We walked forever to find *Dhobi* Ghat, the world's largest outdoor laundry. First, we came upon the mosque in the sea—the Haji Ali Mosque and Dargah, the tomb—reached only by a small causeway with the sea on both sides. We rode a public bus uptown and took a long, hot walk to Crawford Market, where we bought pashmina shawls as gifts. The marketplace was a zoo, crowded with too many people. Why was I surprised? All of India was like that.

That evening we walked from the Hotel Lawrence to the Colaba, where we ran the gauntlet of eager shopkeepers. We bought souvenirs for friends as remembrances from India. It was our last night at the Hotel Lawrence. The communal bathrooms looked like they hadn't been cleaned since our January stay.

Someone in India warned us, "Nadia is not your friend. She would just as soon cut your heart out with a dull knife." Nadia was anyone who wanted to sell you something, get something over on you, or rip you off without the least bit of conscience.

At last, we packed to go home—to our respective homes—and both of us experienced the anxiety of knowing all our belongings simply wouldn't fit. We planned to spend our last two days at the Marriott I had booked for us. I wanted to make sure we had all the mod cons—AC, hot water, and a good night's sleep in a real bed before our flights home. It was a treat to relax and spend a beautiful day of rest and relaxation with Trevor at the Marriott. It felt like a five-star resort compared to the places we had stayed throughout our entire India adventure. We ate Caesar salad for brunch. Lettuce at last. I craved leafy greens. It was the first lettuce I'd enjoyed since Chez Christophe in Gokarna, where the owners grew it organically. We spent a day watching movies and savored the time together.

CHAPTER 20: *Homeward Bound*

The Delta boarding experience was awful and lasted two hours after we passed through security. I was grateful I wasn't seated next to the screaming little French girl who blasted her lungs nearby. There were screaming children—in multiples for most of the flight—and ghastly meals, and I sat next to someone whose breath was even more foul than the Varanasi sewers. It was heart-wrenching to leave Trevor in the Mumbai airport. Saying goodbye to a long-distance lover who lives on a different continent just plain sucked—every time. Our Marriott reprieve had been just what we needed to wrap up our three-month odyssey.

Trevor kissed me at the airport and said, "I want you to visit me in Cornwall this summer."

PART II
Cornwall 2013

CHAPTER 1: *London. Brick Lane*

We were on the Tube from Heathrow.

"Why Brick Lane, love?" Trevor asked.

"I heard it was like Brooklyn before gentrification."

"We're staying in a warehouse?" Trevor looked skeptical.

"Don't worry, sweetheart." The owner had sold his dot-com business, and the warehouse was the office and the couple's living space.

"Hey, babe, well done finding the Airbnb," Trevor said. "Lucky the owners are on holiday, eh?"

Our reunion, after three months, was delightful in the new digs. We had the converted warehouse to ourselves.

"Fancy a bite to eat, Jesse?"

The waiter poured hot Moroccan mint tea into little glasses at Damascu Bite, a Lebanese restaurant two blocks from where we were staying. It was a beautiful evening, warm enough for all the doors to be open. The waiter arrived with a feast—lamb shish-kebabs, a spinach dish, hummus—exotic tastes made to order in the kitchen that was part of the small restaurant. All accompanied by steaming pots of delicious mint tea.

Brick Lane. I loved the graffiti, the murals on buildings, the secondhand clothing shops, and the fabulous restaurants. The designers' shops reminded me of life in New York.

"What fabulous street art," I said.

Trevor posed beside a large mural of Jimi Hendrix, and a blues guitar player on the street entertained us. I dropped a few pounds in his guitar case and he nodded.

"Do you know how much money you gave him?" Trevor didn't approve.

"Life is tough on the street, babe," I said.

I spied a mural of James Gandolfini, a black-and-white portrait on the side of a private residence, inside a locked gate. The artist's rendition looked like a charcoal drawing.

"It's tragic he died in Rome two weeks ago," I said.

The next morning we went sightseeing. Our Airbnb was near the Tube and buses, so it was easy to get around.

"London!" I felt like a kid in a candy store. "It's been years since I've been."

"Your tour guide grew up here." Trevor hugged me.

Having lived and worked in London until he was in his forties, when he moved to Cornwall, Trevor was the perfect guide. We walked to Tower Bridge, saw the Traitor's Gate at the Tower of London, and visited the old Roman parts of All Hallows Church. We walked to magnificent St. Paul's. And we walked some more. I think I saw it all—the Tate Modern, Buckingham Palace, the Horse Guards, Big Ben, the Shard, and the Gherkin.

"Here's the pub we called in after work at the Stock Exchange," Trevor said.

We visited Piccadilly Circus and eyed shoes that could only be described as gravity-defying sculpture.

"Be still, my heart." I pointed to purple Doc Martens.

I wanted to see it all. We packed a lot in during our three brilliant days in London. As a surprise, I'd bought tickets for the musical *Top Hat*—winner of three Olivier Awards—at the Aldwych Theatre.

"I read reviews that the costumes were fabulous," I said.

"Fred Astaire and Ginger Rogers," Trevor said. He grabbed my hand, and we twirled around. "Loved the old movie."

We walked down Brick Lane our last evening in London on the way to the Aldwych.

"Let's take the bus," Trevor said.

"We don't want to be late, Trevor."

He didn't ask me what I had paid for the tickets.

"Let's get a cab," I said. Trevor's lips pressed tight together. We took a cab to the theatre.

Our last morning in London, Trevor was in the shower while I packed. His phone rang. Then it stopped and rang again. I opened the bathroom door.

"Sweetheart, your phone is ringing. Maybe your daughter is trying to reach you." We were meeting her later at Victoria Station.

"I'll check the messages when I get out, Jesse."

The phone rang once more and stopped.

We met Trevor's daughter Heather at Victoria Station before we traveled to Cornwall. She had just flown into Gatwick from a film shoot in Germany. Trevor embraced his daughter—a pretty, slender blonde in her mid-thirties. She was on her way home outside London, where she lived with her partner, Charles. We chatted about the film industry.

"Dad said you worked in Hollywood," she said.

"It's a crazy business—smoke and mirrors." I laughed. "I enjoyed my life in L.A."

"Have you been to Cornwall?" Heather asked. "It's beautiful. Great weather ahead for your walking tour." She gave me a warm smile.

"Can't wait!" I felt relieved. I'd been anxious about how Trevor's grown daughter would respond to my dating her father. One of my stepsisters was brutal to my mother after she married their father.

"Trevor, what time is our train?"

"I bought bus tickets before I left Newquay," Trevor said.

No more needed to be said. Trevor was footing the bill, and although the bus took longer, it was less expensive than the train.

CHAPTER 2: *Cornwall—Tregurrian Camping & Caravanning Club on the Clifftops*

Trevor woke me with a kiss, a cup of Earl Grey, and a McVities digestive biscuit. The sun poured in through the caravan windows. I hadn't heard him stirring. That was unusual for me.

"Hey, sleepyhead," he said.

"What a day, Trevor," I said. The sun shone and it was warm.

"It's brilliant." He asked, "Do you fancy a bacon sandwich for breakfast?"

I took a shower in the small loo. The window faced a hedgerow where flowers bloomed and birds flitted in and out.

"So that's a hedgerow," I mumbled to myself. I'd read about them, of course, but this was up close and personal. Sometimes the little things brought joy.

After breakfast, we walked past the store and office at the campsite and headed toward the clifftop. When we reached a wooden fence leading to the next field, Trevor climbed through first and turned around.

"Wait, babe," he said.

I was puzzled. "Why?"

"This is a kissing gate." He leaned over and kissed me. "Now you can cross it."

We walked through the field to the public path near the cliffs. The sky was brilliant blue, and waves crashed against the rocks far below. I stopped to take pictures of the wildflowers—Queen Anne's Lace and others I couldn't name. Trevor put his arms around me and kissed me.

"It's magnificent," I said.

"Thought you'd like it."

We walked down to Watergate Bay and back. It was a proper walk, and since the weather was so pleasant, I enjoyed every minute. "Remember how hot July was, even in the early morning, back in Fairhope?"

Trevor laughed. "Let's head back. I want to show you Newquay."

We watched surfers on Fistral Beach from the hill overlooking the Atlantic in town, after walking by the high street stores—most of which catered to tourists, with souvenir shops, surf shops, video arcades, candy shops, ice cream vendors, bars, cafés, restaurants, and clothing stores. It wasn't what I had expected.

"Surf city," I said and watched little children lick ice cream cones and run to keep up with their parents.

"Lots of surfing competitions are held each year," Trevor said. "One competition is the largest in Europe."

Who knew? I was amazed but not in love with the scene in Newquay. We walked down toward the ocean, past the shops and a restaurant with a large outdoor space that was filled with a raucous bunch of guys dressed in the most bizarre costumes.

"What's that about, Trevor?"

"It's a stag do." He looked at me, laughed, and explained, "A bachelor party and they're pissed."

"Wow!" I said and watched the young men stagger on the wooden deck. "It's early to be that drunk."

"Come on, babe." Trevor took my hand. "I want you to meet a friend of mine who owns a clothing store."

CHAPTER 3: *Roche Rock, Cornwall*

"*L*ostwithiel means lost within these hills," Trevor said.

We left the small caravan on the clifftops near Newquay early the next morning. It was a gorgeous sunny day for our picnic in Lostwithiel. It was the second day of my walking holiday in Cornwall, after our beautiful stay in London. I saw ruins of stone buildings atop a tall granite rock formation.

"What's that?"

"Roche Rock," Trevor said. "It's an ancient monastery on the granite tor."

"Let's stop, sweetheart. I want to take pictures."

We walked toward the ruins through knee-high ferns and bracken, large boulders surrounding the tall spire. It was inconceivable to me how anyone had managed to engineer the stone buildings on top. Trevor climbed up on one of the boulders.

"Not me." I walked around the boulders to take photos from the other side. The ferns were denser, but I made my way on the narrow footpath to the back of the monument. Walking was a little more difficult because of the uneven terrain and rocks. I ventured farther away from Trevor to capture shots of the ruins from different angles. I was cautious as I stepped down and around small granite boulders. I reached a spot where I had to take a small step around a small boulder and down to a flat granite rock surrounded by flattened ferns and bracken. I stepped forward, planting my left foot with all my weight on the ground where I saw the flattened bracken. Instead of finding granite beneath the undergrowth, I realized my error in judgment a split second too late. I'd stepped into a hole and lost my balance. I fell backwards but I couldn't free my foot as I fell, and I felt a sickening snap.

Jarred by the sudden fall, I lay still for a moment to catch my breath. I thought I'd get up and go back to find Trevor, but when I looked down at my foot, I realized my ankle could no longer support me. It took a few moments, because I wasn't in pain, for me to accept the fact that I'd broken my ankle. In fact, my foot just flopped around. I took off my backpack and the jacket I was wearing and placed the jacket on top of the backpack to create a pillow where I could elevate my ankle. It was a serious break.

"Trevor, I need your help." I called out to him, but I couldn't see him.

"Where are you?" He answered from the other side of the rocks.

I waited until he found me behind the landmark stone outcropping.

"I've broken my ankle," I said. "I'm not going to be able to walk back to the car."

"Are you sure?" He looked stunned.

"You need to call the paramedics, babe." I pointed to my left foot where it lay limp against my jacket.

I lay back on the ground, stared at the sky, and lost track of time. I felt emotionally numb and realized I'd shifted into witness mode. I sat up, reached into my jacket pocket, gingerly working around my ankle, and I started taking pictures. After a few minutes I heard voices.

Trevor arrived with the paramedic first on the scene.

"I'm Melanie." She put her bag on the ground and knelt beside me. As soon as she saw my ankle, she said, "I'll give you morphine for the pain."

"It doesn't hurt," I said. "I don't need it."

"It might be a good idea before the pain kicks in," Melanie urged me. "The other paramedics are bringing a stretcher."

"Babe, I'm going to lead the others here," Trevor said.

I read the expression on Trevor's face as terror, and I gave him a little wave. "Do you mind if I take pictures, Melanie?"

I hadn't given much thought as to how I'd get out of the place where I'd fallen. It became clear that the terrain was simply too difficult for the paramedics to carry me on a stretcher when I heard a man shout as he tumbled down on the way to reach me.

"It's too dangerous for us to carry you out of here," Melanie said. "Our rescue helicopter can't come because they're on another call-out."

"We contacted the Royal Navy," the male paramedic said. "They're flying from the base in Culdrose."

"Are you sure you don't need morphine?" Melanie asked. "It's going to be a while before the helicopter arrives."

"My ankle is aching a little, not a lot," I said. "Okay, go ahead, but I don't need much."

While we waited, I watched Trevor wringing his hands and biting his lower lip. I handed my camera to him. "Please take pictures."

I heard the helicopter's approach before I saw it. It was massive and hovered over the nearby field. I watched an airman in his dark olive flight suit and helmet descend from the helicopter and walk up the hill toward us. The young man was take-your-breath-away handsome. He and Melanie talked while a second airman descended to the ground to join his colleague. They discussed a rescue plan, though I could only catch phrases because of the noise.

"We're going to put your ankle and leg below the knee in an air cast," Melanie said. "I think you're going to want a morphine injection."

As soon as she and the airman began pulling my leg to position it, I said, "You're right." She gave me the injection, and I began to feel as if I were enveloped in a warm cocoon.

The airman explained, "We're going to bring the helicopter in closer. Then we'll lift you."

I looked at Trevor.

"I'll meet you at the hospital, babe," he said.

The Royal Navy airman said, "I'm going to put a harness under your arms and under your knees, and when I say 'Go,' I want you to fall back into my arms."

"No problem," I said. I felt no pain. He was gorgeous.

Halfway to the helicopter, we started a slow spin in tandem with the helicopter blades. From my vantage point, I saw Trevor with my camera pointed skyward toward me. I waved and as we continued to spin, I saw other spectators in the field below taking pictures.

I felt no pain or fear until the last moment when the airman swung through the helicopter's open door, and I dangled in midair for a few seconds before he pulled me into the helicopter. I propped myself on my elbows and turned to look at the pilot, who was equally handsome. In that moment, I understood why my mother had fallen in love with an RAF pilot and war correspondent who was stationed at Maxwell AFB in Montgomery, Alabama, during World War II.

While I wondered what had happened to my mother's Englishman, I saw Melanie swing through the helicopter's open door after the second airman.

"I'm going to accompany you to the hospital in Truro," she said. "I've always wanted a ride in a Royal Navy Sea King helicopter."

It was too noisy to talk. With the helicopter doors closed, we soared upwards, and I turned to my left to sightsee and admire the English countryside. I looked on the bright side like Van Morrison. What was not to enjoy about a spectacular aerial tour of Cornwall with four gorgeous young men?

The Roche Rock paramedics met us on the landing pad at Royal Cornwall Hospital Truro and transferred me to a gurney.

"We're taking you to A&E, love." Melanie patted me on the hand.

I waved goodbye to the airmen. "Thank you, Melanie," I said. "What's A&E?"

They wheeled the gurney into the hospital, where the blue skies and sunshine outdoors morphed into a grayish blur with overhead fluorescent lighting.

"We'll take her from here," a nurse said.

Melanie handed me my small backpack. My mobile phone chimed. It was a message from Trevor.

Trevor: Hiya babe, pls give me a call when you can.
Me: I'm in A&E in Truro and there are some things I need in the caravan. xxx.
Trevor: Just about to ring you, so hold on. I've seen the WhatsApp for bits but will double check before I leave. xoxo

I don't remember the move from A&E to a hallway where I waited on my gurney outside a set of double doors that swung open from time to time and revealed nurses and doctors attending to another patient.

An hour later, I sent Trevor a message:

I'm in hospital gown, so don't bother with a bathrobe. One leg out of jeans. I think they're going to dope me up for whatever they're going to do. I have two magazines and a book in backpack. They don't want me to eat and, yes, it seems I'll be here overnight although I hope not. Too hard to get around right now babe. Hope you will still be my beau. I need you. It's a bit scary, Trevor. xxx

CHAPTER 4: *Royal Cornwall Hospital Truro (RCHT)*

Scene 1. The First Night

I awoke after midnight, lying in a hospital bed in Cornwall. It was my first night in the hospital after breaking my ankle, and I was on the orthopaedic trauma ward. I was in a private room like a glass cage. I could see into the larger ward just outside my room through the windows and the open door. A male patient slept in the large ward, which had at least ten beds. That's why they hadn't put me in the big ward. At least that's what the nurse told me when they wheeled me into the room and transferred me into the bed. I was so drugged with morphine that I don't remember leaving the operating theatre where the skilled surgeon had removed the second cast and put on the third cast. I asked him to go ahead and knock me out with the morphine for the third cast and third attempt to get my anklebones back in place.

A faint light shone through the windows to the left of the bed, facing another part of the hospital. I needed to have a wee. I think it was the first one since I'd broken my ankle and gotten to the hospital hours before. I pressed the button for the nurse. A large, rather stern-looking nurse answered my call and asked what I needed. I told her and she left the room briefly, returning with a bedpan. She handed it to me and left. It was small.

I lifted myself with my good leg and one arm, sliding the bedpan underneath me as well as I could, moving the hospital gown out of the way. I tried to be careful, but I knew there was no way that bedpan was going to work—at least not with me shifting onto it. I didn't want to wet the bed. I was terrified of wetting the bed. I managed to use the bedpan successfully, and I was relieved until I tried to reverse my procedure to remove it so I could lie back down. There was no way I was going to be able to remove the bedpan, but I tried anyway. I spilled the contents all over the bed and hospital gown and myself. I started crying.

The nurse came back into the room, and I confessed my accident. She was that kind of stern person whom I didn't want to upset because I felt so vulnerable. She took the bedpan from me and left the room. A few minutes later she returned with clean sheets and a box of wipes. She turned me onto my right side to remove the bottom sheet from the left side of the bed. Then she turned me onto my left side to perform the same procedure. I still don't remember how she managed to get the clean sheet on the bed, but she helped me get into a fresh hospital gown and handed me the box of wipes. She placed a trashcan on the side of the bed where I could dispose of the used wipes properly. I was mortified. She seemed angry with me. I was afraid, alone, and in pain.

Scene 2. *First Day in the Orthopaedic Trauma Ward*

In the morning, the nurses moved me to a bed in the ward. I was next to an open window that overlooked the rooftop of an adjacent building and out at green fields. Thank heaven, a room with a view. The nurses wheeled several new women patients into the ward as they came out of surgery. For a while, they were kind of doped up. The man was gone.

I told one of the nurses I needed to use the loo. She brought a bedside loo, closed the curtain around my bed and helped me transfer from the bed into the chair. It did afford some privacy. It was akin to having a wee in a department store restroom where the adjacent stalls were filled with women while others waited in line. Ten beds filled the ward, and I asked, "Are there that many patients?"

"Oh, yes," she said. "This is a busy ward."

I'd never been in a ward; during the few hospital experiences I'd had, I'd stayed in a private room.

It was already noisy with a bit of construction work going on, workers sawing a pipe, one patient shouting into her cell phone, and a poor older woman who'd had a stroke crying out for her mother.

The nurse showed me how to transfer to the handicapped toilet, and it dawned on me, albeit slowly because I was still in a fog from the anaesthetic and morphine, that I was about to acquire a new skill set. By the time she helped me back into the bed, the last dose of pain medication had worn off. I began to feel the pain when she propped several pillows under my foot with the new cast, split down the middle. I learned later it was to allow for swelling.

An older lady came with a metal trolley with an urn and cups.

"Would you like milk tea, dear?" she asked.

I nodded and she handed me a slip of paper and a pencil. "Just mark what you'd like for lunch and dinner."

I thanked her and looked at the menu in wonder. What was a *bap*? What was a *pasty*? Mushy peas? *Figgy hobin*? It was a complete mystery. I checked familiar foods—chicken, fish cake, and broccoli. Noisy seagulls on the rooftop across the way flew on and off their nests and kept up quite a racket. It was amusing to watch at first.

My iPhone chimed—a message. It was Trevor.

Trevor: Hiya, babe. I hope you're feeling okay this morning. I'm so worried.

Me: Hi, sweetheart. Last night was a bit rough, but I'm doing okay this morning.

Trevor: I'm coming to the hospital in a little while and I'll bring your computer backpack.

Me: They moved me into a ward. I've never been in a ward.

Trevor: What else do you need me to bring you?

Me: Please bring my silk kimono. I want to cover up the ghastly pink hospital gown. Oh, I need some makeup and my journal.

Trevor stopped by with my backpack. "Sweetheart, you look very pretty this morning." He leaned over and kissed me.

"Maybe I can come back to the caravan until the surgery." My thinking wasn't clear.

"Bad news, Jesse. I asked Hugh about the Duchy Hospital private rooms, and they are £1500 per night."

"Guess the ward is my temporary home."

"Right." Trevor looked stressed.

"Do you know when your friends are visiting this afternoon?" I asked.

A group of medical students surrounded a doctor who arrived at the foot of my bed and examined my chart. I felt a bit like a specimen on exhibit. The doctor introduced himself. He said he was a consultant.

I looked at Trevor, puzzled.

"Jesse, a consultant is a specialist in the NHS."

Yet another instance of my foreign language crash course in Cornwall. He was an orthopaedic surgeon.

I asked, "How long will it be before I have surgery?"

"We can't operate until the swelling goes down," the consultant said.

The entourage stared at me and at my elevated foot with hot pink toenail polish. I was surprised they hadn't removed the polish before they put on the third cast while I was knocked out. The color was a lovely contrast to the white linens.

He continued, "We'll check again on Sunday."

"Sunday?" I was stunned.

I realized that the consultant, stern and unsmiling, his expression aped by the medical students around him, was the bearer of bad news. It was Tuesday.

"Just how long will I be here?" I asked.

"Probably ten days." He and the flock were off to see the next patient on the ward.

"You never do anything halfway, do you, babe?" Trevor said.

I felt sure Trevor's expression mirrored mine. We were stunned.

"I can't believe they're not going to operate for such a long time," I said.

"Patience, my patient."

"Okay, sweetheart." I felt so weird. A stranger marooned in a strange land. I looked in the backpack. "Thanks for bringing my laptop and the silk kimono." At least I could check my email. "Trevor, the Wi-Fi signal isn't great here. It's sporadic."

The seagulls squawked and circled just outside my window.

"Scenery's great, babe." Trevor laughed. "Free entertainment."

What was I supposed to say? I didn't feel patient. I felt afraid and frustrated. I didn't understand the NHS.

"I need to see if Chris wants me to write another draft of the article."

"Right."

"I need a mobile hotspot, babe."

"I'll get you a dongle." He held my hand. "I'm going back to the caravan for lunch, but Charlotte and Paul will call in when I'm here this afternoon."

He kissed me goodbye.

Scene 3. Holding Court in My Hospital Bed

Time passes slowly when you're in pain, I discovered. It was as foreign to me as the ward and more distressing. After badgering the ward nurse, I finally received the medication dose I had requested earlier. She argued with me about all the times I received meds, but I was in pain and whatever they had given me wasn't working. The nurse asked two other people on the ward if they were in pain. I didn't understand why it was so difficult for me. The doctor okayed upping dosage, but the nurse refused to give me the medication until the next scheduled time. Put the round peg in the round hole and the square peg in the square, but God forbid my pain wasn't on their schedules. Unbelievable. I could receive meds at teatime, lunchtime, breakfast, and before bed, but the nurses hadn't done that. It was all about checking boxes. I know I was moaning, as Trevor called what I referred to as bitching or kvetching. I felt bitchy. I had to adjust my attitude before Trevor and his friends arrived.

Charlotte took a photo of me, perched like the queen holding court from a hospital bed, dressed in my beautiful silk kimono, makeup on, smile on my face, holding the bouquet of flowers she had brought me, silver bracelets on my arm, and my foot propped up in the air, hot pink toes matching some of the flowers. I picked up my iPhone and took a quick snapshot of Trevor and his friends. Charlotte wore a big smile, as did her husband Paul.

"You know who was piloting the helicopter, don't you?" Paul asked.

"No, I don't."

"It was Prince William."

"No way." I started laughing.

Trevor's former brother-in-law sat to my left. He crossed tattooed arms against his chest in a manly fashion. He was buff, obviously spent a lot of time in the gym, and was pleased with himself, I thought, his blue cap pulled over his forehead. He grinned. Trevor, on the other hand, bit his fingernails and looked to be a minute away from a panic attack. We passed the visit with laughter and promises of getting together after I was back at the caravan. Trevor looked a lot more relaxed after the jovial conversation about new motorhomes, curry dinners, and how an American felt about the NHS. I totally got how the Bing Crosby character must have felt in the movie *A Connecticut Yankee in King Arthur's Court.*

Later that day, Trevor sat by the bed and held my hand. "Babe, it's lonesome in the caravan without you." He leaned over and kissed me. "I'll be back tomorrow morning."

"I had a bap for lunch," I said laughing. "It's all foreign."

"When do you see the surgeon again?" he asked.

I shrugged. The older woman in the far bed moaned and cried out, wrestling with her bed linens. One of the nurses hurried over to her and held her hand, soothing her in a quiet voice. The young women in the bed next to me greeted her husband when he arrived with her three-year-old and six-year-old. He carried a Starbucks cup and handed it to his wife.

"It's a bit of a scene here," I said.

Trevor turned to see the commotion. "Has it been like this all day?"

I nodded. "Even when the visiting hours are over."

"Ethan and Candace want to visit tomorrow," Trevor said. "Is that okay?"

"Sure." I couldn't help laughing. "What a terrific first impression I must make."

"Honey, my friends are glad to meet you," Trevor bit his lip. "Hugh and Emma got caught in a traffic jam and couldn't get here."

"When is their daughter's wedding?"

"Just a few weeks."

"Oh, Trevor. I can't wear my gorgeous sexy heels."

"You still can wear one." He leaned over and whispered, "We'll make sure you're glowing for the occasion."

The next morning, Trevor entered the ward waving a small American flag. "Happy Fourth of July, sweetheart." He kissed me and sat down beside the bed.

"Oh, joy. Let freedom ring." I was not in a celebratory mood. "It's a beautiful day. I want to have a picnic on the beach."

"And you will." He squeezed my hand. "Did you talk with your brother? I emailed him."

"Yes, babe. He wants me to fly home right now and have surgery in the States."

Trevor's brow wrinkled.

"He doesn't think highly of the NHS." I sighed. "Turns out the Overseas Visitor Liaison at the hospital isn't my ally after all. She makes sure the NHS gets paid. Her official title is Paying Patient & Overseas Visitor Liaison."

"You didn't expect it to be free."

"Of course not. That's why I have travel medical insurance."

"Honey, do you need to sort all this now?"

"I've had medical insurance logistics blues," I said. My eyes filled with tears.

"Oh, sweetheart." Trevor hugged me.

And at that moment, Ethan and Candace arrived with chocolate and smiles—the antidote to the blues. Trevor was my anchor in the storm, and all his friends became instant buddies. It felt good since friends and family were 4,000 miles away.

Scene 4. Please Don't Give Me Senekot

A rare heat wave visited Cornwall. Unusual, but of course it happened while I was stuck in a hospital bed in a ward without air conditioning and minus fans. Windows were open, and for that I was grateful, until the wee hours when the seagulls and their chicks in the nests on the roof of the building across from me started squawking. Their cacophony was relentless. Irritating at 2 a.m., 3 a.m., and basically 24 hours nonstop—a noisy nuisance or entertainment. I wore earplugs at night, and while it didn't completely end the problem, it helped.

The upside was that I had a fantastic window view from my bed. I watched baby seagulls growing up on the rooftop across from me.

The countryside was lush, green, and beautiful. I had a grand view of fields and rolling hills. It reminded me of life in Virginia.

"No, you can't come visit," I said, crying into the iPhone. I sobbed. "No. I can't . . . I'll send you a message on WhatsApp." I knew no one wanted to overhear a conversation about my bodily fluids.

Me: "I'm sick as a dog, Trevor."
Trevor: "WTF?"
Me: "I'll spare you the details, but I'm sick at both ends. It's awful."
Trevor: "Sweetheart, what's going on?"
Me: "I begged them not to give me a laxative."
Trevor: "Bloody hell."
Me: "We're quarantined."
Trevor: "Can I bring you anything?"
Me: "No."
Trevor: "R u quarantined?"
Me: "The whole ward. They think it's Norovirus."
Trevor: "For fuck's sake."
Me: "It's not a virus. My body went mad with the Senekot."
Trevor: "Did they give you too much?"
Me: "Who knows. I begged them not to give me a laxative. I can't take them."
Trevor: "Honey."
Me: "Everyone on the ward is upset with me. The weekend is visiting time."
Trevor: "Oh, sweetheart."
Me: "I'm dying in here."

Maybe the cloud had a silver lining. When heavily drugged, as I had been, I felt as if I were floating. I floated until the hospital saw fit to lift the quarantine.

Scene 5. *Quarantine Lifted & Visitors Allowed*

"I met my surgeon," I said. "He's good looking, wears skinny jeans and Beatle boots."

Trevor gave me a funny look.

"Are all the doctors in the NHS so good looking?" I asked.

"Whoa, girl, we better get you out of here quick if you're hot for the doctor."

"I can't help myself," I said. "I don't think it's the drugs." I grinned. Maybe it was the drugs. I didn't care. "They're handsome and young, but not as young as your harem."

"What's the harem got to do with it?"

"Trevor, those beautiful young girls I met were young enough to be your granddaughters."

"They were my friends in India."

"So you say, Major Tom." I gave him the eye. "If I want to lust after a good-looking young surgeon, I think I will."

"Babe, you're stoned on the drugs." Trevor laughed. "Save some for me when you get out of here."

"Dr. Hawkins said the swelling's gone down," I said, "just not enough to operate on Monday."

"Seriously?"

"He thinks it will be Tuesday."

"And when can you leave after that?"

"Who knows? It's still a mystery to me."

Scene 6. *Escape from the Orthopaedic Trauma Ward*

Dr. Hawkins repaired my ankle with a metal plate, eight screws, and a wire. The three broken bones were ready to knit back together. The morning after my surgery I asked the folks not to give me pain medication. I had to conduct a telephone interview from my hospital bed with Mark, editor of *Wind Turbine World* magazine in Washington, DC. I was grateful to have the assignment. I decided all I needed to do was put my earphones on and conduct the interview. I dressed for the day in a sleeveless black dress, suitable business attire I thought, with makeup and hair in place. After all, it was to be a business meeting via telephone. I had to be the working woman. Who else would think such folly necessary?

Mark was flabbergasted when he learned I was in the hospital and calling him a day after major surgery. He said, "You've gone above and beyond the call of duty to meet a deadline."

I laughed. "Yeah, suit up and show up."

"I'm gonna tell Chris to pay you double," he said. "You earned it!"

The hospital discharged me that afternoon. Trevor somehow poured me into a rental car. I was grateful it wasn't his vintage VW Westfalia. It was difficult getting in. My foot was propped on a pillow on the floor. The drive back to the caravan was a nightmare. I wasn't used to driving on the left side of the road, and I was terrified by curving roads, oncoming cars, and the occasional bump. I was tense and in pain.

CHAPTER 5: *The Caravan—Tregurrian Camping & Caravanning Club*

Trevor pushed my wheelchair on the grass to the caravan.

"Oh my God," I said. "Steps."

How was I supposed to get into a caravan? I couldn't walk. The crutches and I had had a disagreement in my three-minute orientation with them on the orthopaedic trauma ward. And then—the moment that I hadn't expected—steps at the caravan.

"Trevor, I can't walk up the steps."

"Blimey."

"I have an idea," I said. "Hold the wheelchair steady so it doesn't move, babe."

I hopped on my good foot out of the wheelchair, turned around, and managed to situate my derrière on the caravan floor. Surely that was progress, but how was I supposed to get from the door to my bed on the bench seat in the caravan? An aha moment: I scooted backward on my bum like an upside-down crab, using my hands and my good right leg for leverage while keeping my leg with the cast in the air. It wasn't perfect, but it was effective. I had made slow progress to the bench seat when I realized I had another problem—how to get up on the seat. I looked at Trevor. He stood there holding the crutches.

"How are you going to get off the floor, sweetheart?" Trevor bit his bottom lip and looked as if he wanted to cry.

I was dead weight on the floor, and he couldn't lift me. There was nothing I could use to leverage myself up by increments. I tried pushing myself up from a kneeling position. No luck. The wheelchair didn't fit between the bench seats in the caravan. I had a dilemma. I asked Trevor to pull the cushions down onto the floor and make something that looked a bit like a ski ramp. I tried to climb backwards up the incline until I could position myself on the bed. Thank God I had strong arm muscles and was in good shape, other than my broken ankle. I was exhausted and in pain.

"Can you please bring me my tablets, Trevor?" I needed my pain medication. Trevor looked haunted. I don't remember much about the first night back at the caravan other than that I popped pain tablets and heavy-duty Tylenol most of the night.

I sent an email to my brother and sister-in-law:

Trevor took my picture after we got back to the caravan from Royal Cornwall Hospital in Truro. Can't remember if I told you, but Dr. Hawkins said he put eight screws and a plate on the left side of my ankle and one screw and wire on the right side of my ankle because there wasn't enough bone on my ankle for two screws. Whew! Glad that's over. Sutures come out and this cast comes off in two weeks. Cast will be replaced with an air cast for two weeks, then a grey ski boot (whatever that is) for two weeks. No weight at all on foot for six weeks. On crutches, or using "Zimmer frame" (i.e., walker), or a wheelchair. Lots of excitement, huh? Experiencing discomfort forty-eight hours after surgery but not terrible pain, thank heaven. Here's my mailing address:
Trevor Green
c/o Tregurrian Camping and Caravanning Club Site
nr Newquay, Cornwall
TR8 4AE
United Kingdom

The first few days were a blur. I had crutches in the caravan, but it was hard to use them in the small space. I found I could hold onto the cabinets and hop one step at a time to the loo. Thank God the caravan had a separate bathroom because there was no way I could have walked to the facilities at the campsite.

"Cuppa tea. Cheese and pickle sandwich or a bacon sandwich," Trevor said. "How about a good book?"

"Hey, babe, will you read to me from *The Innocents Abroad*?" I asked.

Trevor looked chagrined. "I don't have it." He paused for a moment. "I gave it to a girl from Amsterdam who was camping here."

I wasn't sure what to make of that, but I'd given it to him as a present. It was his to give freely. I was disappointed, however.

"Isn't it time for you to give yourself a jab?" Trevor asked and distracted me.

Each evening, I had to give myself an injection in the stomach. I suppose he thought I needed a reminder, but he couldn't look when I stuck the needle into the skin I pinched between two fingers. "At least my stomach is really colorful," I said.

Trevor gave me his iPhone before he went to sleep because I couldn't get a signal on mine. I signed into my email account and read messages from home. I felt vulnerable and wished my friends weren't 4,000 miles away. My ankle, propped up on two pillows to prevent swelling, hurt, and it was difficult for me to go to sleep. I had the little light over the bed pointed away from Trevor, but he was fast asleep, as usual.

A text message popped up on his iPhone—Sarah. *Who was Sarah?* I wondered. I stared at the phone as if it were an alien creature suddenly alive in my hands. I wrestled with my curiosity or nosiness, take your choice. I blamed it on the pain meds. I knew I shouldn't pry but that didn't stop me from reading the message, or several preceding it. How I regretted my poor decision. Surely it was the Tramadol and brain fog that made me do it.

The text messages went back for weeks, and I understood from the tone of the messages that there was an ongoing flirtation, but was it more? That's when I read the message that sent me into a mental spiral downward. I felt numb. Trevor's message to Sarah was, *"I've got a tentpole under the sheets thinking about your call."*

What the hell? I felt disgusted—ashamed of myself for succumbing to an invasion of Trevor's privacy and opening Pandora's box, and sick at heart with new knowledge. Trevor had sent the text the week before I arrived in London. Was I reading more into the message than was intended? After a year-and-a-half with Trevor, I understood Brits weren't shy of a joke with sexual innuendo. Whatever the intent, I was stunned. I tethered my phone to his and wrote a long message to a friend. It didn't go through. That was just as well. My rambling rant was incoherent and bordered on hysteria. I needed to use the loo. I grabbed the crutches propped at the end of the bed and made it into the small bathroom without a hitch, although once in the bathroom, I had to prop the crutches against the closet door and hop around to sit down. It was simply too small a room for anything else.

As I made my way back to the bed, I cleared the bathroom door with the crutches, but I lost my balance. I must have been drugged out of my mind on pain medication. I fell backwards in what seemed like slow motion in that moment. I let go of the crutch in my left hand and reached out to grab the counter on the storage cabinet. Instead of the counter, I managed to catch the cord to the electric kettle on top of the microwave, and as I fell, the microwave and the kettle, filled with cold water, came tumbling down. Surely it was through the grace of God that both hurtling objects missed me by inches. Otherwise, I would have been seriously hurt. I was, however, drenched with the water from the electric kettle.

Trevor shot up from the bed like a bolt and stared, a deer in the headlights stare. I sat up, checked myself out, and realized, with great relief, that I wasn't hurt—just a bit bruised and battered. The microwave stood on its side on the floor next to me. I didn't see the electric kettle, only its base and the wires from both. I buried my face in my hands and began laughing and sobbing, tears running down my cheeks, at the same time. He must have thought I had lost my mind. I knew with absolute certainty that I had.

"What the hell, Jesse?"

I didn't answer. I couldn't look at him. I needed to get into dry clothes, as mine were soaked. "An unintended baptism?" I muttered under my breath.

"Are you hurt?" He wore a pained expression.

I couldn't tell if he was scared I'd hurt myself in the fall or if he was annoyed. "I lost my balance."

"Right. That's it," he said. "I'm taking the crutches."

"What?"

Trevor helped me back to bed. It was 2 a.m. and, thank heaven, I had the presence of mind not to bring up the text I'd read. Seeing that stung more than any bruises from my fall, and I'm grateful to say I didn't remember anything more from that dreadful night.

CHAPTER 6: *Trevor Pitches a Fit*

Saturday morning, Trevor's phone rang while he was at the campsite shower. It wasn't one of his buddies or his children. Their calls had familiar ringtones. This ringtone was a harp. I didn't answer it. It rang again and again—maybe five times until it stopped.

"Trevor," I said, as he walked in the door, "Someone's trying to reach you."

He picked up his phone.

The phone rang again with the harp tone. Trevor turned off the ringer and pocketed the phone.

I asked, "Do you have any stamps?"

I perched on the bench seat in the VW Westfalia, the sliding door open, and waited for Trevor to load the wheelchair into the van.

"You okay, babe?" he said.

I nodded, but I felt bruised and battered.

"Let's have lunch by the sea after we go to the post office," I said.

He slammed the sliding door of the van closed and got into the driver's seat. "We're not going to a seaside restaurant, Jesse."

"Trevor, normal people go out for lunch on a beautiful sunny Saturday."

We drove in uneasy silence. Tears filled my eyes.

Trevor pulled up to a little store in St. Columb Major. It was a beautiful little village.

"How many stamps do you want, Jesse?" he said in a flat tone.

"That's a post office?" I asked.

I waited in the VW, my heart heavy, my state of mind confused, confounded, and troubled.

Trevor returned with a huge smile on his face. "I'm calling in to the ironmongers, babe."

"What's an ironmonger?" I asked, but he was off at a trot, leaving me with my thoughts. I knew I hadn't been easy company after the accident, but Trevor was no picnic with his light-switch moodiness. I watched passersby and wished I could walk past shop windows.

We drove down small lanes and through charming seaside coves and villages. Sunlight sparkled on the sea. Cornwall was magnificent with its blue skies on a brilliant summer's day. I watched waves break from the tops of cliffs and down near boats in the harbors. My spirits lifted. Having a grand explore was tonic to soothe my troubled soul.

"Let's take a stroll, babe," Trevor said. He unloaded the wheelchair and smiled. His mood changed from foul weather to fair to foul without warning.

He pushed me on narrow cobblestone streets. I felt like a mannequin in a shop window on display moving through efforts not of my own making. I was uncomfortable. Dark sunglasses afforded some privacy. We passed small boutiques, thrift shops, outdoor shops, little tearooms, ancient pubs, and flowers everywhere. The wheelchair bumped along rough lanes, and occasionally I asked Trevor to stop so I could take pictures. We headed down a small incline toward the harbor. Boats rocked on waves coming through an opening in a massive concrete breakwater where I watched a fishing boat headed out to the Atlantic. Trevor pushed me as far as the wheelchair allowed, until steps prevented my moving any farther. He wanted to go up the steps and he left me sitting next to the quay.

Something large and black popped up out of the water next to the stern of one of the boats where a fisherman threw out small fish. And then another large, black creature popped out of the water. Seals! What a grand surprise. I saw three women walking toward me. Tourists, I deduced from the clothing they wore and peculiar large hats. The cameras hanging round their necks were a dead giveaway. I watched them pass and thought perhaps flowered cropped slacks weren't the best choice for a woman rather wide in the beam. In fact, all three had broad derrières—cropped slacks on the first, a dress that hung well below the knees on the second, and wrinkled chinos on the third. They stood close to one another, and since they had their backs to me, they appeared as if melded into one broad beam. I couldn't help laughing.

"What's so funny?" Trevor asked.

I shrugged. "Did you see the seals?"

He pushed my wheelchair back up the quay toward the center of the village and the VW.

A short drive later we pulled into a small cove and parked in a lot overlooking a sandy beach. A couple walked on the sand, their children running, shouting, and laughing, the family's golden retriever in heaven in the waves. Trevor pushed the wheelchair up to a small ice cream stand with picnic tables out front.

"Fish and chips, babe?"

WTF, I wondered. We sat at the picnic table and waited for our order. I had no words.

CHAPTER 7: *Telephone Drama*

Scene 1. The Harp

Monday morning was beautiful and promised another gorgeous day in Cornwall. Trevor fixed breakfast and, while we ate, said, "We'll call in to the Red Cross and get a Zimmer frame."

I nodded. "Good idea."

Trevor's phone rang. His friend Paul's ringtone was the distinctive *ah-ooga* sound of an old-time car horn.

"Hiya, mate," Trevor said and paused a beat to listen. "I'll check with her."

He turned to me. "Hey, babe, Paul and Charlotte want to call in this evening and bring dinner. Are you up for a visit?"

"Sounds great." An evening with new friends was just what I needed, and I hoped it might relieve Trevor's restlessness. I felt I'd been an anchor with a cast and a wheelchair.

Trevor confirmed with his buddy. "They'll be here at five."

"What are you working on, Jesse?"

"Editing the article on decommissioning a nuclear facility," I said. "I have to send it to Chris."

"What if MI6 storms the caravan?" he asked, and we both laughed.

"Trevor, the Wi-Fi isn't strong enough to connect to the Internet."

"What about the dongle?" he asked.

"I'm out of minutes."

Trevor handed me his iPhone and I tethered it to my computer. "Thanks."

He said, "I'm off to the farmer's stand."

Trevor's phone rang. I let it go to voicemail. Then it rang again—a harp ring tone, and again. After the tenth call, I answered.

"Hi, Trevor will be back in a few minutes."

A woman's voice came over the line. "Who is this?"

"Can I give him a message?" I asked. She hung up.

Ten minutes later, Trevor's daughter called. "Hi, Janet, your dad stepped out for a few minutes."

"Hope you're feeling better," she said. "Please ask him to give me a ring."

The phone rang again—the harp. I didn't answer. It rang four more times and finally stopped.

"Thank heaven," I said aloud and went back to work.

Twenty minutes later, Trevor walked in carrying a tote bag, lettuce poking out of the top.

"Hiya, babe," he said. "How's the article?"

"I sent it."

He grinned. "Brilliant!"

"Janet called," I said. "She wants you to call her."

"Did she say when she's coming to visit?"

"No. Trevor, before Janet called, your phone rang ten times."

"Who was it, Jesse?"

"I don't know," I said. "The woman asked who I was, but she hung up after I asked if I could take a message."

Trevor pulled carrots, onions, and lettuce from the tote bag and put the vegetables on the drain board next to the small sink. He called his daughter and listened, biting his lower lip. "Okay, sweetheart," he said. After their phone call ended, he busied himself at the sink rinsing the lettuce.

Scene 2. Flowers and Laughter Over Dinner

That evening, Paul and Charlotte pulled up in her red Mini Cooper convertible. From the moment they walked into the caravan, the laughs began and didn't end until they left. Charlotte brought flowers, a delicious Beef Bourguignon, and a bottle of red wine. Paul and Trevor shared stories about growing up in their neighborhood that still bore the scars of London's bombing during World War II. It was a window into a childhood marked by austerity, if not deprivation, but the men were comedians as they recounted their escapades.

Laughter and good company were the perfect way to end the day.

Scene 3. Truro Fracture Clinic

The next morning, Trevor brought me a cuppa and a biscuit. He gave me a kiss and asked, "How are you, babe?"

"I'm fine," I said, "But the cast hurts."

"Your ankle?" he asked.

"No. Hard plaster," I said. "Can we go to the fracture clinic?"

"After breakfast. We'll go to the Truro clinic and then get groceries."

"Your Zimmer frame helps, Trevor." He watched me walk to the loo. I turned the frame sideways to get it through the door and did a two-step hop to get in, fold the frame, and close the pocket door.

The consultant on duty changed the plaster cast a week before my next official appointment with the surgeon. My new cast was lighter, more comfortable, and bright blue.

Trevor wheeled me through a packed parking lot at Tesco's and into the busy grocery. Summer holiday travelers filled the store and stocked up on supplies.

"It's crowded," I said. The wheelchair took up a lot of real estate. My leg and blue cast were elevated and stuck out in front of the wheelchair, creating an added challenge when navigating turns.

Trevor asked, "Want to wait at the O2 counter to buy minutes on the dongle?"

"Fine with me." I didn't want to tell him how anxious I was that someone would bump my foot by accident.

When Trevor returned with his shopping, he brought a produce box with the Union Jack emblazoned on the front. "Jesse, I brought this for you."

The box, which contained Ben & Jerry's ice cream and Jammie Dodgers cookies, fit across the arms of the wheelchair. People turned and grinned when we left the store. "Trevor, please take a photo. I want to send it to friends."

Scene 4. Ring Tone Blues. Another Day

Since the caravan wasn't hooked up to water, Trevor had to fetch it in huge barrels that he rolled along with a clever device. When it was time to do the dishes after we ate our evening meal, he piled the dirty dishes in a small plastic pan.

'I'll wash the dishes in the camp's kitchen," he said.

"See ya."

I relaxed and watched the BBC. The harp ringtone startled me. Trevor's phone was on the counter next to the door.

"I'm not hopping across the caravan to answer," I told Poirot.

The phone rang and stopped repeatedly. Finally, the calls stopped.

Trevor returned with clean dishes and a big smile. "How about a cuppa with a biscuit?"

"Okay," I said and continued to watch the Agatha Christie mystery.

His phone rang again. The harp.

He turned off the ringer.

"What is going on, Trevor?" I asked.

"I'll be back." He stormed out the door and paced with his ear to the phone. I couldn't hear what he was saying, but he looked stressed.

When he came back in the caravan, he fixed two cups of tea with milk, pulled out the dark chocolate McVities biscuits, and sat down.

"Jesse, the woman I used to date in the islands needs help."

I stared at him a moment. "You haven't seen her in how long?" I asked.

"Two years," he said. "I told you we broke up before I met you."

"And now?" I said in an icy tone.

"If I don't answer, she calls my children and her friends who call me."

"Why?"

"Her electricity was turned off," he said.

Scene 5. Flowers on a Day Out

Candace, one of Trevor's friends who had visited me in the hospital with her husband Ethan, drove up in a new Audi station wagon. It was her day off. She popped into the caravan with a huge smile. "Ready?"

She watched me hop across the floor. "Where are your crutches?"

"She can't use them," Trevor said. He stood outside with my wheelchair facing the door.

"I had an accident, Candace."

I knelt awkwardly at the door, holding the counter to steady myself, positioned my derrière on the floor, and stepped out with my good foot. I grabbed the arms of the wheelchair to brace myself, hopped around, and sat down, a bit out of breath.

"It's my workout." I laughed while Trevor pushed my wheelchair to the car.

I sat in the front seat of the Audi, my foot propped on a pillow, and Trevor loaded my wheelchair into the cargo area of the station wagon.

We drove to Lostwithiel with its twelfth-century bridge crossing the River Fowey. Afterward, we went to the Duchy of Cornwall Nursery, where I wheeled myself through the greenhouse to admire the beautiful plants.

"Prince Charles is an avid gardener who supports sustainability," Candace said.

"The bumblebee garden is over there." Trevor pointed.

"Beautiful plants flourish in Cornwall," I said.

Lunch in the café at the nursery was outstanding. "The food is gorgeous and fresh," I said.

"The chefs source the food locally," Candace said.

"We splashed out for lunch." Trevor frowned.

"What?" I asked.

"Fourteen quid for your salad," he said.

Candace said, "It's my treat, Trevor."

"Thank you," I said. "It's delicious."

Candace dropped us off at the campsite. "Why don't you call in for tea tomorrow evening?"

"That's so kind of you," I said.

"What time?" Trevor asked and added, "I want to see if Ethan got the part for the Westfalia."

Candace explained, "Ethan has a specialty repair shop."

"We'll see you tomorrow," Trevor said.

"I had so much fun, Candace." I thanked her. I'd fallen in love with Cornwall.

Scene 6. Tea in Tregaswith

We called into Ethan and Candace's beautiful farm, Orchard House, where their copper-colored cocker spaniel named Bella and beautiful shaggy German shepherd named Cleo raced around the VW after we pulled into the courtyard and locked the gate. The couple owned a stone cottage they let for holiday makers on adjoining property and were converting a barn for their own home on the property where Ethan had his large workshop.

We gathered round a wooden table outside in a spot overlooking green fields bordered by hedgerows. Summer days in Cornwall were long, and the light was lovely in the evening.

Candace asked, "Are you excited about the wedding?"

"I can't wait to see the twelfth-century chapel and what guests wear." My only experience with British weddings was watching movies and television. Candace said something but her reply was drowned out by a formation of red jets doing a low flyover.

"The Red Arrows," Ethan said. "The RAF Hawk T1 jets."

"Beautiful," I said. "We have the Blue Angels in Pensacola."

CHAPTER 8: *Wedding at Caerhayes Castle*

Getting dressed for the wedding involved a shower, fixing my hair, and putting on makeup, all of which under normal circumstances would have been a breeze, but there is nothing normal about trying to balance against a small sink in a tiny bathroom in a caravan when one is ten days out of major surgery for a broken ankle and cannot put any pressure on the leg encased in a cast. It was exhausting. Nonetheless, I managed to pull myself together. I zipped up the Jenny Mawes halter dress I'd bought at Hertha's secondhand shop, put on an unlined silk jacket, and stuck the fascinator on my head.

"You look stunning," Trevor said. "Well done, babe!"

I was proud of myself. What I could see in the small mirror outside the loo looked presentable—the blue cast didn't clash with the taupe dress, the cream silk jacket, or the one brocade high heel I could wear on my other foot when I was in the wheelchair. This was not the way I'd envisioned making my chic entrance to a wedding in a twelfth-century chapel at a castle. Damn.

I made my way on my butt, then on my knees to the bench seat of the chameleon-green vintage VW Westfalia and hauled myself up. Thank heaven for strong arms. And there I perched, ready to be chauffeured to the chapel. Trevor had dressed for the occasion in jeans, a yellow striped shirt, and his winklepickers.

"I thought you had a suit," I said.

He didn't reply as he put my wheelchair in the VW and closed the sliding door firmly, a little too firmly, I thought. And off we went on a beautiful blue-sky day in Cornwall to the wedding.

We pulled up next to an ancient dry-stone wall and parked. "Trevor, I need to have a wee."

"Love, there's no toilet in the chapel."

"What am I going to do?" I panicked. A car drove slowly past us on the lane.

"You'll have to use the toilet in the van."

There were no curtains on the window. I couldn't pull them shut for privacy. How the hell was I supposed to have a wee essentially in a telephone booth in which I was going to sit on a box? I didn't have an alternative and I needed to go. To hell with modesty. At least there was a portable loo in the box Trevor had built around it. All I had to do was lift the lid. And so I did. I pretended I was simply on a seat in the van—the windows were high enough that no one could see exactly what I was doing. Thank God. Trevor stood outside the van in the lane and waved. Paul and Charlotte drove up in the red Mini convertible just as I finished my business. I rearranged myself to the best of my ability and asked, "Trevor, will you get the wheelchair out for me?"

By the time Trevor's friends got out of their car, I had made my way to the floor of the van and had my good leg positioned to get out and into the wheelchair. Thank heaven it wasn't July on the Gulf Coast. The weather in Cornwall was pleasant—in fact, just right. I wasn't a sweating mess by the time I climbed into the wheelchair. Success in uncommon hours. I was proud of myself, although I prayed no one had been able to figure out exactly what I was doing in the van.

Trevor wheeled me toward the chapel. I was grateful we were early. Three worn stone steps led down into the chapel. Uh-oh. The Parish Church of St. Michael Caerhays was 700 years old.

"How do we get you down the steps?" Trevor asked.

"They're too steep for the wheelchair." I sighed. "Here. Hold my shoe."

I held onto the rail and hopped barefoot down one step at a time into the chapel. Fortunately, I had no witnesses.

"Blimey, love." Trevor brought the wheelchair into the chapel.

A nicely dressed older woman introduced herself and suggested we push the chair to the back of the chapel on the main aisle. The aisle where all the guests and the bride would walk. I wanted to sit in the pew. I desperately wanted not to be conspicuous, but it was not to be. Guests poured into the small chapel. The older women were dressed to the nines in gorgeous silk outfits and fabulous hats. The younger women were dressed in beautiful summer frocks. The men wore suits or morning coats. Oh, crap. I glanced to my right where Trevor sat in the pew in his jeans and the winklepickers. I felt like an idiot with one brocade high heel on my right foot and my blue cast on my left. I suppose the primary benefit of my seating was that I had a bird's eye view of the wedding vows, as well as the bride and groom leaving the chapel at the end of the short ceremony. In fact, I perched while all the guests filed out of the chapel and into the church yard.

The chapel was empty, save Trevor, me, and the pastor. Trevor took the wheelchair outside, and the pastor asked how he could help me. I stood barefoot on the cool stone floor on my right leg. I handed my brocade high heel to the pastor and hopped up the three stone steps. Getting up wasn't quite as easy as getting down, and I stubbed the big toe of my leg in the cast by accident. Oh, hellfire and damnation. I didn't say it out loud, but I wanted to swear. Instead, I bit my lip, became a stoic, and didn't allow myself the least little groan.

At last, the three of us were outside the chapel—me in the wheelchair, now wearing the brocade high heel, my fascinator mashed down on my head, Trevor by my side, and the pastor chatting with me about his daughter in America. We talked outside under the trees on a green lawn near ancient graves with Emma and Hugh, the mother and father of the bride, and made our way back to the VW.

"Trevor, isn't the reception after the wedding?"

"No, babe. It's a wedding breakfast, and it doesn't start for several hours."

"Oh," I said in a small voice.

"Are you okay?" he asked.

All the activity of the morning—getting dressed, climbing into the VW Westfalia to drive to the chapel, hopping down into the chapel and hopping back up and out of it—came to a head. The physical exertion took the steam out of me. I felt like a balloon losing its helium. I was about to crash.

"I think I need to rest."

"We don't have to go to the breakfast, sweetheart."

We drove on the lane past the castle's gatehouse. Nothing was more beautiful than the English countryside on a brilliant summer's day.

"Where are we going?" I asked.

"Mevagissey."

The drive was spectacular. I fell in love with Cornwall. Trevor had history in this seaside port. In his younger days, he had converted two old fishermen's cottages overlooking the harbor. He had lived in one and rented the other as a B&B. One was so small it could be measured with a hand span from the left to the right. He told me how he had lost them in his second divorce. I knew every story has two sides, and I wondered what the ex-wife's story was. He called her the Crazy Welsh Woman. I never heard him give her a name.

Trevor pushed my wheelchair through the cobblestone streets of the old town on the harbor. A brazen seagull dive-bombed an unsuspecting tourist who didn't take precautions with the fish and chips she ate while she sat on a bench and looked at the boats bobbing on the water. She screamed. I was glad we'd eaten the picnic Trevor prepared in the Westfalia since the tourist-savvy seagulls were an aggressive lot.

He wheeled me into an ancient pub and ordered a pint for himself. I had a Diet Coke and looked around. We were in Trevor's pub—steps from the houses he had lost—worth hundreds of thousands of pounds. He seemed a little maudlin, less effervescent than his normal self. I wondered what had happened to the Crazy Welsh Woman. He told me she had filed a warrant for Third Wife's arrest. What a lot of drama in his life! A fleeting thought passed through my mind as I reflected on the text message.

CHAPTER 9: *Bells Are Ringing*

"Hiya, babe." Trevor walked into the caravan, a big smile on his face. I rolled my eyes at him. "The insurance labyrinth. Bureaucratic red tape in the US. I wasted an hour with clueless customer service reps. Utterly futile. Then I got on the computer and wrote sarcastic queries."

"Remember, your brother told you to save the big guns for the battle."

"I want to find one human. One direct phone number. One personal email address. I don't want to spend time pulling my hair out or having a nervous breakdown."

"We'll go for a drive after lunch, Jesse."

A tear rolled down my cheek, unbidden. I brushed it away.

"Stir-fry okay with you?" Trevor asked.

Every day, Trevor's phone rang. It was her. Again. Island Girl. Relentless phone calls. Twenty calls a day. Sometimes thirty calls. Her behavior was off the charts.

A Skype Call

"I'm trapped in a tin can on the clifftops in Cornwall," I said. I sniffled and swiped at the tears that escaped. "I feel desperate."

"What's going on?" Maggie asked.

"Island Girl phones thirty or forty times every day," I said. "She sends texts. She's going blind. She has cancer. She needs money. She doesn't have anything to eat. Her utilities are cut off."

"That's nuts."

"She's lost the plot," I said. "She's calling her friends and Trevor's children. She phones, messages friends, and asks why everyone is abandoning her."

"Come home," she said.

"Can't fly until September, the doc says." I sighed.

"What about the weather?" she asked.

"It's damp today, a mizzle Trevor calls it. First time since I got to England almost a month ago. How time flies when you're having fun."

"What's Trevor doing?"

"On a cliff walk." I took a deep breath. "I'm glad he's not here."

"What's wrong?"

"Too much together time," I said. "He's frustrated with how long it takes me to do everything."

"No," she said and shook her head. "That's just wrong."

"You know him. The Energizer bunny in constant motion," I said. "Like a hyperactive kid. He has to do something all the time."

The afternoon in Newquay was a disaster. Trevor parked in the paid parking car lot in the center of town. He dug into his pocket for the coins and inserted them in the meter to get a receipt. He slapped it down on the dashboard. It cost £3.

"Trevor, let's stop in that coffee shop."

"We'll get a cuppa when we get back to the caravan."

"Seriously. What's wrong with just hanging out in a coffee shop? I'm buying."

"Jesse, leave it."

"Don't you get it? I'm so glad to get out of the caravan that I can hardly stand it. I just want to do normal things."

"Why are you bickering, Jesse?"

He couldn't see the tear roll down my cheek, but he heard my sniffle and saw a passerby stop and stare.

"For fuck's sake, Jesse."

He pushed the wheelchair faster. I swiped the tear away. We bumped along over the cobblestone street. A candy store stood on the corner, and the door was wide enough for Trevor to push the wheelchair through.

"You'll enjoy the Cornish fudge, Jesse."

I saw the hard candies, "sweets" in U.K. speak, in the cases and wondered why in hell he wanted to get me fudge. It was as expensive as a coffee. I shook my head in disbelief and I couldn't help myself. "Will wonders never cease?"

Trevor walked away from the wheelchair. I rolled myself to a display with hard candy and picked up a small bag. I looked through a rack of postcards with lovely scenes of Cornwall, picked out four, and handed over £3.50. Trevor paid for a bag of fudge and broke off a piece for me to sample.

"What do you think, sweetheart?"

Sweetheart? At that moment, I despised him, and I wondered, *WTF*? "Delicious."

"Let's save the rest."

After he washed the dinner dishes, Trevor sat across from me. The look on his face alarmed me. It should have given me a clue as to what would follow.

"Jesse, all we're doing is bickering. I'm sick of it."

"And you think I'm not?"

"I don't think our relationship is working out." He was furious. "We need to talk about ending it."

"Trevor, can't you see what's happening here? We're under serious stress in this situation. We've had more disagreements since my hospital discharge than we've had in the past fifteen months."

"That's what I'm talking about. I can't handle it."

"Don't you see the correlation between the stress and what's happening between us? It's difficult being a caregiver. I know I haven't been a pleasant companion with my emotional highs and lows."

"Jesse, it's just too much."

"What am I supposed to do, Trevor?" I burst into tears. "We're in a fucking emotional pressure cooker, and I feel like the lid just blew." I watched his face as he shuttered all expression. Oh, no. "I can't leave the U.K. for two months." I yanked out a Kleenex and blew my nose. The tears wouldn't stop.

"Let's sleep on what we ought to do," he said. "You shouldn't just leave here. We can be friends about this."

"I can't afford to move to a hotel, and even if I could, I'd still need your help while I'm here."

"Maybe this is good." He continued, "We need to think about where we want our relationship to go." Trevor shut down completely. "I'm going for a walk." He picked up his phone and left without a hug or a kiss.

Everything was sucked out of me. I was empty. Numb. Dissociating. A survival mechanism that served me well when I was experiencing such emotional pain.

CHAPTER 10: *Desperation*

Trevor looked up from his iPad and said, "I'm writing my friend Sarah." He paused. "She might come next Tuesday." He watched my reaction.

"I thought Heather was coming next week." I was confused.

"I told Sarah she could borrow my tent and use my utensils." Trevor gave me a big smile. "I could take her to the store to buy things, and since she's job hunting, maybe she could get a job here for the month of August."

I was gobsmacked. "I'm uncomfortable with her staying here on the campsite for a month."

He was silent for a few minutes and my words hung in the air, gathering weight.

"You're restricting me and telling me what my restrictions are." Trevor was enraged. He turned his back on me, mumbled something under his breath, and walked out the door without another word.

I was emotionally frayed and started sobbing. Maybe it was all the drugs, but I felt helpless and trapped. I picked up my phone and called Maggie. I didn't reach her. She wasn't in. I left a frantic message on her machine, "I don't know what to do." I took a deep breath. I couldn't speak for crying so hard. "I'm at a complete loss. It upsets me terribly to watch the drama unfolding every day. I've lost my objectivity." I couldn't continue the message. I hung up, crossed my arms on the table and put my head down, sobbing uncontrollably.

Email to my brother:

I'm trying to make some tough decisions in what is a less than ideal situation for me . . . and for Trevor. We're both under incredible stress. No point in going into the gory details, but I'm looking at whether I can plan to travel home as soon as possible.

Since I'm going back to the fracture ward on Wednesday to remove the sutures and replace my cast, maybe I can talk to the surgeon. It's not Dr. Hawkins but it's another orthopedist. Maybe I can get a cast the airline approves that will allow for swelling in my leg, and I can get out of here.

It's all so complicated, and maybe in the light of day I'll feel different. Suffice it to say, it's been hard. I don't think this is a good situation for me right now to be with Trevor under such stressful circumstances. I know he doesn't want me to leave just because we're having disagreements, but this sure isn't the holiday either of us envisioned. It's unfair for me to think a sixty-seven-year-old man can be a caregiver.

Email from my brother:

I'm sorry for you and Trevor, Jesse. I don't know all the details for sure, but I can imagine the stress. Times, life deals us bad cards, and we have to play them as best as we can.

I know you're frustrated with trying to deal with the medical insurance while you're over there. It does seem to be one of the top causes of your stress. I doubt the NHS wants to keep you captive in the UK any longer than necessary and have to provide any more of their "FREE" care.

Maybe tomorrow's visit to the doctor will give you more insight to your healing progress and your relocation options. As for you and Trevor and the disagreements, please think of all the wonderful times you've had together and the things you've agreed upon. And yes, my dear sister, a sixty-seven-year-old man can be a caregiver. I think of our stepfather. When Mama became disabled, she often was upset with her situation and her caregivers, and she lashed out at those who cared the most for her. They were equally frustrated, saddened, and upset with her disease and the grief it brought to both of them. Your current situation might not be the same . . .

Email from Maggie:

Dear Jesse, I'm so glad you got in touch with your brother. Though I've never met him, I'm confident you'll get his loving support. You've been so brave, but from what you've told me I really believe you're thinking along the right lines.

The situation where you are with Trevor has become untenable. You need the support of a loving family and have longtime friends who can share among themselves the responsibility of helping you recover. I can't imagine that the added stress of being in a foreign country, in a small trailer, with a gypsy man—as sweet as Trevor is—and no family or friends can be conducive to healing.

Good luck at the doctor's tomorrow. I send my love and prayers to you, and to Trevor. We know he is probably just as overwhelmed as you are. I'm not saying this to imply that you need to worry about him, my dear and sometimes overly caring and compassionate friend. I just know this must be hard for both of you. I hope you make your decision, however, based on what would be best for you right now. God bless and much love.

CHAPTER 11: *Crying Over Curry*

*T*revor's phone rang. It was Paul's *ah-ooga* ringtone. Trevor stepped outside the caravan. He looked tense, unhappy. I didn't want to face another day of his unhappiness, and I felt sure he didn't want to see me unhappy, cranky, crying.

"What's up, babe?" I asked.

"Paul and I are going to go see the tractor exhibit," he said. "Don't you have a deadline for Chris?"

He didn't want me to go with him and Paul. "That sounds like a lot of fun for you," I said.

"What do you mean just for me?"

"I didn't mean just for you, Trevor. It sounds fun. I do have a deadline." I said a silent prayer that we not bicker again. And I said to myself, *please don't cry, please don't cry.*

Trevor gathered his small rucksack and made a cheese and pickle sandwich. He looked at me. "Want me to make one for you?"

"No, sweetheart, but thanks. I think Candace is going to drop by later."

I stared out the window of the caravan, checking out spider webs on the hedgerow and the little blue cornflowers. I felt supremely sorry for myself. What was a girl to do in such a fix?

To heck with deadlines, I thought, and turned on the television to watch the show about house hunting in the English countryside. I loved the BBC. I could while away the hours and lose myself completely. And that's just exactly what I needed to do.

I heard a tap at the door. Candace burst in with a huge smile and a big container of curry. It was so good to see her.

"Hiya, luv," she said.

I started sobbing.

She stopped in her tracks and set the bowl down on the counter. "What in the world?"

I tried to tell her between sobbing and gasping for breath.

Trevor and Paul came in unexpectedly, laughing. Trevor carried a bag of lettuce and carrots. Trevor's smile became a grimace.

Paul said, "Great day, mate." He saw my face, turned, and walked out the door.

Trevor stood at the sink and attacked the carrots with a vengeance. The lettuce was draining. Candace and I set the table. I could see our tea was going to be a bit strained, to say the least. With the task of putting the forks out and setting plates on the table, I managed to pull myself together.

"What's going on between you two?" Candace asked.

"We're at each other's throats," Trevor said.

"It's hard being in a small space together and unable to do much for myself at all without Trevor's help," I said. "It's a pressure cooker and the lid blew off." I laid my head on the table and sobbed.

Candace took my hand. "We're going out tomorrow."

"You don't mind taking Jesse to the hospital to change her cast?"

Candace gave him a look.

"What time is your appointment, Jesse?" she asked.

CHAPTER 12: *Girls' Day Out. St. Mawes*

Trevor put my wheelchair into the cargo area of Candace's Audi wagon, and we were off! Praise God and the Hallelujah Chorus all-in-one on a beautiful sunny morning in Cornwall. My first taste of freedom in almost a month since I'd left the hospital ward.

"Candace, I can't begin to thank you for getting me out of there."

"You need a Girls' Day Out."

"The caravan with Trevor and his hamster-in-a-wheel personality wipes me out emotionally and feels like a prison. He hovers when I'm editing the article for my client."

"We'll go for a drive, get lunch, and go shopping after the hospital."

The wait at the clinic in RCHT wasn't terribly long, and before I knew it, I was in a small room with a doctor, a tech, and Candace. The tech cut through my cast with what looked like a small power saw.

"How can you do that without cutting me?"

He must have noticed the alarmed look on my face. "Lots of practice."

The doctor stepped out of the room and the tech entertained Candace and me with a quick-witted repartee reminiscent of Monty Python.

"Do you do standup comedy?" Maybe he just wanted to keep me distracted while he removed the cast.

"No, just a hobby to pass the time here."

Once my cast was off, I got a good look at my purple and yellow bruises and the surgical cuts. The tech removed the sutures, which looked like plastic tape, and I saw my scars.

"That's quite a beauty." I pointed to the seven-inch scar starting at the ankle and going up my outer leg. The scar on the right side of my ankle was only two-and-a-half inches.

The doctor returned to examine my ankle.

"Looks like it was really difficult," I said.

"It's routine surgery for us." He didn't smile.

"Easy for you to say," I said, "unless you're a very active sixty-three-year-old who sees nothing routine about the situation at all." The doctor had perfect bedside manners for a sadist. He wasn't pleased. I guess he was God in his eyes.

"I want to fly back home earlier than two months from now. Is that possible?"

He didn't know, and frankly seemed clueless.

"Come back in two weeks for x-rays." In less than a heartbeat, he was out of the room.

I turned to Candace. "I need to schedule an appointment with Dr. Hawkins for a private consultation." She nodded. I was frustrated with a system I didn't understand.

The tech said, "Talk to the receptionist and ask her to set it up for you." He applied the new cast and asked me what color I'd like.

"Hot pink works."

He helped me down from the examining table and back into the wheelchair, and before we left, I asked if I could look at the x-rays of my broken ankle. I took photos of the images on the screen as Candace, the tech, and I gathered round. The images were horrific. It's remarkable that it hadn't hurt like hell when I broke it.

The drive was beautiful. I'd never seen such a dramatic landscape, with the cliffs and the coastline, the beautiful villages, and storybook houses. One highpoint of the drive was taking the King Harry Ferry across a tidal river on the way to St. Mawes. Candace and I laughed until we cried on our adventure, and I felt restored.

St. Mawes. Oh my gosh, how I wished I weren't in a wheelchair.

"What a beautiful seaside village. I love the thatched roofs."

Cornwall was made for walking, not for an adventurer with her leg in a cast and dependent on someone pushing her around. Candace wanted me to get a good taste of Cornwall and leave with a sense of its beauty.

We watched the sailboats and the ferry leaving the harbor for Falmouth.

Candace said, "It's considered the third largest natural harbor in the world and was a busy fishing port until the early twentieth century."

The trip by ferry was one mile, but it was a thirty-mile drive to reach St. Mawes. I dreamed of staying in one of the hotels or perhaps leasing a small cottage by the sea.

Candace wheeled me up a narrow street overlooking the harbor and into a restaurant that wasn't handicapped-compliant according to standards in the US, but I wasn't in the US. She was adept with the wheelchair, having had loads of experience because she helped people who needed care.

We were seated at a table in the restaurant where I had a perfect view of the harbor and the sailboats. It was an upscale eatery—more sophisticated than any restaurant where Trevor had taken me. We ordered, and when our meals arrived, I said, "The presentation is lovely."

"I'll take you to Jamie Oliver's restaurant at Watergate Bay."

"Jamie Oliver has a restaurant near the campground?"

"Yes, you haven't been?"

I shook my head no.

"We'll remedy that. Trevor can fork over a few bob to get you out of the caravan."

"We've eaten a lot of cheese and pickle sarnies. I love Branston pickle and Cornish cheddar, but bacon sandwiches are his favorite."

During our beautiful lunch, Candace clued me in to what was going on.

"Candace, the phone calls have almost driven me out of my mind. I can't leave the caravan unless Trevor and I are going somewhere."

"Trevor's been in contact with Island Girl the whole time he's been back from India.

"Lying by omission? Doesn't she know Trevor lived with me most of 2012 in Fairhope and we traveled in India for months?"

"I'm sorry you're having to live with the chaos."

"She must be desperate. Her phone calls are relentless. The phone rings twenty to thirty times until Trevor turns off the sound."

Candace nodded.

The afternoon clouded over to match my mood, and by the time we got out of the grocery store, our last stop, it was raining. A fitting end to a beautiful sunny day.

"We're going to teach you how to use your crutches," Candace announced.

I must have looked like a deer in the headlights.

"You'll be more independent when you get some confidence using them."

"You're right." And for the first time in quite a while, I felt my spark of enthusiasm. "Let's do it."

We drove back to Ethan and Candace's farm, Orchard House.

"You're going to learn to use your crutches." Candace paused and looked at my face. "Now."

"Umm." I wasn't convinced.

"No more wheelchair unless it's essential."

Candace instructed me and made me practice until I'd proven to myself, as well as to her, that I was able to self-propel.

It was awkward at first, but with her guidance I took a few steps. Then a few more. And we even mastered a small step up. I could walk into her home, and I did.

"Time for a cuppa." Candace grinned.

"Freedom." Thank God.

Trevor drove up in the VW Westfalia and grinned when he saw me heading towards him with the crutches. Candace waved.

"I'm not getting in the back." I hauled myself up into the passenger seat and laid the crutches down on the floor between the two bucket seats.

"We're going to dinner at Jamie Oliver's restaurant at Watergate Bay Friday night," Candace said. "You're coming, too."

On the drive back to Tregurrian, I thought about my conversation with Candace. What was I going to do about Trevor and Island Girl? I wouldn't betray Candace's confidence and confront him directly. I was furious, but I knew it would be better for me to act when the time was right rather than react in hysterics.

CHAPTER 13: *A Night on Bodmin Moor*

"*R*eady, babe?"

Trevor was over-the-moon excited. It was the first time for us to go camping, and he was in his element in his restored VW. I set the crutches down in the space between our seats in the Westfalia. The morning was as spectacular a Cornwall summer morning as either of us could wish for. Yes, I was armed with information that was heart-breaking and infuriating all at the same time, but I decided to keep the peace. After all, what could I do?

We drove through such beautiful countryside that I couldn't feel sorry for myself under the circumstances. We stopped for petrol, and Trevor came back carrying two Cornish pasties.

"I was feeling a bit peckish." He grinned and handed me one of the meat and potato pies.

The drive past Daphne Du Maurier's Inn and through Bodmin Moor was fun, especially with a tour guide who had spent so much time in Cornwall with various wives, but I wasn't going to allow myself to think about them and spoil a brilliant day.

The campground at Bodmin Moor was spectacular, with the setting sun on the lake and with the hills and fields beyond. Trevor set up our tea and cooked over his little propane burner. The sunset was to die for, and as he put his arms around me, I relaxed into his embrace.

Stars in the night sky, no city light pollution. It was beautiful and romantic. Only two other campsites were occupied—one by a group of young girls in tents and the other by a couple in a caravan, but we were isolated from them.

A late afternoon rain cleared, and our warm summer day became a chilly summer eve. I tried to help Trevor make up the bed, but he gave me the aluminum screens to put in the windows instead. We were private as bugs in a rug. He turned on the little electric heater to warm us and we crawled into the bed in the camper.

"Your cast is a cheese grater," Trevor said, laughing.

It was a challenge to work a way around it, but we managed beautifully. For the first time in quite a while, we showered one another with the affection we had for each other.

After Trevor blew out the candle, I lay there thinking about my conversation with Candace and wondering just how and when I could bring up the subject with Trevor without causing more animosity and bickering between us.

The air was clear the next morning and we set out on another explore. Trevor wanted me to see some of his favorite places in Cornwall. Why? Why had I picked a man who didn't have "sorry" in his vocabulary? I didn't understand myself, much less him.

CHAPTER 14: *Jaguars and Trewithen House*

Hugh and Emma drove up in a blue Jaguar convertible with cream leather seats. They parked next to us at the entrance to Trewithen House. The day was overcast, and my mood matched it. I had on my puffer jacket because it was cool and damp.

"Babe, the drive to the manor house is too far for crutches," Trevor said. "Let's stick to the wheelchair."

Hugh decided he was going to push me in the wheelchair and race up the long drive past the gate houses to the estate house.

We all started laughing. Emma was dressed to the nines as always, and Hugh was in high spirits. Thank heaven. It was a good idea to spend an afternoon with Trevor's friends. He and Hugh had met while working at the London Stock Exchange, back in the day. Hugh had managed to build his fortune, just as Trevor had managed to lose his. The contrast, oh geez. But I could tell they loved him, nevertheless. He was, after all, a hail-fellow-well-met-charmer in the company of his friends, and it was fun to be around him.

Trevor didn't want to pay an admission fee to enter the manor house, but there were steps, and I couldn't have mastered them anyway. Hugh pushed the wheelchair through the courtyard, past fantastic stables, and around to the gardens, where he and I had a good chat.

"How are you feeling, luv?" Hugh asked.

"I'm having a great time with you and Emma."

Hugh gave me a look. "He isn't easy."

"We take the good with the bad because we're all, all of us, not easy at times. It's tough for Trevor to have to take me on while I'm stuck in the caravan. I'm not the most pleasant of patients."

Hugh gave me a hug. "Sweetheart, he's lucky to have you in his life."

Emma strolled up. "We're heading to our vacation home in Arizona in December."

Hugh chimed in. "We have a lot of good friends in the States, and we love the West."

Emma said, "We haven't spent any time in the South where you're from, but we've visited New Orleans."

"That's only a couple of hours from my home."

Trevor walked up and joined our conversation. "I won't forget New Orleans with Jesse as my tour guide . . . especially after a jazz funeral in the rain."

He grinned and kissed me.

CHAPTER 15: *Heather Comes to Cornwall*

We picked up Heather at the bus stop in St. Austell. She was glowing and happy to see her dad and she embraced me with a hearty hug. Trevor wore a huge smile.

"I'll take the tent and you can sleep in the caravan with Jesse, Heather."

I turned to Heather where she sat on the back bench of the VW. "I'm so glad you're here."

"Glad to be here, too."

Trevor asked, "How's Thom and how's your mom?"

"Thom and I are working on the house," Heather said. "We plan to sell it next year. And mom and Chris are doing great. They just got back after sailing to Italy."

Trevor bit his bottom lip.

Heather continued, "Janet flew to Italy and sailed back to London with them."

When we got back to the campsite, Trevor and Heather went for a walk on the clifftops down to Watergate Bay while I worked on revisions for the wind turbine article.

As we set the table for tea, Trevor said, "Heather's decided to stay in another caravan on the other campsite."

Heather laid the silverware on the table and handed me the plates and napkins while Trevor prepared the vegetables for stir-fry.

"We'll go into Newquay tomorrow. Heather wants to see my friend Ellis who owns the clothing stores. We'll have a picnic after."

***

"Three pounds." Trevor frowned. "Can't believe how much it costs to park in Newquay."

"I have change." I handed him the coins to put in the meter.

Trevor said, "Ellis has three clothing stores in Cornwall."

Ellis gave Heather a huge hug as soon as she walked in the store—a surf shop with cool, expensive clothes. Trevor introduced us, and Ellis asked, "How'd you like London, Jesse?"

"Trevor was a great tour guide. It was lots of fun and, irony of all ironies, we went to see the musical *Top Hat* with fabulous costumes and dance—you know, the Fred Astaire and Ginger Rogers glitz." I pointed to my cast.

Ellis said, "I stay in a pub across the street from that theater in the West End when I'm in London. It's cheap for London but I put up with noise since the music carries on until the wee hours."

Heather picked up my crutches while I leaned against the counter, and she walked around the store with a lot of skill.

"Your dad told me about your accident in Germany, Heather."

"It was awful. I was airlifted back to London for surgery, but I'm doing great now."

I confess I was jealous of a young person's ability to heal and adapt so quickly. Heather handed me the crutches.

Trevor said, "Great to see you, mate. We're on our way to Pentawan Sands for a picnic."

Heather spread the picnic blanket on the ground while Trevor carried the lunch he had prepared. I awkwardly made my way down the slope with the crutches and managed to sit down without falling.

"Heather, I can come help you and Thom in London with the renovations this fall."

"Sure, Dad. That would be great."

I stared at the ocean while dad and daughter chatted. It was a spectacular day and wonderful to sit in the sunshine and watch waves crash against the rocks. My mind wandered back to India and Varkala—the cliffs, waves, and lots of steps I climbed with ease. I didn't think about the future.

Snippets of conversation interrupted my reverie.

I heard Trevor say, "Late September. I'll come down."

I watched the surfers take the boards out. All the surfers wore wet suits.

I couldn't hear what Heather said, but Trevor asked, "Iran? You're going to . . . " Trevor's voice faded in the wind.

"Yes, Dad. A group of us have been invited."

I wondered what my friends were doing back home. I thought how much I didn't know about Trevor's life. I didn't know Thom, I hadn't met his other daughter who called her dad almost daily, and I didn't understand what Trevor had done with the stock market in London, or why he was hell-bent on not spending on anything other than the basics.

Candace called me the next morning. "How'd you all like to go to the Duchy of Cornwall restaurant for lunch? I haven't seen Heather in ages."

"Sounds wonderful. I'll check with Trevor and Heather."

"Hey, babe, how'd you and Heather like to have lunch with Candace at the Duchy?" I watched Trevor's face. "My treat. Candace wants to catch up with Heather."

We got out of Trevor's VW at Orchard House to say hello to Ethan, who was working on a fabulous Porsche Carrera. We climbed into Candace's Audi. I was relieved to see her. As lovely as the visit with Heather was, I felt like an outsider.

Candace included me in the conversation with Trevor and Heather. I appreciated the gesture, but they shared a history I wasn't a part of. Why did I feel sorry for myself? It was a glorious day. I told myself to get over myself. I watched hedgerows march by as we sped through the countryside toward Lostwithiel. I was lost in a daydream, and I didn't realize when Trevor addressed me.

"Jesse? Jesse, where are you?" Trevor laughed. "She's usually lost in a book when she's reading, but I haven't seen her get lost looking at a hedgerow."

"What?"

"I told Candace and Heather about fishing from the pier near your house."

"Tell us about Fairhope," Heather said.

"It's beautiful and on the water. It's not as dramatic as Cornwall, but it's also a tourist attraction—especially after *The New York Times* wrote about Fairhope as a great vacation destination. We were discovered. Retirees with lots of money are pricing out people who could afford the modest homes."

Candace nodded. "Sounds like Cornwall."

"Candace, it's lucky you and Ethan own Orchard House so you can let it as a vacation home." Did I see a hint of regret or jealousy cross Trevor's face?

Lunch at the Duchy was delicious, a treat in good company with lots of laughter. When the server brought the bill, I gave her my credit card. Candace said, "I'll leave the tip."

CHAPTER 16: *Bickering Over Bacon*

We saw Heather off at the train station in St. Austell the next morning. Trevor had decided we needed a picnic. The most fabulous part of my prolonged visit in Cornwall was seeing the countryside. And, after reading novels that mentioned hedgerows, a hedgerow wasn't a mysterious object anymore.

We parked at a boat landing somewhere near the River Fowey and Trevor got out his little propane burner and a skillet. It was sunny and warm—the day inviting me to go outside. I didn't want to sit in the VW with bacon cooking next to me. I made my way to the edge of the caravan, grabbed the crutches, and hopped out.

"I'll have a little explore, babe." Maybe it was my tone of voice, maybe it was the expression on my face. I felt irritable. Why was Trevor adamant about not spending any money? Why did he think I wanted to go out to lunch? Maybe I needed some alone time, and I had little opportunity for that unless he went off with one of his mates. That was it. I wanted some alone time.

Trevor was in constant motion. I suppose he was simply born with kinetic energy, and he never stopped during the day. I was tired. I wanted to sit by the river and read a book. I wanted to watch the birds and the butterflies. I really didn't want to be with a cranky man, especially when I was feeling cranky.

"What's wrong?" His tone was unmistakable.

"And we're off to the races again," I muttered *sotto voce*.

"I'm sick of the bickering."

"Can we please have a nice lunch?"

"Get in, it's ready."

I didn't want to get back into the van because the smell of bacon would be overpowering, and though it would taste delicious, I didn't want the propane burner's fumes to asphyxiate me.

"How about if we eat outside, Trevor?"

"There's no place to sit on the slope."

He was right. I got into the VW. He handed me a plate, but we didn't talk for the next fifteen minutes.

"That was delicious. Thank you, Trevor."

"Right." Trevor put away the dirty dishes and didn't look at me.

CHAPTER 17: *Seeing Daphne du Maurier's House and Fowey*

Paul called Trevor and invited us to join him and Charlotte at the camping store and campgrounds where they had parked their brand new Hymer travel caravan. Charlotte was preparing a picnic lunch for us.

Paul assured us, "We have an awning set up where we can eat and stay dry."

I wondered how Trevor was feeling. I didn't know what a Hymer was but the word "new" sent up an alarm signal in me.

We pulled up to the camping store, where Trevor went in to buy a small propane tank. I walked around the store with the aid of my crutches and Paul came to greet us. He was excited and grabbed Trevor's arm. "Come on, mate."

Paul and Trevor moved quickly towards the campground. Trevor turned and looked at me as I followed on crutches at my own pace. I gave Trevor a grin and a wave to let him know I was okay. They hurried off and left me eating their dust.

I learned all about the shiny new mobile travel vehicle, made in Germany and to my mind remarkably like a Mercedes motorhome. It was gorgeous. Charlotte prepared our lunch in the kitchen. I peeked inside and saw it would be cozy for two. Paul set up chairs under the awning.

The boys drank beers while I nursed a Diet Coke. Charlotte brought me a plate of a beautiful pasta salad. Despite the gray day, it was fun to spend time with Trevor's friends and out of the confines of the caravan.

Trevor asked, "Paul, how's the tenant situation in those new flats you purchased?"

"It's blue. Really blue. The tenant painted the walls, the baseboards, the windowsills, and the doors dark blue. It's a fucking mess."

Charlotte looked disgusted. "It's going to take several coats of paint to cover it and prepare it for the next tenant."

Trevor explained, "Paul isn't exactly a slumlord, but he buys small flats and rents them to people who receive a government check each month."

"The good thing is I know I'm going to get the rent paid, Trevor. On the flipside, I don't know how the tenant is going to treat the property because half of them are druggies or batshit crazy."

"They're on the dole, Jesse."

"The government pays the tenants' rent?"

"Yes. Paul has enough property to let that he's more than paid for all the flats in his portfolio."

"It's getting tiring, mate. I'm ready to start selling the flats."

I couldn't help Charlotte with the dishes, but I walked with her to the toilets.

"What a shame to break your ankle your second day in Cornwall, Jesse. I know it's frustrating to be handicapped in a foreign country and staying in the small caravan with Trevor."

I wasn't sure if she was fishing for information, so I was cautious. "It's a shame. Neither of us bargained on the accident."

Paul and Charlotte piled into the red Mini convertible with the top up because of the mizzle. I thought it was a brilliant word to describe the gray day and the mist. We drove to Fowey, where Charlotte was to crew in a sailboat race later.

We parked in one of the pay parking lots Cornwall seemed to have in abundance. There was no way around it, you had to take pound coins. It irritated Trevor no end, no matter where we went. He tried hard to find places without paid parking to avoid spending a few pounds.

Cornwall had tourism down to a science. It was magnificent, and each of the little villages had figured out a way to keep up their infrastructure, I imagined, with paid parking. Perhaps I was wrong, but it did seem extraordinary.

I walked slowly toward the harbor, toward the River Fowey. Charlotte pointed out Daphne du Maurier's house across the river. I'd read every one of her books, and I was thrilled to see the home where the famous author lived and wrote. We strolled through the charming little town. I called my progress with the crutches "strolling," and I looked in shop windows, stopping at one bookstore with photos of Daphne du Maurier and all her books. I wanted nothing more than to go in and buy a book in the bookstore across the river from where she lived, but Trevor was in a hurry to get back to the van. He didn't understand how much writers love bookstores.

Paul bragged, "I haven't read a book since I graduated from public school."

That was inconceivable to me. I'd never met anyone, or at least I thought I'd never met anyone, who didn't enjoy reading. After all, books could take a reader so many places. Trevor had told me confidential things about his friend that I really didn't want to know. I guessed we all kept secrets. Trevor certainly did. I didn't know how I was going to broach the subject of his ongoing relationship with Island Girl. I put it out of my mind and shifted gears into a tourist mode in a lovely English Village.

"We grew up in London after the war, Paul and me. Our playground was a bombed site. Later, when we had skateboards, we used to grab the back of the bus and hitch a ride with our boards. We've been mates all our lives. We wore mod boots and clothes in the sixties. You know, the whole Piccadilly Square scene."

"Did you have a band, too?" I asked.

"Neither of us had any musical talent. And we both had to have jobs when we were growing up because our families didn't have the dosh."

We reached the van before the time on our meter expired. The weather was blustery, and I thought Charlotte had to be a stalwart sailor, and a grandmother to boot.

CHAPTER 18: *Trevor Turns on His Phone*

Sometimes things go from bad to worse, and that certainly was the case with the two of us jam-packed into the caravan. Things got especially tense when Trevor turned his phone back on.

"I need to hear from Janet. She'll be here next week, and I don't want to miss her calls."

"Of course."

Trevor attacked the celery with a vengeance, chopping it at angles for the stir-fry. "What time is your appointment with Dr. Hawkins?"

"2:30 p.m."

"So, what's he going to do?"

"Don't know." I wondered if I could leave Cornwall sooner rather than later.

"Let's go grocery shopping after your appointment, Jesse."

We sat in the waiting room of the medical center in Newquay, waiting to see Dr. Hawkins. They called us back into a small office where my surgeon—the cool dude wearing skinny jeans and Beatle boots—was waiting.

When we went back into the examining room, I could see by the x-rays that my ankle was mending relatively well.

He looked at his notes and seemed perturbed. "I don't know why you weren't scheduled to have the cast removed today." He left the examining room for a few minutes and when he returned, he said, "I've set up an appointment for you at the hospital in Truro for tomorrow morning at 11 a.m. We can remove that cast and get you into a boot."

"A boot?"

"Yeah, it's time to get you out of the cast. Your leg is healing nicely."

When we got back into Trevor's van, I asked, "Why don't we stop for coffee?"

Trevor didn't look at me. "We're going shopping at Aldi."

By the time we got to the grocery, the skies were gray with the mizzle Cornwall seemed to have in abundance. I guessed the Gulf Stream made the environment inviting for all the beautiful plants. English weather was Girl Scout weather: always be prepared. I remembered how much I had disliked camping as a Girl Scout, but I didn't mind being in Cornwall with its mizzle. I didn't like it when Trevor was in one of his moods or when I was in one of mine. I couldn't point a finger at him without acknowledging my own part in the friction between us.

"Hey, sweetheart, I'm gonna stand by the fence and watch the waves crashing while you pick up the bits we need. Let me give you a few pounds," I said.

"No need, Jesse. I'll be back in a jiff."

The fierce Atlantic crashed against the rocks. I could see all the way to the hotel on the promontory. Trevor said he and Candace went to tea there. I wondered why we couldn't do the same. The gray skies began to reflect my mood. I had to get my head in gear before Trevor came out of the store, or else we'd be two miserable pensioners going back to Tregurrian campsite in stony silence in the VW. I certainly didn't want that.

On the way back to the campsite, Trevor's phone rang. It was his daughter, Janet.

"Would you answer it, babe? It's against the law in England to use a cell phone while driving."

"Hi, Janet, we're on the road." I put the phone on speaker so Trevor could talk with his daughter.

"Hi, Dad, can't wait to see you. I'm taking the train to St. Austell. It's a lot more comfortable than the bus, and anyway, it's a bank holiday."

"Okay, love. We'll pick you up. Just text me the time."

"Oh, Dad, Island Girl called me several times since she can't reach you. I'm sick of it. She's calling all your friends here and the Caribbean."

"Fuck me."

"I stopped answering the phone."

"Just block her, Janet. I've had to do it."

"Okay, Dad. Love you. See you soon."

Trevor didn't say anything about Island Girl's phone calls to Janet, but I could see how upset he was. Obviously, if she had phone numbers for his children and his friends, their relationship had been significant. Was it still? No one had mentioned her to me other than Candace, who had explained the whole situation. It made me feel sick at heart, and once again I felt excluded from his life. Why was I so insecure? Of course, he had a life that had existed before, during, and after our times together. After all, we were survivors of six decades of living and all the things life had thrown at us over the years.

We were in the x-ray department at the Royal Cornwall Hospital in Truro, waiting for my appointment with Dr. Hawkins. Trevor and I sat side-by-side in a room with fluorescent bulbs above our heads and a linoleum floor. It wasn't great but it was nowhere near the hospital in India where we had waited for the doctor to take care of my bed bug reaction.

Dr. Hawkins looked at my x-rays, which were affixed to a light box. I could see the contrasting x-rays hanging side-by-side, and I was happy to see how much my ankle had healed over the two months I'd been in Cornwall.

"Can I leave Cornwall after we change the cast?"

"I'm going to put you in a boot, but I still want you on crutches. I want to check your progress in a month. It's not a good idea for you to fly until the end of September."

Trevor watched my face. I couldn't hide my feelings. My heart sank. As we walked out of the hospital, I stopped. "Babe, I need to use the loo before we leave." It was an excuse to go into the handicapped bathroom, sit there, and wipe the tears from my face. I gathered myself together, emotions tightly packed away.

Trevor drove to a nearby park on a beautiful lake, a tidal pond in Truro, and we walked to the water's edge where swans swam up to us, eager for treats. He pulled a thermos from his rucksack and poured us each a cup of hot milk tea he'd prepared before we left the campsite. I folded myself down awkwardly to the ground and laid my crutches beside me. We had nothing to throw to the swans, so they lost interest in us quickly. Some magnificent new buildings were going up across the tidal river.

"What's going on with those, Trevor?"

"Upscale flats for sale."

"How much?"

I read the real estate section of *The Telegraph* every week, looking at the adverts for beautiful places in Cornwall and dreaming about places where Trevor and I might live, although things were difficult. I imagined a life filled with kittens, puppies, and hollyhocks growing outside a charming cottage. Who was I, anyway? Pollyanna? I watched Trevor climb into the driver's seat and thought, puppies not so much. Hollyhocks probably. Kittens? I'd ask. Didn't all couples have conflicts from time to time? Being neck to jowl in a tin can wasn't conducive to romance if one of the partners was hamstrung as I was. I remembered my friend Molly's mother had warned her, "Never consider marrying someone until you've spent a week together on a small sailboat." Since I'd never sailed overnight with anyone, I changed the admonition to *caravan*.

CHAPTER 19: *Trevor's Other Daughter Arrives in Tears*

The day began with Cornwall's mizzle. I stood under the train shed on the platform in St. Austell. Janet's train was late, and Trevor paced. I leaned against the wall with my crutches, since no seats were available. Trevor looked at his watch. I glanced at the station's clock, and Trevor passed by me.

"Babe, she'll arrive any minute."

He was distracted and walked in the other direction. He looked at his phone, read a text, and turned to me. "Train's pulling into the station in two minutes."

I gave him a thumbs-up and heard the train whistle, its light heading toward us. As soon as it stopped, Trevor went into high alert and ran towards the second car as a young woman with dark hair got off. She didn't have a smile on her face. In fact, she fell sobbing into her dad's arms. That was certainly not what I had expected. Trevor held her in his arms until she stopped sobbing and gasping for breath. He took her backpack, slung it over his left shoulder, and put his right arm around her. They moved toward me slowly, his daughter wiping away the tears with the sleeve of her jacket.

When they reached me, Trevor introduced us. "Sweetheart, this is Jesse."

Janet gave me a weak smile, and by the time they both got under the train shed, the heavens opened. Janet started crying again. Trevor put his arms around his daughter.

"I'll get the van and bring it up to the station, so you don't get soaked."

We made our way through the station to wait for Trevor outside under the awning. Janet looked at me.

"I'm sorry to be such a watering pot meeting you for the first time."

She looked away at the van and her dad pulling out of the parking space. I felt a little uncomfortable. Maybe I was nervous meeting daughter number two for the first time. There's that whole thing about fathers and daughters, and the other woman. I've never been the other woman, at least not to my knowledge. Trevor got out of the van, opened the sliding door in back, and, with his umbrella opened, put Janet's backpack into the VW. Once he had her settled in the back, he opened the passenger door for me, and helped me into the van, handing me my crutches.

"Sweetheart, want to stop for coffee at Costa's before we head back to the campground? The weather's miserable."

"Sure, Dad." Janet sniffled. Trevor looked in the rearview mirror and gripped the steering wheel even tighter. I looked straight ahead at the road.

The coffee shop was crowded, no doubt because of the weather. I sat at a table for four while dad and daughter went up to the counter to order their coffees. Trevor turned to me and asked, "What do you want, babe?"

"Tea's fine."

"How about a little cake?"

"Whatever you pick out will be great, Trevor."

Trevor set a tray down on the table with their coffees, my tea, and a couple of cakes. He handed me my cup, looked at Janet, and asked, "What's wrong, babe?"

Janet had started talking about her boyfriend when we first got in the van at the station. I thought her boyfriend had broken up with her and that explained the tears, but the story began to spill out. It sounded like the problem started at his family's vacation home in a seaside village.

"Dad, he asked me to marry him."

"Why are you crying?"

"I told him I wanted to break up."

The conversation made no sense to me, but I didn't know Janet, her boyfriend, or anything about their relationship. I decided it might be advisable to be sympathetic. "I'm sorry you're so sad, Janet."

She glanced at me and turned to her dad. "What am I gonna do? I love him, but I just don't think I can marry him."

"Janet, you've been together for years. You know each other."

"My bureau's at his house. I need to get it."

Okay, I thought, their conversation was going well, but I didn't have a clue what was going on.

"I don't want to take care of him again."

There was no explanation of what take care of him meant. On the way back to the campsite, I learned a little more.

Janet said, "I met a guy running the 10K race in Manchester. I didn't tell, but he's been calling me, and we've met for coffee a couple of times."

By the time we reached Tregurrian and the caravan, the weather had cleared, and the sun was out. Cornwall's weather was fickle and fabulous.

I made my way to the bathhouse where I could use the toilet. And by the time I got back to the caravan, Trevor had made a thermos of tea, and he and Janet were ready to go on a father-daughter walk on the clifftops and down to Watergate Bay. She had the same Energizer bunny personality as her dad and couldn't stay still for more than a few minutes at a time. Were they both ADHD? *Oh, fabulous,* I thought.

Trevor gave me a quick kiss and they were off to the races. I breathed a sigh of relief. I was slow getting my start off the mark, because I had to sit down at the edge of the caravan, put my crutches beside me, and step out on my good foot, turn around, pick up the crutches, and close the door. Jump down, turn around. I couldn't do that. I hadn't mastered getting down the caravan's step with the crutches. The step up into the caravan was too high for me. Breaking bones when you're sixty-three is a whole lot different than when you're thirteen. I hadn't broken my ankle then, but I had flipped over the front of my bike when I raced down Dexter Avenue in Birmingham and broke my collarbone. It had hurt, but I didn't recall anywhere near the problems with my collarbone that I had experienced after breaking my ankle.

It was dusk by the time Janet and Trevor got back to the caravan. She seemed to be in much better spirits after the clifftop walk. She and her dad chattered like they hadn't seen each other in years. Although Janet phoned every other day, I guessed it had been months since they had really had a chance to catch up. Once again, I needed to ignore my insecurities and accept that daughter would always be closer to dad than I. I told myself to get over myself. It was easier said than done.

I started the salad we were going to have for dinner and pulled the salmon out of the fridge to defrost it.

Trevor gave me a hug. "Thanks, babe. Salad looks great."

"Janet said she wants to stay in the tent next to the caravan." Trevor put the dirty dishes in the sink.

"Yeah, Dad. Will you take a picture of me in the tent so I can send it to my running buddy?"

And so it goes. Like father like daughter? No. I faced a real dilemma. What was I going to do?

The next morning, Trevor prepared a picnic for us.

"Janet, Mike wants to see you. He's coming along for our picnic."

"How's he doing, Dad?"

"He asked the same question about you, babe."

As if on command, tattooed ex-bro-in-law Mike drove up in his old Range Rover. It was chilly outside, but he still wore a tight T-shirt to show off his tats and six-pack. Mike, as odd as he was, spent a lot of time at the gym, I thought, staring in the mirror and admiring himself.

Mike gave Janet a huge hug. "Stella called this morning and asked about you, Janet."

Trevor explained, "That's his girlfriend. She's a personal trainer."

Mike and Janet went outside to chat while Trevor packed our lunch. It was another spectacular, sunny summer's day in Cornwall. A day you could fall in love with. In fact I did fall in love with the day even though I sometimes felt like the third, or fourth, or fifth wheel. Janet and Trevor huddled in the VW to prepare our plates for lunch. Mike and I chatted about his puppy and how he planned to keep it safe. He lived near a road and the farm nearby had cattle. The topic of wife number three was forbidden. Mike's sister, whom Trevor had married, had walked out on him on Christmas day several years earlier. I wondered if the experience had contributed to Trevor's fear of intimacy.

Mike was a character. His six-pack moved when he flexed his muscles. He seemed a rough and ready chap. I wondered about other family members and where number three was.

I glanced back at the VW and saw dad and daughter in a huddle, whispering to one another. Yep, I felt like a third wheel, and I beat myself up for my insecurity.

Mike spread the picnic blanket out and I lowered myself to it, setting the crutches beside me.

"Mike, what do you do around here?"

Mike had bought an old concrete grain silo on a small parcel of land near St. Mawes. It looked more like one of those gun turrets scattered around Cornwall that kept the Nazis at bay during World War II. He was on a mission.

"I'm getting estimates on materials to renovate the silo. I plan to put a deck around it so there's a nice perspective to watch the sunsets."

"It ought to be cool in summer and warm in winter," I said.

The gun turret, I mean recycled silo, was buried half in the ground. I'd have to climb a metal ladder to get down into it. Easy-peasy for someone who wasn't on crutches.

Janet and Trevor joined us. Janet carried a bottle of wine, and Trevor had a tray with our lunch. Mike poured himself a healthy glass of wine while Janet went back for our plates. Sun shining. Not a cloud in the sky. Waves broke against rocks below the cliff. We had driven into a farmer's field. I was surprised but guessed it must've been the thing to do in Cornwall if you wanted to have a picnic in the field. I didn't understand the rule book.

"Janet, how's life up north?" Mike asked.

Janet turned to her dad and gave him a look. "I got promoted at the University."

Mike nodded. "How's your boyfriend?"

"I want to break up with him." Janet got a bit teary.

Trevor interrupted, "We're not gonna talk about that right now, Mike."

"Got it. How's your cute roommate from Germany?"

Ever the Romeo, I thought. Janet and Trevor laughed.

After we ate, Janet jogged up and down the hill leading from the VW toward the clifftop. Trevor jumped up and joined her.

"Good Lord, do they both have adrenaline coursing through their veins?" I asked.

Mike laughed and poured another glass of wine. I lay back on the blanket, my hands underneath my head, staring up at the blue sky and a few cumulus clouds. I was in England, on a fabulous summer day, thinking of poets and writers, and wishing for a retreat where I might explore my own creativity.

I heard Janet and Trevor's faint laughter in the background, and Mike's monologue lulled me as I got lost in my reverie. I had a funny thought. Mike was a nice guy, but he was someone who would terrify me if I met him in a dark alley and I didn't know who he was.

CHAPTER 20: *Seeing the Water Garden at Veryan*

We dropped Janet off at the train station in St. Austell.

"I want you to see Veryan, Jesse."

We drove to the Roseland Peninsula, and Trevor talked about his aunt and uncle, both artists, who lived next door to poet John Betjeman. Betjeman described the beautiful village as a mild tropic garden. We drove past two matching houses shaped like beehives. What an extraordinary place Cornwall was!

"Trevor, let's stop and take pictures."

Veryan was a small village. We parked across from a beautiful water garden. I walked to a white bridge that crossed the little pond. Tropical plants grew so tall I could hide behind them.

"Trevor, take a photo of me leaning against the railing."

After our photo op, Trevor walked off in one direction, and I walked around the small pond until I came upon a bench at the base of a beautiful stone wall. I sat down and read the dedication on the back of the bench. Tears filled my eyes. My heart ached. The man who built the water garden had dedicated it to his wife in memory of his love for her after she died.

In memory of my dear wife
Eppie MaCleod
Who loved flowers and beautiful things
and her neighbour as herself

I ducked my head and hid my tears when I saw Trevor walk past me. I decided not to share my thoughts about the husband's love for his wife. The moment was sacred to me. What was love all about anyway? Trevor went up a path, through a gate, into the ancient church graveyard and disappeared. I sat on the bench a little longer. Time in Cornwall had given me opportunities to see who he was. And I supposed it had given him the same about me. I wasn't on my best behavior since I felt sorry for myself a lot of the time. I felt vulnerable being dependent because independence was my middle name. I didn't like to rely on anybody for anything. I knew one person in my life I could count on and that was myself. It was a lonely and devastating realization. I wondered at what point in my life I had reached the conclusion and, sadly, I realized that it was when I was a very young child. The beauty and peace of Veryan's water garden soothed my soul. I thought about one of the most beautiful hymns I knew, "In the Garden."

I made my way up a little path of stepping stones and dirt, with my crutches, into the ancient graveyard outside the Gothic church. Trevor was nowhere to be seen. I took photos of the aged graves leaning this way and that—some moss-covered, others covered in a dark lichen, and some broken. What was it about old church graveyards that intrigued me? When I read the names and birthdates, as well as their dates of death, I glimpsed into lives from centuries prior to my own. It was heartbreaking to see how short some lives were—days, in cases of infants. Perhaps, as I sat in the water garden, the dedication of love triggered emotions I didn't expect.

I caught up with Trevor outside the church. He said, "I figured out a way to make money visiting graveyards. Take pictures and find relatives in the States. Charge to send photos. Genealogy is hot."

I looked at the gravestones and thought about Trevor's idea. He was the master of ways to make money. Maybe it was because of the way he had grown up in London after World War II without the necessities we all take for granted. I couldn't imagine his bathing once a week in a washtub in the kitchen or making his first scooter with a piece of lumber his father brought back from a construction site. I turned away from the gravestones and headed to the entrance of the church.

The interior of the church was magnificent. An arched ceiling soared above me with timbers like those a shipbuilder used to construct ships. Cornwall was all about fishermen who may have been boat builders and smugglers hiding contraband in its caves, at least those who were the rum runners, pirates, and shipwreck scavengers. I sat in one of the wooden pews, stared up at the ceiling, and thought about all the people who had come before. Stained-glass windows were dedicated to men who had lost their lives on the sea, and the altar was magnificent. Veryan was about those who had been lost at sea, as I was at that moment. Less than a quarter of a mile away The Homeyard Homes stood in a little enclave for the widows of the fishermen who died. Residents still lived in the charming homes behind a tall white wall with slate stone steps leading to each home, flowers growing on either side of every entry. What a joy it must have been to live in such a peaceful community. Veryan was magic.

CHAPTER 21

The Field Behind Orchard House

Seven red jets flew in formation low over the field behind the house. Bella and Cleo barked at the noise.

"The Red Arrows are fabulous, Candace."

"We're on the flight path for training fly-bys."

Like our Blue Angels—only RAF. I thought, not for the first time, about the RAF war correspondent whom my mother had met at Maxwell Air Force Base when the Brits were stationed in Montgomery during World War II. According to her best friend, she had fallen in love with the Englishman. I never knew the whole story, but I told Mom's best friend Louise that I'd met an Englishman and fallen in love. Wearing her dressing gown and playing bridge with three other ladies wearing dressing gowns in a retirement home, Louise gave me her unforgettable smile and said, "Your mother fell in love with an Englishman, too." My mother had died twenty years earlier of ALS, but as a young woman she had looked like a young Elizabeth Taylor.

I waited with Candace at the outdoor table while Ethan and Trevor set up the caravan in the next field the couple owned. The field was down a gentle slope from the house, the barn, and the workshop.

Earlier, Trevor had told me we had to secure everything in the caravan. We had to move the caravan from the campsite. I didn't understand exactly why we were moving. He told me you can stay on a campsite with the Tregurrian Camping & Caravanning Club only a set number of days. I felt uncomfortable about the whole situation. It seemed odd we weren't moving to another camping site with the caravan.

"Why don't we just go to another campsite, Trevor?"

"Why spend the extra dosh when Ethan and Candace said it's okay for us to stay in the field behind Orchard House?" And that was that.

Since the field wasn't flat, Trevor and Ethan had to adjust the caravan to make sure it was level.

Ethan said, "You can't use crutches to get into the caravan, Jesse."

He was right. The step up was higher because the caravan faced the bottom of the next field rather than the house. Ethan created a wide landing platform with an old crate. I put my crutches on the crate, moved across it, and easily got into the caravan.

Why in the name of all that was holy hadn't Trevor come up with a solution like that earlier? I suppose one of the advantages of my having had to enter the caravan backwards was that my arms looked great in a sleeveless dress or blouse. The things I did for love.

Wouldn't you know? The next day disaster struck. Not for me. I was fine. The refrigerator in the caravan stopped working overnight. The food was spoiled.

"For fuck's sake," Trevor said. He checked the fuses, turned it to the gas mode, tried the electrical connection for the second time, and it was clear the refrigerator wasn't going to be an easy fix. "It's packed up."

Trevor panicked and stormed up the hill to Ethan's garage. Moments later, Ethan and Trevor returned and tried to repair the refrigerator. I watched long enough to realize I had to get the hell out of the caravan to save my sanity and serenity. The day had been going so well.

I sat at the outdoor picnic table and patted Cleo's head. The German shepherd waited eagerly for me to throw the ball she gripped loosely in her mouth, her tail wagging. I obliged and flung the slimy tennis ball down the field for her. She raced away barking and skidded to a stop on the grass still damp from the mizzle we'd had earlier.

Candace came out of the barn carrying a basket of laundry and saw me playing fetch with her dog. "I'm going to fold this. Want to come in for a cuppa?"

I sat on the couch in the caravan Ethan and Candace had chosen as a temporary home while they renovated another old barn. I looked out the window and down the hill, but I didn't see either Trevor or Ethan. I guessed they were both still working on the refrigerator. Candace handed me a cup of tea which I set on a table nearby.

"I'll help fold the laundry."

"What are they doing, Jesse?"

"They're trying to fix the refrigerator. It 'packed up' last night, according to Trevor. I suppose having things break down is part of owning a caravan."

"Maybe Ethan can help him."

"I hope so. Trevor's in a state." I folded the towels and put them beside me on the sofa. "You and Ethan are awfully kind to let Trevor and me stay here. I'm embarrassed because it seems like such an imposition."

"It's not a bother."

"Maybe not right now, Candace, but how often has Trevor stayed here with you for extended periods of time?" I couldn't help but feel that the situation wasn't right. "After all, he's a sixty-seven-year-old man. He's not hurting for money. I don't understand why we didn't just go to another campsite for a few days until we could move back to Tregurrian."

Candace looked at me and nodded. "Would you like another cup of tea?"

"Have you ever thought you and Ethan may be enabling Trevor by allowing him to stay here? It's not as if he can't afford an alternative."

"I suppose you have a point, but we like Trevor. You know how charming he is and how funny he can be. He's good company and he tries to help Ethan by painting things for him, like the fence on the property."

I saw Ethan and Trevor making their way to the caravan. Moments later they joined us.

"We have to get a repairman out here," Trevor said and clenched his fists.

"When can he come?" I asked.

"He'll be here tomorrow," Ethan said.

"It's going to cost bloody fifty quid." Trevor was upset.

I watched the refrigerator repairman work his magic on the little fridge in the caravan while Trevor paced and looked frantic. The night before had been less than stellar. We'd gotten into another exhausting bicker session about money.

"Trevor, I'll pay for the repair."

Trevor looked relieved and gave me a kiss.

The day before we were supposed to return to the Tregurrian campsite, Trevor suggested we camp overnight at a campground he liked. We launched through the English countryside, picnicked along a river, and drove through forests with beautiful blue wild hydrangeas and ferns. After picking up a few bits we needed at the grocery, we stopped at Costa for a cuppa and cakes. What a surprise. After every low moment, Trevor did something to make up, but he never said he was sorry.

"Blimey, I used to manage this campground."

Campers, caravans, and motorhomes filled the campground. August was the high season for caravanning in the U.K. The good thing about being in a VW bus on a chilly night was that the bed was small and candlelight was romantic.

CHAPTER 22: *Dante's Inferno*

When it all went to hell in a handbasket . . .

Trevor was halfway out of the caravan when I called him. "My draft is due." I was on the computer and starting to panic.

"What's wrong?"

"I can't get the campground's Wi-Fi signal."

"What about the dongle?"

"I'm out of data and I need the Wi-Fi to refill it online."

"Babe, just tether my iPhone."

Things heated up while Trevor was at the bathhouse for his shower. The phone rang. I didn't know who was calling—no caller ID. I let it go to voicemail and went back to work. I had had fun drafting the article about wind turbine repair and seeing wind turbines dotting the landscape in Cornwall. We didn't have wind turbines where I lived. The last time I'd seen wind turbines was outside Thousand Palms, California, when I drove across country back to Los Angeles.

My article was polished, ready to send. My income depended on it, and I needed to pay the guy housesitting for me.

Trevor's phone rang again. I tried to ignore it, but after five consecutive calls, I turned off the ringer. It vibrated. Twenty more times. I knew who it was. "She's a nutter," I muttered.

Trevor walked into the caravan, rubbing a towel over his wet hair. "What?"

"Your phone rang twenty-five times. I turned off the ringer after five calls."

Trevor's expression was a mix of anger and frustration. He picked up the phone and listened to a few messages. I'd never seen Trevor's face turn white.

"What's wrong?"

"She says she's going to kill herself."

"Oh my God, Trevor. Do you think she'd really do that?"

"She's left threatening messages before." He made a phone call and paced back and forth, distressed.

"Seriously, how many times can she kill herself, Trevor?" As soon as I opened my mouth, I regretted it.

Trevor freaked out. "She called from one of my mates' phones. If I don't recognize the number, I'll answer."

"You realize how crazy this is, don't you? She's manipulating you."

"I feel terrible . . . so guilty."

" . . . if that doesn't take the cake," I said in a tight voice. "I'm trapped in a sardine can, a nutcase calls thirty or forty times a day!"

"How do you think I feel?" Trevor interrupted me.

"Change your phone number."

"You don't understand, Jesse."

"No kidding."

"We were together when I was on the island. I helped her financially. She tried to stop me when I packed my suitcase before I left."

"And you left two years ago?"

"Jesse, she couldn't imagine your life, how you traveled, the career you had, the home you own."

"But you left. And you didn't tell her if or when you were coming back, did you?" Trevor's face hardened. I was critical. I judged him. It wasn't my business, but I couldn't help myself.

"So what if I did?"

"What are you gonna do?"

He shrugged his shoulders.

"Change the phone number, Trevor. That's a simple choice but you're gonna have to decide."

Trevor's phone rang and rang. He turned off the sound and set it on the table where it vibrated. It grew still. It vibrated again, and again, and again. Island Girl called at least ten times in the fifteen minutes that Trevor and I had the discussion. Things grew more heated by the moment.

"Welcome to Dante's Inferno, Trevor."

Trevor slammed his fist on the table.

"Right. That's it."

He turned his back to me, stormed out of the caravan, and slammed the door behind him.

I put my head down on the table and sobbed.

When he returned, he said, "I'm not sure how I feel about our relationship."

"Well, that makes two of us."

Dinner was dreadful. Stony silence, except for the phone. Every time it rang, my blood ran cold. I ignored it.

"Trevor, we really need to talk."

"Not tonight."

End of discussion, and that was that.

CHAPTER 23: *Having a Picnic with Friends*

Trevor drove into the field overlooking a protected cove where children splashed in the surf and raced across the sand with colorful kites. Hugh stood up and waved. Trevor parked the VW facing down toward the beach, next to the couple.

The day was windy, sunny, and magnificent. I made my way slowly around the VW and toward the well-dressed duo who'd spread their lunch on a lovely wool blanket—a large wicker basket beside them. Matching china, cloth napkins, and silverware graced the luncheon tableau. That's when I noticed the vintage red convertible MG-TD Roadster behind the couple.

"Fabulous car, Hugh!" I could hear the children on the beach shrieking with the abandon only children have in such abundance.

Trevor spread an old sheet on the sloping ground. I laid the crutches down and made my way to terra firma awkwardly. He brought a tray with plastic containers and utensils, the paper napkins weighed down by the pasta container. He set it beside me and held up his thermos.

"Care for a cuppa, babe?"

CHAPTER 24: Changing the Phone Number

*T*revor was frantic.

"How many calls is it now, Trevor?"

Island Girl had called sixty times in the past two days, and it was driving him mad. In fact, it had pushed him over the edge.

"I'm at my wits' end, Jesse." He looked helpless, pitiful.

"She's holding you hostage, babe."

"I know I have to change my phone number." The muscles in his face tightened.

"She's stalking you." I paused. "It's sick behavior."

"I don't want to lose all my contacts."

"You won't."

"Jesse, will you help me change it?"

I nodded. "Of course."

After two-and-a-half months of intermittent calls and two days of nonstop calls, I was beyond being over it. I'd stopped talking about it, though. You could lead a horse to water, but you couldn't make him drink . . . until he got thirsty.

Trevor paced around the caravan and gnawed at his nails. I'd never seen him do that. The phone rang again.

"Hiya, sweetheart." Trevor scowled as he listened to his daughter on the other end of the line. "Well, fuck me. She called Janet four times this morning."

"Janet, I'm going to take care of it today. I'm changing my phone number, sweetheart." He paused. "Jesse's going to help me. I'll call you later and give you my new number."

I fixed a glass of orange squash and took a 900 mg ibuprofen. My head was pounding.

"What time is your appointment with Dr. Hawkins?"

"It's at 1 p.m."

"We'll go to the phone store after, Jesse."

Thank heaven! *That's a relief*, I thought.

CHAPTER 25: *Tasting Freedom*

I sat in the waiting room in the Trelawney Wing at RCHT, with its linoleum floor and fluorescent lights overhead, rows of plastic seats in the middle of the room, with exam rooms all around it. It wasn't as crowded as the waiting room in Varanasi. I felt depressed. *How many more visits did I have to make to the hospital?* I wondered.

Trevor took my hand and squeezed it gently. "I know you're anxious, babe."

"I'm scared what Dr. Hawkins is going to say."

Wearing his skinny jeans and Beatle boots, my handsome surgeon studied the x-rays on the light box in the small exam room. "We can take off the boot."

I exhaled, realizing I'd held my breath.

"You're free to wear shoes."

I felt on top of the world, like I'd just been given $1 million, and I had lunch plans with Liam Neeson.

"That's great news." Trevor grinned.

"Jesse, I want you to continue to use the crutches," Dr. Hawkins said. "Don't put all your weight on your foot yet. The bones are still healing."

"But I'll be able to go home soon, right?"

"At the end of the month."

I was euphoric. It was brilliant news.

We drove to a small village where Trevor took his phone to a shop to get a new phone number. I sat in the passenger seat of the VW and watched him walk down the hill toward the shop. I started crying, overwhelmed with a sense of relief after spending nearly three months incapacitated by my broken ankle. Although Trevor was a good companion under most circumstances, he'd proven to be a less than ideal partner under the strain my accident placed on our relationship, and I wasn't a good patient. "I'm free!" I shouted, startling a magpie in the tree. Passersby eyed me with suspicion. I wiped the tears from my face and continued to cry and laugh at the same time. Was I going mad?

Trevor climbed into the driver's seat and took my hand. "What's wrong, Jesse?"

I couldn't explain the mix of elation and sorrow I felt. My emotions were on overdrive. "It's been so long since I've been able to have a normal day." I was over-the-moon Tim Buckley happy sad.

He looked like he might've understood.

It was a perfect Cornwall day, and I was free.

We called in to see Ethan and Candace on our way back to the campground, and Candace fixed us a cuppa while I played with the dogs.

"I'm so glad to see you're out of the boot," Candace said.

"It's a relief."

"I have an idea, Jesse. It's a bank holiday weekend. Why don't we go for an adventure so you can see more of Cornwall."

"Sounds great."

"Let's go camping, Ethan. It would be brilliant for Jesse to see Penzance and The Lizard."

"Trevor, I'd love to go. How about you?"

CHAPTER 26: *Trevor Sends Ten Quid to Island Girl*

My nose was buried in a book while Trevor cooked bacon. I didn't pay close attention to what he was saying until I heard him say Island Girl.

"What?" I was gobsmacked.

"I'm going to send ten quid to Island Girl." The tone of his voice issued a challenge. Like, "So what if I do?"

My blood ran cold. I stopped myself from screaming. "You've got to be shitting me."

"She doesn't have as much as you and me. I'll do what I want."

"Of course you will. You're keeping her hanging on."

"It's none of your business, Jesse."

"Oh, for Christ's sake, Trevor. Put her out of her misery."

He scowled at me.

"It's cruel to do what you're doing to her."

"We were together for several years, Jesse." Trevor stared me down as if to dare me to say anything else.

Suddenly it was all clear. "That's it. I've had enough."

"Right." He turned his back to me.

The smoke detector shrieked. The bacon was burning. Trevor grabbed the skillet with a mitt and ran outside.

We ate breakfast in stony silence. It's hard to digest food when your stomach is churning, and your emotions are tumbling in a crescendo.

We sat on the clifftop overlooking Watergate Bay in uneasy peace. I knew I couldn't go on with things the way they were. I felt as if I were on a stormy sea being pitched one way and the other, like the fishermen who went out in their boats from the ports in Cornwall. I simply couldn't find my emotional balance. It was no longer the effects of anesthesia or pain killers. I couldn't attribute my ups and downs to the medication.

"What do you want, Trevor?"

He stared at me.

"I mean you can't jerk this poor woman around. I'm tired of being in the middle. I don't understand what you're doing. What do you want?"

"I don't know."

"Oh, for heaven's sake. You're not a teenager." I stared him down. "Either you want a romantic relationship with me, or you want one with her. You can't have it both ways. At least not with me."

"I'm sick of the bickering, Jesse."

"Trevor, this isn't bickering. I want to have an adult conversation and stop avoiding the elephant in the room. I want to get to the bottom of what's going on and what you want."

I wondered why I was wasting my breath because I knew men detested The Talk. Okay, so I wasn't the easiest person in the world to get along with while trapped in a caravan with the wild camper who thought he was thirty years old and who acted at times like a three-year-old. His mother had spoiled him. His brother had been ten years older than he when he was born, shortly after the war. He was treated like an only child. And I gathered from things Trevor had said that he struggled in school. Did my education and career experiences intimidate him? Island Girl had limited education and financial means. He was a god to her. And he was an ordinary bloke to me, albeit one I loved. Damn.

"I'm going for a walk." Trevor stormed off.

"Fine!" I shouted.

CHAPTER 27: *Limping on the Last Leg of the Journey*

I couldn't stop thinking about the pair of Doc Martens I'd seen in the window in Carnaby Street when Trevor and I were in London. I'd drooled over the Doc Martens. Maybe if I'd been wearing Doc Martens when I photographed the old monastery on top of the rock, I wouldn't have fallen and broken my ankle. Then again, I wouldn't have had the opportunity to see so much of Cornwall. However, Trevor was the Energizer bunny and couldn't stay still long enough to explore things thoroughly.

My heart was stomped on. Plain and simple. It seemed to me the day after a major confrontation in which I was terrified of losing a relationship, I was so emotionally drained I was unable to function normally. I was aware of it, and I didn't like it. I needed to look at it, but it was difficult to have any time for reflection with Trevor in constant motion. Unless it was midnight of course, and I was so tired I couldn't think while he slept like a baby beside me. How was he unfazed by our argument the next day, almost as if it hadn't happened? Had I lost the plot? I envisioned someone doddering around, and that someone was me.

"Where are you, Jesse?" He sounded none too pleased that I hadn't paid attention to whatever it was he wanted me to notice.

We were parked by one of Cornwall's marvelous drystone walls. Rising above me, beautiful stone cottages overlooked a harbor.

"Where are we, Trevor?"

"Portloe."

It was a small fishing village, typical of one of the coves in Cornwall that I'd grown to love. We walked down the hill to the boat ramp, where I saw a cottage for rent, a small restaurant, and a hotel in a boathouse. It was charming.

Trevor put his arm around me and gave me a passionate kiss. He had caught me off guard, and I was thoroughly puzzled. Was this an effort to apologize? To make up? Relationships were confusing.

There was something romantic about discovering an old mill wheel next to a renovated cottage with a stunning view of the beautiful cove. Maybe it was contagious. Trevor rediscovered his charming spark as we walked toward the cottage. I took photos of the mill wheel and thought what a glorious spot it was to live in the reclaimed Cornwall cottage. Trevor played along with me. How could he blow so hot and cold from one day to the next?

He dashed up a narrow path behind the cottage. Since it was a steep slope, I couldn't follow. I watched with envy because I wanted to walk up the slope. I took photos of another cottage near the old mill wheel. It was larger and grander and had been landscaped professionally. I wondered who lived in those cottages and how they could afford them. Real estate in Cornwall was expensive, but it didn't stop us from dreaming. We scoured the real estate ads that came out in a supplement each Wednesday and picked up magazines when we went to Sainsbury's and Aldi.

I walked up the hill as far as I could to see where Trevor had disappeared. The only thing marring the landscape was an old gray concrete World War II gun turret overlooking the harbor.

I made my way back down the path and turned to see Trevor and a beautiful young woman descending from the clifftop, a border collie racing circles around them. By the time they made it down to me, Trevor had magically transformed himself with his mesmerizing cloak of charm. It was certainly what had seduced me, although I didn't like the drama with Island Girl.

The young girl followed her pup as it raced ahead and returned to herd his mistress along with an impatient bark. Trevor and I made our way back toward the VW and met another couple around our age who seemed interested in learning about what had happened to me. The husband was very funny when he learned I didn't have much longer to spend in Cornwall.

"You're on the last leg of your journey." He hopped on one leg and laughed.

Yep, I thought, and watched them walk away.

CHAPTER 28: *A Whirlwind Weekend Getaway*

It was a spectacular morning to launch from Orchard House on our big adventure with Ethan and Candace. Trevor and I followed their van in the Westfalia. I wore my Merrill trainers for the first time in almost three months, and though I had my crutches, I felt free. Trevor and I were on great terms during our romantic getaway. Maybe the romance was in seeing the Cornish countryside, but I wanted to think it had something to do with the Englishman next to me. Surely it did.

Candace insisted we had to go on the camping trip before I went back home. She wanted me to experience how fabulous Cornwall was—even if it was a whirlwind tour. She'd been my salvation throughout my convalescence and recovery. Without her, I'd never have known the truth about what Trevor was hiding. The sins of omission were as deadly as those we confessed. There were some secrets I didn't share with Trevor. We all have our secrets. Was it a form of self-deception or self-protection? Everyone had filters. Well, almost everyone.

Riding through the single lanes with hedgerows and sitting high in the VW allowed me to view the fields behind them. We stopped by Goonhilly Downs—Arthur, Merlin, and Guinevere. The earth's largest listening system. The oldest satellites named after Cornish legends. The English had extraordinary names for things. Trevor dashed around Goonhilly Downs on his Swan Vesta legs. He had told me his legs were like matchsticks. I loved his Swan Vesta legs and his endearing smile. Why was love so darn complicated?

I think we saw it all. HMS *Seahawk,* Lizard, Cadgwith, St Ruan, Porthleven, Marazion, St. Michael's Mount, 'Mergh Gwyn,' Lamorna, Penzance, Newlyn, Mousehole, the Minack Theatre in Porthcurno, Land's End, and Sennen Cove.

We spent the night in a small campground. Candace set up a picnic table between the vans. She and Trevor set out the food and we enjoyed a splendid picnic. Since Cleo was with us, I wondered how she would behave. She was a beautiful shepherd, and she waited patiently while we ate. I was grateful for Candace's kindness during our trip. We watched the sunset and Cleo lay at my feet.

We stopped in Mousehole. I watched Trevor's face as he engaged in animated conversation with Candace, and I saw the charming man I had met and fallen in love with. I hadn't seen him look at me that way in a long time. It gave me pause for thought. Maybe we were having a great time. On the other hand, maybe Trevor was showing his true colors. He loved women. Candace was a good friend. I looked at Ethan as he watched the interaction and wondered what his thoughts were. The specter of Island Girl haunted me. The presence of her absence was always with us.

CHAPTER 29: *Asking Trevor What He Wants*

Trevor hauled out my suitcase. I folded clothes to get ready, taking them out of the small containers where he'd put my belongings. We'd had a beautiful weekend away with Ethan and Candace. Our last night at Cape Cornwall, a storm raged, lightning flashed, and fierce winds off the Atlantic rocked the VW. It was an unforgettable experience.

I turned to Trevor. "When are you coming to the US, babe?"

"Don't know."

"Winter will be here before you know it."

"I'm going to the farmer's stand, Jesse."

And with that, he was out the door. I shook my head trying to figure out what had just happened. How things could go from a hundred to zero in seconds flat without warning. I felt uncomfortable and wanted to continue the conversation when he came back. I kept packing. Another couple of days and I'd be home. It seemed as if I'd been gone an eternity. All the emotional ups and downs. The revelations—unhappy and happy.

After I washed the lettuce and set it on the drain board, I was standing at the kitchen sink and looking out the window, lost in a daydream, when I heard the caravan door open.

"Hiya, sweetheart." Trevor put his arms around me and gave me a kiss. "What can I fix for lunch?"

I pointed to the salad I was making.

"How about a bacon sandwich?"

I nodded.

We sat at the table eating and listening to Sting play "Englishman in New York."

"Why don't you fly to New York, Trevor? I'll meet you there."

"I don't know when I'll come to the US."

"What's that supposed to mean?"

"I promised Heather I'd come help her and Thom."

"You can fly from London." I tried to make it easy, but he acted as if he hadn't heard me. Things were getting stranger by the minute.

"Let's take a walk, Jesse." He handed me my crutches.

"Why are you changing the subject?"

He didn't answer. We walked up the road towards Watergate Bay. When we got to the general store at the campgrounds, I sat down at one of the picnic tables outside the store. "I need to rest." It was hard work walking that far without being able to put pressure on my foot.

Trevor returned with two ice cream cones, handed me one, and sat down next to me.

"Trevor, we need to talk."

He frowned.

"I'm leaving in two days," I paused a beat. "I want to know where I stand."

By the time we got back to the caravan, it was late afternoon. We were like two caged animals. Trevor paced and I packed. When I got to a good stopping point, I sat down. "Trevor, sit down."

He whipped around and gave me an ugly look, but he sat down.

"What do you want, Trevor?"

"I don't know."

"When will you come to the US?"

"I don't know, Jesse."

"No, Trevor."

"What do you mean, no?"

"Just plain no. I don't want to do this anymore. I've had enough. More than enough. I don't know if I ever want to see you again. Your idea of a relationship is one-sided. Maybe Island Girl is okay with your coming and going whenever you feel like it and leaving her hanging. I'm not. Either you're in a relationship with me or you're not. This has been one of the most crazy-making experiences I've ever had, and I don't want the drama in my life. I'd have to be a complete masochist to continue doing the same thing, dancing this insane courtship dance, and expecting things to be different when the music stopped. Instead, it's like musical chairs in which you always have one for backup and I'm scrambling to find the safe spot. There is no safe spot. It's crazy."

Trevor looked like a deer in the headlights.

When the overnight bus to London Heathrow reached St Austell, Trevor helped me get settled and waved goodbye. The bus drove off into the dark Cornish countryside. Once again, I was on a solo journey.

We stopped at a station to pick up passengers, and a drunk young woman sat down beside me with a cup of beer. It wasn't allowed, but what was I going to do? She talked my ear off for several hours before she passed out. Lucky me. It was lonely on the bus in the dark hurtling towards London. I was used to being with Trevor. As angry as I was, I still felt a hole in my heart. How dare he play with my emotions?

It was dark in the early morning when we reached Heathrow. The wheelchair American Airlines had promised me wasn't waiting for me. No way would I be able to transport my bags and myself with crutches any distance. People were arriving for a morning shift. The lady at the information desk promised that someone would help me. I waited an hour, grew impatient, and asked an older woman in a sari who sat next to me to watch my bags. I made my way into a hall and flagged down a golf cart in the long hallway at Heathrow. Within a few minutes the Indian woman who had watched my bags and I were perched on the back of the golf cart on our way to the check-in desk. What was easy when I was part of a couple was a logistical nightmare at Heathrow. I cursed Trevor. My phone rang. Speak of the devil.

"Why are you calling me?" I paused to listen. "How do you think it is? I'm on my own and didn't have a wheelchair waiting for me when I got off the bus. If you were so worried about me, why did you put me on the bus by myself? Don't call me again, Trevor. I'm done."

PART III

India 2014

CHAPTER 1: *Never Say Never.
New Delhi, India*

I'd vowed I'd never go to India again. When I left Bombay in April 2013, I never wanted to smell curry again for the rest of my life. And yet here I was in India. Again.

How had that happened? I wondered. As if I didn't know. Trevor's phone call came in mid-November, the week before Thanksgiving. I'd been tempted not to answer, but he'd sent WhatsApp messages and emails imploring me to speak with him. I listened. He told me how he was gutted after his daughters read him the riot act, telling him he was going to die a lonely old man without love. They were angry at the way he'd driven me away from Cornwall. He asked me if he could come to the US so we could spend the holidays together. He wanted a second chance, an opportunity to give our relationship more time under a less stressful visit. I'd given in. Maybe my resolve was weak, but I still loved him.

And so he had come. Life was sweet. We'd celebrated holidays with our friends, enjoyed a romantic early Christmas with a special night at the Grand Hotel, and even hosted a New Year's Day party where we entertained thirty. Everything had gone smoothly. We were closer than ever, and Trevor brought up the idea of an odyssey. A seven- or eight-month trip. A return to India where he wanted me to have an uninterrupted time to write my story about train journeys.

I told Trevor there were two places I wanted to visit before we traveled to Varkala. I wanted to see the Taj Mahal and visit Rishikesh, where the Beatles stayed with the Maharishi.

India was in my blood.

We reached New Delhi in the late afternoon after our flight from Heathrow. I had thought, until the very last minute, that I would have to fly to India by myself because Trevor's Indian visa had expired. A day earlier, he had gone into a complete panic when he realized his mistake in not getting a new visa. We were in London, and a quick Google search yielded the office where he could get a visa—the Indian Visa and Consular Application Office. We showed up, without an appointment, first thing in the morning after a night in a hotel near St. Pancras. The room was so tiny, we had to put our luggage on the bed to get out our toothbrushes.

How had Trevor forgotten about the Indian visa? I'd made our flight reservations when we were in the US weeks earlier. Fortunately, Trevor had managed to get his Indian visa, although it was a tedious process in which he was overcome by anxiety.

The first night in India was memorable, though not eventful. Before we left the U.K., I had made reservations at the hotel in the Pajar Ganj where we stayed on our first trip to India and watched the Holi festivities from the window overlooking the main thoroughfare.

On this occasion, our inaugural night before our odyssey, we didn't have the lovely room we had had a year earlier. Instead we were in a room without windows. A bat cave at the top of several flights of steps. The hotel didn't have an elevator.

"Bloody hell, Jesse." Trevor was less than thrilled.

"It's just one night, and surely we can get a good night's sleep in a dark room."

Wishful thinking. The stairs were right outside our door, and the noise from anyone ascending the marble steps and walking down the hallway toward other rooms was amplified by the hard surface. Guests arrived throughout the night. They stomped up the steps, shouted into mobile phones and to one another, and stumbled down the hall, obviously inebriated. Trevor slept through it all.

CHAPTER 2: *Taj Mahal*

After a sleepless night in the windowless room, we hauled our luggage down the street and enjoyed a long, peaceful breakfast at the Brown Bread Bakery with its delicious omelets and great Wi-Fi.

Trevor was restless. "Let's go explore."

"Why don't you go for an hour? I'll use the computer to make hotel reservations and catch up with friends." We'd roughed it on the first trip to India, but this time I had put my foot down. "Trevor, I don't want a do-over of the Gap Year Experience."

I made our hotel reservation in Agra and selected an air-conditioned room. The hotel boasted hot and cold running water, and the pictures online promised a comfortable, although not luxurious, stay.

The train trip to Agra from the New Delhi Railway Station was just over two hours. We arrived at dusk, and upon walking out of the station, we were accosted by the tuk-tuk drivers. One driver was especially persistent, and we surrendered to his sales pitch. He said his name was Azeel. He put our luggage in the tuk-tuk, and we were off.

My first impression of Agra, at least by the route Azeel chose, was less than stellar. I was horrified to see dead dogs lying in the street. My heart ached. I saw hungry, emaciated dogs scavenging for food and dodging traffic. Perhaps if we'd been headed to a resort hotel, we might have had a different experience.

After Azeel dropped us off at the hotel, he said, "I'll pick you up at dawn. It is the best time to see the Taj Mahal." He puttered off in his tuk-tuk.

Our hotel room was clean and cool; the bathroom was in two parts. The toilet and sink were in one small closet on the side of the room, and the shower was in a broom closet. At least that's what it appeared to be. I could hardly call them rooms.

I got up at 4 a.m. and tried to shower. There was no hot water, and the showerhead was blocked with calcium or some other mineral.

Trevor said, "Babe, there may be seventy-five pinholes but only five are working."

The water from the five working pinholes didn't fall straight down. It shot out at angles. It was impossible to get wet or bathe. I turned off the shower and filled the bucket below the faucet. The water was icy cold. I used a little measuring cup that goes with every bucket in India in every wet room aka bathroom. I poured the cold water over my face, then over my head, then over my body, two cups at a time, until the soap lathered, and I washed myself. Finally, I picked up the half-full mop bucket and poured it over my head to rinse my body. I was clean.

Our tuk-tuk driver had decided he was going to be our personal guide for all things Agra. The early morning was cool, and the day could not have been more perfect. I thought about the iconic photo of the reflecting pool and the Taj Mahal mirrored in the water. Azeel dropped us off near one of the entrances to the grounds. I'm not sure what I'd expected on arriving at the Taj Mahal, but I was surprised I'd not known about the massive red gates at each entrance. The gate framed the Taj Mahal perfectly. I stood on the steps, the early morning sun lighting the magnificent tomb, and tears ran down my cheeks. I was overcome by the majesty and beauty.

"Babe, are you crying?" Trevor wore a worried look.

I sniffed and nodded my head, unable to speak. The first sight took my breath away.

We were grateful we weren't in a huge crowd of tourists early in the morning. I took photos, and we asked a young Indian woman to take our photo in front of the reflecting pool and mausoleum. I noticed a professional photographer, his tripod stationed before a model in a flowing red dress who stood on one of the concrete benches. He snapped photos and waved his hand as he directed her. She twirled around, and the diaphanous gown floated around the beautiful woman.

We followed a line of tourists into the mausoleum, where photography was not allowed. The workmanship of precious gems forming flowers and vines in the marble was phenomenal. The depth of love the Mughal Emperor Shah Jahan must have felt for his wife to build such a monument was beyond my comprehension. The walk around the inside of the tomb inspired reverence. I whispered to Trevor. I looked at the other visitors—Indians in beautiful saris and young well-dressed Asians, and I felt self-conscious and underdressed in my wrinkled outfit.

When we walked out of the grounds, our driver, who'd said he'd wait for us, was nowhere to be seen. Trevor looked down a tree-lined avenue and spied parked tuk-tuks. He went down the street at a trot to find our ride. During the several hours we'd spent on our exploration of the grounds, the temperature had risen, and it was hot. I mopped my face with one of the cotton bandanas that went with me everywhere in India. We were hungry and asked our driver to take us to a restaurant.

Azeel was entirely too enthusiastic about being our guide. He took us to an expensive restaurant where I felt certain he received a kickback. Trevor was irritated. I was hot, tired, and hungry to the point of being cross. I didn't want it to show, but I was having a hard time concealing it. I couldn't face spicy food. My stomach was queasy. I looked at the menu and didn't see anything that appealed to me.

Trevor asked, "What do you want to eat, Jesse?"

It was a reasonable question, but I was cranky. "Nothing appeals to me. I wonder if the kitchen can make a cheese sandwich."

Trevor eyed me as if I'd sprouted horns. "Seriously?"

When the waiter arrived to take our order, I asked him for a cheese sandwich.

He said, "Not possible."

I said, "I'd like a bottled water."

"You're not eating, Jesse?"

After lunch, Azeel was adamant. "I take you to Agra Fort now for sightseeing."

Trevor said, "It's too hot for us to visit the fort."

The temperature in Agra that Sunday was over 100 degrees. We had to take the train back to Delhi later that afternoon.

"Why don't we just wait at the train station, Trevor?" And that's what we did.

CHAPTER 3: *Rishikesh. Five Israelis, a Brit, a Sikh, and Me*

The next morning in Delhi was a scorcher. We thought we could go to the train station and get a ticket to Haridwar. No such luck. Every ticket was sold out. A religious festival was being held there, and a million pilgrims were expected to attend. After all Haridwar was regarded as a Holy Place. We had no idea what lay ahead of us.

We always tried to avoid buying train or bus tickets at the hotels where we stayed because we knew we'd get ripped off, but we were desperate. The travel agent across the little alley from the hotel said he could get us an air-conditioned car. I was ecstatic. We had an eight-hour drive ahead of us according to the agent. He said it would be an SUV because parts of the road were under construction, and it was the last vehicle he had available. Who knew whether it was the truth? The only thing I thought was how much easier it would be on both of us in an air-conditioned vehicle with a driver. While we'd had taxis with AC on rare occasions, a car and driver for a long road trip would be a first. Little did I know what was to come.

We went out into the marketplace to find the white SUV the travel agent described. The driver, a Sikh with his turban, gestured for us to get in. The engine was running and the air conditioner blasting. Why didn't the driver get in the vehicle? He'd put our luggage in a luggage rack and fastened it down with bungee cords. What was he waiting for? Trevor and I looked at each other and saw the same question in each other's eyes.

Within a few minutes, a young guy—not an Indian—arrived and climbed in the front seat. Then another guy came and climbed in the back seat beside me and Trevor. I had to move into the middle—over the exhaust. A few minutes later, two young women and another young man approached the vehicle, and suddenly it dawned on me. The travel agent had sold as many seats as he was able in the vehicle. Why had I thought Trevor and I would have the ride all to ourselves? We all shuffled around.

So there we were—the Sikh driver, five young Israeli soldiers—the wild bunch on vacation—Trevor, and me. All packed like sardines into the SUV, and I was wedged in the third-row seat between the two young women. At last, we were off. I asked the driver a question to which he replied in English, "I don't speak English." Fabulous. *Could it get any better?* I wondered.

Of course, there was a festival in the Pajar Ganj where we'd been staying, and we were parked off the Main Boulevard of the old Delhi marketplace. The traffic was godawful as the driver wound his way through alleys and back streets until we were finally on a four-lane road, although it was still in the city. Did I say it was hot? Even with the AC going full blast, I was sweating profusely. My tunic was soaking wet. I was miserable, and I wondered if we'd ever get to the highway, when we stopped at a traffic light in bumper-to-bumper traffic.

There was a light tap on the driver's window, and I saw a hand with bright painted fingernails, a forearm decked out in bracelets, and a *hijra* who sought a handout. The driver opened his window and dropped some coins into her palm. It was bad luck otherwise not to give alms to the men/women, India's third gender.

Open discussion of gender other than male and female was a recent cultural shift in Western societies, it seemed. In India, people of nonbinary gender played important roles for more than 2,000 years. Hindu scriptures speak of the third gender and can be found in the holy texts like the Ramayana and the Mahabharata.

The road was under construction a good deal of the way, and our Sikh driver, who spoke no English, had a death wish. He drove like an absolute maniac, weaving in and out of traffic around cars and buses. I finally closed my eyes when I couldn't take any more of the driver whose racing skill put our lives in danger. The last half hour of the trip was gravel and dust and not necessarily in that order. That was the road from Haridwar to Rishikesh. The driver stopped in the marketplace and gestured for us all to get out of the vehicle. That was as far as he was going to take us.

We got a tuk-tuk to take us from the center of Rishikesh to our hotel. I'd made reservations online when we were in Delhi. The hotel had good reviews. It was in the back of beyond, perched on the side of what had to be a mountain overlooking Rishikesh. I didn't panic at the outset. I was too relieved to have arrived.

It was dusk. The hotel looked promising from the outside. It wasn't as spectacular as the online description, but it seemed to promise what I hoped would be a comfortable stay. It was a huge concrete structure, much larger than most of the low-rent hotels where we had stayed. I had reserved air-conditioned rooms for our special trips to Agra and Rishikesh. I thought we deserved special treats before going to Varkala. After paying for a couple of nights in advance, we hauled our bags up several flights of steps on the exterior of the building to the top floor. The balcony overlooked the city and the river. The entire top floor was a suite, and it was to be ours for the next couple of nights.

We opened the door and stepped back in time. At least that's what it felt like. The place looked like a set for a James Bond movie. It was a time capsule. It hadn't changed since the 1960s. It was garish and exotic. The large room with marble floors featured shabby but fancy furniture. The bathroom was pink, all pink, with a massive pink bathtub. The bed was on a platform. At one time it had been surrounded by curtains that fell from ceiling to floor, but there was only one pitiful curtain hanging and empty tracks on the ceiling for the missing curtains. It must have been extraordinary when it was new.

I couldn't wait to take a bath in that huge tub. The faucets didn't work. I couldn't fill the tub with water. At least the shower worked, and we had warm water.

The next day, as we walked down the steps for breakfast, a large, hostile monkey appeared out of nowhere and bared his sharp teeth. Monkeys were aggressive if they'd been fed and were around people a lot, especially in a tourist town. I was terrified. Trevor scared the monkey off, and I stepped around the poo it had left on the steps. It remained there for the duration of our stay. The hotel employee—I only saw one—wasn't cleaning. Who was cleaning? And why weren't they? The neglect of the building was a mystery. It was in such contrast to the exotic hotel room with its vintage furnishings from the 1960s.

The first evening, a group of motorcycles roared up, and handsome young Indian guys, all well-dressed, congregated in the office, a sitting room in a separate building—the older part of the complex. They stayed an hour, and all left at the same time. The next night, the motorcycles arrived at roughly the same time, and the guys gathered in the office for an hour and left as a group, the motorcycles all roaring off into the night.

It seemed odd because it happened each night we were there. I was intrigued and wanted to know why. So I asked the young man in the office why the guys met in the evening. He gave me a blank look, a wave of his hand, and went back to his computer. What an odd non-reaction. Given my wild imagination, it was mysterious and intrigued me. I decided the key to the puzzle had to be money. The motorcycles were brand-new, and the guys were well-dressed. It must have been a money laundering scheme. The hotel, which did a cash business with its guests, was simply a front. And there I was in a James Bond movie set in Rishikesh where the Beatles had descended for spiritual enlightenment. Capitalizing on enlightenment struck me as ironic.

CHAPTER 4: *Durga Puja. New Delhi*

We got on the Kerala Express train to Varkala by the skin of our teeth. The Durga Puja Festival blocked streets in Delhi's Pahar Ganj Market Bazaar. We couldn't get a tuk-tuk from the Brown Bread Bakery, where we ate breakfast, to the New Delhi Station a few blocks away.

Trevor swore under his breath. "Bloody hell."

We snaked our way through alleys, between buildings where vendors' shops lined the narrow passage, and spied a tuk-tuk off the alley on another street. We were in luck. We piled our luggage into the noisy, albeit relatively clean, auto-rickshaw with a Sikh driver.

"What's the charge to take us to the New Delhi Station?" I asked.

"Money doesn't matter. You tell me what you want to pay when we get there," the Sikh said.

I'd heard other Sikhs say the same thing, and I was curious about the philosophy behind the statement.

"Do you mean you believe in the abundance of the universe? That all the things we need are provided by God, Allah, Buddha, Krishna, or whatever deity to which one prays?"

The driver made an abrupt U-turn, narrowly avoiding a collision in the traffic jam. It was incredibly hot—over 100 degrees Fahrenheit. The streets were packed. We had lingered too long over breakfast, or rather I had, using the bakery's Wi-Fi to chat with a friend on Skype. I needed her help to rent my empty home. I had to rent my house to carry out my mission and reach my goal to write in India.

Trevor bit his lower lip and glared at me.

"Sorry," I whispered. It was my fault we were pushing it way too close to the time our train would leave. The Sikh tuk-tuk driver was confident and collected. He navigated with skill through the incredible traffic. He cut in front of taxis, cars, motorcycles, and pedestrians. He took shortcuts. He passed a man who pushed an ancient bicycle loaded with huge blocks of ice that were melting in Delhi's heat.

Throughout the mad ride from the Pahar Ganj, Delhi's discordant and deafening symphony of car and motorcycle horns bombarded us. The noise was never-ending, and in the heat as well as under the stress of trying to get to our train, it was overwhelming. The city was more crowded than usual for the Durga Puja celebration. The driver wiggled the tuk-tuk through impassable traffic without a scratch. Drivers shot us angry looks, shouted, and shook their fists, the road rage accompanied by nonstop horn blowing.

The driver dropped us off in front of the station and Trevor paid him

"We have fifteen minutes to get on our train, Trevor."

Under normal circumstances, it was difficult to find the train number and track. Nothing was normal that morning. The New Delhi Railway Station was a madhouse. Porters surrounded us, asking to carry our bags.

"One hundred rupees per bag," one man shouted in our faces.

Trevor said, "No. Go away."

They followed us as we wove our way through the crowded station. We tried not to step on the people who slept on the floor. We dodged stray dogs and people who surrounded us.

"I help you."

"Where you from?"

"Where you go?"

It was difficult to ignore someone who was in your face, and it was doubly difficult to ignore ten people who badgered you to get your attention and a handful of rupees. We searched the board above the ticket desk for the track where we would board our train.

I saw the obstacle. To reach the train, we had to haul our bags up one flight of stairs, cross a small landing, ascend another flight of steps, cross the pedestrian bridge, go down the third flight of stairs, and find our car on the train that stretched forever on the tracks. My heart sank.

"Trevor, I'll pay anything for this man to carry my bags." I pointed to the porter who followed me.

"Jesse, hurry!" Trevor dashed in front of me.

I struggled up the first flight with my bag. The wheels bumped up every step.

"Jesse, I'll get your suitcase," Trevor shouted from the landing above.

The hopeful porter watched me. "Madam, forty rupees. I help you."

I did the math. It was less than a dollar. Trevor turned around and saw me as I was about to hand my bag to the porter.

"Jesse, I said I'll get your bag!" Trevor yelled. "Leave it."

The porter dropped back when he heard Trevor shout over the noise in the station.

I stopped. I couldn't take another step in the heat. I was exhausted and the train journey hadn't begun. Through our efforts, and much to the amusement of other travelers who crowded the stairs, we hauled our bags. Trevor's expression frightened me. He was so angry.

We finally reached the platform and track where our train waited. Trevor raced ahead to the right and passed train cars to search for our car. I looked to the left toward what I thought was the front of the train and dashed in that direction. Wrong way. I turned around and followed Trevor to a group of conductors and uniformed men standing by the train.

"Where is car number eighteen?" Trevor asked.

We had less than five minutes. I was wringing wet. My fresh clean clothes were soaked with perspiration. Sweat poured down my face, and I knew I was beet red.

"Our train car is eight cars away, Jesse."

Trevor panicked and ran. So did I. Train cars had never looked so long. I thought for sure we'd need to jump on the train and haul all our belongings through countless carriages. I wasn't up to the challenge.

"Here it is, Jesse."

Two car lengths were between us. I tried to run faster. He shoved his bag onto the train and raced back to grab my suitcase. He handed my suitcase to a passenger who saw our plight and came to the rescue. He grabbed my hand and helped me up onto the train. I looked for our compartment and our seat numbers.

We sat down—rather I sat down to catch my breath.

"I'll stow the luggage, Jesse." Trevor scowled. "I've never met anyone who liked to cut it so close."

"Well, that wasn't my intention." I'd forgotten about Durga Puja and the fact that the Main Bazaar was blocked. "We have two minutes left."

Trevor gave me a dirty look, got off the train, and bought a large bottle of water from a vendor whose cart was nearby.

The train whistle blew. We were on our way in the 2AC car of the Kerala Express. Oh, rah for air conditioning. The heat outside was unbearable. My internal radiator was set at a different temperature than most people's. I drank my warm 7UP and looked out the window. There were four berths in our small compartment, separated from the aisle by a tatty curtain with well-worn Velcro closures.

I wrote in my journal:

There are water buffalo in a pond by the train tracks. A small herd of white goats crowds under the shade of a tree with an old woman who wears a tattered sari. Small children, some of whom are naked, huddle beside her. The poverty made my heart ache. Makeshift bamboo huts with blue tarpaulin roofs are homes next to the railroad tracks for millions of people. The miserable dwellings under the overpass have prime real estate and more protection from the heat and the monsoon rains. A naked man sits on a square of ragged cloth under the rusting sign for Mathura Junction. A woman washes her saris by the train tracks using water from the pipes meant to refill the tanks for the toilets on the trains when they stop at the station. Two men take showers from the water spigots along the same pipe that serves as the woman's laundry room. One man washes his leather shoes under the faucet. That is puzzling. I watch a man carry a woman across the train tracks toward the station. The woman's lime green sari has sequins that sparkle in the sun. A farmer drives his herd of water buffalo across a field. A cane pole is in his hand and a sand-colored rag is draped around his head.

It was a two-day, fifty-one-hour journey to Varkala in India's state of Kerala.

CHAPTER 5: *Varkala, Kerala, on the Arabian Sea*

We reached the Varkala Railroad Station in the early afternoon, the last hours of our journey, with spectacular views of lakes, canals, and the sea. Green Kerala. The landscape was distinctly Kerala. Palm trees, water, and green.

The train didn't stop on the platform next to the station. Instead, it stopped one track over and away from the platform. We got off and carted our luggage across the tracks, disoriented and unsure where tuk-tuks were parked.

When we reached Om Beach Resort, where we'd stay for the four months we planned to be in Southern India, we stored our luggage in the modest room we had booked. Sanjay, now manager of the small hotel where we'd stayed a year earlier, welcomed us with his unforgettable smile.

"Let's take a walk, Jesse."

We walked down the beach road toward the ocean.

"We're winter visitors on the Arabian Sea, Trevor."

Big surf, waves crashed on the sand. Trevor said, "It's the second monsoon season."

"There's a second monsoon?" News to me.

"Sanjay said we'll have rainstorms for another month."

"We're still travelers without a clue, Trevor." I laughed.

Little remained of the beach in early October. It was dangerous to swim, but we were in Paradise. It was hypnotic watching the ocean, all sounds muffled except for the surf. The wind blew in off the sea. The sand was golden and black in areas. I wondered if it was volcanic since the black beach wasn't too far from where we stayed.

Sanjay said, "The black is from ashes the families of the deceased have released into the water on Papanasam Beach over hundreds of years."

Later I told Trevor, "That sounds far-fetched."

Rocks that had fallen from the eroding cliff appeared to be volcanic material infused with reddish-brown, suggesting a high ferrous content. I wondered if Varkala's cliffs were part of a caldera created by a volcanic eruption like Santorini, but there was no information to support my hypothesis.

Life's irony. In my memory, I had imagined Varkala as the quiet getaway from home. My writer's paradise. Trevor and I looked at each other, awakened by the call to prayer at the temple. It was before 5 a.m. We laughed and Trevor fell asleep before I pulled the pillow over my head and nodded off.

An explosion jolted us out of bed.

"What the . . . ?" Trevor asked.

"The blasts of gunpowder at the temple, babe. Remember what Sanjay told us last year? Pilgrims pay a guy to light gunpowder in the barrel outside the temple to make sure the gods know they've said their prayers."

"Bloody hell."

We were awake.

At 6 a.m., tuk-tuks puttered by and motorcycles roared past the hotel.

"They're beeping their hooters," Trevor said.

"I don't see any pilgrims on the beach road."

"Wankers." Trevor looked disgusted.

Our room was simple, modest by Western standards. It wasn't air conditioned. A small rotary fan mounted to the wall stirred the air opposite the bed. We'd requested the room at the front of the hotel because it had a small balcony with chairs where we could sit.

Trevor made a cup of ginger, lemon, and honey tea for each of us. He took his tea and a book out to the balcony. I wrote in my journal. It was cool, perfect weather in the early morning.

I once read in a tiny book of lovely thoughts a quote from French dramatist, poet, and novelist Alfred de Musset: *A happy memory is perhaps on this earth truer than happiness itself.*

At 7:30 a.m., Arjun, the resident Indian yoga guru, chanted a prayer in a booming monotone on the rooftop directly above us. His deep voice reverberated off the walls. He instructed his students to start the pranayama, breathing exercises, during which he counted in a loud sing-song voice, "Inhale. Two, three, four, five. Hold to the count of ten. Exhale to the count of eight."

He repeated this over and over. And then, the thumping and pounding began as the yoga class started their asanas to Arjun's commands.

"For fuck's sake," Trevor said.

I nodded in agreement. "Time for breakfast."

Our second night in Varkala I had a terrible cough from the cold I'd caught on the train journey. We experienced a severe electrical storm with thunder, lightning, and torrential rains. It went on and on. We lost electricity. I heard a scream. Was it an animal in the jaws of a predator? Was someone having a bad nightmare? The screams continued and I hoped no one was in trouble. It was unnerving.

Someone on our travels told us, "Thunder is the sound of gods throwing coconuts at each other." There were loads of coconuts in Varkala, but I wasn't sure there were enough coconuts in the entire world for the number of gods and goddesses in India's panoply of 33 million deities.

My journal entry:

Today is Gandhi's birthday. Hindu pilgrims walk down the beach road from the 2,000-year-old temple to the beach where they will receive a priest's blessing—puja—and toss their offerings into the sea. We are on the Arabian Sea here in Varkala. I think it was, or still may be called, the Malabar Coast. Romans, Greeks, Phoenicians, Arabs, Dutch, French, English all came to what's now Kochi and Kollam for the spices. So valuable, so precious—like gems. How difficult it must have been to sail to Kerala, to its ports. How did people know it was here? Plot your course, navigate by the stars. Follow your bliss . . . oh, please!

CHAPTER 6: *Puja Ceremony. Papanasam Beach*

Rain or shine, Hindu pilgrims walked down the Papanasam Beach Road from the Janardana Swami Temple to the sacred beach. After the holy men at the 2,000-year-old temple blessed them, the pilgrims walked to Papanasam Beach to perform puja with the Sadhus or priests who were sanctioned by the government to pray on their behalf. The pilgrims paid priests to guide them in the spiritual ceremony to honor a deity or pay respect to someone who had passed away. Sometimes the Hindus released the year-old ashes of a deceased family member into the Arabian Sea.

At the priests' instructions, men knelt on the sand and bowed forward until their heads touched the sand. The men were shirtless and wore *mundus* to enter the temple. The long skirt was a South Indian tradition. It took some getting used to, I had to admit. The men walked along, wrapping, and unwrapping their mundus around their waists. It was a long piece of material they pleated and tucked into the waistband they created. Before the men knelt on the sand, they pulled the fabric up and the ankle-length skirt became loose shorts to make it easier for the men to kneel. Most of the women wore traditional saris or the *salwar* tunics. The little girls' dresses fascinated me. They were fabulous, frilly dresses in all the colors of the rainbow—purple, fuchsia, yellow, brilliant blue, turquoise, white, and they were lacy, with layers of netting, gathered at the hem. Some dresses had sequins that caught the sun and reflected its brilliant light. Parents bought little girls funny, cheap black plastic hats from vendors whose concessions were close to the beach. The small hats stayed on the little girls' heads because an elastic chinstrap anchored them in the stiff breeze off the sea. Incredibly, I saw young boys wearing knitted Tibetan caps with earflaps. It was 90 degrees Fahrenheit in the sun.

We were close to the equator, and Varkala was tropical. The jungle had reclaimed abandoned old homes. Coconut palms were heavy with fruit. Hibiscus grew everywhere. Other tropical flowers I didn't recognize dotted the lush green landscape with their colors.

Varkala's dramatic landscape had surprised me the first time we visited India. The cliffs overlooked a wide beach in February, but the water now covered most of the beach. Two restaurants were on the beach, and one was built into the hillside that marched up to the cliffs. The restaurants were built on different levels. One was a crude bamboo structure that felt wobbly on the second floor. The steps leading from the sand to the second level were hazardous. The other was more stable, built with more money and forethought, perhaps.

We sat at Marina Bay Restaurant overlooking Papanasam Beach. One of the Nepalese waiters said, "Good morning, Mr. Honey Lemon Ginger."

I laughed. The Nepalese waiters called Trevor "Mr. Honey Lemon Ginger" since he drank pots and pots of tea.

"So that's what you do while I'm up on the roof garden writing," I said.

Trevor grinned. "Yep." He patted the book on the table.

The restaurant was Trevor's go-to place where he read and watched passersby, surfers, and fishermen and met other winter visitors.

Trevor said, "It's another C&B Scene."

"C&B Scene" was the nickname he'd given to Page & Palette's Latté Da coffee shop back home. I supposed there was one everywhere—a primo spot to watch the action in town.

Later I sat on the steps at Papanasam Beach to watch the puja ceremony. A large extended family gathered around the priest, who sat beneath his beach umbrella atop a red cloth on the flat-topped mound of sand he had built. He was the only priest performing the ceremony. The others looked bored. One of the priests talked on his mobile phone. Moments before, he had gestured to me to come sit with him. Not this time, I told myself. I was on a mission to observe the ritual.

The Indian family who surrounded the priest knelt on the sand. Younger women knelt with grace in their saris. The older women and men sometimes needed help kneeling on the sand. Three men, shirtless and wearing the traditional mundu, bowed their heads down until their foreheads met the sand. They rested back on their knees and the puja ceremony began.

The priest poured holy water on his fingers and dabbed it on the forehead of each person who performed the prayer ritual. The priests were allowed only with government-sanctioned guidance. I saw female priests at the beach for the larger celebrations like Durga Puja, or Diwali Puja, or Holi. The priest placed a banana leaf before each of the kneeling pilgrims, and the Hindus dropped flower petals—jasmine, marigold, and hibiscus—and grains of rice on the leaves. The men raised their hands with palms together to their foreheads in prayer. They rose in unison and turned around three times before they bent down and waved clouds of incense up over their bodies and into their faces. They lifted the banana leaves and took their offerings to the sea. A police jeep blew its loud horn and interrupted the otherwise peaceful scene where I heard only the sounds of the sea, crashing waves, crows, and brahminy kites that caught the air currents.

One of the Indians who walked toward the sea was young, fit, and handsome. He held a banana leaf wrapped around a thick packet on top of his head. The packet held his relative's ashes, and the family performed puja to honor the memory of their deceased family member. The young man turned his back to the sea and released the banana leaf packet and its contents into the water. Then he immersed himself in the powerful waves that crashed onto the beach. The other two men stood on either side of the young man and took his elbows to help him rise out of the sea. It appeared to be more ceremonial than necessary, but as I watched the young man's face, I realized how profound an emotional experience it was.

A strong onshore wind blew off the Arabian Sea. I was the only person who didn't fit in the moment. The priest had a large white stripe painted across his forehead and a bright red and orange scarf wrapped around his neck. He wore a white mundu and sat cross-legged on his makeshift temple where he talked with the family members.

I sensed that someone was watching me. Where there had been two men watching me scribble in the Moleskin journal, I now saw three groups, maybe fifteen men, all staring, all curious. I felt uncomfortable. One group appeared to be businessmen dressed in working attire—slacks, nice shirts, leather shoes. Others wore the traditional Keralan mundu. I turned around and looked back at the waves. Seven stray dogs were nearby—four were asleep on the sand, one sat up and watched the passersby, and the other two were mothers whose teats were filled with milk. A puppy followed one and tried desperately to gain a firm hold, time and time again.

Forty precious elementary school children marched to the beach with their teachers. They held hands and stood at the edge of the sand where the waves splashed them. They shrieked with laughter and jumped back from the waves, absolutely thrilled with the experience. *What a marvelous field trip*, I thought.

Papanasam Beach was a holy place where Hindus had come since the twelfth century. Papanasam means "Destroyer of All Sins." The waves at Papanasam Beach had the mystical power to wash away one's sins.

An Indian family arrived together, at least three or four generations, and the parents and grandparents carried the smallest children and the babies. I hadn't seen one Indian child in a baby stroller. The children were always in their parents' or grandparents' arms, or they held the hands of a sibling, a parent, or an older relative. Seeing four generations of a family gathered around the priest seemed remarkable. It was the norm rather than the exception. One day, I watched an older man wearing a mundu walk on the beach holding a young girl's hand. He was fit, healthy, and proud to be with the girl, who was likely his granddaughter. The little girl, about six years old, wore a beautiful frilly dress. She looked up into her grandfather's smiling face with a smile that shone on her own lovely face. It took me back six decades to memories of my own grandfather, "Papa," whom I adored.

CHAPTER 7: *Writer's Room*

It was 5:15 a.m. and gunpowder blasts in the drums at the temple on the beach road boomed every few seconds. I sat on a little bright-pink stool in the wet room aka bathroom with my MacBook Pro perched on the toilet seat. Trevor slept in the adjoining bedroom. Why, I asked myself, was I typing on the toilet? Simple answer, I didn't have a private place I could go without having to dress first, and I was naked as a newborn babe. It was cool in the early morning, and my thoughts stirred madly.

The evening before, Trevor had said, "I don't want to put a downer on the day, but what if I can't give you £500 for November to help pay the mortgage? If the house isn't rented, what are you going to do?"

"I don't recall asking you to help." I was gobsmacked.

He reminded me, "You didn't ask the realtor to lower the price."

It was 7 p.m. I was exhausted and wanted to call it a day.

"I'm going for a walk," Trevor announced. "I'll be back in five minutes or twenty-five minutes." He was angry.

By 8:15 p.m., I was concerned. I couldn't sleep. I got up, tempted to check email or Facebook. I wanted an escape from the stress. I tried to pray, I tried to meditate. I repeated my mantra from Deepak Chopra's meditation course Melissa taught me. I repeated a prayer repeatedly. I wept. Nothing took away my fear and pain.

How could I blame Trevor for wanting to get away from me? I wanted to get away from me. I thought maybe I needed to pack my bags and leave. Go back home. Throw in the towel. The house wasn't rented, and the financial burden was impossible without a tenant.

Before going on his walk, Trevor had asked me, "Are you writing?"

Not just plain no. Hell no. When? Where? He got up early, made tea, and I had no effing place to go, to have time, to have privacy to write. How could I write if we were constantly doing? There was no writer's space or place, and Trevor didn't understand. He was supportive in many ways, but he didn't understand my spiritual life or its importance. He didn't understand how difficult it was to write when there was no place to write. I was beyond frustrated with the situation and didn't know what to do.

If I went home, it would be without the cash flow from my writing business. And if I returned now, leaving Trevor in India, I knew it signaled the end of our relationship. We couldn't sustain a partnership if we were worlds apart. I prayed for trust, for faith to be restored, for inner peace. I had lost my way, my focus. I was responsible for my life, and I felt like a complete failure.

A friend was writing her second book and celebrating the publication of her first. Everyone raved about the book, and all her friends gathered 'round. I wouldn't have a book if I didn't write every day. I hadn't returned to India to live like we were living—for a day at the beach. I had come with a mission.

The next day, Sanjay brought a table and chairs up to the roof garden for me to have a space where I could write. A Writer's Room. I was happy, even if I couldn't write more than a word or two. I awoke and started my day with a routine to bring me closer to my goal. I was grateful to be sitting at my new writer's table because my morning started with depression and another anxiety-producing chat with Trevor. It wasn't easy being together 24/7 in close quarters. I needed quiet time to reflect, to write, to recharge.

"Trevor, you're in constant motion from the time you get out of bed in the morning to the time you go to sleep at night."

His face fell, and I knew I'd hurt his feelings, but it was true. When his head hit the pillow in the evening, he was out like a light. I envied him that ability to sleep so soundly.

"I'm going down to breakfast, Jesse."

I didn't enjoy talking about tough stuff because it was emotionally exhausting. Still, we had to talk about tough stuff to be real. Trevor dodged discussions with practiced skill. Instead, he entertained folks along the beach road because he was charming and delightful.

It wasn't all paradise in Paradise. There were no easy answers, no platitudes to dissipate discomfort miraculously. There was no magic bullet, nor was there one voice in the wilderness we called life that had all the answers. There were no shortcuts to being happy. One simply was or wasn't, I thought.

Trevor was happy most of the time. He said he was a simple man. I didn't know if that was true, but he could be a funny, sweet partner.

I'd read a Facebook post about Oprah and Elizabeth Gilbert on a spiritual tour and an article in *The New Republic* about Oscar Wilde meeting Walt Whitman. I thought about the gurus of the hour. Whitman encouraged Wilde to become a celebrity and push the old poets out of the way, essentially kick them off the stage to get in the limelight.

I hadn't considered that showmanship was as important a part of the creative process as the writing. I needed to promote myself, and I wished I were more comfortable with it. I wasn't uncomfortable with public appearances, but it felt unnatural for me to pull a Barnum & Bailey routine. I understood no one would know what I was doing if I didn't talk about it and about myself.

When Oprah and Liz held court, folks paid their respects and listened avidly. In fact, they hung on every word. Liz said following your bliss is "not a day at the beach." No kidding. It was painful—emotionally, and in some cases physically—staying in a jungle, battling heat, humidity, and mosquitoes.

Participants raved about *The Oprah Life You Want Weekend*. I imagined the experience generated a high, euphoria, and bliss. The concept was praiseworthy. Was I living the life I wanted? I thought so, but I experienced self-doubt. Everyone needed inspiration and affirmation. I read words of wisdom written by different people or attributed to the Hindu gods, Buddha, and the Dalai Lama. I thought Rumi, Kahlil Gibran, Oprah, Deepak Chopra, Tony Robbins, and Dr. Phil were all seekers who had followers, and perhaps had found what matters to them.

Sanjay came to the roof garden with one of the waiters from his Passion Fruit Cafe.

"Thanks, Sanjay. You helped me get my groove back," I said.

"You're welcome." He gestured for the waiter to put a beautiful bowl of fresh fruit on the table beside my computer.

"Writing restores my batteries. The roof garden is a beautiful place to think."

I saw the real India in contrast to glossy tourist brochures, and I was grateful. I hadn't thought my travels, first to India, then to Cornwall, and now to India again, were part of a spiritual journey. I was wrong. It was all part of my spiritual journey. I was starting to find myself again.

My original spiritual journey was born of my own mystical experience. I recalled the quote that fit then, that still fit. William Blake wrote, "If the fool would persist in his folly, he would become wise." Had I gained wisdom in four decades? A little, perhaps. The exploration of India and my own creativity was daunting.

Was I in the right state of mind in India to accept what was and stop trying to swim against the tide? I was grateful for all I had experienced and for the gifts I'd been given. It was time to multiply talents and embrace my understanding that we are all one. That love is the most important thing in the world.

CHAPTER 8: *Janardana Temple*

I sat on the deck of the roof garden overlooking the beach road to Papanasam Beach. It was a brilliant Sunday morning. The beach road was crowded with a steady stream of Hindu pilgrims who walked from the 2,000-year-old Janardana Swami Temple, where they had received a blessing.

Janardana Swami was a form of Lord Vishnu. Whenever the world was threatened with evil, chaos, and destructive forces, Vishnu descended in the form of an avatar (incarnation) to restore the cosmic order and protect *Dharma*. The temple was dedicated to the gods Vishnu and *Hanuman*, the monkey god.

On the way back from lunch, Trevor and I stopped by a small store where we met a delightful and handsome young man, Malik, who managed his family-owned store near the beach. Tibetan items and beautiful jewelry filled the elegant store. It was a proper bricks-and-mortar store in contrast to other vendors' plywood, bamboo, corrugated tin, and tarp huts dotting the beach road. Malik said he was a Muslim and told us about his home and houseboats on a beautiful lake in Kashmir. He showed us a photo of his five-year-old daughter. "She's coming for a visit next month."

We stopped by the crude wooden coconut stand covered with a rusting tin roof. The wrinkled and stooped coconut lady was Trevor's ancient go-to-girl every day for fresh coconut milk. She held a fresh coconut in one hand and deftly whacked off the top with her machete.

I held my breath, certain she would lose a couple of fingers. After Trevor sipped the coconut water through a straw, the coconut lady cut a scoop with her machete, and then cut the coconut open. Trevor used the scoop to dig out fresh coconut meat. I wasn't keen on the taste, but I did love the fresh pineapple juice in India.

We stopped by for a quick chat with the old man Gopi, a lean man whose long white hair and beard made me think he was a holy man. He set up his shop in a small tin hut he had built with corrugated metal he'd found. Gopi had a small table and an easel set up inside to do small paintings on leaves. There was no electricity, and one night, when we walked back from the beach in the rain, a candle burned inside the hut where Gopi slept. He had cut a window out of the tin siding and propped it open with a wooden stick. He and the old coconut lady were resourceful seniors.

Large, healthy crows in Varkala cawed all day long and the crow-caphony was deafening. Nevertheless, I was grateful to sit at my table in the roof garden and tap away at the keyboard. Since the roof garden was part of the restaurant, I knew I wouldn't have the privacy after the restaurant opened.

CHAPTER 9: *Running the Gauntlet*

We had to run the gauntlet on the clifftop. Every day it was the same. If we walked up the stone steps from the beach to the clifftop, we had to pass vendors' shops on the sides of the steps. Tourists bought everything from tie-dyed T-shirts to prayer beads and incense, statues of Hindu gods, Tree of Life bedspreads straight out of the 1970s, flowing dresses à la Woodstock, pipes, and bongs. Hippie heaven.

"Come see my shop?"

"Where you from?"

"How long you staying?"

"You come back tomorrow?"

"Look. No have to buy."

"Here, here. I give to you. No have to pay."

The sales pitches took place not once, or twice, but from every vendor on the clifftop, up or down the steps, to or from Papanasam Beach, on the beach road, and into the hotel. Of course, I'd buy something during our four months in Varkala when it suited me.

As I sat in the roof garden, I watched men lower red clay tiles from the rooftop of a small hotel across the road to the ground. It was like the stone age. Two men worked on the roof and two men worked on the ground. All the men who worked wore mundus hitched up to make shorts, and only one man wore a shirt. They rigged up a crude bamboo goal-post–type scaffolding, threw a long rope over a pole, and filled a sorry-looking straw basket with tiles they lowered to the ground.

One man, obviously the supervisor, wore a shirt, white trousers, and sandals. He watched.

I mused that the scene was repeated in India wherever manual labor was performed. The supervisor either sat in a chair under a beach umbrella, stood in the shade, or hovered over the workers to check their every move. He gestured wildly, and a stream of the *Malayalam* language spoken in Kerala gushed forth. The next time I looked up, I saw two men supervising the two workers on the ground as they stacked the tiles neatly next to the road. The question that begged to be answered was, will the tiles sit there with weeds growing around them in a matter of weeks, or will someone come along with a rattle-trap lorry or rusting bicycle-powered cart to haul away the tiles? It was another day at the beach.

In two days, we would celebrate Diwali, Devali or, Dilwale, depending on whom you asked. I gave up on trying to figure the correct spelling of the all-India holiday. I wasn't clear on exactly what we were celebrating, but Sanjay said it involved exchanging gifts and eating sweets. I googled it to find out because, when I asked, I got a different answer from each person.

Diwali—the festival of lights, is an ancient Hindu festival celebrated in autumn each year. The festival spiritually signifies the victory of light over darkness, knowledge over ignorance, good over evil, and hope over despair.

How wonderful! A celebration of the victory of light over darkness and hope over despair lifted my spirits. Festival preparations and rituals took place over five days. The main festival night of Diwali coincided with the darkest, new moon night. Diwali fell between mid-October and mid-November.

Before Diwali, people cleaned, renovated, and decorated their homes. On Diwali night, people dressed up in new clothes or their best outfits, lit *diyas* (lamps and candles) inside and outside their homes, took part in family puja—to honor Lakshmi, the goddess of wealth and prosperity. Fireworks followed puja, prayers. A family feast including *mithai*, sweets, took place while family members and close friends exchanged gifts.

Activity on the rooftop across the beach road ended. Crows took a caw-break. It was hot. I checked the sky. Heavy cumulus clouds gathered moisture from the Arabian Sea and moved in over the coast. We were minutes away from a spectacular thunderstorm that might compete with the temple drums' gunpowder blasts.

Our arrival in Kerala for the second, and supposedly less rainy, monsoon season meant everything was green, clean, and beautiful. I was grateful every day I sat in the shade of the roof garden under its bamboo and palm frond roof and watched people on the beach road. It was the perfect place to write and dream. I felt happy and fulfilled.

CHAPTER 10: *Celebration of the Black Moon*

"They're all beeping their hooters," Trevor said.

The cacophony on the beach road woke me. I looked at my watch. "It's 5:45 a.m. What's happening?"

Hundreds and hundreds of pilgrims walked down the beach road. It was usually quiet before 6 a.m., but cars, tuk-tuks, and motorcycles all honked their horns. The gunpowder booms blasted from the tin drums at the temple, timed one after another in rapid succession, just a few seconds apart.

"Sounds like they're bombing the bloody temple," Trevor said. "I'm going downstairs."

He dressed quickly, kissed me, and walked out. I stuffed my earplugs in as far as they would go and pulled the rock-hard pillow over my head. Silence . . . and sleep.

Trevor handed me the morning's cup of ginger, lemon, and honey tea.

"It's a celebration of the Black Moon, *Onam*."

"A festival? What kind of celebration?"

"Ain't got a clue, but the road is absolutely jammed with people walking to the beach."

I dressed quickly and we walked down the beach road along with the hordes of people, noisy motor vehicles, and bicycles. Papanasam Beach was dotted with more Hindu priests than we usually saw.

"I wondered what they were doing last night," I said.

On the way back from the clifftop the night before, we had seen priests setting up shop on mounds of sand they packed hard with sea-water, using their trowels to dig the sand and their hands to pat it down. Watching the priests perform puja at the altars they set up was the beautiful part of the day. The other part of this day was, for me, a nightmare. Trevor said there were beggars all along the beach road, that someone must have brought them down because they couldn't have walked. I looked down the red steps, paint badly chipped away—their new paint job waiting for the monsoon rains to end—all the way down the steep staircase and through the archway leading out of Om Hotel and down to the beach road. I looked first across the street at the vendor who had set up his cart the night before and covered it to protect it from the rain. Now, I saw there were baskets full of nuts and grains—yellow, brown, chestnut-colored—and other things I couldn't name.

Then my waking nightmare began as cruelly as if someone had taken a sledgehammer and knocked the breath out of me, hitting me in the solar plexus. The beggars. I wasn't prepared for what I saw. I walked into a Hieronymus Bosch painting of Hell. It was an involuntary, visceral response. The first beggar sat a few feet from the vendor's cart. He had no legs and sat on a tatty rug with his hand held out to the passers-by. But it wasn't the first beggar without legs that took my breath away, it was all the beggars, one after another, no more than twenty feet apart. All with tragic afflictions, all on tatty mats, all brown-skinned but filthy and wearing ragged clothing. All with hands outstretched.

The pilgrims, in colorful saris and mundus, all fit and well-fed, walked past the beggars—most of the people unseeing, not giving any alms. Because of the number of pilgrims, my view was blocked farther down Papanasam Beach Road. We walked toward the beach. Oh, dear God. A slight, brown-skinned man wearing a bright blue short-sleeved shirt and blue shorts lay on his back. His mat was larger than most. He couldn't sit up. His right leg stuck out straight from his body, normal-sized, but his other leg, undeveloped and tooth-pick thin, bent back at an unnatural angle almost sixty degrees from his knee toward his left hip.

Broken beggars lay on the right-hand side of Papanasam Beach Road, one after another for the length of two football fields, all the way to the beach. I saw only one woman. My heart was breaking. I couldn't get the image out of my mind.

"This is a news story, Trevor, but I don't have the courage to photograph the beggars. It's overwhelming."

It was impossible to help them all. There were simply too many. I wondered if I could help just one person. I tried to do that every day—give a little. The crippled man in the blue shorts—a victim of polio perhaps—waved his outstretched left hand.

He wailed, "More. More. More."

"Do you think he was born with that deformity, babe?" I asked.

"Jesse, children are maimed to elicit sympathy as beggars."

"Who on earth would do that?" I recalled the film *Slumdog Millionaire* in which a young boy was blinded.

How was it that I was devastated by the scene, but Trevor could detach from the horror of it all? How could all their fellow country-men and women walk past, unseeing, and not give a little? Pilgrims visited the Janardana temple, gave money to the Brahmins or Holy Men there, and paid for gunpowder in the drums to be lit and explode with loud booms to say, "Hello, God. I am here."

Holy Men in the temple talked to God on behalf of the Hindus, and pilgrims walked to the beach, barefoot, in sandals, flip-flops, wedge-heeled mules, trainers, or leather shoes. At the beach, they paid priests or Sadhus to pray for them, to perform puja. After the pilgrims washed away their sins in the fierce, unpredictable waves of the Arabian Sea, they bought ice cream, bottled water, or Coca-Cola, and they threw paper cups and plastic bottles on the beach. They littered the beach and the beach road. They walked past the beggars, filthy and pathetic as the trash beneath their sandals, flip-flops, and bare feet, unseeing.

I was numb, dissociating after seeing the crippled beggars some-one had stationed on the beach road. Meanwhile, majestic brahminy kites with white heads and necks swooped and dove and circled over-head, soaring on air currents above the cliffs. A beautiful butterfly, black with a tail like a colorful fan and larger than a hummingbird, reminiscent of a luna moth, lit on flowers in pots on the terrace. A school of dolphins swam south, their black fins breaking the surface of the sea. I breathed and embraced the beauty to ground myself.

Trevor had taken a photo of a beggar I'd forgotten on purpose. The man's back looked like a tiger's black stripes. At first, I'd thought he'd been whipped severely and left with badly scarred skin, but as we got closer, I'd seen he had a skin disease. He was marked all over his body—black tattoos—stripes on his arms, chest, and face.

Later, we sat at Marina Bay Restaurant on Papanasam Beach, drank a pot of ginger, lemon, and honey tea, and waited for a rainstorm to pass. We walked back to the hotel on the beach road, and I wished with all my heart not to see the crippled beggars.

CHAPTER 11: Friday Morning in the Roof Garden

Trevor brought me a beautiful fruit salad from the Passion Fruit Café. Earlier, he had made me the morning cup of ginger, lemon, and honey tea. For several days, he'd been generous, sweet, and supportive of my writing. At times his moods were unpredictable, and I attributed it to the 24/7 proximity. I had encouraged him every day to go for a swim or a big explore while I wrote for a few hours. My precious time.

I hadn't planned for the trip to India to be a spiritual journey. I had only wanted to test myself. Despite my intentions, I realized it was a journey into the spirit, the mystic. It didn't seem to be my will. Maybe it was my interpretation of God and her/his will for me. As I talked with Hindus, Muslims, and Christians on my travels, I knew in my heart of hearts we were all one. The understanding was profound and beyond words.

I reflected on the walk back to Om from the beach on Sunday. I had dreaded seeing the horrors again, but I need not have feared it. I lingered at the beach, writing in my journal, in part to record the experience in its immediacy and in so doing to dispel some of its horrific power over me.

The beggars were gone. Most of the pilgrims had gone. Trevor and I walked up the muddy street to the hotel. And I saw him. The man without legs, who sat on his tatty mat across from the hotel. He walked down the road on his hands, dragging his stump of a body along. We couldn't imagine such deformity in our perfect little bubble world back home.

I remembered the man I had seen on the sidewalk in town a few days earlier when we went to the family restaurant for lunch. His legs were stumps cut off above the knees. He walked on the stumps unaided by crutches or prostheses. And what did he have to help him navigate the concrete sidewalks? Flip-flops. Using the thong part of the cheap rubber sandals, he attached the flip-flops to the stumps of his legs sideways. Flip-flops. He walked by rocking from side to side on the flip-flops that cushioned his limbs. He didn't walk putting one leg in front of the other. It was a painstaking process for him to rock back and forth, and painful to watch. He made slow but certain progress forward on the sidewalk.

"Prostheses would help him so much," I said. "I wonder why he doesn't have them?"

"He doesn't have the dosh, Jesse."

Trevor was intent on going into the restaurant, and seeing the handicapped man didn't faze him. We walked past him, entered the restaurant, and took our seats. Two young English travelers at the table next to us said they were on a three-week holiday in India. Their faces were beautiful, unlined, rosy, and tan. I ordered the Tomato Uthappam, and Trevor got the Masala Dosa.

When the waiter brought our bottled water, Trevor said, "We'd like glasses, too."

The waiter looked at him with a wrinkled brow, confused.

I pointed to the metal cups at the next table. "Two cups, please." Sometimes gestures communicated better than words. The waiters spoke Malayalam.

Out of the corner of my eye, I saw the man who walked on his stumps enter the restaurant confidently. He walked to a table on the far side of the room and pulled himself up onto a chair. He smiled at the waiters who poured him a cup of water from a metal pitcher.

"That blows my mind," I said.

Trevor didn't notice. He tucked into his Masala Dosa.

Hunter S. Thompson said, "I'm a word freak. I like words. I've always compared writing to music. That's the way I feel about good paragraphs. When it really works, it's like music."

I understood what he meant. Music transported and transformed us. When I wrote, I was transported to another place. I saw and heard what was going on around me, but the writing took me to my happy place, where I felt fulfilled. I might have written garbage, but my intention in Varkala was to write without trying to be perfect. I let go of control.

CHAPTER 12: *Elephant at the Temple*

"What's that?" I asked. I had seen something move out of the corner of my eye. It was an elephant, or rather the back half of an elephant. It walked down a small lane that intersected the one we were exploring.

Trevor looked at a family compound with two large new homes.

"I saw an elephant, Trevor. Let's hurry back and catch up with it."

We walked to the end of the lane at the junction behind the temple, looked right, and looked left.

"Jesse, there's no elephant."

"I swear I saw an elephant."

"Hmm," Trevor said.

The elephant had vanished.

"I can smell the elephant, Trevor. We can follow the smell."

I pointed down the lane to the right. The elephant stood inside a walled garden and was having a grand time drinking water from a running faucet. It wasn't a very large elephant. Its tail swished back and forth.

Later, I learned she was a female. She was a small elephant, as elephants go. Her hide was mottled with small spots like a jungle cat. She was named Sarasvati for the Hindu goddess of wisdom, who was always seen with a musical instrument.

Sarasvati put her trunk under the faucet, filled it as much as she could, raised her trunk to her mouth, and drank. We heard water gurgling down her throat. The elephant's home was poor, the yard bare and muddy. A man wearing a mundu swung a machete with a dull blade and cut tall grasses in one corner of the walled area.

A young boy sat on a bale of hay to the left of the entrance gate. He was excited to see us and spoke rapid-fire Malayalam. He gestured for us to come in and see the elephant. The child didn't understand any English, but he continued to shout and wave to urge us into the compound.

"Do you think he wants money?" I asked.

"Jesse, he's probably looking for . . . "

The roar of a motorcycle drowned him out. A neatly dressed man rode up and parked his motorcycle outside the elephant's home. He walked toward the entrance, took a long appraising look at us, and marched into the compound. He approached the young boy and chastised him in Malayalam for the child's obvious misstep in asking us to enter.

"Let's get out of here before he hits the little boy," I said.

Trevor and I turned around and walked back the way we had come.

I took a quick look over my shoulder. The elephant played with and drank the water, obviously having loads of fun, indifferent to the scolding the child had received.

CHAPTER 13: *Behind Every Journey is a Story*

The yoga teacher's sonorous chant woke me and reminded me of the pallbearers who carried bodies on bamboo stretchers to funeral pyres on the Ganges.

"Let's take a walk before it gets too hot, Trevor." He was always keen to be on the go.

"I'll put on my trainers." He adjusted the laces on red Salomon sneakers.

We headed up the beach road to the temple, climbed steep steps past its second entrance, and walked to the Surf and Soul resort on the clifftop south of Papanasam Beach.

"It's as high as the north clifftop, Jesse."

"Let's keep walking. I want to explore the alleys."

"Babe, this road takes us back down to the beach."

I hoped my lightweight white cotton Punjabi pants and print cotton salwar would help in the heat. I mopped my face with my ever-present cotton bandana and opened my purple brolly for shade in the morning sun. We wandered down a lane shaded by coconut palms and papaya trees, walked past shoulder-high stone walls on either side of the narrow lane, and reached a gate. The wrought-iron gate was old, beautiful, and divided into two curved sections, verdigris with age. The middle of both sides of the gates was painted white to show off the design, a stylized rising sun.

"Trevor, there's no lock on the gate."

I was tempted to walk through the gate and onto a path, its rust-colored stones covered with dark green mold. Papaya trees, palms, and other tropical plants lined the path that curved back into a lush garden surrounding an ancient Keralan home. The elegant architecture was striking in its resemblance to a Chinese pagoda.

The home was one story, its roof tiles almost black with age. The windows had no glass, only bars set about six inches apart in dark brown wooden frames fitted into the stone walls. I saw someone through the open front door. The person stood in silhouette near another door on the opposite side of the house.

Trevor, who wasn't constitutionally capable of standing in one spot for more than a minute or two, was no longer by my side. He stood across the narrow, paved lane.

"Cor!" He gestured toward a massive new home.

The contrast was startling. It was a fortress.

High walls surrounded the property, and a tall black wrought-iron gate prevented entry into the compound. Paving stones of different sizes and shapes covered the drive and courtyard and formed a pattern from the street to the front door of a large, white home. A new white car stood under a portico to the right of the entry, with potted tropical plants artfully arranged under the portico. The only other living green plants were coconut palms that overhung the courtyard from the home next door.

A smaller white house stood near the front gate. Perhaps it belonged to a grown child who had married and was raising a family. One Keralan custom was for a family to buy a large plot of land and to build their first home on one quarter of the land. As generations came along, the family divided the land—the quarters into halves and so on, but it was all in the family. That was just one beautiful thing about India—multigenerational families everywhere. I lamented that the same was no longer a custom in America.

Amin walked up to the roof garden where I sat. He was small and dark-skinned with beautiful brown eyes. He had set up his practice in the Ayurveda Center at the hotel for the tourist season, and gave massages to men. I had to have a female masseuse.

"Is the roof garden a good place to write?"

"Yes. It's lovely."

"Are you writing about Varkala?"

"I'm writing stories about train travel. We're all travelers here, and behind every journey is a story."

Amin was a Kerala native who had a good heart and radiated kindness. Some of the vendors, hotel owners, and tuk-tuk drivers we had met were thieves, liars, charlatans, and con artists. We couldn't always trust a smile because it might not be a friendly gesture. It might be a ploy to suck a gullible tourist into someone's drama. It was disheartening to meet a charming person only to learn that he or she had money problems, was ill, had a sick relative, needed to pay the moneylender for a relative's funeral, or had an emergency.

Trevor reminded me of the Bob Dylan song lyrics, "They rip you off with a smile instead of a gun."

CHAPTER 14: *Awareness or Awakening While Reading in India*

E mail to a friend:

I enjoy the luxury of time to read in India: Shantaram, White Tiger, Three Cups of Tea, The God of Small Things, and The Last Mughal (William Dalrymple's historically based account of the 1857 Indian uprising against the British in India and Delhi, in particular).

What I've come away with is an understanding that there's nothing new under the sun. I researched information about Hinduism, Muslims, Islam, the madrasas (schools the Muslims set up), mujahidin, jihadists, Sunni, and Shia. I don't understand why headlines isolate current events as if they were one-off incidents. Isn't history repeating itself? Am I naïve to think it's absurd to believe bombs dropped from the sky will eradicate religions, or religious extremists, in existence for 1400 years?

The shoe thief visited Om. He stole up to the front door of the guest-house in the wee hours. He was discriminating and didn't touch rubber flip-flops, crocs, or cheap knock-offs of name-brand sandals.

"The thief has good taste in shoes," I said.

Trevor laughed "Right."

"He likes leather."

Sanjay scrubbed his fingers through his hair, as if it would aid his sleuthing.

"He didn't take both shoes," Trevor said.

"He didn't even take a whole shoe."

"He gnaws at the tender leather bits."

We eyed the pile of shoes.

"And he leaves a shredded mess." I tried not to laugh.

Sanjay said, "The thief has distinctive features—black around his mouth."

"You know who the shoe thief is?" I felt sure my surprise was obvious.

An attractive, well-dressed Englishwoman joined us on the porch and shrieked, "My new shoes!" Her designer sandals—leather and expensive—were a gnawed mess.

An older guy, an aging hippie who'd done one too many psy-chedelics, took one look at his mangled leather sandal and shrugged. "Don't sweat the small stuff, man."

The fashionista got in Sanjay's face. "You'll pay for my shoes."

"Madam, I am most sorry." Sanjay tried to calm her. "I will refund the money for your stay."

"You most certainly will. And I'll check out as soon as you do."
She walked off in a huff.

Sanjay said, "She's staying in the 1600-rupee-a-night room." That
was about $25 USD or sixteen pounds sterling. I did the math. Since
she'd already spent ten nights, the refund would compensate her for
the $200 leather sandals.

After the incident, Sanjay brought all the shoes in for the night.
He said, "He is the only dog in Varkala that eats shoes, or parts of
leather shoes."

Trevor started laughing and I fought back a grin.

Sanjay continued, "He causes problems for the hotels and guesthouse managers who request that guests leave their shoes outside
the door."

"It's a reasonable request, Sanjay," I said. "The beach comes back
with all of us who walk down to the sea."

It was a tragedy. The shoe thief was a hungry dog, one of many
strays that roamed the streets, slept on the beach, hid in the tall grasses,
and bred like crazy. It made me sad to see the dogs, hungry for affection, wary of sudden movements. Some were crippled after being hit
by cars, motorcycles, tuk-tuks, buses, taxis, or the people who drove
them away from their shops with sticks and stones.

The dogs had mange—sometimes so bad that they had no fur.
Their ribs protruded. Especially the dogs with puppies. Sometimes the
puppies had spindly legs and wobbled to stand, and I only saw them a
day or two. I wondered if the shopkeepers or other dogs killed them,
or if they wandered off the beaten path and became prey for the kites.
The mama dogs walked on the beach with a pup or puppies grasping
for a hanging teat and dying, literally, for mother's milk. Sometimes
the puppies grew into the next generation of strays to starve, become
crippled, get killed by a motor vehicle, or to have another generation
of puppies. When I spoke in a soft voice to one of the sad creatures,
it followed me and begged for a stroke—at the same time terrified a
loving gesture might become a blow.

The little dog that feared thunder slept outside the locked gate at
the back of the second floor. She was brown, tan, black, and white. A
sweet dog. When I reached out to pet her, she whined loudly, rolled
onto her back, and left her throat bare, unprotected. Occasionally I

slipped her crackers between the spaces in the folding gate. I had to warn her. "Shhh. Shhh. Shhh." Or else Susie, Sanjay's little street dog, would race up the stairs and bark like mad—not intending to harm Scaredy Pup, putting on her major intimidation act. Poor ole Scaredy flattened herself into upside-down submission. Once, after having Ajay's attempt at a cheese sandwich, I took Scaredy all the crusts from the bread.

I wanted to pet the dogs, feed the dogs, but I knew none (other than Susie, the adopted former street dog) had had rabies and distemper shots. It would have been dreadful to have a stray dog bite me. I didn't feed them. When I saw them, it felt like someone had put a hand around my heart and squeezed it, and it hurt, not physically, but emotionally. I imagined my visceral reaction was strange to someone who didn't love pets as I did—even the scrawny, ugly little white-and-tan cat that visited the balcony.

Trevor gave the little cat a few slivers of Amul cheese, the strange white all-vegetarian cheese in the tin can, and Little Scrawny Cat gobbled it up. Once, when I gave the little cat some cheese and tried to pet her, she bit my finger, not hard enough to draw blood, but sufficiently hard to warn me away from trying it again. She was feral, hardly larger than a kitten. And she either was pregnant or had just had her first litter of kittens. Trevor gave her pieces of crackers, some cheese, a little *idli*, and fresh bottled water in a blue glass ashtray, and she lapped it up like crazy. She sat on the balcony with Trevor when he read. Not next to him, but at a safe distance.

She came to the door of our room on the balcony and either sat or stood in the doorway and meowed her rather dreadful little meow whenever we gave her food. It was the best I could do in India. I chose one dog and one cat to feed whenever the dog, Scaredy Pup, or the cat, Little Scrawny Cat, appeared.

Same-same for the beggars. I was sitting on the clifftop at Abba, having an avocado sandwich, when the professional beggar arrived. She was an old woman who haunted the volcanic brick path with hand outstretched and gestured toward her mouth with her hand that she was hungry. How did I feel about ignoring her? Putting the Big I-G-N-O-R-E into action wasn't involuntary. I felt awful because I'd lost trust in beggars, vendors, tuk-tuk and taxi drivers, hotel managers, train conductors, and waiters in restaurants. It felt like each was out for something. Gimme. Gimme. Gimme. Children in school uniforms asked me for rupees—for ice cream, for the bus home, for no reason at all. The vendors on the steps as we walked down from the clifftops hounded us.

"Give me orange."

"You buy me something."

It was annoying. I became inured to their plight, and I didn't like myself at all. It wasn't as acute as the moral dilemma and shock I had faced on my first visit to India.

The group of young people who joined us—three or four Americans, two English youngsters, and one Frenchman—talked about the stray dogs in Varkala. The discussion led to spay and neuter programs in the US, and the young travelers asked why Varkala didn't have the same types of initiatives. I didn't know.

CHAPTER 16: *Passion Fruit Café*

"Still no sign of Scaredy Pup or Scrawny Cat after two days," I said. "I'm worried."

"Is pup giving birth?" Ajay, the waiter and sometimes cook, asked.

"I felt a pup moving in her belly." And I wondered if Scrawny Cat had had a new litter of kittens. Was she safe? Two new street dogs showed up in the back area near Mango Cottage behind Om Hotel.

CHAPTER 17: *Celebration of Spirit*

"Let me make this day a celebration of the spirit. There is a part of me that keeps a childlike sense of curiosity, wonder, enthusiasm, and delight."

One morning I tried to write about letting go of Lily and Lulu, but it was hard to unearth pain and loss. I missed my precious cat and dog who had crossed the rainbow bridge. I had adopted Lily, the white cat, sometime after Thanksgiving 2002. Lulu, my white German shepherd, was born on Good Friday, two days before Easter 2004.

I didn't feel like writing. Would I stare at the page for two hours? It wasn't that I didn't have anything to write. I didn't want to think about the morning I made the decision to let Lily and Lulu go together.

The rain hammered on the roof, a torrential downpour. Scrawny Cat devoured cheese on the balcony, slipped into the room, and planted herself in Trevor's suitcase. What was I to do after she found a safe spot to wait out the storm? I dared not touch the cat for fear of being bitten.

CHAPTER 18: *The God of Small Things*

Iberated myself for slacking on my writing the day before. I tried to write when I was on the roof garden, but the new waiter was on the phone, Sanjay arrived with Amin (who needed a bath) to put up paper stars, and customers arrived. It was impossible to write. I was in a bad mood, and I packed up after a few minutes of writing crap.

I hadn't set off for India the first time, or the second time for that matter, on a spiritual quest. The first time I traveled to India in 2013 was to jolt me out of my comfort zone, to push the edge of the envelope. On the second trip, I found myself accepting India as it was—a mass of glorious contradictions. I couldn't change a thing and didn't try to change anything except myself and my infrequent negative thoughts.

Earlier that morning we had enjoyed a lovely breakfast at Marina Bay aka C&B Scene with Tatyana from Bulgaria. She had told me about her guided meditation, led by a musician who had the people in the class envision love as light coming from within, opening themselves to love, sending love out into the world, and bringing it back into themselves.

I gave Tatyana my copy of *The God of Small Things* about Kerala.

It was an extraordinary book I had read when we were in Alleppey, where I saw the Communist signs and posters. The restaurant association had been on strike the Wednesday we arrived. The irony had reminded me what workers could do when they united.

Later, we got lost during the ferry ride and ended up on a boat landing in the middle of nowhere. We walked past a rice paddy where men worked, mud up to their knees and elbows, with the crudest of tools. We discovered Toddy, the restaurant for the workers. I reflected on conversations about the men with whom we talked and about India's caste system. Were these workers in the rice paddies the untouchables? Were they like the untouchables described in Arundhati Roy's book? The men were surely the poorest of the poor. After our lunch at Toddy, we waited at the bus stop overlooking the rice paddy and talked with one of the men from the restaurant about life in Alleppey decades earlier.

He said, "The people only ate tapioca."

"Why were people starving when there were canals, rivers, and the sea all teeming with fish?"

"A group of Hindus didn't eat fish," he explained.

CHAPTER 19: *Celebrations in India*

"We're closer to Christ's birthplace in India, Trevor. Maybe two of the three wise men came from Kerala, bearing frankincense and myrrh on camels from Pushkar, or at least the beach at Alleppey."

He laughed and tucked into his breakfast, a delicious green curry at Aramam Restaurant at the temple junction.

"I can't keep up with the number of celebrations in India, Trevor."

"Jesse, I don't think anyone in India can name all the gods or tell you stories about those they do know."

"That's for priests in the temples, Brahmins, the high holy men who preside over sacred occasions," the waiter said.

"The frequent sacred occasions," Trevor added, with a grin.

It was the first day of forty days during which food was prepared and served at the temple.

"Today is our hotel's day to serve a meal at the temple, Trevor," Sanjay said. "I'll bring food back for you and Jesse to eat after the priests bless it."

After Sanjay left, Trevor groaned. "No more food this morning."

"Sanjay will be offended, babe."

"Let's get out of here."

Sanjay captured us before we made our great escape, and we were still full.

"I don't want to hurt his feelings, Trevor."

"Yeah, we have to eat whatever he's bringing us."

Sanjay arrived with a bowl of the delicious food: plump, short-grained rice, coconut, peanuts, tiny bits of carrot, and little beans. It wasn't too spicy or too mild. It was a perfect combination of ingredients.

"Sanjay, is there a ritual we need to perform? Do we say prayers for people before we eat?" I asked.

"If you want," he said.

After we finished our temple food, Trevor said, "I'm going to check out a small guesthouse on the south cliff." He gave me a kiss and left for his afternoon explore.

CHAPTER 20: *Longing for What Cannot Return*

There are no choices without consequences. Or conversely, we always have choices. Always. Ipso facto: our choices always have consequences.

I reflected on my choices and the challenges I had faced before my second trip to India. It was time for a reality check. Be. Here. Now. I might be in Varkala, in this moment, but I was homesick. I longed for things that would never be again.

Two months before we set out on our odyssey, I had faced a dilemma—the decision to let go of Lily and Lulu when it was their time to cross the rainbow bridge. We are stewards of the animals we choose to have in our lives. It's easy to forget when we adopt, buy, or foster our animals that we likely will outlive them. We grow attached. We receive unconditional love.

Lily, my thirteen-year-old cat, let me know she was dying when she sought dark places and slept. When she heard Lulu, my ten-year-old white German shepherd lap up water, she drank water from Lulu's bowl at the same time. Lulu licked Lily's head. The cat and dog were inseparable.

Lulu's hips bothered her. She was in pain when she sat down. She panted loudly, almost nonstop. She had trouble breathing when she lay down. I faced a devastating choice and remembered Meryl Streep in *Sophie's Choice*. It wasn't that kind of choice, but my heart didn't know. Lulu and Lily were best friends. Lulu wasn't well. When Lily died, Lulu would go into rapid decline. Was it fair to keep her alive knowing she suffered? Was it more humane to let her go at the same time as her best friend?

When I came home afterwards, the house was still. No Lily in hiding. No Lulu bringing me her little hedgehog. The only sound was the click, click, click of the ceiling fan.

CHAPTER 21: *Things Get in the Way of Writing*

I started out with the best of intentions every morning and inevitably wasted time. I tried to write early, before I left the room, but Trevor wanted me to join him for breakfast.

"Gordon Bennett, getting out of here is worse than the steps to the clifftop, Jesse."

"We have to ignore them." I dreaded walking in and out of the hotel.

"They're bloody wankers!"

We filed past an ever-growing number of chefs, waiters, housekeepers, Ayurevedic ladies, and others whom Sanjay had hired.

"I'm uncomfortable, Trevor."

We didn't want to eat breakfast at the hotel restaurant every day, but we felt guilty when we didn't. At breakfast, the chef only made Masala Dosa and omelets. A day earlier, I had asked for one piece of toast with melted cheese on top. Ajay, the waiter, had brought me three pieces of bread with butter and jam.

Trevor cursed under his breath. "Bloody hell."

"Maybe he didn't understand, babe."

The next morning, Ajay brought our breakfast with his interpretation of cheese toast. Trevor eyed his plate with three slices of untoasted white bread and something resembling cheese between the slices.

Ajay held up canned vegan cheese. "This is all we have." He shrugged his shoulders.

"Pathetic," Trevor said when Ajay was out of earshot.

It was past time to accept that we wouldn't get toast for breakfast. It was ridiculous for us to continue to ask for toast. Sometimes we wanted to laugh. Other times, we wanted to cry.

At times we felt dysfunction knew no bounds. We read about it. We heard about it. We experienced it. Every day. What happened at the hotel restaurant was no exception. The case of toast was one instance. In loads of countries 'round the world, people made toast. They browned bread in the oven, under the broiler, or in the toaster on the kitchen counter. All over the world. Except in India. Toast appeared to be a mystery to the Indian waiters and chef. Had we morphed into dreadful tourists rather than travelers who accepted cultural differences?

Trevor and I surrendered. We wouldn't get toast at the hotel. Abba Restaurant on the clifftop understood toast and had a kitchen equipped with ovens to make homemade bread. Delicious bread. Real toast. It was worth the walk up to the clifftop in the heat to get toast. Trevor bought a beautiful loaf of the bread for Sanjay. He wanted the guesthouse manager to see what delicious bread a competitor served. While I wrote, Trevor counseled Sanjay on things he could improve. He wanted the manager to succeed.

Eight weeks after we arrived in Varkala, thirteen people were on staff. The housekeeper, who also prepared breakfast and lunch for the staff, had left after a blow-up with Rahul, the new chef. One morning, she'd found the kitchen in a complete mess and argued with Rahul because he hadn't cleaned up the night before. Sanjay had fired her and said she was from a lower caste than the chef, who threatened to quit. Then, the waiter walked out in a huff over some slight. Trevor and I kept our fingers crossed that things would improve once Rahul started cooking. Two housekeepers replaced the first. The new housekeepers, who spoke only Malayalam, didn't do a good job. The new housekeepers often sat on the steps leading to the roof garden. I had never seen the original housekeeper sit during her workday. She was always cleaning, sweeping, mopping, or cooking while the men sat around and talked.

Two Ayurevedic practitioners worked in the Ayurveda center. Amin seemed a bit at loose ends, although he did have clients for massages on occasion. Chef Rahul finally agreed to cook, but he wouldn't open the restaurant until Sanjay hired a new waiter.

Trevor said, "The bloody chef can't be bothered to take food orders or carry plates."

When the restaurant finally opened, Rahul made Masala Dosa and nothing else for a while. I tried his *idiyappam* with *veg korma*, hoping against hope it was as delicious as the veg curry I had enjoyed at Aramam up at the temple junction.

"Oh my god, Trevor, what is this?"

We stared at the bowl in which four little round balls of something floated.

"Maybe it's rice."

Perhaps it was rice, steamed and puffed. Whatever it was, it didn't look appealing.

"This isn't veg curry."

We stared at our plates. My plate held small containers of the identical condiments Trevor had received with his Masala Dosa. I vowed I wouldn't eat at the restaurant again. Two more waiters arrived. One hung out on the balcony overlooking the beach road. The other sat upstairs in the roof garden, talked on his mobile phone, or surfed the web. When they weren't working, all the men hung out together. Yoga Arjun sat on one side of the steps, Diva Chef Rahul on the other. Trevor and I ran the gauntlet of staff when we walked down the steps. It was awkward.

The week before, we'd tried the restaurant. "Let's give them a shot, Trevor."

"Okay, babe." Trevor looked skeptical.

"Maybe things are better now after Rahul tried new dishes in the kitchen."

I got a tasty omelet, but I didn't get the toast I ordered.

S anjay locked Susie in the little cage under the steps to the roof garden with another dog. It was the high tourist season in Varkala, and Susie had come into season. She was in heat. Sanjay wanted her to mate with another white dog, the little guy just a bit fluffier than Susie. Why in the name of all that was holy did that man want to create another litter of puppies?

Days before Susie went into heat, two strange dogs had appeared on the terrace outside Mango Cottage behind the hotel. Both dogs wore scars that spoke of arguments with other dogs. One dog had lost an eye. I didn't want to make any sudden moves because I thought One Eye might bite me in a heartbeat. Neither of the dogs had a collar. People killed dogs every year to purge the numbers of stray dogs that formed packs at night. Only dogs with collars survived mass slaughter, the annual genocide of furry four-foots. It made me sick at heart to hear it.

CHAPTER 23: *Moving to Mango Cottage*

We had two more nights in the front room with the balcony. Olga from Russia booked the room for three months every winter. We were moving to Mango Cottage behind Om Beach Hotel. Even in the back cottage we wouldn't be immune to the cars with loudspeaker systems that blasted our eardrums with messages in Malayalam, that I didn't understand, and with Indian music that jolted me out of moments of concentration and reverie.

It had rained during the night, and when I awoke, I saw Trevor standing beside the bed.

"Showered, shaved, had my cuppa, and read twenty pages," Trevor said, and he kissed me. "I'm off to breakfast downstairs."

I nodded, still groggy. The night before, I had read too late. I had heard the rain and I had also heard Sanjay's pup Susie crying in the little closet under the staircase where she was locked in behind the wire gate with the male dog, who seemed interested in nothing other than sitting.

Trevor returned to the room. "The veg curry looks good."

"Give me a few minutes. I'll be down."

He sat alone on the upstairs terrace just outside the kitchen. I sat down with him.

"Can I have a wee taste?" The curry was delicious. I waited for someone to take my order. It was too spicy for my tastes with the dark red chili floating on top.

I walked up to the kitchen when no waiter arrived and asked Chef Rahul, "I'd like the same with two *parathas*, but no red chili on top."

Amin, who still needed to bathe, delivered my breakfast. Gregory, a visitor from Estonia, sat down at our table, uninvited. Gregory liked to talk. A lot. Too much, in fact. He took hostages. He said he was on his way to swim, thank heaven. Instead, he settled in for a chat. My hopes were dashed. He told us about his world travels. He said his family was wealthy, but he preferred to travel as cheaply as possible. He wrote poetry. He wanted to be free of obligations and commitments. Relationships confined him too much.

He boasted, "I can be with a woman maybe two hours a day. One hour for conversation and another for sex." He looked at me as if it were a dare. "I guess that's too European a discussion for an American."

"If you say so." I stared him down. Trevor watched the motormouth Estonian and me.

"I have a Jewish girlfriend in New York. We meet all over the world, but she's puritanical on a nude beach. She won't disrobe completely." He didn't understand how she could be so different when she was in private.

"Haven't you seen the Indian women walk into the sea in full saris here in Varkala? Have you seen an Indian woman here in a bathing costume or a bikini?" I asked.

Gregory stared at me and launched into a diatribe about how intelligent Americans were in some areas, how advanced, and how completely backwards they were in sociology, geography, and world history.

"Even a moron in Estonia knows where Uzbekistan and Kazakhstan are."

I said nothing. He was a jerk.

"I don't understand how Trevor and you can travel together and be together every day."

"We decided to go on our seven-month odyssey because we enjoy each other's company."

Of course we got on one another's nerves at times. We all needed privacy, alone time, time for reflection.

I'd listened to Gregory pontificate long enough. I stood up and looked at Trevor. "See ya, babe. I'm heading upstairs to write." Big mistake.

Gregory put his hand on my arm. "I want to ask a favor before you go."

Alarm bells rang, and I could see it coming. Gregory had thirty-five poems he wanted to send to a publisher. He asked me to proof them, to make sure his spelling was correct, and to make sure the words were the right words.

No. I wouldn't allow myself to get sucked in. I knew it would turn into a nightmare. I shook my head. "I don't have time. I came to India to write."

CHAPTER 24: *New and Different. Not Necessarily Better.*

We made the move to Mango Cottage with bags, suitcases, backpacks, and daypacks with all our bits and bobs from our room with the balcony. I looked at all our possessions with dismay. It was always chaos making a move.

I returned to the cottage after breakfast. The fan kept it cool inside, and it seemed quieter. I hoped I'd enjoy writing in the new setting. I took my computer outside to the small covered porch, but it was too hot, even with the breeze. So, I wrote inside on the bed.

I walked to Marina Bay Restaurant for ginger, lemon, and honey tea. It had been a sunny, hot, and humid morning for our move to Mango Cottage. After a light rain, it was damp and cool with a dark cloud cover.

I was tired. I hoped to fight off my scratchy throat and lethargy. The switch to the new room wasn't ideal, but the price was right. We were spoiled by low prices and delicious, inexpensive food. By the time we traveled to Thailand, we would have been in India for four months, conserving our finances. I was ready for Thailand and, who knew, maybe Myanmar, Laos, Cambodia, and Vietnam.

We had met amazing young travelers in India. The young people we met had made a break from what was expected of them. They questioned their lives and felt there must be more to life than the corporate world.

Tatyana and Liza had come up to the roof garden during a rainstorm while I worked at my writer's table. I wore my ear plugs, my back was to their table, and I ignored them while I wrote. At some point, I turned around and looked at them with a smile.

Liza asked, "Are we bothering you?"

"Not at all. I've written my quota for the morning and my brain is drained." I asked if I might sit down with them.

Tatyana was a delightful spirit from Bulgaria. She called Liza, a beauty from Soviet Georgia, and me her Sunshine Sisters. She addressed us as goddesses. Our chance meeting was "the refreshing."

CHAPTER 25: *Sanjay's Special Dinner*

Sanjay invited Trevor and me to share his birthday dinner. Special mutton. I took a tiny taste because, other than seafood, I didn't eat meat in India, especially not chicken. In Kerala, the cities of Alappuzha and Kottayam were under duress because deadly H5N1 virus had infected thousands of ducks and chickens and killed humans. Photos in *The Hindu Times* showed that none of those who were destroying the fowl wore protective gear or masks. They burned the infected and slaughtered animals. Villagers downwind from the toxic smoke were alarmed.

Did India have systems in place for epidemics? The papers reported there weren't enough antiviral drugs to take care of people. The first report said that four isolation rooms were prepared some-where. Trivandrum, maybe? In a rest home? Had the powers-that-be in India figured it was better to risk killing old folks? Shortly after the first news article, the papers reported that all the hospitals in Kerala had ramped up to deal with the epidemic and created isolation wards. Keralan authorities made sure they had enough of the antiviral drug to counter an outbreak. Oh, sweet Jesus. First there was Ebola. And now H5N1. I chose not to focus on the negative. I accentuated the positive. I kept on the sunny side. I was delusional.

Chef Rahul outdid himself in the kitchen and prepared a lovely veg curry with loads of vegetables and coconut milk that gave the dish a sweet, mild sauce. We had coconut rice with fresh curry leaves, raisins, almonds, and only one chili pepper. The mutton curry was ultra-spicy and tough, chewy, and not to my taste. One small piece was enough for me. Rahul prepared a lovely *palak paneer*. It was a beautiful green color. We enjoyed a special tapioca dish, although the one Rahul prepared didn't include the rhizomes like the tapioca at Toddy, thank heaven. All in all, it was a beautiful birthday dinner Sanjay shared with us.

The next morning, Scaredy Pup returned. She had given birth to her puppies, and she was overjoyed to see us. She talked in a loud, plaintive whine. She needed affection and food for the puppies. I fed her every day. Then Gregory, who took hostages, didn't respect boundaries, and loved to hear himself talk, moved into the small room adjoining Mango Cottage. The energy vampire was our new next-door neighbor. His fangs appeared and sucked our souls.

CHAPTER 26: *Strikes in Kerala.*
A Communist State

I sat at Bennie's little café cum coffee shop cum bookstore on the beach road and enjoyed a delicious iced coffee. Kerala was the striking-est place I'd ever seen. All the shopkeepers were on strike. Not only the shopkeepers from Varkala but shopkeepers from all over Kerala. They'd been to Trivandrum and descended on Varkala in droves. Men and women filed down the beach road in great numbers. The men wore mundus and the women dressed in saris. It was a colorful parade for a strike.

On Monday, bank workers went on strike. That threw things into a real kink. The ATM at the temple junction ran out of money on Sunday. It was another special holiday. At least, that's what I understood. I was never certain. There were oodles of Hindu pilgrims. As a result of the strike on Monday, Trevor didn't get money from the ATM at the temple junction for the second day in a row. He and Sanjay drove into Varkala and found a cash point in service.

The rainbow parade headed to the beach. Strikers blocked the beach road, and the cars, motorcycles, and tuk-tuks couldn't travel down the road at the usual breakneck pace. Since not many walkers returned from the beach, I imagined a mob scene on Papanasam Beach. The number of people in India never failed to amaze me.

CHAPTER 27: *Mission Hospital*

My nose was stuffy, my throat scratchy, and my undercarriage, as Trevor called the bits, itchy. I had a dreadful heat rash. It wasn't as bad as my allergic reaction to bed bugs in 2013.

The entrance to Varkala's Mission Hospital felt like the invitation "Abandon all hope, ye who enter here" from Dante's *Inferno*. It was a madhouse of saris, mundus, and hijabs. A hornet's nest of limps, crutches, wheelchairs, pregnant women, men, and boys and girls in Western garb. Trevor's ear was stopped up. He chatted with two patients who waited for the Ear, Nose, and Throat Doctor. I sat in the dark, bleak, sand-colored hallway with its one fan blowing hot air in the faces of the infirm. The lights went out shortly after we arrived. I didn't feel well, and I didn't want to talk to anyone. Did I have a sinus infection? I didn't want to join a queue to see a doctor. I felt paranoid about infirmity. Germs thrived in the Tropic of Capricorn heat and humidity. I imagined little germ cheerleaders with pompoms in a sideline routine.

An Indian man wearing a filthy mundu walked past and sneezed without covering his nose. Aargh! I screamed a silent scream. The lights went out again, flickered, and turned back on. I was curious about hospitals in India. Why were entire families crowded into the doctors' offices? Even the gynecologist's office had eight family members jam-packed into and outside the small room, separated from the poorly lit hall by a sheer curtain. A hospital worker painted the floor gray with a filthy mop and dirty water.

CHAPTER 28: *Cultures, Countries, and Other People's Dreams*

We went to Abba Restaurant for breakfast on the clifftop and joined Liza.

Liza said, "I'm from Russia, but I was brought up in Kazakhstan." She talked about the breakup of the USSR and how difficult it was for Russians who were born in Russia and whose families, farms, and businesses were in Russia to be thrust into a newly formed state.

I'd never considered the impact of such a divide, but why would I? I'd led an insular life in the US. It was only on this adventure, and my last visit to India, that I had learned so much about other people's cultures, philosophies, and dreams. We shared one thing in Varkala. Most of the people with whom I talked were on a spiritual path. Some people found it in an ashram. Others found their spiritual life in yoga. And others found their spiritual truths through meditation or by going to the temples or to the mosques or to the Catholic Syrian churches. Who was to say what was the right path?

"Liza, I came to Varkala to write." I expressed my regret for not taking part in yoga classes with all the opportunities in Varkala.

Liza asked, "Do you mean the Asanas?"

"And the pranayama."

"But yoga is focus," she countered. "You practice yoga when you focus."

I realized I was more at peace, more in balance, less stressed, and far more content than I had been for a long time. I felt a strong center. I was glad to have the opportunity to write and grateful for Trevor's support when he showed it. I was thrilled to meet all the young people who shared their dreams and their youthful energy.

I embraced an understanding. Although I wasn't practicing yoga asanas, I hadn't failed in my mission in Varkala. I had come to write. It was inexpensive to live in India, compared to the United States, but Lorenzo, a young Italian who'd joined us, and Liza said, in unison, "Varkala is expensive."

Lorenzo said, "Where I stay, the floor is sand. It's a bamboo hut with a cot and a mosquito net, no electricity. The facilities are communal."

I didn't want to do that again. The treehouse in Gokarna had been a sufficient test of my Girl Scout skills. I preferred modern conveniences that included an en suite bathroom, even if there was no hot water.

Liza, Lorenzo, Trevor, and I talked about how all of us—on our respective journeys from our individual countries—could share experiences, have fellowship, and accept one another as we were. Political differences, religious choices, even the warring factions didn't divide us. We held our own United Nations assembly over shared meals in Varkala—U.K., US, Russia, Bulgaria, Ukraine, France, and Italy.

"The Russians are fed misinformation through the media," Liza said.

"I think it's a problem no matter what country you claim as home," I agreed.

What we knew, in most instances, was what we were told. We didn't question. We didn't challenge. And, if we did question, we were labeled un-American, or in Thailand, we risked being thrown in prison.

Liza said, "In Russia, we might find ourselves thrown into a gulag."

How did we get along? When I sat down for a cup of *masala chai* with a lovely young Russian woman, a Cold War didn't divide us. I visited Muslim shopkeepers with beautiful young children, and we were interested in one another. We weren't at war, but many Americans I knew had hearts full of fear. Some people grouped all Muslims into a collective terrorist cell. I was dismayed when I read social media posts and saw friends of friends who wanted to "nuke all the goat-humpers." It never occurred to our American friends that the Europeans, Muslims, Russians, and others saw our country as the most violent in the world, and the most racist with the black and white divide.

While I was out of the country, I watched Ferguson, Missouri, implode and set off another great racial schism. I watched as a choke-hold verdict in New York launched another wave of protests with coffins in the streets and signs telling folks to stop racism and racial profiling. It must have been so disheartening to the black community to have gained so much since the 1950s only to see there was still such hatred and prejudice in our country, nearly seventy years later.

"I rent a little house near the black beach and the shrimp hatchery," Liza said. "It's in a Muslim community, and it's a place where I feel accepted." She continued, "I have a dog and a white rat."

"A white rat?" I was surprised.

"An albino."

Liza said she was respectful of the Muslims and wore a cover-up to walk to the beach, but she said many of the children didn't wear head coverings. It was fascinating to learn about the young Russian woman who followed the yoga path instead of working as a veterinarian, for which she had trained. A woman who lived in a Muslim neighborhood and felt safe and accepted. Wasn't it wonderful we could enjoy peaceful coexistence in Varkala?

After Lorenzo joined us at the table, our conversation turned to literature and writing. He asked if I had read the Japanese author Murakami.

He said, "Murakami's magical realism is fabulous."

Liza asked questions about the writing process. "I'm writing. How is writing a film script different from a novel?"

"Film scripts are lean."

"What do you mean?"

I gave her an example from a script opening. I hadn't forgotten screenwriter Shane Black's words. "Snowflakes assault the windowpane." The first words in his script said it eloquently. The image of soft white snow assaulting anything was a powerful way to begin a thriller or an action-adventure script.

CHAPTER 29: *Sunday Night at Papanasam Beach*

We listened to the waves sound on the sand. The lights of a hundred fishing boats twinkled on the horizon where the night sky met the Arabian Sea. Hindu Karaoke competed with the sound effects of the waves. It was Malayalam music. We heard sitar and flute, as well as electric organ. Whoever held the mike seemed to know what he was doing, at last. Thank heaven. The other singer had sounded as if he were gargling out of tune. A breeze blew in off the sea. It was a gentle night after a very hot day.

The beach road was packed with cars and motorcycles when we left the hotel. Sundays were a circus on the beach, especially at sunset, when a mad rush of Indian men, women, and children splashed in the sea fully clothed. No bikinis in sight.

CHAPTER 30: *Mission Hospital. Again*

It was our third visit to Varkala's hospital. The second visit had been to see a skin doctor for the infection I couldn't shake with baking soda and water splash baths, or cortisone cream. The skin doctor visit was an in-and-out experience, efficient and quick. We thought our third visit would be short—a pro forma chat with a psychiatrist who would write my prescription for an antidepressant refill. Wrong. We waited in a rundown building across from the main building. Painted a sickly industrial green, the building hadn't seen a facelift in its lifetime.

The Psychiatrist's Office and the Physiotherapy Department were on the ground floor where we waited to see the doctor. It was open to the elements, with only metal screens between us and the outside road where tuk-tuks, motorcycles, cars, and pedestrians polluted the air with fumes, smoke from a rubbish fire, and coughing, sneezing, and gob spitting to clear throats. My eyes burned.

Two ladies in saris sat across from me. Both women looked depressed. Three men sat on a white wooden bench outside the psychiatrist's office. An older man with his two sons, I guessed. The father sat, a broken man, his head in his hands. The sons, unhappy with the wait, paced back and forth inside and outside the grimy building.

Student nurses walked past and up to the second floor School of Nursing, wearing crisp white short-sleeved coats over a gray uniform—tunic and pants. They smiled as they caught my eye. We waited an hour and a half. The father went in and out in a few minutes. The lady who had ushered us to the building said we were next. We finally saw the doctor and got my prescription. It was remarkable and baffling how things worked in India.

A day earlier, when we entered the Casualty Ward at the hospital as we had been instructed by one of the doctors, I had been struck again by how dilapidated the room was. A badly crippled young boy lay on one of the three beds. He wore an oxygen mask and was hooked up to a machine recording his vital signs. His pulse was too rapid, and the machine kept stopping. I feared the child was dying. The boy was surrounded by family members draped in worn saris. The child had tiny little twig legs. One was badly bent at an unnatural angle with his left foot turned round on his leg, so it pointed the wrong way. He wouldn't have been able to walk. He was a baby bird fallen from the nest, a soft gray body with feathers unformed. I marveled at how the child survived, and my heart went out to the family. Trevor and I declined the doctor's invitation to sit on the hospital bed next to the bed the child occupied while we waited.

CHAPTER 31: *Fawlty Towers*

I cast John Cleese with his Indian counterpart, and his sidekick Manuel with an Indian as well. The scene at the hotel resembled the theatre of the absurd. Every day, we saw something baffling. One morning, while Trevor and I ate breakfast, we watched a new waiter walk halfway down the steps, where he was met by another new waiter with a plate with two pieces of bread.

The Passion Fruit Café downstairs was on the street level. The restaurant was on the terrace between the entrance and the hotel's first floor. The new waiter walked up the steps from the café and handed the plate to New Waiter Number One, who walked up the steps to the terrace and the kitchen. He handed the plate of toast to the chef, who added an omelet.

The chef arranged the toast that was kind of toast, but not really. He handed the plate back to New Waiter Number Two, who carried the plate with breakfast up another flight of steps to the roof garden dining area, where an unknowing customer had no idea his or her toast had completed such an illustrious journey from street level to rooftop before he or she ate it. The toast couldn't have been hot or even warm by the time it reached the customer. Trevor and I were stunned.

"Chef Rahul has lost the plot," Trevor said.

"Why doesn't he have a loaf of bread in the kitchen?"

"Why not get a second toaster?" Trevor laughed.

Meanwhile, our dirty breakfast dishes sat on a nearby table where Trevor set them, the bowl with leftover fruit attracting a host of swarming flies.

The derelict building site across the road was under noisy renovation. The machine sawed metal. Added to the noise on the beach road, loudspeakers at the temple pumped out bizarre music. Tuk-tuks puttered past, motorcycles whizzed by with loud mufflers, and an old white Ambassador cab with a huge loudspeaker mounted on its roof blasted Bollywood songs. I'd dropped into an Indian music festival, spirited away, and I was tied to a chair facing speakers set up on stage. I couldn't escape the noise. Not on the beach road, not in the small café, not on the terrace where we sat, nor on the roof garden. We couldn't escape the cacophony in the privacy of Mango Cottage where it seemed we were in a fishbowl at times.

CHAPTER 32: *Fawlty Towers' Revolving Cast of Characters*

The two new housekeepers fought with each other. A young cleaning woman swept while an older woman made the beds, but neither cleaned as well as the former housekeeper. The young housekeeper swept nonstop. She attacked leaves outside Mango Cottage twice a day with a crude straw broom and peered at me through the windows. It was disconcerting and interrupted my writing when Trevor went for a swim. The broom's *scritch, scratch, scritch* irritated me. She swept at 8:45 a.m. and engaged her clean-sweep broom again in the early afternoon. The young woman leaned over to sweep with her right hand, her left hand behind her back, palm facing outwards, because the homemade broom was too short for her to sweep upright. I wondered if the method, as well as the means, were leftovers from the days in which Untouchables swept and moved backwards to exit a room. The pecking order at the hotel was clear, and cleaning women weren't on top.

When the two housekeepers had completed their tasks, they sat on the steps to the third floor where Arjun held yoga classes. The women ignored each other on the staircase under a large, wooden spinning wheel set in the masonry wall. The spinning wheel window, which had no glass or screen, offered ventilation, and mosquitos had access to unsuspecting guests, free of charge.

One afternoon, I met the hotel's new Ayurvedic female masseuse. I walked down the uneven, rocky slope between the hotel and an old brick wall because the staircase entrance to the hotel had wet paint.

The woman, maybe in her forties, pushed her skills while I made my way down the awkward slope, punctuated by uneven rocks. She took advantage of my slow descent.

"Come to my Ayurveda treatment. I will make you look fifteen years younger."

Her annoying sales pitch implied I needed to look fifteen years younger.

"I give you massage today."

Her pushiness irritated me. "Not now, but thanks." Oh boy, was that a mistake. It opened the door of possibility.

"Tomorrow, I give you massage."

"Thanks, but no thanks. I'll let you know."

The woman stalked me for days. Whenever she saw me descend the slope, she approached me, hawking her skills.

"You look fifteen years younger after Ayurvedic treatment."

To shut her up, I told her my husband wouldn't give me any money. Eventually, the middle-aged masseuse left, and two new young, attractive sari-clad Indian women appeared. Their sandals sat outside the Ayurvedic Treatment Center. Occasionally, I saw a woman go inside the center and leave with oily hair. Unfortunately, the young women availed themselves of the terrace outside Mango Cottage daily. They picked berries and talked on their cell phones.

CHAPTER 33: *The Menu Mystery*

Meanwhile, back at the restaurant, Chef Rahul expanded his culinary repertoire. A new menu featured more than 150 dishes.

"I'd like Kashmiri curry," Trevor said.

"Not possible."

"What about . . . ?"

No matter what we ordered, it wasn't available.

Trevor was irritated. "Oh, for fuck's sake."

"Let's just ask what is available."

"Bloody hell, Jesse." Trevor swore loudly.

"Trevor, he's a diva." It didn't matter that we were guests at the hotel.

The night before, when Trevor and I returned from dinner at Marina Bay, I had spied Sanjay watching us from his bedroom.

"Trevor, Sanjay is housemother at the hostel checking up on us."

Trevor nodded. "Constant surveillance."

Sanjay lurked, listened, and kept an eye on all things at the hotel.

"It's unnerving, babe. Please don't encourage any more familiarity."

"A fat lot of good that's gonna do, Jesse." Trevor put his arm around me.

I didn't want to engage in more than a polite *hello, good morning, good night,* or *how are you* with the staff. Hadn't we learned the lesson in our travels? Familiarity bred contempt and opened floodgates for people to recount their woes—illness, hunger, money problems. No one hesitated to ask us for money.

CHAPTER 34: *Running the Gauntlet.*
Third Black Moon.
Papanasam Beach

Some days I felt as if the whole world had gone mad. The Sunday before Christmas was one of those days, and the tears locked inside me—though they wanted desperately to be released—refused to fall.

I walked to the beach in the morning and headed toward Marina Bay. Of course, I ran the gauntlet of cars, motorcycles, tuk-tuks, men in mundus, women in saris, and babies whose eyes were blackened with kohl. The mayhem increased the closer I got to the beach. The Ambassador cab with the huge amplifier strapped on top blasted its deafening tunes. Hindu pilgrims on the beach ignored the cacophony. I imagined for a nanosecond what would happen if I leapt on the roof of the old white taxi and ripped out the massive loudspeaker's wires. I stared daggers into the driver's face and suddenly the sound stopped. It was dead quiet for a blissful moment. As soon as the loudspeaker was silent, the other background noises erupted.

Papanasam beach was a teeming, swarming mass of pilgrims, colorful beach umbrellas, saffron-clad priests, stray dogs, the tea wallah, and Western tourists with cameras. It was the third black moon celebration since we arrived in Varkala. I debated, as I sat in the restaurant, whether to celebrate my mother's death in the ritual. How was honoring one's loved one on a beach in India any different than in any other part of the world? I concluded there was no difference, but I decided not to join the hundreds of people on the beach.

Incongruously, amid the sacred I viewed the profane. People filled bag after white bag with sand and lined the bags, one after another, on the sacred part of the beach. The visitors erected a net and set up a sand volleyball court between the beach umbrellas. It was a zoo. Indian pilgrims by the hundreds, priests on the beach by two score, and in the middle of it all—a volleyball court. Tall palm trees lay on the sand near the court and two stacks of red plastic chairs perched on the edge of the uneven volcanic stone sidewalk.

CHAPTER 35: *Not Every Day's A Diamond*

I was depressed. I'd allowed Trevor to see my vulnerability. Was I a burden to him? Did my despondency weigh him down and prevent him from enjoying travel? It seemed as if that was what he implied.

"Jesse, I'm not going to come to America without traveling to other parts of your country."

I felt as if he had punched me in the gut. "Where did that come from?" The timing couldn't have been more painful.

"I don't want to feel responsible for you financially."

"I never asked, Trevor."

When I returned to America, I'd continue freelance writing. I had accepted Trevor's help for two months while I waited for the realtor to rent my house. Meanwhile, he had stayed in my home when he visited, but he didn't pay my mortgage. I was desperately sad. I'd opened my heart. Did I feel sorry for myself? I needed to let go of control and have faith. I had prayed all night long the night before, awakened by a puppy crying in the unfinished building nearby. Desperation in the hours after midnight. My way wasn't clear. I had to detach, or I wouldn't survive. Not every day's a diamond, but I sure didn't want to be shoveling coal.

After a good cry and a talk with Trevor, we walked downstairs to the roof garden where Chef Rahul prepared a beautiful Kerala meal on a banana leaf. I enjoyed finger painting with food and mixed all the colorful sauces—at least eight—with the short-grained rice. It was delicious.

CHAPTER 36: *Maya Means Illusion*

It was Christmas Day and I felt downtrodden, as if I were an old shoe in a pile of single shoes in a rundown Salvation Army donation bin. The numbness that kept sorrow at bay was a carefully honed survival skill. Mia, a Swedish lady and one of the investors in Abba Restaurant, had invited Trevor and me to join the fun on Christmas Eve, have dinner, and meet Santa on the lawn to exchange small gifts. Christmas holidays on the Arabian Sea.

Christmas Eve had turned into a very strange affair. I dressed up for a fun evening celebration in the Christmas spirit on the clifftop at Abba Restaurant. We showed up at 6 p.m., after buying some trinkets for the Grab Bag that Santa carried when he gave out the gifts. It was an annual tradition, and we were the first guests to arrive.

Tables with candles, flowers, and chairs were set up under a tent for those Mia had invited to the special dinner. Everything was going smoothly until our hostess said, "Our Santa is sick and won't make it."

"I'm sorry, Mia. Everything looks beautiful. Trevor and I put our gifts in the Grab Bag."

She turned to Trevor and asked, "Will you be Santa tonight?"

Trevor looked stunned and had a strange look on his face. I couldn't read it.

"Santa's costume is over there." Mia pointed to the white beard and red suit draped over one of the chairs. "You carry the Grab Bag and hand out the presents to all the guests."

How fun, I thought. I could not have been more wrong.

Trevor flipped out. "I ain't doing it." He turned his back to us and walked away.

Mia looked shocked. "What on earth?"

"I have no idea what just happened."

I shook my head, torn between staying or following Trevor, who stood next to the brick path on the clifftop and waited for me, his expression like a gathering storm.

"Something's wrong. Forgive me, Mia. I need to leave." I started to cry.

She put her hand on my shoulder. "Please don't worry, Jesse."

I followed Trevor past the restaurants and shops, all brightly lit to celebrate Christmas. Tourists crowded the brick path. We walked in silence and in single file until we reached the helipad, where I grabbed Trevor's hand.

"What in the world is wrong?"

"I don't want to talk about it."

"Help me understand. It was rude to walk away from our hostess."

He pulled his hand away. "I ain't playing the fool."

He didn't say another word for the rest of the night. Nothing like being shut out on Christmas Eve. Trevor's demons must have plagued him, but he refused to spend time in self-reflection. And my own demons haunted me.

CHAPTER 37: *Ten Days till Thailand*

During our travels, I had time for reflection. I thought a lot about character. According to the British psychiatrist who spoke to our screenwriting group in Los Angeles, character reveals itself through action over time. I thought about the significance of the number forty in Hindu culture as the period of mourning a death. The number forty represented closure. At least, that was what I understood. I wanted to let go of the last vestiges of my people-pleasing. Another awareness was about individuals I had met along the journey. Each one had a lesson for me, if I was attuned to it. What was Trevor's lesson for me, and why did I bend over backward to make things go smoothly?

CHAPTER 38: *C&B Scene*

"Breakfast, Jesse? How about Marina Bay?"

On our walk to the beach, I spied an ancient bicycle parked outside the Donkey Cada Café. The bike rack behind the seat was loaded with two-by-fours.

"Crikey, babe." Trevor pointed to the bike.

"It's Indian ingenuity."

We passed a man in a dirty mundu with a filthy turban wrapped around his head. He was rail thin with skinny legs and carried a bamboo ladder and a hemp rope. We watched as he climbed the coconut tree.

Somehow, despite and maybe because of the dysfunction we saw, everything worked. If there were rules, they were broken.

"Maybe there aren't any rules, Jesse. Nobody knows what to do, so they just play it by ear."

The signs at the beach were clear. *No Parking by Order of the Varkala Police.* Motorcycles lined up at the entrance to the beach. We walked sideways to reach the sidewalk and headed to Marina Bay Restaurant aka C&B Scene. The beach was packed with more sightseers than pilgrims, the Brahmin priests, and the puja ritual. By the time we reached the restaurant and ordered breakfast, my nerves danced like Mexican jumping beans. Trevor picked up on it. The morning's chaos had thrown me.

Earlier, three kitchen staffers had clambered over pieces of tin roofing over the wall from our terrace. I lost my train of thought and commotion interrupted my writing. They were on a mission to retrieve five puppies in the abandoned building at the back of the lot next to the hotel.

Trevor popped into the cottage. "Bloody hell, Jesse. The chef left and no one is cooking."

"A new twist in the drama at Fawlty Towers."

"People are sitting at tables in the restaurant. There's no food upstairs."

"What about downstairs?"

"You can get an omelet or coffee in the café downstairs, but the kitchen staff are milling around on the terrace. They ain't doing a thing. Not one of the wankers is cooking."

I gave up on my writing and went downstairs.

"Trevor, is there a sign to let people know the restaurant is closed?"

"The chef lost the plot."

No one was minding the store. Dysfunction junction. Trevor's expression was glacial. He clenched and unclenched his fists, beside himself with frustration. I had a moment of clarity. I had allowed myself to get caught up in the chaos. It was impossible to write.

Three hours later, I returned to Mango Cottage and hoped to get back on track with my writing. Fireworks went off with loud explosions at the temple, sounds for the tympani section of the Varkala symphony. Crows entertained with raucous caws. Motorcycles beeped their hooters. I put in my earplugs, but I heard Scrawny Cat gnawing, crunch, crunch, crunch, on Purina Dog biscuits. She wasn't scrawny anymore.

Later, we walked to Kerala Spice Shop, where we met Swedish yoga instructor Britt, *ja*, like Eklund. She told us she came to India each year to teach an eight-week course. While I talked with the shop-keeper, Britt turned her body toward Trevor who sat beside her about eight feet away from me. He talked, joked, and charmed as only he could, and Britt posed, one knee crossed over the other, toe pointed down like a ballet dancer. She removed the scarf she had draped around her shoulders and faced Trevor with her head resting on her palm, devouring every word. Trevor ate up the attention from the attractive woman. Britt wore a small tank top with spaghetti straps, *OM* written on the front. She pushed out her braless chest with her tiny breasts and nipples, proud to invite attention and touch. She leaned toward Trevor.

When we first met, Trevor had introduced me to Britt as his partner. Her behavior was cheeky. I watched the drama unfold, and

I'd had enough. I finished my pineapple juice and muttered *sotto voce*, "I'm outta here." I'd choke on fresh pineapple juice and die if I had to watch Miss Little Nipples' courtship dance.

"Hey, babe, I need the keys to the room. I'll see you later."

Before I left, the toothless former drug addict walked into the scene. He was a Swedish guy about our age, overweight, a heavy smoker. Wild white hair curled, unruly and desperately in need of a trim, in a nimbus surrounding his florid face. His one tooth appeared to be loose on the bottom gum. The night before, I had learned that he'd OD'd on drugs nine times. It was a miracle he had lived to tell the story, whatever that was. The drugs had fried his brain. He knew what was going on and was able to carry on a normal conversation. Kind of. However, his affect was off. In the middle of a conversation, he would turn his head and face away from the person to whom he was speaking and laugh like a loon at some private joke. More likely a misfiring in the brain. His behavior was unrelated to the situation at hand. It was disconcerting, to say the least. Between his heavy smoking and the bizarre behavior, the guy had become an anathema to Trevor. Fortunately for me, the big nutter showed up.

"I ain't staying," Trevor said. "I can't stand the wanker."

CHAPTER 39: *Morning Mayhem*

 amiliar sounds punctuated the morning's brief peace. Arjun sang his prayer for his rooftop yoga class. His picture adorned a large poster on the side of the building facing the street—a true Indian yoga contortionist. *In-haaaaaale . . . ex-haaaaaale.* The crows' cacophony. Cleaning lady with her broom, *skritch, scratch, skritch.* Gunpowder explosions at the temple, motorcycles revving up, tuk-tuks' chug-a-lug motors, and beeping hooters of various vehicles. Perhaps it was a meditation as well. I longed to escape Varkala, but when we reached Thailand in nine days, I wasn't sure whether I'd find relief or frustration. Would I have time to write?

I wanted to order breakfast downstairs, but Chef Rahul had been gone two days. The kitchen was closed. Ajay in the Passion Fruit Café was the only person available to make breakfast. Maybe it was irrational, but I was afraid his negativity would infuse the food he prepared for me—negative voices in his head, the world too sad a place. I smiled at Ajay, but it wasn't in my heart. He didn't return the smile. *Like Water for Chocolate* and the characters in Salman Rushdie's book *Midnight's Children* came to mind. The emotions they felt went into the foods they cooked. Bitterness, jealousy, anger, and hatred were the negative spices in the food the characters prepared.

"Ajay, I'd like an omelet, please."

"Not possible."

Over the months we'd been in Kerala that was the standard answer when anyone in the kitchen didn't want to be bothered. Since the chef left, Ajay hadn't wanted to prepare meals.

CHAPTER 40: *Extraordinary Times in India*

Xi, Putin, and Obama courted India. Extraordinary times, I thought, when *The Hindu Times* reported Narendra Modi's international travels with the purported goal of international alliances. One writer said, "India succumbs to the allure of good PR and believes the aggrandizement of the publicity."

It wasn't grounded in what I saw as reality. India was in a sea of messy change. Sometimes transitions were bloody. The border of Assam in the far northeast of India was closed by Bhutan, the neighboring country. Terrorists massacred tribal peoples in Assam. Dissension and terrorism took place at India's border with Pakistan. The Taliban attacked a military school and killed more than 140 children to send a message. What was the message?

And when I thought I'd seen it all, I read a newspaper article about a case being filed against Guru Ram Rahmin for alleged castration.

"Trevor, you're not going to believe this."

He looked up. "What?"

"This article in *The Hindu Times* is about a bizarre twist on life in an ashram." I read the article out loud. "Dera Sacha Sauda's Gurmeet Ram Rahmin Singh forced the castration of more than 400 of his followers—himself included—at his ashram Sirsa in Haryana."

"It's a load of old bollocks."

"I don't know, Trevor. India's Central Bureau of Investigation (CBI) is investigating the guru. He's already facing a trial for alleged murder and sexual exploitation of female disciples."

CHAPTER 41: *Do Our Desires Jibe?*

It was New Year's Eve. How had it arrived so quickly? At 3 a.m., a tuk-tuk powered noisily down the beach road, beeped its hooter, and woke me. Gunpowder blasts resounded from the temple in rapid succession, starting at 6 a.m. Trevor slept through it all.

Thousands of yellow-clad pilgrims walked from the ashram to Papanasam Beach on New Year's Eve and would do it again on New Year's Day. Cars, tuk-tuks, motorcycles, and large passenger buses filled with pilgrims rolled down the beach road.

I limped toward gratitude. I didn't want to venture out of the cocoon into which I had retreated. I'd grab hold of gratitude for what was and release my death grip on the old as well as the endless, imagined tomorrows. We'd gotten to know other travelers while we stayed in Varkala, but we were too familiar with the hotel staff. Trevor wanted to help and got involved in the drama at Fawlty Towers every day. I wanted nothing to do with the dysfunction, even though it was entertaining at times.

The night before, on the walk back from dinner, we had stepped around piles of trash. ChocoBar wrappers by the hundreds, little ice cream cups, all the flotsam and jetsam and rubbish the Indian visitors threw on the ground at the beach littered an otherwise beautiful view of the Arabian Sea and sacred Papanasam Beach. Beach sweepers arrived in the morning to clean with homemade brooms, blue lab coats over their saris and baseball caps on their heads—the cleaning lady's uniform. For every instance of dysfunction we experienced, I witnessed the functioning opposite.

I tried to stay in the day. I fought not to worry about my future. It wasn't easy to replace my fear with my life-preserving, sanity-making faith. Letting go daily was a struggle. I tried to think of ways to fix it, and I knew money would make things easier. If we had more money on our travels, I'd move into an AC accommodation in a heartbeat. A week of air conditioning would help get rid of the skin rash I'd had for the past two months. That didn't include the fungal infection that had sent me to the hospital, albeit reluctantly, for a consultation and medication to get rid of ringworm blisters.

Trevor wasn't bothered by the heat, didn't get skin infections, didn't have a clue how painful and debilitating it was, and appeared to have no empathy. I didn't feel sorry for myself, but it put a damper on any kind of romantic thoughts. I didn't know if I would ever return to India, but I'd learned never to say never. Trevor said he saw himself alone in his old age. I preferred not to imagine myself alone. It was past time to think about how my desires and his wishes jibed or didn't, as the case might be.

The early-morning sounds of songbirds, the brahminy kites' shrill whistle, and a monkey's hoots greeted us our last morning in Varkala. I felt apprehensive. Despite the dysfunction and our frustration, Fawlty Towers had been home for four months. Our last night was wonderful. We ate delicious Fish Malabari, only fitting since we ate our evening meal overlooking the Arabian Sea on the Malabar Coast; and we watched a beautiful sunset on Papanasam Beach while we drank a large pot of ginger, lemon, and honey tea.

The past two days had been stressful. Another fucking adventure. SpiceJet had sent us an email at the last minute. Our flight to Bangkok was canceled. SpiceJet had changed the first leg of our flight to Mumbai. Our flight arrived after the flight from Mumbai to Kolkata left. How bizarre to send out a new flight schedule with an impossible connection to reach Bangkok. How perfectly predictable!

Trevor came to the room in an absolute panic as I sat down to write. I was so happy to get back into a routine, but as Robert Burns wrote, "The best-laid plans of mice and men . . . " We spent two hours on SpiceJet's website. It was impossible. An illogical, maddening infinite loop returned me to the starting point. I wondered what sadistic programmer had created it.

"Trevor, there's only one thing we can do."

"What?" His face was contorted with anxiety.

"Go to the airport in Trivandrum and sort the dilemma face-to-face."

He looked stunned. "You're kidding."

"The phone lines will be impossible, babe. And even if we reach Customer Service, we won't understand one another to explain the problem."

Trevor balked at my suggestion. It took an hour to convince him because my solution would cost a round-trip cab fare. He finally agreed to my plan. Sometimes, he worried so much about money that it got in the way of what we needed to do to take care of ourselves. He couldn't sort the problems, so the stress became mine. I grew impatient and irritable. I couldn't control SpiceJet and its dysfunction. Our plans to fly to Bangkok were an utter mess.

After the tense breakfast that I had choked down because Trevor misdirected his anger over the circumstances at me, we took a cab to Trivandrum—an hour-and-a-half ride. We weren't sure whether it was the International Terminal or the Domestic Terminal. Finding a helpful person at the Domestic Terminal, we sorted the problem quickly. However, it meant we had to go to Mumbai at least one day early if we were to fly on SpiceJet.

"Let's go on Sunday," Trevor said. "We like Mumbai. We'll spend a day there, stay at the Hotel Lawrence, and we won't have such a long flight to Bangkok."

"Sounds like a great plan." It seemed reasonable at the time.

We returned to Varkala. OMG, what a trip! You'd think a cab ride—it was air conditioned, thank heaven—would be an uneventful experience, but nothing was ever as it was planned. We had near accidents, near misses in which I gasped or squeezed Trevor's hand. Why did I find it stressful in a motor vehicle in India on highways, such as they were, under construction or in poor repair? Maybe I'd feel safe riding in an armored truck.

By the time we got back, it was after five o'clock. A day wasted and I was wasted as well. Since we were starving, we ate at the hotel. I had a delicious veg curry with coconut rice and Trevor had *Paneer Kadala*. Paneer was misspelled Pioneer on the menu. Chef Rahul, who had returned after his disappearance, worked miracles in his small open-air kitchen. Trevor watched the chef, talked with him, and recorded videos of Rahul making his dishes. The chef was flattered and loved Trevor's attention. He enjoyed talking with the chef and the guys who worked in the restaurant. So much for too much familiarity. I fell asleep quickly, and the next morning, I looked forward to a pedicure and relaxation after I packed a box of clothing to ship back home. Of course, things changed.

CHAPTER 42: *Muslim Parade and the Post Office*

I awoke excited about a day dedicated to writing 1,000 words. The morning's meditation brought focus, and I felt calm, looking forward to a well-planned day. Trevor said he'd take care of shipping the box. We talked about our lodgings in Mumbai. Trevor planned to book the Hotel Lawrence with its nasty shared bathrooms. I should have known I wouldn't have a leisurely morning to pack my suitcase and enjoy a relaxing pedicure in the afternoon.

"I'm heading downstairs for coffee, Jesse."

"What do you think about asking Sanjay to help you phone the Hotel Lawrence and book our room for two nights?"

Trevor nodded. "See ya."

I leapt through my morning's cold shower while Trevor made reservations. At least we knew what to experience at the Mumbai hotel aka flophouse. It was 9:30 a.m. I took the box downstairs.

Trevor and Sanjay called a number with the wrong area code for Mumbai. The first delay. Then they discovered the Hotel Lawrence was full, as was every other low-rent, hole-in-the-wall lodging for a penny-pinching, senior traveling man. Trevor paced back and forth, stressed. I had to escape the chaos.

"I'll take the box to the post office while y'all sort hotel reservations."

Trevor pressed his lips together, the muscles in his face tense.

I figured it would take an hour to mail the package. I could come back to the hotel, have a nice breakfast, pack my suitcase, and get my pedicure. Sanjay phoned a tuk-tuk driver for me in between phone calls to Mumbai. He and Trevor had a strange conversation with a dodgy character in Mumbai who wouldn't give them the nightly rate for the hotel.

Dodgy Character said, "I will tell you the rate when you get here at 11 p.m. Sunday night."

Sanjay asked the Indian, "Where are you from?"

"Trivandrum," Dodgy Character said.

Sanjay switched from Hindi to Malayalam and listened a moment. "He hung up on me."

I got into the tuk-tuk and off we went to town. We were on our way, or were we? Out of the blue, we found ourselves in the middle of a parade. Last weekend, a Yellow Parade had celebrated the Indian Guru. Saturday's celebration was a Green Parade for Muslims. Thousands of Muslims of all ages walked along the road and carried green flags. The men wore white tunics, trousers, and caps. The little girls' heads were covered. Everyone chanted. Big trucks with loudspeakers blasted songs and young guys sat atop the speakers with legs dangling.

"What's going on?" I asked the driver.

"Festival."

Good Lord, folks in Hindustan loved a good party, or festival, or parade. It was always colorful and at an ear-splitting volume. I took a video of the parade. We reached the shop where the man packed boxes, next door to the man who ironed clothes with hot coals inside an iron. A narrow alley near the post office was festooned with colorful ribbons. An archway of pink and white covered the length of the alley to a large building at the end of the lane.

The tuk-tuk driver said, "Post office is closed. Is holiday."

Oh, shit, I thought.

We took the box into a packing shed, a tiny room lit with a single naked bulb and a wooden plank for a shelf. Packing Guy got a double-lined box and said, "Watch me."

I was puzzled as I watched him repack the box. He took every item from my box and placed it in his box in a different order.

"Hold the box and help me tape it."

I followed his instructions. He wanted me to know he hadn't taken any of my belongings. After he packed and taped the box, he wrapped it in a white waterproof bag. I was in the way. I went outside on a narrow concrete porch where I watched the Muslim Green Parade. Packing Guy stitched the four corners at the end of the box. He didn't tape it. Instead, he sewed it with a strong thread.

Before he finished sewing the box, I asked, "The post office is closed?"

"No, open."

After Packing Guy wrapped and sewed the box, he sealed the edges with wax.

"You write address to and from on outside."

I paid him for materials and labor. It was a lot more interesting than going to the UPS Store. The tuk-tuk driver picked up the package and carried it to the post office, where I waited in line. The back of the room was antiquated. Eight workers hand-sorted mail at a long wooden table. Three women stood on one side of the table and five men sat on the other side. The post office was a place out of time.

When I returned to the hotel, I stumbled up the steps to the terrace and spied Trevor at a table.

"We didn't make a hotel reservation in Mumbai."

"Why not?"

He scowled at me but didn't answer.

"Let me guess. You couldn't find a hotel room for less than a thousand rupees a night."

"Last weekend of the holidays. Rooms are expensive until Monday." He spat out the words.

"Trevor, we have to book a place in Mumbai."

Trevor didn't want to spend any money. He walked off. After he left, I booked and paid for a hotel with decent ratings. We were set for our travel to Bangkok.

PART IV

Southeast Asia 2015

Thailand

CHAPTER 1: *Siam Gypsy Junction. Bangkok, Thailand*

*E*arly one morning, as we were leaving to go see Wat Pho palace in Bangkok, I learned that a good friend had died of pancreatic cancer. I was sad and had a sore stomach from a twenty-four-hour bug.

Trevor didn't get it. "I'm ready to explore."

Why did he ignore me when I said I felt ill? The night before, he had been in his fear place over money.

"I don't think I have enough money to travel in Thailand."

"We're here, Trevor. Why did you agree to fly here?"

My question set him off. He launched an attack.

"How are you going to go back to the USA without a job?"

"What makes you think I'm not able to live on my own?"

He was furious.

"Don't project your own fear about money. I live in today, in the moment."

"That's stupid. You ignore reality, Jesse."

"No, I'm looking ahead at my life and planning to do freelance writing again."

"Yeah." He snarled.

"I don't live in a state of constant fear."

Why the hell were we arguing? Where had this discussion even started? Oh, yeah. With Trevor's fear, and the fear morphed into his displaced anger. Friends had flown to New York for a birthday weekend and celebrated at Le Bernardin. The last time I had visited Le Bernardin was when I lived in the city. I started to get angry at Trevor, but I wondered if I needed to get angry at myself instead for allowing myself to be upset by his fears of financial insecurity.

"You don't think about the future at all, Jesse."

"It feels like you want to place the blame for your anxiety on me, but I won't let you."

"I have to take care of you. That's why I'm worried."

"I didn't ask you to take care of me." I had to let go, or I knew I'd be sick. I was sick at heart. I wouldn't live in fear.

Why did Trevor insist we go by riverboat to visit the famous temple of the Reclining Buddha? Why hadn't I put my foot down and told him I was staying in bed? I wanted to visit the temples, but I needed a day of rest. Trevor was the Energizer bunny who couldn't stay still and had to be doing, doing, doing until he fell asleep at night.

He gave me a hand as we stepped off the riverboat and headed toward the entrance to the temple. We needed to eat. We sat on little plastic stools at a crude wooden table. I felt as if I were in kindergarten because we were so low to the ground. I was nauseated and in a cold sweat.

"Trevor, I need a 7UP or ginger ale."

He looked at me like he was put out by my lack of enthusiasm.

"I feel sick."

He nodded and ordered lunch. I had a bowl of soup and my 7UP. It helped to eat. And after lunch we went into the temple of the famous reclining Buddha. It seemed we were now tourists, and any hope of my writing daily went out the window.

CHAPTER 2: *New Friends and a Haircut*

I thought about my haircut in the salon in the alley between Number 3 and 4 Udom Suk, at the corner of Watson's drug store. Thanks to Waan, the lovely Thai lady we had met at the Dim Sum restaurant, I had found the beauty shop. Waan held my hand, led me to the salon, and explained in Thai that I wanted a haircut. Initially, I wasn't sure, but the team met me with smiles and so much enthusiasm that I changed my mind. A new experience.

The reception desk sat back from the front door with a gold Buddhist altar on the floor. Four massage tables covered with burgundy blankets were behind the reception desk. The white pillow on each of the beds had a burgundy towel folded creatively into the shape of a swan, or perhaps a duck, or maybe a goose. Who knew? Trevor and I had watched a man who carried two lively, very good-looking roosters, one under each arm, as he crossed a busy intersection. Maybe the burgundy towels were roosters.

On the left-hand side of the salon were two beauty stations with the requisite mirrors, chairs, and shelves for tools of the trade. A couple of old-fashioned bonnet-style drying chairs sat with their backs to the front window of the salon. To the right of the stations, a tall screen separated the beauty area from the hair washing station with two black porcelain sinks and comfortable chairs.

Waan made the introductions, and Pai, a beautiful young woman who spoke English, became my interpreter and hand-holder. A shy young woman from Laos gave me a head and neck massage and massaged my scalp. Heavenly. A prissy young man with plump cheeks and a beautiful complexion watched. I wondered if he was my hairdresser.

A chic Thai lady walked up. She wore cool glasses like the Theo special edition I had seen at the Paragon Mall. She took the scissors. I was confused. Was the plump young man the salon owner? Who was she? It turned out that Boom owned three salons in Bangkok and taught hairdressing.

Pai said, "Boom hasn't cut a customer's hair in ten years."

But she cut mine! It was edgy, fun, and took off about ten years for me.

Boom said, "It didn't take off ten years from me." And we all laughed.

Throughout the haircut, Pai and I snapped photos. Everyone watched, chatted, laughed, and had a rollicking good time. I loved every minute of it. I hadn't even asked Boom what she charged for a haircut. After I paid her, I gave her a deep bow of respect, and thanked her, "*Khàawp khun kha*. I want to come back and get the whole works, a manicure and pedicure. All twenty fingers and toes."

Fun and new friends worked magic and dispelled the darkness of the night before. Trevor had been irritated with me and had let me know with his stony silence during a tense evening meal. His light switch, on-and-off moods confused and distressed me. He blamed me for imagined transgressions.

CHAPTER 3: *Overnight Train to Chiang Mai*

It was quiet in the hours before dawn on the overnight express train Number 13 from Bangkok's Hua Lamphong Station. Trevor slept across the aisle from me. The curtains on my lower berth in the immaculate train car were closed. A porter had made up our beds the night before with pristine sheets, a better quality than those in any place we had stayed in India—thanks to Trevor's miserly ways. The toilets were clean and didn't reek of stale urine. I was grateful to have quiet time to reflect and write. I hoped to watch the sun rise with precious solitude.

The night before, we had met and talked with Fatima and Juan who lived in Copenhagen where they worked. Juan was from the Basque Region of Spain near the Pyrenees. He and Trevor talked about surfing on the coast in the north. Fatima was from Hong Kong—her father Indian (five generations living in Hong Kong) and her mother Pakistani. Both were involved in film making. Juan was a photographer and editor, and Fatima said she edited film also. When she said her mother was from Pakistan, I asked her if she, Fatima, had read *Three Cups of Tea*. She said her mother had told her she loved the book and said it accurately described life in Pakistan as she had known it growing up.

We'd reach Chiang Mai at 9:55 a.m. Our Airbnb host had said he'd wait by the elephants to give us a ride to his house in Hang Dong because it was twenty minutes outside Chiang Mai. Trevor and I laughed.

"We're riding elephants, Jesse."

It was kind of him to fetch us from the station, but Trevor seemed disappointed to find the elephants were statues. If I had to choose one word to describe my impression of Thailand after seven days, it was kindness. Thai people had generous hearts.

First light before the dawn. I saw it creep up in black with gray. I knew color was there, but it would be a while before I saw it. I was happy to have quiet time in my lower berth. Alone, behind the blue curtain and in a chilly nest. The train rocked gently, and the whistle blew.

I saw the silhouette of mountains in the distance. We were in the countryside. The gray hills and landscape revealed bits of color—yellow-brown grasses, dark green on the hillside, and red clay roads. The trees had lost their leaves. I liked the dawn, and I thought I'd have to get up every morning to write. I had a sinking feeling that it wasn't going to happen on this leg of my trip with Trevor. Sometimes I felt as if I were dealing with a demanding toddler who pitched a fit if he didn't get his way. Pink clouds reflected the light of the rising sun, white clouds, and a lovely pale blue sky. Where the sun hadn't touched the sky, the clouds were still a milky gray. I greeted the morning in blissful solitude.

We stopped at a station where a monk in a bright orange robe ate his breakfast. The flag of Thailand hung next to the yellow flag for the King. The night before, while we waited in the train station, an anthem had played through the loudspeakers at 6 p.m. and everyone got to their feet. Everything stopped. The soldiers in uniform saluted. Images of the King showed on the large-screen televisions on either side of the huge train station. When it was over, everyone sat down again.

Finally, it was light. Markets buzzed with early-morning activity in the small towns we passed. People wore jackets, and it looked cold outside, but I saw leaves on the trees, flowers, banana plants, and an occasional palm tree. We were in a different climate zone, and I was confused. We passed temples with gold wings lit by the sun into fire, startling green rice paddies, and humble dwellings outside small towns. Mist rose from the creeks and fields and hung below the mountain range in the distance. It reminded me of mornings in the Shenandoah Valley outside Charlottesville and the Blue Ridge Mountains.

The train was waking. People washed their faces, brushed their teeth, and combed their hair. I reminded myself. Be. Here. Now. In that precious moment, I embraced who I was, where I was, and what I was doing. The train climbed a mountain, the valley floor still in shadow below me. The rising sun streamed through the leaves of the trees, green lace filtering the light, softening it.

I had had a delightful conversation with Fatima about her desire to write a screenplay without dialogue. She said she wanted it to be lyrical and thought-provoking, eliciting emotions with visuals that morphed organically from act to act. It was a gift to talk with people from different cultures and religions. Young people I met inspired me with their drive and ambition.

We traveled through a dark tunnel, and when we emerged, I spied two white stone elephants near a picnic table set under a small pagoda. I was ready to get off the train and have new adventures.

CHAPTER 4: *B's Bungalows in the Bamboo. Chiang Mai*

We were in B's Bungalow and were roughing it, compared to the air-conditioned Bangkok condo with its beautiful swimming pool. Solid like a rock described the mattress. The steps leading up to the bedroom and bath were hazardous and reminded me of a cartoon. All the steps were different sizes, broken pieces of teak. Some slanted down. When we opened the door, it blocked the handrail.

It was 6:15 a.m. in the bamboo. Roosters crowed but it was still dark outside. Dogs started barking like mad at 5 a.m. Not B's dogs, but the twenty-two dogs down the street. One of B's dogs barked for an hour in the middle of the night outside our teak treehouse. B, our Airbnb host, had clearly set out to make money at the expense of his guests' comfort. When I wrote my review, I'd say:

Bring your own soap. Just in case, bring your own toilet paper, too. Make sure you're careful using the steps to your upstairs bedroom and bathroom as they are all different sizes of pieces of teak—broken, slanted down, and slanted sideways. The door blocks the handrail. Must love dogs because B has eight of them that bark. A lot. Need supplies? The 7-Eleven convenience store is a quarter-mile walk up the road. Leave the end of the cul de sac where Bob has his construction site, aka his Airbnb compound, and walk up the street, zigging, zagging, and dodging dog poo. Pass the house where the junkman collects rusting playground pieces and the auto body shop with its pile of fenders.

B supplied bottled water, but the kitchen left a lot to be desired. The tabletop was filthy and hadn't been washed for ages. Cups and plates in the glass-fronted cabinet were dirty. The microwave didn't work, nor did the electric hot plate. The mattress on B's grandmother's antique brass bed was rock hard.

Everything at B's Bungalows was in a state of disrepair, under construction, or simply chaotic, as far as I could tell. B had lived in Thailand for twenty-five years, didn't like tourists, and wasn't a gracious Airbnb host. He was in the game to make money and build teak treehouses as fast as he could. I thought he'd misplaced some of his gray matter along the way. He was scattered, running this way and that, wheezing from asthma and holding his sore chest where he had broken two ribs in an unspecified accident.

"Do you have soap and toilet paper? We don't have any in the room."

"I don't supply soap. The toilet paper is over there." He gestured vaguely toward the house as he dashed to his truck past the dogs and two elderly Thai men who were working on the next tree house. Trevor found the toilet paper and took a photo of the sad, rain-stained little roll. The bedside lamp didn't work, nor did the extension cord next to the bed.

B asked, "Did you bring the lamp down to read?"

"No, it packed up, and the extension cord is broken." Trevor's tone conveyed his disgust.

"Oh, it probably needs a new bulb." B left us in the dust.

Hang Dong was twenty kilometers outside the old city of Chiang Mai, and the Airbnb owner dissed us when we asked about the state of our treehouse and the workers he employed.

"Oh, yeah, it's good for the locals to make money. We don't even see the tourists."

But you're glad to take our money, I thought.

"Trevor, I'm furious about B's false advertising on his Airbnb listing."

"Everything looks like it's from a jumble sale." Trevor described the dirty dishes in the cabinet and the mismatched knives, forks, and spoons in filthy drawers. I had paid for a week in advance, or we would have left after the first night. The broken lamp still sat on the dirty table.

We walked up to a six-lane highway. Crossing six lanes of highway traffic at a bit of a jog, Trevor shouted, "Look right and dash!" We made it to the middle of the highway and the elevated median.

"Look left, and run like hell to the other side, babe."

We flagged down a yellow bus. The little yellow and red openair buses were the mode of transport into and out of Chiang Mai. We crowded into the little vehicle the size of a small pickup, its bed converted into a covered conveyance with benches on either side. We squeezed in beside the locals—no other Westerners were on the bus. One woman, who taught at an orphanage, spoke English; the other passengers were silent. The ride into the old city took half an hour going and forty-five minutes returning. It wasn't the easy twenty-minute ride into the city B had advertised. I dreaded returning to B's Bungalows after a lovely day in Chiang Mai.

First light. The birds were waking up, and a chorus of roosters joined the tree frogs and frogs in the rice paddies beyond the creek next to the teak house. The resident gecko added his or her *cheep . . . cheep . . . cheep* to the cacophony. The dogs weren't barking, and I had a rare hour for myself, as I sat with my pillow propped on the footboard of the brass bed. I was under the musty comforter B had supplied.

"B couldn't be bothered to put the comforter in a clean duvet cover," Trevor said.

There was trash under the bed from the last guest. B offered a sad excuse for Airbnb hospitality. His dogs started barking, and the twenty-two dogs down the road barked in reply. Good morning, Chiang Mai.

CHAPTER 5: *Old City Chiang Mai*

After a few days Chiang Mai made me think of Disneyland minus Mickey Mouse ears. The sacred and the profane met in the old city with its extraordinary temples and temple complexes. A moat and the ruins of a brick and earthen fortification surrounded the old city. Coffee shops sprouted on every corner. The city was geared to tourism. We stumbled upon one of the few hidden noodle shops where locals ate and enjoyed a delicious lunch. Later in the day, we stopped by a coffee shop with prices for tourists. It could have been a Starbucks. We felt disillusioned because we had expected something entirely different.

We were in the middle of nowhere in Hang Dong. Trevor was frantic. "My ATM card won't work. I need cash."

"What about calling the bank?"

"Later. HSBC can sort the problem."

I suggested a solution, and that irritated him. He had tried to withdraw too much money on Sunday in Bangkok when we went to Chatuchak Market, and the ATM wouldn't allow him to withdraw anything. He blamed me for the problem with the machine.

"You talked to me while I was trying to withdraw the money, Jesse."

Oh, FFS, I thought.

"Look, Trevor, you're mad at the situation. Not me. Don't displace your frustration."

After that incident, we hit a rough patch for a couple of days. I wasn't sure what was going on. I got over tiffs quickly. Trevor, well, not so much. He carried resentment and gave me the silent treatment. I ignored his passive-aggressive behavior, but it drained my energy. B's dogs started barking again. Barking, barking, barking. I wanted a few minutes for reflection, a rare commodity since we had reached Thailand.

CHAPTER 6: *Leaving Chiang Mai*

We traveled back to Bangkok via overnight train from Chiang Mai. The Airbnb experience had been disconcerting, and I had lost my emotional balance. I told Trevor I didn't think it was a good idea for us to visit Chiang Rai and Chiang Khong. We'd planned to travel north and make our way into Laos and south through three cities in that country.

"Let's regroup," I suggested. "We can map out a plan to stay in Thailand until we have to leave when our tourist visa expires."

We planned three nights of luxury on the twenty-sixth floor of a high-rise apartment in Bangkok to celebrate my birthday. I was overjoyed. Maybe we could go south to one of Thailand's beaches or islands for a week and return to Bangkok, I thought. We planned to go to Cambodia and Vietnam. Maybe we could take a train from Bangkok to Vientiane, Laos.

"We can plan a manageable travel circuit, Trevor. We don't have to travel pillar to post like twenty-something backpackers."

Trevor nodded, but his expression showed he didn't agree.

B the Builder with his cartoon chaos might have been entertaining, but he was one of those people I needed to avoid. His energy was dark. His aura was a gray shadow. It wasn't good for me, and I couldn't think straight. I lost my focus, felt afraid, and was confused. Thank heaven, I found enough clarity amid the chaos to tell myself to listen to my instincts and simply stop. I needed to think things through, clear my mind, plan, and act. We could do that in Bangkok, or so I thought.

Our new friend in Chiang Mai, Ying, had been our bright spot, source of sanity, and fount of knowledge about Thailand and the King. She was an extraordinary single mom with a seventeen-year-old daughter and a fifteen-year-old son. One day, when Ying didn't have to teach class at the University of Chiang Mai, she said she'd pick us up at noon and we'd have lunch and visit. Afterwards, she would take us to the train station. I was looking forward to our return to Bangkok. It was almost noon, and I listened to hammers and saws, the construction work going on in the courtyard. Time to let go of chaos and return to center.

Ying was kind and generous, a gift to us. On our last day in Chiang Mai, Ying took us to Waan, her favorite restaurant in Hang Dong, a fabulous coffee shop with great food. She told us that *Waan* meant sweet in Thai. We had a wonderful lunch and shared beautiful desserts. The architectural details and décor at Waan were exactly what we needed to dispel the miasma from our time spent with B the Builder. The front door was a work of art in wood and glass. Five stools built with tractor springs stood near the front window. The staircase leading to the second floor was built of wooden steps jutting from the wall to an upper level of concrete, unfinished on the ceiling above us. Everything in the room had function and purpose as well as artful design.

CHAPTER 7: *It's My Birthday and I'll Cry If I Want To*

Bangkok was foggy in the early morning. I gave myself a present and took time to write. I felt like I hadn't been true to myself by not writing since we arrived in Thailand. I was relieved to be in Bangkok again. The day before, Waan at the Dim Sum Restaurant and Pai and Nong at the hairdresser's salon had welcomed me with huge smiles and hugs. It felt like home. After the dreadful experience at B's Bungalows in Chiang Mai, the positive energy had refreshed me.

My relief turned to despair after Trevor arose.

CHAPTER 8: *On the Bus to Trat*

Unfortunately, the 8:30 a.m. cab we had scheduled didn't arrive to take us to Eastern Bus Terminal from Ideo Verve Condominium. We had to haul our shit up and down several flights of stairs to take the BTS Sky train two stops from OnNut to Ekkamai. I was drained spiritually, physically, and emotionally. I had serious doubts about whether I ought to be going anywhere with Trevor after our talk on my birthday. It certainly wasn't the birthday I had envisioned. I wanted time to myself to relax. We'd gone to the Tesco's grocery store, and our Thai friend Chakrii had called. That was when everything fell apart. Not for the first time.

The trip to Bangkok was supposed to be a time of rest and restoration after Chiang Mai. Instead, it turned into an extension of chaos and miscommunication with Trevor. Friday, after very little sleep on the overnight train to Bangkok, we checked into our glorious Airbnb apartment on Sukomvhit 79, Ideo Verve. The apartment was right across from the Sky Train BTS OnNut and Tesco's. We were in a primo location, but it wasn't a day of rest. Instead, it turned into a day to sort out Trevor's bankcard problems. It took hours and was no fun on my birthday. I was frustrated and angry, and I felt as if I had been taking care of a child.

"It's my birthday, Trevor." I couldn't keep the anger penned up.

Trevor scowled. "I've lost my confidence in myself. I don't know if I can travel alone because of you."

"What? That's absurd."

"I'm tired of the bickering between us."

I wasn't sure if that had taken place over the past few weeks, or was it years? On my birthday, Trevor chose to tell me everything that was wrong between us.

"Why now, Trevor? Birthdays are meant to be celebrated. Your timing is hurtful."

We couldn't have a discussion. Trevor parroted everything I said. He was defensive, got his back up, and didn't listen. I lost my joy. The timing struck me as odd because the disagreement, or whatever it was, took place on my birthday. I recalled the year when he had started a fight the day before my birthday. What was that about? I was confused. I felt as if I'd been sucker-punched emotionally. A blow to my soul.

"I thought we'd go on the water ferry to Wat Pho so you could have a massage to celebrate, Jesse."

"Did you think to ask me what I'd like?"

He was furious. "It would have been special."

"Trevor, I can walk around the corner for a massage."

Time passed on the bus, but my heart hurt. Trevor had agreed to meet Chakrii and his friends for dinner on my birthday. Not my choice. I was wiped out and felt numb. I dissociated to protect myself. It wasn't the first time. A sign on the road caught my eye. *Elephant Crossing. How amazing,* I thought, and I embraced a moment of joy to soothe myself.

CHAPTER 9: Trat, Thailand. Garden Home Guest House

"What is it we are questing for? It is the fulfillment of that which is potential in each of us. Questing for it is not an ego trip; it is an adventure to bring into fulfillment your gift to the world, which is yourself."
—JOSEPH CAMPBELL, *Pathways to Bliss*

What to do? What to do? A beautiful Mynah bird called out, "*Sawadeeca*" and "Hello."

"I'm afraid you're gonna lose the plot if I take a shower." Trevor gave me a look that could kill.

"Trevor," I said, in as calm a voice as I could muster, and paused a beat. "That's not going to happen."

I didn't get it. His reactions seemed to be those of a victim. When Trevor morphed into high-alert defensive mode, he lashed out at me in over-the-top hostility. What the hell?

CHAPTER 10: *From Trat to Hat Lek.*
Cambodian Border

Earlier that morning I had talked with an old monk at a temple complex in Trat. His saffron robes were dirty and tattered. He had the kindest eyes. His lips were stained orange and looked as if he had outlined them in a deeper orange with a pencil, but it was applied with a shaky, palsied hand. The temples in Trat differed from the ones I had seen in Chiang Mai, with a strong Chinese influence and, in some instances, hints or definite influences of Hindu gods and goddesses.

We returned to the Garden Guest House after breakfast, and everything was hunky dory until I sat down on the wet toilet seat. Again. The seat was wet from the spray of the hose Asians used instead of paper.

"Trevor, bring me a towel." I knew I sounded angry. I was. "The seat is wet."

That pissed him off. He handed me a towel, gritted his teeth, and slammed his fist into the bathroom door after handing me the towel.

"What the fuck?" I was stunned and closed the bathroom door. I was angry, too. Once again, I asked myself, *Do I leave now?*

I hadn't left. Instead, I was in a minivan traveling to the Thai border. Yes, I'd lost my cool, too. I'd said the F-word to Trevor several times. That didn't improve the situation or make me feel better. I prayed the Serenity Prayer over and over. I was too stressed to think straight. I didn't know what to do anymore. "Hear my prayer, O Lord." Maybe it was time to listen.

Cambodia

CHAPTER 1: *Near the Market. Koh Kong, Cambodia*

Trevor and I sat in the Bay Chha Restaurant, the only Westerners, and listened to a tinny radio playing a squeaky song. Motorcycles puttered by and supplied background noise. The sound reminded me of old black-and-white movies with Charlie Chan. I wanted to cry, and I didn't understand why my emotions were raw.

Without warning, a motorcycle skidded across gravel and crashed into a flat woven tray filled with hundreds of tiny snail shells. A bystander picked up a little girl wearing a pink knit cap who had fallen from the motorcycle with its wheels still spinning in the gravel. She wasn't hurt, but the small mollusks, some covered in red chili flakes, lay on the gravel where the motorcycle had skidded. The young vendor, a woman about twenty-five years old, swept the mollusk shells into a dustpan. The unfortunate vendor, who wore flannel pajamas, had lost a day's wages, I felt sure.

Cambodian soldiers in camouflage uniforms sat in the small café with us. The soldiers finished their meals with cigarettes and the sweet coffee the café served. The world passed us by. A young girl, maybe the café owner's daughter or granddaughter, stared at me. The owner's son had studied English in school. He helped us order a meal and have an idea about what we would get. Half the women I saw wore flannel pajamas in a variety of prints, patterns, and colors. Sometimes it was Hello, Kitty. At other times, red roses appeared on a yellow field. Everyone was quite colorful.

CHAPTER 2: 99 Guest House. Koh Kong, Cambodia

I was good for nothing as I sat in the little sea-view café, Samet Meas (Golden Sea). I had a delicious baguette with bacon, lettuce, and tomato for breakfast, and the resident kitten fell asleep in my lap. I was glad to be chilling in Koh Kong for a few days, especially after seven nights too many with B the Builder, the overnight train to Bangkok, three dreadful nights in Bangkok with our tension-filled relationship, and two nights with the ants and flying bugs at the Garden Guest Home in Trat, where the old lady told us not to worry, she would clean them up. She offered her solution to the problem after I pointed to all the dead bugs in the room.

CHAPTER 3: *Bay Chha Restaurant.*
Koh Kong, Cambodia

A television blared in the background. Ladies dressed in colorful flowered pajamas sold their wares in the marketplace across the street from the restaurant. A toddler who looked like he hadn't been bathed for days, dirt coloring his face, legs, and arms, wore a man's dirty orange Tshirt that swallowed the barefoot child. He held onto a massive black motorcycle to stand.

A monk stood in front of the restaurant, his saffron robes more like a dark mustard. He held an alms bowl. The proprietor went out to the monk, money in her hand, and dropped it in the bowl after putting her hands together in prayer at her forehead and bowing her head three times. She stood with her hands folded in prayer in front of her chest, heart level, to pray. When she finished, her prayerful hands went back to the center of her forehead, and she bent her head down three times. Prayer completed.

The young woman with the tiny mollusks on the woven tray was back at her stand, where she placed three woven trays on small red, yellow, and blue plastic stools. The sun was behind her. She wore yellow pajamas. Her long black hair was in a ponytail that hung over her right shoulder. She sprinkled hot chili flakes on the mollusks and tipped the tray from side to side to coat all the mollusks in the fiery red flakes. People picked them up like candy, sucked them, and popped whatever it was into their mouths. Indians and Asians had asbestos lining their mouths and tongues. They were fireproof.

The family who owned the restaurant ate with chopsticks, faces over bowls. The mother cut vegetables, and soldiers in fatigues smoked at tables nearby. I missed home and friends, but as I sat in the small family restaurant, I knew it would be hard for me to return to a normal day-to-day routine without Trevor.

CHAPTER 4: *Golden Sea. Samet Meas*

I walked to Golden Sea in the midday heat and stared at the water. It was a peaceful setting to relax. I greeted the man with long white hair that reached to his shoulders. He sported a scraggly white beard, white eyebrows, and pinkish skin, although he wasn't albino. The Irishman lived in the U.K. He drank beer every day. Probably the better part of every day. He was grizzly.

Mick cycled eleven kilometers to the sea for a swim each day. He said, "I work hard for six months, save the dosh, and come here to relax. The guys who sit here in the heat and line up beer bottle after empty beer bottle are brain dead."

I watched the world pass by. A little motorcycle taxi filled with Cambodian families and screaming children sputtered past. The motorcycles passing us carried three or four family members or friends. I stared in disbelief when I saw small children who could hardly walk stand on the motorcycle, their mother or father's knees penning them in, and arms on the handlebars to keep the children from falling out. Fathers held tiny infants in one hand and steered with the other. I wondered how folks back home would react. Vendors parked their carts across the road near the sea, their tables and chairs stacked. Later in the evening, they would be filled with people who sat to dine on meals cooked over charcoal in heavy pots.

CHAPTER 5: *Leaving Koh Kong for Phnom Penh*

We stood in the unpaved parking lot and watched an elderly lady in rose print, flannel pajamas board the bus in the early morning. It was cold because the AC worked. Hallelujah. We had chosen Virah Buntham Express Travel and Tour bus service because the other had a reputation for theft of suitcases and bags during scheduled stops.

We picked up passengers at little markets. Folks got on the bus, stinking of cigarettes, wearing backpacks, and carrying plastic bags with Styrofoam containers—lunch or breakfast—plus the requisite red chili sauce in a small bag closed with a tiny rubber band.

We drove through the mountains, where rubber trees with black cups collected sap. Small, crude wooden huts with rusting tin roofs stood on stilts. We traveled on winding, bumpy roads and over a bridge crossing a river with new homes and a condo on one side. On the opposite side of the road were shacks on stilts and a small market. We stopped at the market with its large *Red Angkor Beer* sign for a break. Smoke from burning rubbish stung my eyes.

Winnie the Pooh minus his ears hung from the mirror on the dashboard, along with Buddha. The dashboard was decorated with an odd arrangement of ornaments—two small jade elephants, two little metal sculptures of guitar-playing, cowboy-hat-wearing men, and red artificial flowers. A movie blasted the soundtrack in the Cambodian language. It could have been Japanese anime with real life because it was a story filled with so much action, I didn't need to understand the language.

After we left the market, we traveled on a red dirt road under construction.

Trevor said, "Look at those blokes carrying bicycles up the mountain."

We descended the mountain in the opposite paved lane, crossed another river, and saw shacks on stilts next to new construction of impressive homes. The contrast baffled me.

No matter how crude the wooden houses were, even those with space between the boards holding up the tin roofs, a modest altar stood in the yards of bare red dirt. For some odd reason, I flashed on Paul Coelho's *The Alchemist* and the magical realism in Salman Rushdie's *Midnight's Children*. Odd how the books I had read in India resonated.

We drove past Chi Phat Eco-Tourism Site on another river. House after house with tin roofs on stilts hugged the riverbank. Old wooden houses with thatched roofs in states of deterioration and ruin dotted the landscape. Wooden boats in the river were in such disrepair it was a wonder they floated. The cows were white and bony. Other tiny, crude shacks were built of palm fronds to form their thatched roofs and sides. The rice paddies were dry. It was winter and 90° F. at midday.

Some humble shacks had one cow tethered underneath to the stilts holding up the homes. Other fields boasted healthy herds of fat cattle. The homes featured a puzzling decoration on which only part of the wood was painted. Some homes had a single exterior wall painted in bright green or blue. I wondered if that was as much paint as the family could afford. So many mysteries to ponder.

The bus stopped at another small market with clean squat toilets. A Winnie the Pooh towel hung on the line to dry. Towel Pooh had ears. We passed more small villages of old wooden houses on stilts and saw families in the shade under their homes. Someone told me 40 percent of the population of Cambodia was under the age of sixteen. If that was true, it was remarkable.

We passed a man with mattresses on his motorcycle. The mattresses, with brightly colored flowers, were folded, covered in plastic, and tied together. It was an impossible load. I couldn't imagine the sight anywhere in the United States. We drove past red clay roads and fenced fields with sandy soil. It might have been an Alabama winter in the countryside except for the very high mountain range ahead. We were almost three hours into the bumpy bus journey by 10:35 a.m.

When I got tired of listening to gunshots and screams from the movie on the bus, I pulled out my earplugs. The noise got old an hour into the journey, and we had three hours to go. I saw pristine new buildings with a sign for Cambodia People's Party. What a contrast to the shacks on stilts. We'd seen imposing headquarters in Koh Kong, and the small building on the road to Phnom Penh was pristine and bright blue.

The bus driver with the earless Pooh Bear loved to honk his loud horn at least eight times to pass every motorcycle and at stops. He honked ten times as we approached a more heavily populated area. There were fewer wooden shacks on stilts. The Brahman cows were fatter. There was more traffic on the road and new buildings under construction. Contrasts of old and new continued to baffle me. I didn't know if we still had an hour or two until we reached Phnom Penh.

We passed temples, industrial buildings, and a lot of litter in Samrong Ton District. A sign in French, *Ecole* ("school"), surprised me. Cambodia People's Party signs were posted everywhere. United Apparel (Cambodia), a large industrial complex, was the second garment factory I'd seen. The litter in the ditches in one town's marketplace surprised me after Thailand's cleanliness. What a curious combination of temples, factories, and the occasional Baptist Church.

CHAPTER 6: *Appearances Are Deceiving. Phnom Penh*

We reached Phnom Penh at dusk, without a hotel reservation. After the bus dropped us off, we walked down the street and stopped at the first guesthouse we saw. From the outside, it appeared to be okay.

I asked one of the guests, a guy with dreadlocks who sat at a table with a beer bottle in his hand and a couple of empties on the table, "Are you staying here?"

"Yeah." He gestured with his beer bottle. "It's cheap."

"Jesse, let's see if there's a room." Trevor grinned.

The owner said, "I have one room left. On the ground floor." He pointed to a door down a narrow hallway.

We agreed to take the room, sight unseen, and paid him. Mistake. The room was a nightmare. A broken window without a screen was an open invitation for mosquitoes.

"Oh my gosh. No, Trevor."

"For fuck's sake."

"I'll be back." I went out to find the guesthouse owner.

"What are we supposed to do about the broken window and mosquitoes?"

He handed me two small rackets that looked like badminton rackets with short, thick handles.

"What is this?"

"Just hit the switch and zap 'em." He turned the battery-powered mosquito zappers on.

"Seriously?" The expression on my face had to convey my incredulity. I carried the zappers back to the room.

"Trevor, I have mosquito weapons."

He hadn't heard me, as he was lost, sorting his own problems.

"Babe, there ain't room in here for our suitcases." Trevor pointed to his suitcase on the floor. "I can't open it."

"What about my suitcase?"

"In the corner. You have to put it on the bed to open it." He swatted as a mosquito divebombed him.

"Darn. I didn't think this place could get more bizarre."

"Where's the mosquito spray?" Trevor pointed at the broken window. "What's he going to do about that?"

"Brace yourself, sweetheart." I handed him one of the badminton rackets aka mosquito zappers.

"What the fuck?" He eyed the strange contraption.

"Flip the switch on it."

"You're taking the piss, ain't you, Jesse?"

I laughed and danced around the small room, pretending to play badminton. Trevor joined me. We were in hysterics, swatting, batting, and zapping mosquitoes. For every mosquito we fried, another swarm flew in through the broken window. It was dusk, the light was on, and the mosquitoes feasted on us until we electrocuted the little buzzing bastards.

"We gotta get out of here, Jesse."

"No shit."

Twenty minutes later, after getting a refund, we found another guesthouse several blocks away and hauled our suitcases up three flights of carpeted steps to our room. It was blissfully cool with air conditioning and nary a mosquito in sight.

CHAPTER 7: *A Noodle Connoisseur*

An elderly lady wearing bright yellow pajamas pedaled a cycle rickshaw down the street. Motorcycle carts carried impossible loads of trash, cardboard, plastic bottles for recycling, and other indeterminate materials. Old ladies, dressed head to toe with gloves, long-sleeved shirts, pants, and hats that covered their necks, picked up plastic and put recyclables in carts. They loaded them to the brim and pulled them by hand through the streets, where motorcycles and cars dodged the carts and the women.

We were in Phnom Penh, and I was a noodle connoisseur. My breakfast at Trunk on a busy corner was maybe a five or a six, with a strange meat, good flavor, thin rice noodles, and fair presentation. I ate with chopsticks and a soup spoon, although I dribbled noodles on my chin. Trevor and I were not enamored with Phnom Penh, and we were tense.

CHAPTER 8: *Tuol Sleng.*
The Genocide Museum

We visited Tuol Sleng, S-21, a chilling and exhausting experience as we viewed the evidence of genocide and ethnic cleansing Pol Pot employed to annihilate Cambodians and create a pure race. I thought the same thing was taking place in Syria with ISIL. It was strange to be in a country where I couldn't understand the language, yet the dollar was the preferred currency.

Viewing the relics of the Khmer Rouge reign of terror was a horrifying experience. S-21, a former high school, looked derelict, its walls topped by barbed wire. The energy field surrounding Tuol Sleng made my heart heavy with grief. S-21 was spiritually and emotionally the most bereft place I'd experienced in my life.

Doctors, lawyers, intellectuals, old, young, men, women, children—yes, children and infants—were brought to S-21 under cover of darkness. They were photographed and measured, had their information recorded, and were assigned a number. Guards tortured and killed the prisoners at the rate of more than one hundred people per day, and 17,000 to 20,000 human beings went through the inhumane brutality at Tuol Sleng.

The only difference between the Khmer Rouge and the Nazis was that the Khmer Rouge didn't tattoo their prisoners. The bodies and still-living were taken fifteen kilometers to the Killing Fields, where any living prisoners were bludgeoned to death to save bullets. The fractured skulls, broken jawbones, and broken bones bore silent witness to the horror, the atrocities.

CHAPTER 9: *Diamonds, Sweet, Sad Music, and Blind Musicians*

For the second morning in a row, I watched the monk in saffron robes walk down the street toward the hospital with an umbrella in his left hand and a bundle under his robes in his right arm. Dogs barked, and the motorcycle shop below the hotel was bustling and noisy. When we booked our room, the motorcycle shop under the hotel had been closed. Ah, the unwary visitor in a strange land.

We sat at a small corner restaurant near Central Market and sipped iced coffees. I studied a wealthy Asian lady, in her late forties, dressed in black with expensive jewelry—a large diamond wedding ring, diamond bracelet, and diamond necklace. She was an attractive woman with lovely cheekbones and well-done makeup. She made several phone calls and looked impatient. A young man, a good-looking teenager, rode up on his motorcycle. He drank a vanilla milkshake and stared at her. It sounded as if she were giving him a tongue lashing that he volleyed right back at her. Their body language spoke volumes about the tension between them. It was not a happy reunion. One didn't need to understand the language to read body language and facial expressions to have a glimpse into two people's lives.

I met Yoki, a precious Chihuahua pup wearing a Pooh Bear sweater. Winnie the Pooh had both ears on his sweater. I didn't understand why Yoki was dressed in a sweater on a hot and humid afternoon. The owner was also the manager of the little café on the corner. She was a lovely lady with welcoming smiles, and she treated us with kindness.

It had been a helluva day so far, but I prayed things were looking up. We were back at the café with iced coffees after a dreadful morning disagreement. I watched a blind musician tethered to a leading string—a little piece of knotted cotton string—and the other man who led the blind man through the café. The musician played a haunting, sweet tune on a stringed instrument with a bow—a *tro ou*. I wasn't familiar with the instrument, which sounded like a violin because the musician had a bow. The younger man who led the white-haired blind man had dark hair and appeared to have a vision impairment as well.

I saw them after they came to the corner of the outdoor café facing me. I heard them—the sad, sweet music—when they entered the café behind me. I knew they were begging, although they didn't have hands outstretched. They used God's gifts, although they were both vision-impaired. A symbiotic relationship—father and son perhaps. The morning's argument with Trevor still stung. I gave them five dollars even though I was afraid it would set Trevor off again.

We had our passports with visas for Vietnam. We had also bought bus tickets for the early morning bus to Battambang. The morning had been horrible. When I checked online for hotels and prices for rooms with AC, Trevor flipped out and went on the attack mode.

"If you want it cold all the time, we might as well go back to Newquay, to the caravan, where it's cold in February."

I didn't reply or react to his taunt. The campsite didn't open until early March, almost a month away. I refused to argue. Trevor's fear about money was irrational and obsessive.

"Trevor, it's not fair to lash out at me because I want an air-conditioned hotel room in the heat." I'd suffered for two months with a hideous skin infection, ringworm, hospital visits, and anti-fungal medication and creams when we were in India. "I can't get over the skin infection with the heat." The infection looked like lesions and was uncomfortable. Sleeping in an air-conditioned room alleviated the problem.

Trevor had turned away from me and left the hotel room. I wept. What the hell was wrong with him? When he had a tiny sliver of glass in his hand while visiting me, I had taken him to an urgent care clinic. The doctor removed the glass and put a butterfly bandage on the tiny incision. He'd used an anesthetic to numb the area before the minor procedure. Trevor acted as if he'd had major surgery and was entirely too dramatic—like he'd been when I broke my ankle in Cornwall. I was stoic while he fell apart. Relationships were hell.

The impact of these bizarre arguments, and Trevor's eruptions, was that I numbed out to protect myself. My affect was flat. I was emotionally drained. Why couldn't we discuss money without his overreaction? I had a flashback to a moment when I, as a seven-year-old, had asked my father for money to buy school supplies. He had said, "You're going to dollar me to death." Stingy father, stingy Trevor. It was familiar turf, but I wasn't a child.

CHAPTER 10: *Sardines in a Minivan to Battambang, Cambodia*

We were sardines packed into a minivan for a seven-hour ride to Battambang. The minivan, or minibus, picked Trevor and me up first. He and I squeezed into two back seats of the four seats in the last row of the four rows in the tiny transport vehicle. The driver was surly, or a particularly unhappy Cambodian.

I'd experienced such despair the night before that I couldn't sleep. I felt like a failure because I hadn't finished writing the first draft of my collection of stories about train travel. I saw author friends talking about options with major film production companies for their books. DreamWorks had bought one friend's book rights and film rights. I was excited for my friends. I wanted to go home with a first draft, the outline for a book proposal, and money in the bank. I was delusional. I'd had little time to write since we arrived in Southeast Asia. I didn't want to feel despair, to experience another dark night of the soul.

We stopped abruptly, the tires squealing on the street. The minibus driver loved to slam on his brakes in Phnom Penh's heavy traffic. *Why?* I wondered. Maybe unhappy, surly Cambodian guy was delivering payback. Who knew? Unfortunately, I sat over the right rear wheel and the bus had no suspension. My poor beleaguered butt was getting pounded. We had paid extra for what we were sold as a faster ride to Battambang (or Battambong—the spelling varied).

It was a sightseeing tour. People slept on the street. Kids played in a nasty concrete garage with black grease all over the floor. Three monks in saffron robes with saffron umbrellas walked by, and a motorcycle conveyance drove past with twenty people in what looked like a covered wooden boat with wooden planks for seats. And just like that, we were on an unpaved road under construction. The poor people in front of us ate a cloud of red dust behind a huge construction lorry. We bounced around like popcorn with the massive force of the minibus almost bottoming out on the rough road. We couldn't have imagined such a hellish ride.

The scene was set in poverty with red dust and litter everywhere. We bumped past dilapidated wooden shacks on stilts with rusting tin roofs. This part of Cambodia reminded me of India and the poverty we had seen, thanks to Trevor's insistence on bargain-basement travel. Poverty and road dust. I saw a child and his mother who sat in the doorway of one of the mean dwellings. He combed her long hair and picked nits from her scalp. My elbow was bruised from bashing against the hard metal window frame.

"Get ready, Jesse. We're going off-road again."

I braced myself. "People pay to do this?"

"Yeah, with an ATV."

Suddenly, the driver slammed on the brakes, and we all flew forward. He hadn't seen the car pull out in front of us. Unhappy, surly Cambodian was a maniac driver with a death wish. We passed four young boys, wearing the saffron robes of monks, in a huddle near a vendor with his cart. The driver followed vehicles too closely. He decided to overtake a black, shiny new Range Rover with a V-8 engine ahead of us. We were in a fifteen-seat tiny transport van, for Pete's sake. How fast could he possibly drive? I didn't want to find out.

We passed six small boys, monks with alms bowls, by the road and overtook a motorcycle whose driver carried a dozen chickens hanging upside down, still alive. A lady sat on concrete with dead chickens all around her. Horrified, I watched as she killed another one of the chickens she had brought to market. Amid all the poverty were pristine temples.

The ride was reminiscent of our travel to Rishikesh from Delhi, with the suicidal Sikh, and our harrowing overnight bus down the hairpin curves from McLeod Ganj when we returned to Delhi in 2013. *How many seniors could claim to have experienced such extreme adventures on a shoestring*? I wondered. Not a likely scenario for people I knew.

We slowed briefly for a herd of white cows and their calves to cross the road. I was shaken, not stirred. Six wooden carts, heavy laden, pulled by pairs of bullocks came toward us at a calm, measured pace. The minibus ride was horrible.

"We need a bootlace instead of a shoestring, Jesse."

"To travel in comfort in Cambodia."

We laughed. Misery does love company. Cambodia was expensive, but it wasn't as nice as our visit to Thailand. Cambodia was India at four times the cost. Did two-tier pricing exist everywhere in Asia, brown skin one price and white skin another?

Two little girls danced naked at a water pump in the yard, bathing and splashing the cow drinking from their fountain. It was hot in the midday sun. We passed a sign, *Sustainable Cambodia,* but I hadn't seen a thing that smacked of sustainability. Someone said the Japanese had bought Angkor Wat and had plans to put a theme park outside it. Rumor mill. Talk about the sacred and the profane. Siem Reap as Disneyland. No.

We passed brick huts, round with domes constructed of brick, just like Henry Stuart, the "Hermit of Tolstoy Park," built by hand back home. Stuart had chosen to leave his home in Idaho in the 1920s after his doctor told him he only had a year to live. He came to Fairhope to die, but the doctor had been mistaken. I had been in what felt like deep freeze for a decade before I made a choice to change my life. As a result of my choice, I had met Trevor; although falling in love with an Englishman hadn't been part of my grand plan.

We bounced past more ornate and delicate temples than I'd seen in other parts of Asia. Girls and ladies wore long skirts.

"Hey, Trevor, you think they got Boudreaux's Butt Paste in Cambodia?"

CHAPTER 11: *A Corner Restaurant in Battambang, Cambodia*

The night before, standing on the corner while waiting for a tuk-tuk, I had seen the little ones approach the corner on the opposite side of the busy street. Cars and motorcycles whizzed by. They stood on their dark corner on the sidewalk. Two very dirty little boys, maybe three and four years old. They were so small. The older boy carried a naked infant—it looked like a newborn, but the babe wasn't crying. He shifted the baby's weight and put it over his shoulder. The two children stepped off the curb cautiously. They were still in the shadows. Then they walked into the middle of the street.

Cars dodged the children but didn't stop. I wanted to go into the street to help them, but I'd injured my left foot the night before. I held my breath until the children made it across the street safely. The older child reached the corner opposite me first. The younger child stopped in the street to pick up and examine a tattered plastic bag. The child tottered along and climbed onto the sidewalk. They walked toward a doorway. What was going on? Where was their mother? I was horrified.

Two teenage girls sat atop a cart behind us on the sidewalk. The girls didn't blink, unfazed by the sight of the babies alone on the street in the dark. A tuk-tuk pulled up after Trevor flagged the driver down. The next time I looked, the children had disappeared. I experienced many haunting moments on the journey, perhaps none quite so heart-wrenching as this.

Battambang was the first town in which I had witnessed what seemed to be the sex trade of young children. I wondered if those babies were a part of it. Days earlier, in Koh Kong, Trevor and I had walked past a group of eight children playing marbles. The girls, up to about age eight, and the boys, possibly four or five years old, and a toddler sat with a large pot of marbles. Two women and a man sat nearby in the shade. Two more children, clean and well-dressed compared to the assortment of dirty urchins reminiscent of Spanky and Our Gang, sat with the adults. I stared at the children. The adults stared at us. It felt like a tense moment between the adults and Trevor and me. The children were friendly when we waved and smiled. Why would a mother give a baby a bowl full of tempting green marbles, so easily swallowed? The adults weren't concerned about the children. Something felt wrong about the scene and I was sick at heart.

It was hard to fathom that we had left India a month earlier. We'd covered a lot of ground in a short time. Trucks, vans, tuk-tuks, and old cars passed by at a dizzying pace, overloaded with goods and people, axles squeaking. I spied a family of five on a motorcycle. Dad was in front, mom was on the back, and three children were sandwiched in the middle. Not one child was over the age of five. Conveyance. Transport. It was big business in this market town and bustling crossroads.

The travels contributed to my growing interest in history's parallels about wars and extremists. With man's inhumanity to man. With greed and the inequalities in distribution of wealth. It was life. The same since the beginning of time. Were men programmed genetically with the kill-or-be-killed DNA that somehow evolved into the hunt that turned into the acquisition of wealth and possessions? I didn't understand the mystery, although I tried to find a logical explanation.

An old motorcycle stopped across the street, behind it a small open trailer loaded with green melons and one boy sprawled atop the load. A second boy joined the first and off they went. Motorcycles drove off with passengers and their goods. Battambang's market was intriguing, but I'd had enough of the city. It was too noisy, with too much traffic, too many people, televisions blaring, snooker balls crashing into one another, and cars and tuk-tuks beeping their hooters and roaring past.

CHAPTER 12: *On the Bus to Siem Reap, Cambodia*

I sat at a small Cambodian open-air restaurant for breakfast—iced coffee and a bowl of soup that featured a strange assortment of meats and what looked like a cow's tongue. I moved the mystery meat out of the way with chopsticks and ate what I thought wouldn't poison me. An elderly man drank a cup of tea, watched me, and smiled. I was the only Westerner, as was the case most of the time because we ate in neighborhood spots where we saw no other white faces. We walked past overpriced places geared to tourists who felt more comfortable with familiar foods on the menu and the company of other Western travelers and backpackers. We rarely saw any Westerners our age traveling as we were.

After breakfast, we hailed a tuk-tuk from our two-star hotel to the Capitol Bus stop. A beggar sat on one of the concrete benches, one of his legs amputated below the knee in a crude stump. His crutches leaned against the bench beside him. Dressed in dirty, tatty clothes, he wore a red towel over his head and another draped around his shoulders. He was desperate to get our attention. He smiled, gestured wildly, and chatted with rotten teeth. He was drunk and quite mad. When he wasn't deep in his charade to charm us and the other waiting passengers, his expression changed—lost, despairing, hopeless.

An elderly woman beggar crowded up close behind me and touched me, startling me, but she had my attention. I bowed to her with my hands folded in supplication, but I didn't give her or the drunk, crippled man any money in front of Trevor. He didn't want me to give beggars any money. When he wasn't looking, I gave them each a few dollars. It was so little. Jesus said, "As ye give unto the least of these, ye also give unto me."

The bus to Siem Reap held forty-two passengers. We had room to breathe. Trevor read my copy of George Orwell's *Burmese Days*. My earplugs helped block out the throbbing bass and tinny treble music, the soundtrack for a movie on the flat screen at the front of the bus. A family of ten, three of the children chatting nonstop at a deafening volume, squeezed into six seats. A couple of the children sat on the floor with their straw hats, tote bags, and bags of produce from the market.

Water lilies and vibrant fuchsia bougainvillea grew in dusty, littered yards and depressions that probably filled with water during the monsoons. Sometimes, when we ate in the neighborhood noodle shops, as I called them, we met wonderful people like Ying in Chiang Mai, Thailand. In Battambang at a marvelous Chinese restaurant, we met precious chatterbox ten-year-old Nita and her parents, who joined us at our table because Nita wanted to practice her English. She studied in an American school and her father worked with an NGO—a foundation based in the U.K. to help landmine victims. Landmines and unexploded ordnance from the conflict still posed great danger after more than thirty years. Someone said it was money supplied by the US and the U.K. that funded the acquisition of deadly weapons that continued to maim, cripple, and kill the innocent.

Large glass bottles filled with gasoline for motorcycles and cars stood at every roadside shack, with whatever food or produce was on offer. *What did it take to escape the poverty in Cambodia?* I wondered, and thought education was the answer. We passed schools—all pale yellow with children dressed neatly. Ecole d'Arts et de Culture Khmers schools served communities like the awful buildings at Tuol Sleng in Phnom Penh. Signs in French dotted the roadside.

We passed beautiful, ornate temples in different cities from Trat, Thailand, to Battambang, Cambodia. India's influence. China's influence. The landscape featured startling green rice paddies, pristine temples and their compounds, new buildings next to wooden shacks that barely stood on rickety wooden stilts, and litter. Cranes flew above the rice paddies, white wings graceful over the bright green fields. I couldn't wait to see Angkor Wat, a world heritage site.

When I sat at small restaurants or watched someone walking down the road, older faces dour, sometimes smoking a cigarette, no joy in their faces, I wondered, *were they victims or perpetrators of the Khmer Rouge atrocities?* We stopped at a market in a small town. Bags of lovely fresh baguettes tempted us, the legacy of French occupation. Tourists, shopkeepers, and tuk-tuk drivers spoke French, and we were surprised when we withdrew US dollars from cash machines.

Our bus left us standing at the rest stop. My backpack with jewelry, computer, and passport was on board. I tried to stop the bus and cried out for the driver to wait. Apparently, that was the modus operandi because ten minutes later the bus returned.

CHAPTER 13: *Angkor Wat, Siem Reap.*
I am Lara Croft.

I sat on a rock in the shade while Trevor explored Temple Bayon. It wasn't just a temple. It was a massive pagoda under reconstruction. Another temple, the Elephant's Terrace, was on the agenda next. A welcome breeze blew, and leaves fell. Thousands of tourists, a hundred guided tours, and massive busloads of Chinese poured into Siem Reap. I hadn't understood until I saw Angkor Wat that it was a massive temple complex on over 400 acres in Cambodia. We had bought three-day tickets to visit the temples, but we didn't have a clue what was in store for us. The entire complex was called Angkor Wat—not just the massive Angkor Wat temple surrounded by a moat.

I never dreamt that I'd have an opportunity to explore the temples by climbing through crumbling ruins as if I were an archaeologist. I was no Indiana Jones, but I could imagine myself as Lara Croft scrambling over fallen and broken stone blocks. I'd been fascinated with archaeology since I was five years old. I remembered my grandmother reading to my brother and me. When she had shown us pictures of pyramids, I simply knew more ruins were under the sands just waiting to be discovered. I couldn't remember where my adult-sized pith helmet had come from, but I distinctly remembered wearing it when I was a little girl and feeling like a mighty explorer. The scale of what we saw was beyond anything I'd imagined. How long had the incredible monuments, the architectural wonders, taken to build? How many slaves? Where did they quarry the massive stones? Hundreds of stones lay on the ground around me; most had been in place long enough to gather moss. While I waited for Trevor, I thought about the temples we had seen, the places we had visited, and the people we had met. Buddhist philosophy and teachings held truth and lessons for living.

CHAPTER 14: *The Mekong Express*

e left Siem Reap in a comfortable air-conditioned bus for the seven-and-a-half-hour journey to Phnom Penh, where we'd board another bus to Ho Chi Minh City, Vietnam. Seeing the temples at Angkor Wat had been mind-boggling, but because Trevor got sick at the end of the second day, we had used only two days of the three-day passes we had bought. We were both whipped by the tropical heat and our adventures up, down, and through the temples—Ta Prohm temple, the *Lara Croft: Tomb Raider* set—Angkor Wat, and Preah Khan. It was rugged going since we climbed among ruins under restoration.

Our first day was eventful when our driver and experienced guide Sky pulled the old bait and switch. He handed us off to another driver, a young guy named Wat, who wasn't what we had bargained for. After spending hours climbing up and over all the rocks at temples in the Angkor Thom complex—Bayon, the Palace, the Elephant's Terrace, and the Leper King's Palace, which was probably a crematorium—we ate an overpriced lunch of stir-fried rice.

"Where's our driver and the tuk-tuk, Trevor?"

"Ain't got a clue. You think he left us here?"

"Wouldn't surprise me after the tour guide palmed us off this morning."

We searched and found Wat, along with six other Cambodian blokes, drinking beer in our tuk-tuk.

"Bloody hell." Trevor was furious.

"Wat, how much have you had to drink?"

His eyes were glazed over. He told us two beers. It was a lie.

"Trevor, he's drunk and stoned."

The six other drunks scattered. We climbed into Wat's tuk-tuk, and he drove off, steering the vehicle badly on the hard-packed sand. I didn't like it one bit.

"Take us to Angkor Ta Prohm. We'll visit Angkor Wat later," Trevor said.

We explored Ta Prohm—much of it still under reconstruction, as was the temple at Angkor Thom. Massive tree roots snaked their way over stones and the ruins. The engineering feat and craftsmanship of stone carvings was astonishing. Nature and tree roots had taken over throughout the centuries, forcing huge blocks of stone out of place, or in some instances becoming part of the ruins—the glue that held the immense stones in place.

The entrance to Angkor Thom was amazing. We crossed a bridge with a series of heads, gigantic stone carvings, set at intervals across the bridge that crossed the moat. The immense gate, South Gate, was topped with carved faces facing north, south, east, and west.

CHAPTER 15: *Having My Nineteenth Nervous Breakdown*

Our express bus broke down on a dusty, dirty road—a highway under construction without gravel or tarmac. Clouds of red dust enveloped the bus every time a car, motorcycle, and especially another massive lorry, passed by. The driver promised we would transfer to another bus, and, fingers crossed, we would make our other connection to Ho Chi Minh City via Phnom Penh.

"This is going to be a test of patience, Trevor."

"Another bus will come along in an hour." The young man who said he was our tour guide promised, his hands clasped together.

"Maybe," I muttered.

"It's all part of the adventure, babe." Trevor wrapped his arms around me and laughed.

"I prefer to avoid today's adventure."

Another large truck roared past and red dust shrouded the bus.

Our frantic tour guide shouted, "Everyone, hurry and get off the bus." He assured us a new bus was on the way.

"Trevor, he told us 'A new bus is coming' thirty minutes ago."

Every passenger who'd been on the bus stood or sat beside it on red clay and morphed into ghostly silhouettes when the red dust enveloped them.

"Bloody hell!"

"I'm not standing in the road dust another minute, Trevor."

I got back on the bus, wet my handkerchief, and tied the bandana around my face and nose. I only needed to don my pink hoodie and

I'd look like I was ready to rob a convenience store. Whether or not we'd reach Phnom Penh in time for our connection to Ho Chi Minh City, Vietnam, remained to be seen.

An hour passed and a second bus arrived. We stood in line waiting to board, but when we climbed the steps and stood next to the driver, we didn't see any available seating.

"Where are we supposed to sit?" Trevor asked the tour guide.

The young man pointed to the aisle.

"You expect us to sit on the floor of this bus for six hours?" I thought, *Not just plain no. Hell no!*

I got back on the old bus, added more water to the bandana, now as red with road dust as I was, and watched a drama unfold outside. Although their voices were muffled, an American, a Brit, and two Italians pitched a fit, along with Trevor, who gave the tour guide a piece of his mind. Meanwhile, the Cambodian passengers—old, young, men, women, children, and infants—sat under a tree across the road in the shade and waited patiently. They must have been through this before. I thought, belatedly, that I should have joined them.

A new bus finally reached us, and we were back on the road. I looked at Trevor. "Why didn't we stay in the last market town?"

"The wanker knew the engine was overheating."

"It would have been a lot easier to wait in town."

I stared out the window and saw live chickens cooped in upside-down woven baskets. Kids and ladies wore what looked like flannel pajamas midday. The fashion choice intrigued me because it was hot and humid. People cooked meals outside over burning charcoal. A man slept in a hammock strung between two posts in the shade of his roadside stand. We endured hours and hours of almost unbearable jostling on our bus trip to Phnom Penh through Cambodia's midday heat and on the red dirt road under construction.

Cambodia's infrastructure was sadly lacking. I guessed Pol Pot and the lingering impact of the Khmer Rouge until 1998 did the country in. Although the country was poor, our purchases cost more than in Thailand. We were white. We were Western. And we paid tourist prices in Cambodia. On the other side of a river, a short distance from the glitz and glitter, the shiny palace, and pristine hotels, lay shanties listing precariously toward the water, defying gravity. How did they stand without falling? Poverty defined the countryside marked by dirt and litter. Massive clay pots outside mean dwellings held families' water supplies. How did the people living in Cambodia stay in balance?

Finally, we were on our way to Saigon aka Ho Chi Minh City. The movie on the bus was *Return to the Planet of the Apes*. It was in English with English subtitles. And it was the third bus ride on which the movie had been shown, started, but never completed. Thank goodness we weren't subjected to six hours of perfectly dreadful Cambodian music by a singer born with a terrible affliction—her voice. Traffic was a dusty nightmare. Chaos ruled. The driver pulled the bus into the wrong lane trying to pass a dump truck filled with wet sand going in the opposite direction. *Another madman hell-bent on self-annihilation*, I thought.

Vietnam

CHAPTER 1: *Valentine's Day. Saigon, Vietnam*

The hotel manager upgraded us to a luxurious, spacious room on our first night. We'd reached Saigon after dark and booked the Le Le Hotel around the corner from the travel office and bus drop-off. The second night we had to move to a room filled with a double bed and nothing more. No chairs or wardrobe. Not even a table with a bedside lamp.

"Blimey," Trevor said. We didn't have room to open our suitcases.

"The bathroom doesn't have a door," I muttered. How peculiar. In fact, the bathroom wall had large openings near the ceiling. We were privy to all the goings on in the hall outside our room.

"Good Lord!" The openings allowed anyone in the hall to hear us.

Trevor got up in the wee hours when noisy guests in the hall woke us. He opened the door. "Can you hold it down? The hall walls have openings to our bathroom. We can hear everything you say."

I couldn't hear the reply, but Trevor added, for emphasis in his inimitable style, "You can hear me fart if you're standing there."

When we awoke, I said, "Happy Valentine's Day, sweetheart." I hadn't slept well but I wanted to start the day with a loving gesture. I'd found a Valentine's card a day earlier, and I gave it to Trevor with a smile.

Trevor's face clouded. "It's just a day."

I didn't react, but the overcast day matched my mood. After breakfast, when we returned to the room, I perched on the edge of the bed and looked at Trevor. He sat on the bed, pillows propped behind him, focused intently on his iPad, and typing away. What was the deal about holidays? It was time to talk, to ask questions, and I prayed I could do that without recrimination or confrontation.

"Trevor, I don't understand," I said as calmly as possible. "What is it about Christmas, birthdays, and Valentine's Day?"

He looked up, irritated.

"I want to know why you ignore holidays when we're together?"

Trevor stared at me, the muscles in his jaw tensing, and met my question with stony silence.

I wanted him to know how I felt. "Why are holidays flashpoints?" As a rule, he picked a fight. "We end up bickering, as you call it, and you blame me." I didn't stop, even though he didn't say a word. "Is it a way to avoid giving me a gift? You're generous with your out-of-the-blue surprise gifts. It's confusing." *In for a penny, in for a pound*, I thought. "Is it that you don't choose to recognize the significance of special occasions?" I paused, while counting to ten and taking a deep breath to keep an even tone of voice. "Is it a way to avoid acknowledging the importance of our relationship?"

"Do we have to do this now?" Trevor spit out the question.

He was fuming. I didn't care.

"It's not me, Trevor. You might want to think about whatever is going on in your head, because it's not me." It sucked big time—just like my Bangkok birthday non-event and his bringing up the problems with our relationship. "I'm heading out. See ya later."

CHAPTER 2: *Saigon (Ho Chi Minh City) to Mui Ne, Vietnam*

Valentine's Day I was a zombie, exhausted spiritually, physically, emotionally. After our fifteen-hour trip from Siem Reap, I felt beaten, discouraged, despondent. I hadn't taken care of my own needs. I wanted Trevor to acknowledge Valentine's Day, but every holiday—Christmas, New Year's, my birthday, and Valentine's Day—we got into a conversation about my negativity, or our bickering, and suddenly I was falling all over myself apologizing to keep the peace. The reality, it seemed, was that all the incidents were a way of avoiding holiday celebrations, the source of the problem. I was worn out. We didn't see anything of Saigon, only wandered around briefly. I went out early to The Sinh Café, The Sinh Tourist, and bought tickets for the 7 a.m. bus to Mui Ne. I wanted to be cherished and loved. Was I getting my needs met? I wasn't writing. Was I merely a convenient tour planner and travel guide?

Be. Here. Now. The bus passed through small villages where yellow and bright orange marigolds, some six to eight feet tall, were sold. Tet Holiday had begun, and we were in the middle of it.

My thoughts wandered to the war. What had grown back after the defoliant Agent Orange? The devastation corporations caused with the deadly chemical dioxin? Since there wasn't a demand for dioxin, megalomaniac monsters had placed their bets on GMO food, ironically selling genetically modified foods in Vietnam where they had destroyed jungles, lives, and the health and well-being of future generations of Vietnamese.

I thought about the heat, jungles, and mosquitoes. How did the young men and women who fought here survive the jungles? How did they cope with Vietnam? Some didn't return, and some of those who did return were forever changed, the changes heartbreaking.

CHAPTER 3: *On the South China Sea.
Mui Ne, Vietnam*

In a gentle way, you can shake the world. The young Russian who wore the Tshirt with Gandhi's words drank beer with his buddies in the Vietnamese restaurant. Trevor and I were disoriented from travel. We weren't sure what town we were in, much less which country. Mui Ne was filled with young Russians. I called it Little Moscow, with loads of young people, kite surfers, and partying kids— Aussies, Brits, some Americans, and mostly Russians. Signs were written in the Cyrillic alphabet. Liquor stores outnumbered retail shops. Mui Ne was a drinker's and backpacker's paradise. A handful of elderly people and a few older, ragged men stumbled in the streets— thoroughly pickled. Dollars, Pounds, Rupees, Baht, Riel, and Dong. Mui Ne was the capital of currency confusion.

I sat by the ocean at Joe's Restaurant, where four overweight Russian women ate plates loaded with fries and bread. We watched the kite surfers and sailboards. At least a hundred rainbow kites skated across the rough sea. The winds were fierce, and waves pounded the bulkhead, spraying us with salty mist. We were on the South China Sea. Traveling as we had been for almost seven months was exhausting. I wanted nothing more than to be home in my bed with my furry family, but my furry family was no more. We booked a sleeper bus from Mui Ne to Hoi An—half the cost of the train, which would have been more comfortable, but with Tet in full swing, it was impossible to get tickets. We'd lucked out with our lodgings for a few days at Green Hills Resort, a beautiful hotel with bougainvillea climbing the walls of cottages and a pool surrounded by banana trees and palms. It was peaceful where I sat under a palm, shaded from the noon sun, and listened to a bird calling in the brush nearby. Sand dunes covered in brush towered behind the resort. I wondered if monsoons wreaked havoc with the dunes. My ankle hurt and my foot hurt. It had been eleven days since I twisted my ankle in Battambang, Cambodia. Bruises appeared after eight days. Had the doctor misread the x-rays in Battambang? A hairline fracture? I didn't think it should hurt so much. Trevor was in the pool and waited for me to join him for a swim. It looked inviting and I felt as if I were on holiday at last.

Later, I sat at Joe's Restaurant and watched waves smash against the breakwater, leaving a salt spray on my lips. I waited for a burger—the first since I'd left the United States. Three Russian backpackers arrived and lit up their fags. Our breakfast earlier had been punctuated by a horde of Russian easy riders who roared up on motorcycles at the Vietnamese family restaurant where we ate most meals. They were a bunch of guys, kite surfers, a bit sleazy looking and covered with tattoos. I saw several young Western women but few Russian women. I figured they came to Mui Ne to drink, smoke dope, kite surf, ride motorcycles, party hard, and sleep. They all acted cool and tough. The posturing was laughable, but I imagined I had been as silly at one time in my own life, minus the tattoos.

After our delightful stay at Green Hills Resort, we had to move to the only place we could find for two nights. Every place we checked was booked during the Tet Holiday. Tien Truc was a hole in the wall where we paid a bundle for our last nights in Mui Ne. It wasn't entirely dreadful. The air conditioner didn't work but we were almost comfortable with high ceilings and an overhead fan. *Keep on the sunny side.* I reminded myself to envision a positive future. Trust. Faith. Hope. I was out of commission with a lousy cold and a nonstop cough. I only hoped I wouldn't cough all the way during our bus ride to Hoi An.

CHAPTER 4: *On a Sleeper Bus to Hoi An via Nha Trans During Tet*

I was a pretzel, slightly salted by the spray of the South China Sea, scrunched in a bus with forty-one other pretzels of various nationalities—mostly young kids whose bodies conformed to pretzel shapes naturally. Trevor and I were off on another Big Ass Adventure on the Sinh Tourist Sleeping Bus to Nha Trans, with our destination Hoi An. We pretzels passed the red sand dunes of Mui Ne on a beautiful stretch of new highway punctuated by a divider with bougainvillea and small pine trees. Streetlights, sidewalks, and flowering trees were on either side of the road. We had a seventeen-hour adventure ahead as pretzels.

Red sand dunes stretched for miles. The South China Sea had to be powerful to have left this undulating landscape. When I saw old people—and I'd seen few older Vietnamese—I wondered how they felt about Americans. The advanced infrastructure in this country was in sharp contrast to the lack of it in Cambodia. Since we'd reached Vietnam, I'd thought about the war. One morning at breakfast we saw an old man, his back as hunched as some of the sand dunes, pushing his bicycle up the hill past the Vietnamese family restaurant we liked. Another day, we watched an elderly Vietnamese man wearing faded, dirty blue clothing and a pith helmet. He talked with an invisible companion as he wandered up the main road in Mui Ne.

"He hasn't forgotten the war, Jesse."

"I think he's still trapped in the nightmare."

The people were poor, I noted, when we passed through small villages. A graphic design decorated homes along with red flags, a yellow star at the center. Some older flags had faded to orange. Our ride turned bumpy as we traveled over a road under construction, although road construction in Vietnam stood in vivid contrast to road construction in India and Cambodia. It was well-organized and well-executed, although it made for a driving nightmare with stops along the way. Rice paddies in the foreground were lush and green. Ladies walked single-file through the paddies, all wearing the broad-brimmed conical hats that reminded me of TV broadcasts from the 1960s and 1970s. We'd grown up in turbulent times in the United States.

We passed a war memorial of three soldiers carrying the flag. I lost count of small cemeteries that I thought might have belonged to families who owned the land, and graves dotted the landscape from Mui Ne to Nha Trans. I was surprised to see a wind turbine farm. It was difficult, as an adult, visiting countries ravaged by wars. Time played tricks with my mind, and I was a child again in Mitylene visiting the old McLemore Plantation. War in Cambodia and Vietnam. Civil war in the United States. Nothing civil about war, as far as I could see. The Sinh Tourist Bus driver had a lead foot on the accelerator, and we flew down the highway. Mountains rose from the earth as if by magic where a conjurer raised the hills from the plains.

We stopped at a rest area facing the sea. I took my shoes out of the plastic bag and tied the laces. Quick break. Shoes off and into the plastic bag. We twisted ourselves back into our seats, akin to slipping into the space shuttle, or folding ourselves into a Ferrari but with better suspension. One had to have a special talent to get into the seats on the sleeper bus. It was butt first, then legs. I was grateful I was limber. Rocky hills and mountains looked as if they sprang from the sea. We passed shanties that spoke of poverty. A goatherd led black and white goats by the roadside. Vibrant emerald rice paddies stretched out across the otherwise dusty gray landscape, punctuated by red flags with yellow hammer and sickle or the yellow star as reminders that Vietnam was a Communist country. The US and U.K. had so much wealth in comparison. I thought of home and all the other places I lived—New York City, Los Angeles, Charlottesville. I worried what would happen to Trevor and me in April. I had to go home. Trevor would go to the U.K. When would we see each other again? Would we see one another again?

Karaoke and billiards seemed to be big forms of entertainment, I noted, as we passed through little towns where motorcycles parked. Homes featured bonsai trees, marigolds, and splashes of bougainvillea, even amidst the poverty. I laughed when I spied a gaggle of geese—more like a hundred gaggles. The light was behind the mountains to my left, and I realized we wouldn't have the pleasure of watching the mad man driving our bus on the road with other maniacs. We had a near miss with a big red bus. It wasn't the first time during the afternoon's drive. A fine gray dust from roadwork and crushed gravel covered the landscape, buildings, and cars.

We neared Cam Ranh, a little town with stoplights, pretty waterways, and mountains in the distance. The sun was setting, so my observations would be limited. Flags hung everywhere. Was it an exhibition of patriotic pride like the Fourth of July in America? Sometimes, I thought about the people who ripped us off and lied. The hotel owner at Green Hills had overcharged for the room he secured for us at hole-in-the-wall Tien Truc. The travel agency had overcharged for the bus tickets from Mui Ne to Hoi An.

"Oh, yeah, Trevor. They ripped us off."

Trevor shrugged his shoulders. "Could have been worse, babe."

"Maybe they feel it's their due. Payback."

CHAPTER 5: *You're Late. You're Late! For a Very Important Date!*

We reached Nha Trans at 7 p.m. Late. We had to transfer to another bus, and we were in the thick of it—the Tet Celebration in downtown Nha Trans, decorated with festive orange and yellow lights strung from every building. Jam-packed streets vibrated with revelers. Massive tour buses, taxis, minivans, cycle rickshaws, motorcycles, cars, and bicycles clogged the intersections. It was a madhouse! Our bus to Hoi An was scheduled to depart at 7 p.m.

"Cor blimey! Run, babe!" Trevor shouted. "I'll get our bags." He raced off the bus into the mass of people crowding the sidewalk. I lost sight of him.

"Jesus, Mary, and Joseph." I ran to our next bus, its engine started and door closing.

"This is our bus to Hoi An." Out of breath, I panted and told the driver, "We have reservations."

"Show tickets."

Our tickets were from Mui Ne to Nha Trans. Not to Hoi An.

"We paid the agent in Mui Ne for the trip to Hoi An." I was frantic.

The bus driver shrugged and closed the door.

I turned and begged the travel agent standing outside. "Help us! We're supposed to be on that bus." I pointed. "We paid for tickets in Mui Ne."

We needed new tickets to transfer from the first bus to the second.

The pretty young Vietnamese travel agent said, "Go get tickets." She pointed to the counter inside a small building that served as the bus terminal and ran alongside me. She explained our plight to the young Sinh Tourist agent who stood behind the counter. She nodded and printed our tickets while I raced to the toilet. Inside the small terminal, chaos reigned with families herding crying children. Elbow room only. I waited in line to use the loo.

The young Vietnamese agent handed me our tickets. Trevor rushed toward me on the sidewalk outside the terminal. He had our bags. I ran to the bus and showed the driver our tickets to Hoi An.

"Go to office and get luggage tags."

"Seriously? I have tickets."

"What's wrong, Jesse?"

"Luggage tags."

I ran back inside the office and rushed up to one of their agents, a young lady who spoke English. I looked out the door. "Oh my god!" I watched our bus to Hoi An pull away from the curb. I pointed gesturing wildly. "Our bus is leaving!"

The young Vietnamese agent went into high gear and got our luggage tags.

"Here." I shouted over the din of voices and revelry in the streets and handed Trevor the luggage tags.

Meanwhile, Trevor ran with two Sinh tourist agents across two streets while the heavy traffic whizzed by. The young woman and another Sinh Tourist man raced with me to help us board the bus. At the bus, the driver, who had pulled to the curb around the corner from the office, was behind on his time schedule, and he wasn't happy. Two Western tourists were pulled off the bus along with their bags. They were pissed off, but they'd been given our seats. The driver handed me a plastic bag for my shoes. I took them off in the street and clambered in an ungraceful manner onto the bus. I couldn't find our seats at first. One was upper, the other lower, separated. I was at the back of the bus with lots of excited, noisy children. Maybe they'd go to sleep soon. People slept on the floor of the bus alongside bags strewn on the floor. Oh, man. The bus for our overnight journey had no restroom or toilet. I looked behind me. Where was Trevor?

He boarded the bus, out of breath. "Bloody hell, babe."

He recounted his experience when he'd told the male tourist agent he needed a wee before boarding the bus.

"Hurry! Hurry!" The Sinh Tourist agent had told Trevor. "Pee against a wall."

"I couldn't pee where the agent pointed because someone's cooking pots and utensils were against the wall."

And we were off—senior pretzels awkwardly fitting into berths on the overnight sleeper bus to Hoi An.

CHAPTER 6: *Truc Huy Villa.*
Hoi An, Viet Nam

Trevor and I caught a lucky break in Hoi An. We'd booked a stay at Truc Huy Villa three weeks after it opened. The morning we reached Hoi An, the town was still asleep. After we downed much-needed Vietnamese coffee at a little shop, we took a long taxi ride to find the hotel. Truc Huy Villa turned out to be a blessing. When we arrived, the manager upgraded us to a luxury bedroom facing the saltwater pool. I needed a break to unkink my body out of the pretzel position. The second day, we wanted to get bikes out to ride, but the manager's intensity in combination with the decongestants I'd been taking made me dizzy. The young woman on staff the first morning was not as pushy about tours, clothes, and souvenirs as the young woman the second morning. When Trevor saw how unsteady I was on the bicycle, he vetoed our outing.

I walked down the street to a temple filled with beautiful flowers—sunflowers, hollyhocks, giant marigolds, and dahlias—where I met a gentle young Buddhist nun-in-training with her new name, Tinh Dai. She had created a heavenly garden inside the walls surrounding the temple. We exchanged Facebook sites, took photos with my iPhone, and went into one of the temples where the young nun lit two sticks of incense. I put a contribution in the alms box.

Tinh Dai showed me what to do when we entered the temple. She and I bowed three times before the Buddha with hands folded in supplication. Then we knelt and bowed with hands over our heads three times, and finally we stood and bowed three times. She led me past a laughing Buddha, surrounded by brilliant yellow marigolds, to the small temple with a female Buddha, Tara, and we repeated the ritual. Tinh Dai handed me a stick of incense to put in front of the white porcelain statue of the female Buddha, and after I performed the three bows standing and kneeling, she left me to have a moment of solitary prayer. It was beautiful and peaceful. I felt refreshed after the unexpected meeting and experience at the temple.

No. No. No. Later the first day, exhausted from the journey on the sleeper buses, I lost my center. After a glorious shower in the marble bathroom, I walked back into our luxurious poolside room with its gorgeous linens and was alarmed when I saw the dark expression on Trevor's face. He launched into a tirade about money, ambushed me again, and made me the target of his anger. His fear of financial insecurity was contagious and overwhelmed me. I tried to replace my fear with faith. Since I didn't want Trevor to see my distress, I put on a happy face and kept my mouth shut. Not a great choice, I thought, but anything to keep the peace.

We walked to Hoi An Ancient Town for lunch and watched a boat race on the river near the famous covered Japanese bridge. Hoi An was extraordinary. The UNESCO World Heritage site had been an important trading port and the old town's well-preserved architectural styles reflected the influence of the nations that traded with Hoi An.

CHAPTER 7: *Waking to Drumbeats.*
Hoi An, Vietnam

I awoke to the sound of drumbeats, but Trevor wasn't in the room. I was confused because it was early. I was about to take a shower when Trevor bolted through the door.

"Hurry, hurry and dress."

"What?"

"They're at the temple to celebrate the end of the Vietnamese New Year."

I splashed water in my face, ran my fingers through my hair, and threw on my clothes. Trevor and I walked to the temple with the owner of Truc Huy Villas, who had invited us to join the celebration. Hieh, the young woman manager, whose name meant "Secret", came with us because the owner, her boss, only spoke Vietnamese. He explained through our translator, "It shows respect for our ancestors, then we pray for a new year of health and prosperity."

We entered the temple, lit incense, and bowed three times, then knelt and bowed three times to the floor, then rose and bowed three times again. I felt peaceful after my prayers. Old silk Chinese paintings were framed and hung inside the altar of the temple. The paintings were stained with age, water damage, and perhaps smoke as if they'd been rescued from a burning place. Food, candles, incense, flowers, and even a red cardboard box of ChocoPies—a mashup of Moon Pies and Twinkies—sat on a stand in front of a large, old photograph of Ho Chi Minh.

The priest invited us to sit with the old and young men who sat cross-legged on bamboo mats in the temple. A server placed dishes of chicken, meats, fruit, and chopsticks in the middle on a long bamboo mat where dragon fruit, apples, papaya, and oranges were displayed artfully. Each man had a can of beer set before him. They insisted on giving us tiny tumblers of rice wine we pretended to sip. We raised it to our lips with an enthusiastic cheer, "Hoh!" as the men raised their beers in the air for a toast.

"What an honor to participate in the celebration at the end of Tet." I thanked the owner.

Trevor and I walked back to the hotel. "That was amazing, Jesse."

"It was great, but I felt a little weird being the only woman sitting with all the men."

After breakfast, I walked down the street to the temple with the beautiful flowers, the white ceramic laughing Buddha, and the white female Buddha. I heard a gong ring three times and saw Tinh Dai and her friend Tinh Sen. Tinh Dai handed me a beautiful origami lotus blossom she had constructed out of heavy paper. It was a precious gift. I felt blessed and at peace.

CHAPTER 8: *Not with a Bang, but with a Whimper. An Bang Beach*

At the beach, but not the beach of our expectations. It was fronted by restaurants, row after row of wooden lounge chairs with cushions, and palm-thatched umbrellas. We hadn't been out of the taxi five seconds before a vendor approached us.

"Come eat at my restaurant."

Another vendor said, "Come sit in my beach chairs for free."

Translation: You can sit in my beach chair for free only if you eat at my restaurant.

"Oh, my!"

"Those wankers want the dosh."

It wasn't what we'd hoped to find on our day at the beach.

I'd talked with Trevor earlier in the morning. I had noticed that, when he talked about his future, he didn't talk about me. I had to be realistic and stop entertaining thoughts of life in England with him. Loving Trevor was a strange thing. I wanted happiness and well-being for him, even if it meant I was no longer a part of his life.

"I'm worried about you, Jesse. I feel responsible for you."

We sat on the beach and listened to "Three Little Birds," my favorite Bob Marley song. "Don't worry . . . everything is gonna be alright." Timing? Coincidence? A wonderful message.

"Trevor, I love you. I don't want to control or manipulate you. I don't need you to take care of me. You're not responsible for me or my life." I thought it was best to say what I felt and not leave it unsaid. When we loved someone, we showed it through our actions, not our words.

The respite in Hoi An was a welcome relief from the flurry of activity after leaving Thailand, going to Cambodia, and making our way to Vietnam. Saigon wasn't a good scene for us with all the chaos. Our week in Mui Ne had been fragmented because of the Tet Holidays. I awoke in the morning crying as I envisioned myself back home without Trevor. My freelance work was on ice because of our extended travel overseas. My future was unclear. In some ways I knew it was best not to know, but the black cloud followed me all morning. I prayed for peace, serenity, and direction.

The Vietnam War haunted my thoughts more than I ever imagined. My feelings caught me unaware and gave me a knot in my stomach. I looked at rice paddies, the people who worked in them, and thought of bombs striking the emerald fields. After I read Lonely Planet descriptions of places in Vietnam where fighting had taken place, I remembered names from headlines, and I was gobsmacked or "gutted," as Trevor said. Danang. China Beach. Hamburger Hill. Hanoi. No longer names in the headlines but cities, villages, towns with people whose lives had been shattered by the war. It had been over four decades, but I felt such sadness about what had happened to innocent people, towns, and temples. Let there be peace on earth.

What was I going to do? Trevor said he wanted me to return to Cornwall with him for three months and take time to finish my book. Reining in the stories about train travel was a challenge. I had to limit the scope of the manuscript. Trevor's mixed messages confused me. I was out of my comfort zone, and I needed to find someone. Me. Again. I wondered where I needed to go after our odyssey—literally and metaphorically. Back home in April? Back to England with Trevor? Wrestling with demons was exhausting. Was it a pipe dream to think my writing could support me? Sometimes, the dark cloud lifted when I wasn't even aware. Nothing ever happens unless first a dream. I had to believe in myself.

CHAPTER 9: *On Leaving Hoi An, Viet Nam*

My heart felt sad on leaving the Buddhist nuns at the pagoda in Hoi An. Tears filled my eyes on the sunny early-morning walk after my goodbye visit. The highlight of my stay in Hoi An had been meeting Tinh Dai and Tinh Sen in the stunning garden at the Buddhist temple. The young women touched my heart with their innocence and their individual sparks of mischief.

As thoughtful as the hotel staff were, the constant attention was exhausting.

"Hello, Jesse. How are you?"

"Hello, Tre-vor. How are you?"

"Where do you go today?"

"What did you do today?"

"Are you going for dinner now?"

"Is your ___ all right?" Fill in the blank: breakfast, room, laundry, and so on, ad infinitum.

We were on the Sinh Tourist Sleeper Bus to Hue. I thought about Paul, the sixty-year-old Brit we had met at the hotel, a man who had an insatiable desire for drama in his life, or his month-long holiday, in Hoi An. One of his lovers was Loang, the Herbal Spa (massage parlor) owner on Cam Island. She arrived unannounced to join him for breakfast one day. I felt sure Lover Number One wanted to meet

Tanh, Lover Number Two, the competition who visited Paul's room for whatever. A massage, or perhaps mutual satisfaction according to Paul. He never admitted he paid them. A third woman showed up on Sunday as well. Trevor and I watched the drama carousel. The variety of lovers were Paul's Vietnamese distractions, or entertainment, or projects. Older men came to Asia for entertainment with young women in a culture where entertainment was a business transaction. Paul gave Number One money, and she in turn gave it to her husband, who drank, gambled, and physically abused her. To add to the excitement, Number One's husband had a girlfriend with whom he had a baby. He and Number One had two children. Paul spent Tet in their village where everyone gathered.

Paul had told us all about himself—his money, his big empty house in England, his two cars, including the Audi Quattro he loved to drive, two ex-wives, and four children away from home—either married, or working, or at university. He said when he was in the U.K. all he did was go to the pub and drink with his mates.

"It's such a drab life," he sighed.

He was in Vietnam for entertainment when we met him. The year before, he had been in Thailand with a beautiful Thai girl. Paul's gray life in the U.K. became 4-D Technicolor, all brilliant colors of the rainbow in Southeast Asia with the young women he paid. He talked with Trevor every day, boasting about his exploits.

"He has a sexual problem and can't get an erection," Trevor said.

"So he compensates with money and by acting like Big Daddy?"

"Jesse, he bought the massage parlor owner's family a refrigerator and then a washing machine so she could stop washing the towels by hand."

CHAPTER 10: *Haunted by the War*

On the way to Danang, I saw an old man lying in the street beside his parked bicycle. Was he dead, or dead drunk and sleeping it off? Other cyclists and motorcycles whizzed by him. It was impossible for me not to think about war and Americans I knew who had come home scarred after shooting children who carried hand grenades. One, two, three, what were we fighting for? Cows grazed, roaming free, by the side of the highway. Trash filled deep holes and craters next to older, roofless brick buildings. Streets without houses ended in fields filled with rubble. New and old schools and temples stood in testament to the country's history.

We drove through a long tunnel, an engineering feat under the mountains near Danang. The jungles were impenetrable with bamboo thickets and vines like kudzu. The Viet Cong had transported supplies through two hundred kilometers of tunnels during the war, and they had three levels of tunnels under Saigon. No war was won with the Viet Cong going to ground.

We emerged from the tunnel in a small fishing village by the sea. Age, black mold, dirt, and years of poverty marked old buildings. Against a backdrop of lush emerald-green rice paddies, water buffalo, and humble dwellings, an elderly woman stacked kindling on the back of her bike. She stood next to another woman wearing a conical straw hat. I struggled to process my emotions and reaction to Vietnam because the war felt like yesterday, not forty or fifty years ago. The tropical landscape, although dotted with scars, was beautiful, with palm trees, bright pink bougainvillea, and majestic older buildings.

When we reached the outskirts of Hue, I thought about our friend who'd been a helicopter pilot during the war. He told us Hue was bombed repeatedly. "The US dropped more bombs on Laos than Vietnam and Cambodia together to stop the VC supply chain on the Ho Chi Minh trail." The former helicopter pilot continued, "We bombed temples at My Son, a Viet Cong hideout, and bombed Hue's Citadel— sacred ground."

CHAPTER 11: *Hue and The Citadel*

March fourth. March forth. We walked to the Citadel from the Hue Charming Hotel that hadn't been bombed during "The American War," as the Vietnamese called it. I was happy to leave Hue after two nights at the hotel I called Way Charming. Not. We walked for hours, with breaks for water and my nonstop face mopping. I wore the air and felt the effects of the heat and high humidity despite the gray skies.

We walked through a public park along the Perfume River. Extraordinary sculptures, all related to the war, in granite, bronze, and what looked like steel or aluminum, filled the park. No matter where we were, I wondered, *Did that building survive the bombing? Is that rubble left over from the war? Did that old man with the long white beard and conical hat fight in the war?* Not to be overlooked, the Viet Cong murdered countless civilians in Hue. The Americans discovered the bodies in mass graves and gave the dead a proper Vietnamese burial. POWs handled the dead.

The Citadel—a massive citadel within walls and a large moat—had been the residence of Vietnamese emperors of the Nguyen dynasties. Because the VC were using it during the war, the Americans had bombed the sacred grounds. Both sides took actions against the terms of the agreement regarding historic or sacred places. Other temples and emperors' residences had been leveled in the war in 1947. Fortunately, many historic buildings had been spared and had been restored. It was a window into the past and unfamiliar ways of life and an opportunity to soak up the beauty of the walled enclosures of the respective emperors who called Hue and the Citadel home over the centuries.

The craftsmanship and carvings in the wooden buildings were colorful, stunning, and beautiful. Pagodas and entry gates to the various walled compounds were built of masonry and decorated with extraordinary carvings or figures in relief—mosaics of dragons, roosters, horses, flowers, birds. Each building and entry was topped with what looked like ornate, fragile porcelain carvings or metal dragons.

We took a taxi back to the hotel, stopping only to buy baguettes, *bánh mì,* with meat, the usual fillings, and hot chili sauce. Then we went straight up to our large room—with windows fronting one street and a full balcony facing the Perfume River. Fishing boats lined up near a bridge crossing the river.

CHAPTER 12: *Leaving Vietnam*

I was distressed the first night in Hue, saddened and confused, because I didn't know what to make of my Facebook messages from Tinh Dai. She said she had had a sad day and been scolded. She didn't like the people at the temple in Hoi An. I had noted that the older Buddhist nuns at the temple rarely smiled at Trevor and me. Tinh Dai said she had a problem. She wanted to travel home to see her grandmother, but she didn't have the money for her return trip. She said she was very confused. That much had been obvious for most of the short time I'd known her. Tinh Sen seemed to be more mature and a lot more content than Tinh Dai, although both girls, Buddhist nuns-in-training, were twenty years old, and it was the first year away from home for both.

I asked how I could help. I felt helpless and sent love and prayers. Trevor read my messages with Tinh Dai.

"You asked her how you could help."

"Yes." I nodded.

"Well, you stepped in it."

Trevor's comment stirred my thoughts, and I felt like a balloon with a sudden puncture. The air rushed out of me. He said I was at fault. Was it about money all along? I thought about it for a while, and I sent her a message.

Dear sweet Tinh Dai, I can send you my love and prayers. I cannot send you money. <3

Sad, sad heart. I wanted to think I misunderstood. Was I deceiving myself? I didn't want to believe I was so naive. I had allowed myself to trust.

"Looks like the week we spent chatting with her was a ploy leading up to her request for money."

"I don't believe it, Trevor."

What was it about Tinh Dai? A winsomeness, innocence, and beauty. A need for love and hugs. She told me she loved me. In my book, love meant love. I adored her and Tinh Sen, precious girls whose smiles and company meant the world to me from the first day in Hoi An. We were leaving Vietnam. Would I ever return? I hoped so.

Thailand

CHAPTER 1: *Bangkok.*
Siam Gypsy Junction

We arrived in Bangkok on a Thursday night. I slept very late on Friday, felt sluggish, and didn't want to go out. Trevor went for a swim, a walk, an exploration of the neighborhood, and was gone most of the day. I took advantage of the quiet afternoon to reflect. He brought food back for our evening meal, marked by uncomfortable tension and little conversation. Later that evening, I decided it was time to have The Conversation with Trevor about our relationship. He planned to return to the U.K., and I would fly back to the US. We didn't have a plan to see each other again. He either couldn't, or wasn't willing to, make a commitment. He knew I didn't mean marriage. I had made it clear I wanted a committed relationship. For three years, I had experienced hellos and goodbyes with nebulous plans to see one another. Three years was long enough.

Island Girl, the nutter in the Caribbean and Trevor's former girlfriend, had tried to friend me on Facebook. Who had told her my name? Trevor had assured me she was no longer a passenger on our bus, but it felt weird. My instincts went on high alert.

Trevor. I had adored him with blind trust, but his behavior dashed my illusions. I wanted a life partner who respected me, who cherished a committed relationship with me. It was past time for pragmatism. It was time to detach, separate my emotions from my intellect.

"Trevor, I'm not going to entertain fantasies about our relationship."

I couldn't muster the courage, but the Universe could. God could. Krishna could. Buddha could. Allah could. I decided to let them, and I prayed for inner peace. When we set out on our odyssey, I had imagined seven months of uninterrupted writing. Travel in Southeast Asia with Trevor, the human kinetic ball of energy, had blown up my writing routine. I was drained emotionally. *Parting is such sweet sorrow.* What was sweet about it? I had a hole in my heart. Love was a bargain with no guarantees, a deal that could be broken.

CHAPTER 2: *Dark Night of the Soul in Bangkok*

I understood full stop how much Trevor rebelled against commitment, and I felt stupid having loved. Part of me knew I shouldn't chastise myself. It wasn't self-caring to continue an intimate relationship in which I couldn't be completely open and trusting.

"I'm selfish, Jesse."

Yes, he was. Was his life simply an example of prolonged adolescence? I sobbed alone in the dark, my face buried in the pillow, on the living room couch. Then I grabbed my laptop and searched for the earliest flight back to the US, but not back home. I could fly to Orlando—to Judy's house where I knew I'd be safe, could fall apart, and regroup before heading home.

The morning after, we sat at his dental office near the BTS station at Thong Lo. Trevor acted as if nothing had changed. "I want to go back to Cornwall and walk on the clifftops, darling."

Heartbreak wasn't a mortal blow, was it? I waited in the dentist's office in Bangkok while she worked on Trevor's teeth, after she replaced the amalgam I had lost in a tooth. Muzak played "As Time Goes By" from the film *Casablanca*. "A kiss is still a kiss . . . " Humphrey Bogart stood in the rain and fog in front of the hangar while the plane taxied off with Ingrid Bergman. It was a fitting end. Sometimes the end was goodbye.

Could I walk away from the man I loved who didn't return my love in equal measure? The man with whom I had shared the adventures of a lifetime in my so-called golden years. It was a difficult choice. Trevor's expression, "I feel gutted," captured exactly how I felt.

"I want to pay for your dental work and for your flight home, Jesse."
His mixed messages were beyond confusing

I thought about our senior love story. It was comic and tragic, funny, and sad, all at the same time. Shortly after Trevor came into my life, in our unlikely meeting, a friend said, "People come into your life for a reason, a season, or a lifetime." My eyes filled with tears. I got up and drank a cup of water from the dispenser.

After we left the dentist's office, Trevor said, "Let's go to Starbucks." He paid for our iced mochas without so much as a raised eyebrow about the cost.

CHAPTER 3: *At the Dentist Again.
Thong Lo*

We returned to the dentist's office for another minor procedure Trevor needed. Our day was easy, no tension. Since The Conversation, Trevor had been sweet and affectionate. He made Vietnamese iced coffee for me and brought me surprises like the tiny, powerful Bluetooth speaker from MBK (the well-known Ma Boon Khrong Center shopping mall.).

"Now you can listen to Paul's recordings [a former Jesuit priest who quoted Anthony De Mello] while you get dressed Sunday mornings, Jesse."

Why now? I wondered. Why was Trevor loving and generous? My thoughts roiled like the muddy Mississippi while I packed for our move to the next seven-day Airbnb. I didn't know where it was, but it had a pool and washing machine—important features.

CHAPTER 4: *Condo at the End of the World*

Friday the thirteenth. I was dismayed when I walked into the Airbnb studio condo near the BTS Wutthakat station. It was a tired, rundown place that smelled of pee and reminded me of a nursing home. I looked out the sliding glass doors directly into the windows opposite and I saw a wheelchair folded on the balcony and a bare mattress on the bed in a room with no curtains. Sad and tired. I wanted to leave as soon as we walked into the dismal place. I hated it. It was on the far side of the world. It had taken an hour-and-a-half by taxi to drive twenty-three miles through Bangkok traffic from our wonderful one-bedroom condo at 58 Udom Suk—iCondo—where we had stayed for a week.

My reality. I'd fly back to the US in a little over two weeks with enough money to last two months. Maybe. If I didn't eat much. Was I delusional? Living in a fantasy world, as Trevor accused me? At times, Trevor had been a wonderful partner, but his on-off mood swings left me feeling as if I were a ping pong ball. I had to detach with love and not leave anything I needed to say unsaid before we parted. Trust. I wanted to handle our parting with love, wishing him only the best in whatever he chose to do.

I felt sick at heart, and there was nothing for it except grieving and healing. I sent a note to close friends to share my choice, my difficult decision to part as friends. To go our separate ways.

My stomach ached and I wanted to weep as I sat by the pool at the dreadful condo. Thank heaven, we had only three more nights at the end of the world. We'd return to the BTS OnNut area for a new Airbnb called The Next, a studio with a full kitchen, washer/dryer, and pool. It was next door to the Tesco Lotus—its food court, shopping, and ten-minute BTS ride to Udom Suk where I planned to go to the little beauty shop off the alley near Watson's to see Pai, Nong, and Boom. Of course, I'd go to the dim sum restaurant a block away to visit Waan. I needed to lick my wounds. They were my adopted Bangkok family after all.

Trevor's flight to the U.K. was booked for five days before I had planned to leave Bangkok. He said he wanted to help his daughter with her projects and buy potted plants for the balcony at his penthouse apartment in the converted warehouse. I didn't have an airline ticket. Did I want to stay in Bangkok? I could live in Bangkok for a fraction of the cost in the US. I couldn't go back home right away to an empty house filled only with memories. It was a healthy choice for me to cut our ties, to detach with love but detach completely.

Trevor's iPad beeped, beeped, and beeped again in the wee hours. It woke me. Trevor didn't stir. I got up for water and looked at the screen. What? Desperate Island Girl had sent two messages, a photo, and a video. I didn't need to read the messages. My wakeup call was crystal clear. Island Girl had been and was still the third party in our relationship. Trevor said she was crazy. He hadn't seen her in four years. I was awake. I couldn't sleep. My mind was a maelstrom of confusion. If Trevor didn't derive satisfaction from contact with her, why hadn't he blocked her? Why did Trevor choose to encourage a crazy woman? I asked myself why I had chosen a man who wasn't willing to make a commitment. I had spent more time with Trevor in three years and felt closer to him than I had to anyone since I had been married thirty-four years earlier. If tenants rented my house, I could stay in Southeast Asia and write. I was tempted to stay in Bangkok with its lower cost of living. I felt calmer and I wasn't as raw with the ache, the sick emptiness in my belly.

Later that day, it was my turn to do our laundry while Trevor went for a swim. And in all honesty, I needed to do something completely mindless. I took the wet clothes out onto the balcony and hung as much as I could on the drying rack. Then I draped clothes over the balcony, one by one until the catastrophe. Trevor's special technicolor Krishna Tshirt, his favorite, slipped off the railing and fell. I panicked, but I thought it had probably fallen to the shrubs three stories below. I peeked over the railing. Oh, no! The Tshirt had dropped to the balcony of the apartment below and caught on the railing. I raced downstairs to the second-floor condo and knocked on the door. I waited and knocked again louder. No one answered. I ran back to the steps and saw one of the residents. She eyed me.

"Do you know when the owners will be back?"

She shook her head, clearly suspicious of me.

"I dropped laundry on the balcony."

"No one lives there."

Oh, man, what was I going to do? Trevor's favorite Tshirt. Back in the stinky condo, I started laughing. I couldn't help myself. I laughed so hard I cried. It felt great to release tension.

When Trevor returned from his swim, I said, "I have a confession." I giggled until I couldn't hold my out-loud laughter in check.

He looked puzzled. "What?"

"You know your Krishna Tshirt?"

He nodded. "What about it?"

"Well," I hesitated, and the words rushed out. "It kind of slipped off the railing and fell to the balcony below."

He went out to the balcony and looked down where Technicolor Krishna hung precariously over the railing.

"No one lives downstairs," I mumbled. "I checked."

Trevor looked at me and in the corner of the balcony where a mop stood in a bucket. He got the mop and leaned over the balcony as far as he could reach to get the shirt. No luck. "Now what, Jesse?"

"I have an idea." I had a flash of inspiration. "Where's your little fishing pole?"

“Seriously?”

“I’m not kidding.”

Trevor assembled the three parts of the pole and went out on the balcony to fish for the shirt. People sitting around the pool pointed up at us, some laughing and others with mouths wide open. He fished for his shirt, while I laughed. Two attempts later, the hook snagged Technicolor Krishna, and Trevor reeled the Tshirt up. Success. We doubled over laughing. Laughter was the best medicine.

It was our last night at the condo I detested. We were lovers. We cuddled, touched, kissed, hugged, and fell asleep holding hands; but I was Patsy Cline: “I fall to pieces.” I ached all over.

The next morning, Trevor sat outside by the pool with his iPad. I unpacked my suitcase, only to repack it for the journey home. Alone. I envisioned early mornings where I couldn’t reach out and touch Trevor while he slept. I knew I would long for our goodnight kisses and “Sweet dreams.” I reminded myself we had parted before and I had survived: two times our first year together, two times the second, and one time in the third year. Nevertheless, at each of our five partings, I felt as if my heart were ripped apart, not knowing when we would see each other again. Would the parting in our fourth year be our last?

CHAPTER 5: *On the Way Out of Town*

We waited for our Thai friend to pick us up for a weekend out of town to see the couple who owned an English language school. I thought, *"Trevor, every minute with you is precious."* He held my hand. We had five more nights together. I held my emotions in check. The language school owners, their young Chinese employee, and a nephew talked about the school.

Trevor said, *sotto voce,* "It sounds like a cult."

"The control and manipulation scare me."

The language academy was successful, but the owner was a control freak. She was studying me, I knew, to see if I would be a good fit.

"You'll become part of the family," she said.

And play by their rules was unspoken but a clear dictate, I thought. School lasted ten hours a day during the week, but the weekend hours were shorter—eight hours a day. The language school was in an out-of-the-way, unattractive area.

Our young Thai friend said he and his girlfriend, who had gone with us, wanted us to see something more international than the school. We were in the car for what they said would be an hour's drive to see who knew what. The young Thai couple were good friends and ribbed one another throughout the drive. Trevor and I sat in the back seat in silence. I reflected on the owners' descriptions of the language school. I focused on the facts. Employees worked seven days a week. The young Chinese instructor was in her mid-twenties and enthusiastic. Learning was new. She was challenged. Been there, done that. The language school was way the heck away from Bangkok. I felt like a deer in the headlights. Fresh meat. What was their agenda? They saw my educational and business background and thought, I imagined, this is what she can do for us. Yes, but what did they have to offer me? Naught. The language school wasn't a good fit for me. Maybe Bangkok. I hated the weekend trip because it robbed me of two days I could have spent with Trevor in Bangkok.

We reached a resort in the mountains. WTH? I couldn't wait to get back to my adopted family in Bangkok. Lady Boy at the little hair salon in Bangkok was a female impersonator in large-scale shows. Lady Boy was *Kathoey* in Thai.

I thought, *The drive was a boondoggle, a wild goose chase, a snipe hunt.*

"We're going to one of the largest national parks in Thailand, Jesse and Trevor."

"Lord, get me outta here," I whispered.

The sun peeked through the clouds at the end of the day. It was 5 p.m., and we were in the mountains. If I worked at the language school, I would be stuck in the middle of Nowheresville without transport. No way. The language school owners offered to get me a Thai work visa so I could give lectures. While we were at the school, I felt strangely insecure. I'd pumped it up to be the "honored" guest in a classroom with Chinese students. I was cautious about what I said because a camera in a corner of the ceiling faced the classroom. They watched me. It was their hidden agenda. I felt manipulated. When we left the room, I saw a guy come out into the hallway with earphones. Had he been listening in? If the school had CCTV, he probably had recorded my talk for analysis later. Why did I feel like a bug pinned under a magnifying glass? We had interviewed one another. Fortunately, Trevor had talked a lot at the end.

The owners put me on the spot. "How do you like it here?"

Thank heaven Trevor launched into his opinion. "I'd prefer Bangkok. You need to start a school in Bangkok."

The owners were too polite to disagree with anything Trevor said.

"Their school was bizarre, Jesse. I thought they'd offer us the Kool-Aid."

"I'm excited about potting plants for my balcony, decorating my flat, buying linens for my beds," Trevor said. He wanted to rebuild his life in the U.K. Had he made his choice based on finances rather than emotions? "Jesse, I don't want to assume the responsibility of taking care of you financially."

"You sound like a broken record, Trevor. I never asked you to take me on."

He was terrified of his own financial situation and fear colored his life. Why did he have a poverty mentality when he was in the catbird seat with a two-bedroom penthouse worth several hundred thousand pounds, his retirement, and a pension?

Bangkok without Trevor. Life without Trevor. My life was changed forever. I saw the world through different eyes because of our travels. Cold turkey withdrawal. It was hard to walk away from someone you loved, even when you knew you wanted different things in your lives. It wasn't right or wrong. It was just what it was.

Of course, I asked myself if I was doing the right thing by cutting off the relationship. Insanity was doing the same thing over and over again and expecting different results. Codependency. Serenity Prayer time. God grant me the serenity to accept the things I cannot change, the courage to change the things I can, and the wisdom to know the difference.

CHAPTER 6: Alone in The Next Garden Apartments. Bangkok

Our last full day together. Our last night together. I didn't want to second-guess my choice. We wanted different things in our lives. Sunday, we went to Chatuchak. Monday, we visited JJ Market. Tuesday, I had an allergic reaction to something, and Trevor went to MBK. Thursday, we visited Chinatown. No more going, please. *We had busied ourselves as a distraction,* I thought.

It was 5 p.m. and Trevor was gone. I thought about the cups of milk coffee I brought him in bed in the morning and the cups of ginger, lemon, and honey tea he brought me. I stared blindly at the crazy Chinese pool walker in the infinity pool across from our balcony as he walked round and round, and I wept.

It wasn't breaking up to go on different paths. Nothing was broken. But I wanted a partner who wanted to grow old with me, and Trevor said he didn't want that for his life. I had to respect what he wanted, just as I hoped he respected what I chose. I didn't want to believe we'd never see one another again.

Before he left, Trevor had stood in the doorway, tears running down his cheeks. My vision blurred through my tears. He left his luggage in the hallway, came back into the room, and held me.

"I love you, Jesse Meredith."

The End

Epilogue

"Well, damn!" I broke the silence. "Every shut eye ain't sleep, and every goodbye ain't gone."

Epilogue 2

"Those who cannot learn from the past are doomed to repeat it."
—George Santayana

Eight years later . . .
Jesse peered down from her kayak through the crystal-clear water where the manatees congregated en masse on the Crystal River and thought about the choices she had made. In those quiet moments of reflection, she was grateful for the heartache. Through the pain of loss, she'd found her voice, reclaimed her dreams, and embraced her fierce independence. She had accepted her mistakes and didn't regret the decisions she'd made before she understood that what she'd imagined was the end wasn't quite the end at all, but a new beginning marked by resilience.

In fact, the tumultuous last chapter of her relationship with Trevor clearly showed her the transformative power of pain and the enduring spirit of the human heart. Things had fallen apart in the most unexpected and shocking way almost a year after they had parted in Bangkok. At Trevor's invitation and with his encouragement, Jesse had rented her home in the US and had been living with Trevor in the U.K. and working to establish a long-term, non-resident visa when everything unexpectedly went to hell in a handbasket. She had thought their relationship had changed and had moved to the U.K. in the mistaken belief that life with Trevor would be different going forward. Her folly!

The last straw was the night Trevor had told her, "I don't want to continue a romantic relationship with you."

WTF, Jesse thought.

Trevor had followed his shocker with a bizarre invitation for her to continue living in his home and had said they could be friends.

"Seriously! That's not going to happen," Jesse had said.

"You're going to write about this, aren't you?" Trevor had asked.

Jesse said nothing.

"People are going to hate me," Trevor said, shaking his head as if it mattered one way or the other to Jesse.

She had left, but not before telling Trevor, "That's it. You won't see me again. Don't expect me to show up crying at your door or to call you twenty times a day in tears. You won't hear from me again. When I walk out that door, I'm walking out of your life and this incredibly effed up situation. I'm outta here."

Jesse thought, *Churchill nailed it when he said, 'If you're going through hell, keep going.'* And so she had.

Leaving England on a miserable cold, wet, and gray February day, Jesse had looked at bright yellow daffodils poking through the snow and had sighed with relief. "I'm not going to be defeated by this."

The taxi driver had asked, "What was that, luv?"

"Sorry," she said, "I didn't realize I'd said anything out loud."

"Heading back to the States?" he asked.

"No," Jesse had told him. "I'm going where it's warm and sunny." She didn't explain that she'd rented her house and was more-or-less homeless at age sixty-six.

And so she'd flown to Bangkok . . .

She'd lived there for six months in 2016. It hadn't been easy and at times she'd felt terribly lonely, but loneliness was far preferable to living with the unpredictable chaos of life with Trevor. During that time and with the distance of continents away from England and the US, she had flourished. Jesse had traveled to Myanmar twice—the first time she'd gone to Yangon (Rangoon) on a visa run to extend her stay in Bangkok. In the airport for her return flight to Bangkok, she'd seen a large group of monks many of whom wore satin bags in vibrant colors even though most of the monks carried cotton bags in the saffron color that matched their robes. She had asked their Chinese translator about the colorful satin bags and had attracted the attention of one monk who looked like he could have been an NFL linebacker. She never learned anything about the satin bags, but the monk, through the Chinese translator, had explained he was curious about her and thought she had a very kind face. He then invited her to visit his temple in Bangkok where he was *phra ajahn*, a venerable monk, second in rank at the Temple of the Golden Buddha.

Jesse had returned to Myanmar, because she wanted to visit the ancient temples on the plains of Bagan. She'd flown to Mandalay and had taken a small bus to Bagan. Her first evening in Bagan, she experienced a magnitude 6.8 earthquake that damaged many of the temples. She was fine and thought it was a fitting welcome on her solo adventures in Southeast Asia. Her friends started calling her Indiana Jones.

Before she returned to the US, she had asked a new friend—a young Thai woman, a supervisor she'd met at a Starbucks—to go with her to the Temple of the Golden Buddha as her translator with the monk. Magic kept happening and, through the young woman's translation, Jesse had learned the monk thought they'd been family members in a previous incarnation. She had asked for his blessing and kept a small silver icon of the Golden Buddha in a Buddhist prayer box, a *gau*, she wore on a silver chain for protection.

Slowly, but surely, over time Jesse healed, and only later understood she had escaped a toxic narcissistic relationship.[1] Who knew? Instead of regret, Jesse was filled with gratitude because the universe had indeed booted her out of her comfort zone. She understood that she would never have found her strength and her agency unless she had experienced it all—the good, the bad, and the perfectly dreadful.

We don't know what we don't know until we know it, Jesse thought, and she thanked the universe for the lessons learned.

---

1. Although there are many excellent sources of information about narcissism, one of the most helpful the author discovered was Dr. Ramani Durvasula. Dr. Ramani's YouTube videos and her podcast are invaluable resources.

Acknowledgments

My heartfelt thanks to Mary E. Murchison, Esq., for her encouragement, skilled editing, support, and lifelong friendship. I am indebted to Mary for her belief in me.

To my friends in the U.K.—Kate Green, Abi Miller, and Sarah Willis—thank you for being part of the journey.

Thanks to Karen Knapik, who pushed and cheered me to launch my podcast and finish the book.

To Savan Wilson: I owe a debt of gratitude for her insightful comments and our wonderful conversations.

Many thanks to Rebecca Barrett for her extensive editing and honest commentary.

A thousand thanks to Judy Herman Shujman, Janet Shelton, Regina Ochoa, Joyce Murray Sullivan, Crystal Rockwell, and Surabhi Kaushik for their feedback on the early drafts. Thank you also to the wonderful authors Jayanthi Sankar, Anju Gattani, Judith Teitelman, Veena Rao, and Alka Joshi who graciously agreed to be guests on my podcast *Bollywood and Books*.

A huge thank you to the Pulpwood Queen, Kathy L. Murphy, founder of the International Pulpwood Queens and Timber Guys Book Club, for her encouragement.

And where would I be without my Writing in Community (WIC) buddies led by Kristin Hatcher? Thank you, Coach Susan Fritz, for reading the manuscript. Thanks to the coaches—Annette Mason, Karena de Souza, and Joyce Sullivan—for leading the Write Now and Out Loud morning sessions. Thanks to Kim Donlan, Win Treese,

Trent Selbrede, Chad Stamm, John Hollenbeck, and all the writers who showed up on Zoom calls. You are all my people.

Thanks to my brother Penn Cook and sister-in-law Shealy Torbert Cook for their interest in my progress on the manuscript over the years: "When is your book going to be finished?"

Thank heaven for the Hail Mary Pass author Mandy Haynes delivered at the eleventh hour.

It takes a village . . .

Glossary

Aloo: potato

Auntie: respectful, affectionate address for an elder female acquaintance

Ayureveda: ancient Indian medical system based on a natural, holistic approach to physical and mental health

Bap: British word—a bread roll

Bira: a mouth-watering sweet in India

Brolly: U.K. umbrella

Chai: Indian tea

Chaiwallah: person who sells chai

Chapatti: round, flat, unleavened bread

Cheese naan: a variation of Indian flatbread

Dal: spicy lentil dish

Dharma: in Hinduism, the eternal and inherent nature of reality; in Buddhism, a universal truth

Dhobi: man who washes clothes for a living

Diwali: Hindu festival of light symbolizing the triumphs of good over evil

Diya: a small clay lamp lit to dispel darkness

Dosa: a thin pancake in South India, served hot with chutney and sambar, a lentil-based vegetable stew

Dosh: U.K. slang for money

Gob-spat: clearing throat loudly and spitting

Hanuman: Hindu deity, a central character of the epic Ramayana

Hijra: a person who was male at birth but who identifies as female or neither male nor female

Hindi: official language of India, widely spoken in the northern regions

Holi: Hindu spring festival of colors that signifies the triumph of good over evil

Idly or Idli: savory rice cake, generally in South India; a breakfast food

Idiyappam: rice noodles prepared in South India and Sri Lanka

Ji: respectful address for men and women

Kathoey: "Lady Boy"; in Thailand, transgender women and men who choose a feminine appearance

Kohl: black eyeliner

Krishna: known as the supreme being in India

Lakshmi: Hindu goddess of wealth and good fortune

Lassi: a refreshing drink made with yogurt

Mahal: palace

Malayalam: language spoken in Southern India

Masala chai: Indian beverage made by boiling black tea in milk and water with herbs and spices

Masala dosa: a South Indian dish

Mithai: sweets

Mundu: four to seven yards of white fabric wrapped into loose pants or a long garment for men

Naan: leavened flatbread

Namaste: Indian greeting with hands pressed together to show respect or say hello

Onam: an ancient Indian harvest festival celebrated in Kerala

Paan: a betel leaf laced with tobacco and betel nut paste, juice spat out or swallowed

Pakora: vegetables dipped in chickpea batter and fried

Palak Paneer: spinach and cheese vegetable dish

Paneer: fresh cheese made at home by curdling milk

Paratha: flat bread, stuffed, made with whole wheat

Pasty: British, a folded pastry case filled with seasoned meat and vegetables

Puja: the act of divine worship

Raita: a refreshing cucumber yogurt side dish served with spicy foods

Roti: round flat bread made with whole wheat or corn

Rupee: the currency in India

Sadhu: holy man

Salwar: loose, pleated trousers tapering to a tight fit at the ankles

Salwar kameez: women's tunic and loose pants

Samosa: a fried snack, sometimes filled with potato, spices, and peas

Sarasvati or Saraswati: Hindu goddess of knowledge, music, art, wisdom, and learning

Sari: a draped women's garment five to nine yards long

Sawadeeca: hello, a traditional Thai greeting

Tomato Uthappam: a South Indian dosa, crisp and crepe-like, with toppings

Uncle: respectful, affectionate address for an elder male acquaintance

Veg Korma: a popular Indian curry

Vishnu: Hindu deity, the god of preservation, whose avatars include Krishna and Rama

About the Author

Lovelace Cook is a storyteller, writer, narrator, podcaster, and traveler. A graduate of the University of Virginia, she has lived in New York City, where she worked in publishing, and Los Angeles, where she worked on films and attended classes at UCLA and the American Film Institute. When she was eligible for Social Security, she challenged herself to change and traveled through India and Southeast Asia like a twenty-year-old on a gap year. Although not recommended for the faint-hearted, the challenge launched adventures. Experiences morphed into the book *Meet Me in Mumbai*. Discovering books, authors, and Indian cinema through travel and from people she met inspired her podcast *Bollywood and Books*. She is an on-call disaster worker who serves as a public information officer in communities devastated by tornadoes, hurricanes, floods, and other disasters. She lives on the Eastern Shore of Mobile Bay in Baldwin County, Alabama, with three mischievous cats.

Lovelace invites her readers to visit her website www.lovelacecook.com, listen to her podcast www.bollywoodandbooks, and write to her at lovelace@lovelace.cook.com. She loves to meet virtually, and in person, with book clubs.

Author photo by Stephen Savage